star-crossed

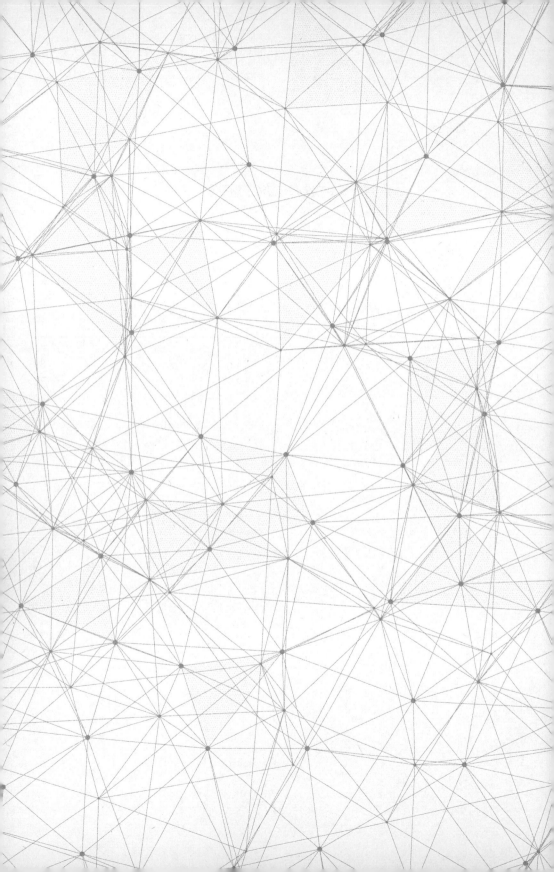

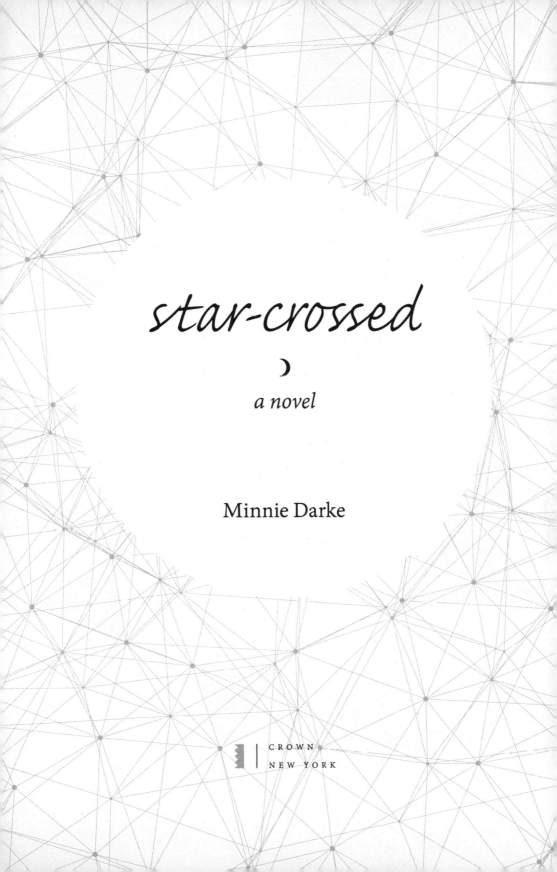

star-crossed

a novel

Minnie Darke

CROWN
NEW YORK

Copyright © 2019 by Minnie Darke

All rights reserved.
Published in the United States by Crown Publishers, an imprint of the Crown Publishing Group, a division of Penguin Random House LLC, New York.
crownpublishing.com

Crown and the Crown colophon are registered trademarks of Penguin Random House LLC.

Originally published in Australia by Penguin Random House Australia, North Sydney, and in Great Britain by Bantam Press, an imprint of Transworld Publishers, a division of Penguin Random House Ltd., London, in 2019.

Library of Congress Cataloging-in-Publication Data is available upon request.

ISBN 978-1-9848-2282-6
Ebook ISBN 978-1-9848-2284-0

PRINTED IN THE UNITED STATES OF AMERICA

Book design by Andrea Lau
Book illustration by K1r1/Shutterstock
Jacket design by Elena Giavaldi
Jacket illustration (hand) by Kristina Jovanovic/Shutterstock

10 9 8 7 6 5 4 3 2 1

First United States Edition

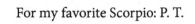

For my favorite Scorpio: P. T.

The stars are the apexes of what wonderful triangles!
What distant and different beings in the various
mansions of the universe are contemplating the same
one at the same moment!

HENRY DAVID THOREAU

)

Astrology is like gravity.
You don't have to believe in it for it to be working in your life.

ZOLAR'S STARMATES

)

No passion on Earth, neither love nor hate,
is equal to the passion to alter someone else's draft.

H. G. WELLS

star-crossed

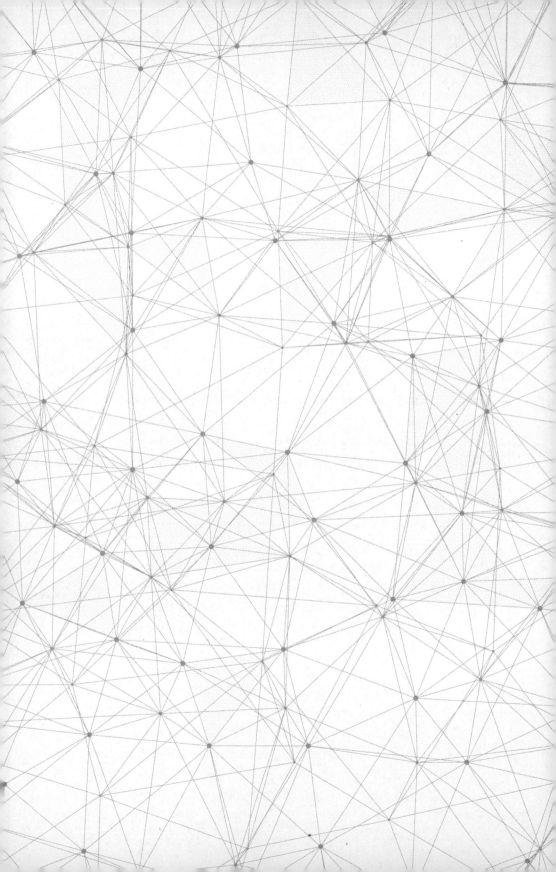

Aquarius

JANUARY 20—FEBRUARY 18

Nicholas Jordan was born not beneath a starry sky, but in Edenvale Hospital—a modest red-brick building on the outskirts of a town that had four pubs, no banks, one swimming pool, six service clubs and bitterly resented water restrictions each summer. The hospital was surrounded by beds of bright pink bougainvillea and rectangles of thirsting lawn, and at the moment of little Nick's birth, the sky above its hot tin roof was the scorching blue of a southern hemisphere noon in February.

And yet the stars *were* there. Out beyond the cloudless heat of the troposphere, beyond the stratosphere's blanket of ozone, beyond the mesosphere and the thermosphere, the ionosphere, the exosphere and the magnetosphere, were the stars. Millions of them, patterning the blackness and orbiting themselves into the precise configuration that would be forever mapped onto the soul of Nicholas Jordan.

Joanna Jordan—Aries, owner-operator of Edenvale's Uppercut hair salon, the freakishly accurate goal attack for the Edenvale Stars netball team, and a two-time Miss Eden Valley titleholder—did not think of the stars in the hours that followed her son's birth. Blissed out and disheveled in the hospital's sole delivery suite, she only stared into little Nick's face, and charted influences of a more terrestrial nature.

"He's got your nose," she murmured to her husband.

And she was quite right. Her baby had a perfect, miniature replica of the nose that she knew and loved on the face of Mark Jordan—Taurus, square-shouldered Australian Rules defender turned polo-shirted financial planner, lover of baked cheesecake and helpless admirer of long-legged women.

"But *your* ears," Mark said, feeling his hands to be suddenly and gigantically out of scale as he smoothed back a wisp of the dark hair that feathered Nick's newborn head.

And so, Joanna and Mark looked over their son and traced back to various sources his cheeks, forehead, fingers and toes. The new parents found an echo of Mark's brother in the wide setting of their baby's eyes, and a hint of Joanna's mother in his full and expressive lips.

Nowhere, however, did they find, or even think to look for, the fingerprints of Beta Aquarii, a yellow supergiant burning some 537 light-years from Earth. Or the more diffuse touch of the Helix Nebula, or indeed any of the other heavenly bodies that comprised the sprawling constellation of Aquarius, within whose auspices the sun was housed at the time of their baby's birth.

An astrologer, looking at the pinpricks of destiny as laid out in little Nick's natal chart, might on the day of his birth have been able to tell you that this child would grow up to be original to the point of slightly eccentric, creative and caring, but with a competitive streak so wide that his siblings would prefer eating Brussels sprouts to playing Monopoly with him. He would love costume parties and have a habit of bringing home any starving dog or flea-ridden cat that crossed his path.

This same astrologer might have allowed themselves a fond smile as they foretold that Nick, from his midteens onward, would be a true believer when it came to the stars. Nick would like the fact that he was an Aquarius—a sign he would associate with innovative and original thinking, as well as summertime, music festivals and hot young hippies who smelled of patchouli and sex.

On the day of Nick's birth, however, there was no astrologer at hand, and the only person who did make an astrological prediction about baby Nick at that time was Joanna Jordan's friend Mandy Carmichael. Mandy—Gemini, dimple-cheeked darling of the regional television network's weather report, radiant newlywed, ABBA fanatic—appeared at the hospital like a good fairy, straight after work. Her face was still thickly plastered with foundation and she teetered on high heels as she balanced in her arms an enormous blue teddy bear and a bunch of supermarket chrysanthemums. Soon the teddy was reclining in a chair, the chrysanthemums were in a Fowlers preserving jar and Mandy was barefoot beside the bed, cradling her friend's firstborn with infinite care.

"A little Aquarius, hm?" she said, her eyes misting. "Don't expect him to be like you and Mark, will you, JoJo? Aquarians are different. Aren't you, little one?"

"Well, he'd better like sport," Jo said lightly. "Mark's already bought him a tennis racket."

"Which is why he'll probably be an artist. Or a dancer. Won't you, my treasure?"

Mandy slipped her finger into the closing star of baby Nick's hand, and for a moment she was uncharacteristically speechless. Then she said, "Jo, he's beautiful. Just beautiful."

By the time Mandy stepped out of the hospital, dusk had fallen, bringing with it a breeze as softly cool as the wistful mood that settled on her as she cut across the spiky grass—carrying her shoes—to the parking lot. The western sky was a smoky blue strung with drifts of low, pinkish cloud, but in the east a few eager stars had already burst through the deepening dark. Mandy slipped in behind the wheel of her car and watched those stars for a good long while. The smell of baby was in her nostrils.

≈

The following Friday, at Curlew Court—a cul-de-sac in a newly built part of Edenvale that was full of concrete curbing and single-story homes with bright-colored roofs, mown lawns and eucalypt saplings in plastic plant guards—Drew Carmichael flopped onto his back and said, "Wow."

Alongside him, on his next-door neighbor's trampoline, was an empty bottle of Baileys Irish Cream, two smeary tumblers and his sweaty, smiling, semiclad wife. Drew—Libra, agricultural consultant, amateur aviation enthusiast, Pink Floyd aficionado and fearsome bedroom-mirror air guitarist—had been home from a two-week business trip for less than an hour, and he had a sense of having been quite deliberately ravished. Drained of his essence, even. Fortunately, the neighbors were on holiday in Queensland.

"Mmmmmm," said Mandy, smiling up into a star-filled sky.

Drew propped himself up on one elbow and looked at his wife. He could see a shadow on her left cheek where it dimpled, and smell the mischief on her damp skin.

"What was that all about?" he asked, putting a hand on the soft paleness of her exposed belly. "Hm?"

"Excuse me," she said, slapping his hand away but grinning widely, "but I'm a married woman. Don't touch what you can't afford."

He tickled her, and she giggled.

"What are you up to?"

"Up to?" she said. "Up to? I . . . am looking at the stars."

Slightly drunk and entirely happy, Drew pillowed his head on folded arms and followed her gaze, up into space.

On that February night, the Carmichaels set in motion a baby girl, who would be born in the early hours of a November morning under the sign of Sagittarius. She would arrive, petite and perfectly formed, with her skull capped in a finer version of the light brown hair that would eventually curl around the sharp contours of her face. Her eyes would be hazel, her chin would be pointed and her lips—like her mother's—would form a pronounced Cupid's bow. Her dark eyebrows would—like her father's—be straight and almost severe.

An astrologer might have predicted that this baby would grow up to be a straight shooter; playful, but also something of a perfectionist. She would love words, appear at age nine on a kids' TV spelling contest (which she would win) and usually have a pen wedged behind her ear. Always her bedside table would groan under its payload of books (read, half read, to read), and there was a good chance that you would find, concealed within this pile of books, an IKEA catalogue, since wardrobe-organization porn would, for this girl, be a lifelong guilty pleasure. Her memory would be as flawless as a gleaming, stainless steel filing cabinet and even her text messages would be faultlessly formatted and punctuated.

It might also have been accurately foretold, with a sorrowful shake of the astrologer's head, that this child would grow up to have scant regard for the stars. To be frank, she would consider horoscopes to be a crock of implausible hog-shit.

"Justine," Mandy murmured, mostly to herself.

"What?" said Drew.

"Jus-tine," Mandy said, more distinctly. "Do you like it?"

"Who's Justine?" Drew asked, perplexed.

You'll see, Mandy thought. *You'll see.*

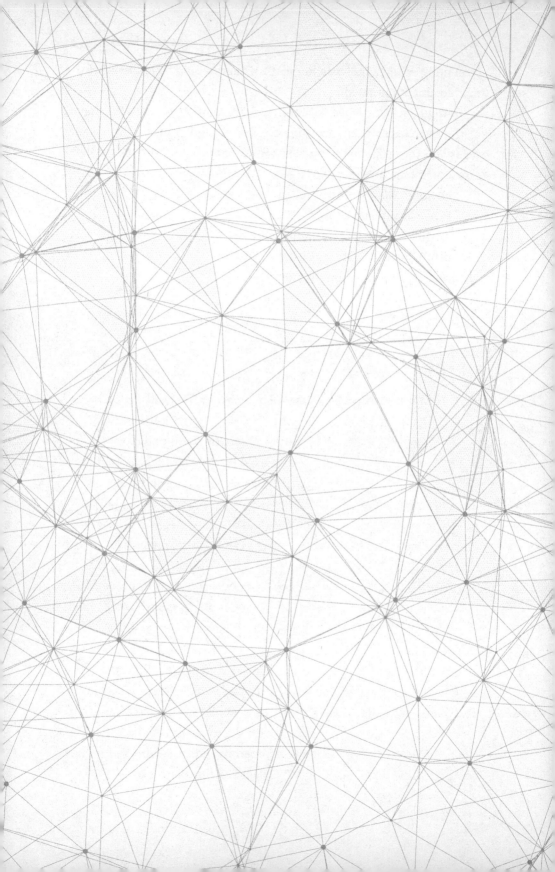

Pisces

FEBRUARY 19–MARCH 20

T ime passed. Moons orbited planets. Planets did laps around the brightest stars. Galaxies swirled. And, as the years went by, more and more satellites joined in. Then one day, as if by magic, there she was: twenty-six-year-old Justine Carmichael, carrying an unsteady load of takeout coffee cups along a leafy suburban street on a Friday morning in March. She wore a cheerful swing dress of green-and-white polka-dot linen and nearly white sneakers that caught the sunshine and shadow as she made her way along the light-dappled sidewalk.

The street—about two hours east of Edenvale—was Rennie Street, one of the main thoroughfares in the dress circle suburb of Alexandria Park. This was a district of late-nineteenth-century mansions and art deco apartment blocks, flower boutiques and cafes, the sort of place where it was easy to get a Vienna coffee in a tall glass with a long spoon, and where dog groomers specialized in cuts for Maltese and West Highland terriers. Justine's destination was the headquarters of the *Alexandria Park Star*, where she worked. Officially, her job description was "copy-runner," although the editor—who was prone to verbal flourishes that in no way resembled the incisive brevity of his journalism—liked to refer to her as "our dear, darling cub-reporter-in-waiting." If he had been writing about her, he'd have called her "dogsbody."

The *Star*'s headquarters were in a gracious, converted weather-board home that was set back slightly from the road. As Justine turned without pausing through an open front gate, she passed beneath one of Alexandria Park's most controversial monuments—the star itself. As ugly as it was unmissable, it was a mosaic sculpture the size of a tractor wheel that swung, high and bright, on a post-mounted bracket above the pavement. It was fat and curvy for a star, and its five not-quite-symmetrical points were crudely covered in chips of acid-yellow tiles and the smashings of a tea set patterned with yellow roses.

Thirty years earlier, when the star had first been hoisted into place, the locals had dubbed it the "yellow peril," and they had tried every trick in the municipal council rulebook to have it pulled down. In those days, most of Alexandria Park's residents regarded the *Star* as a grubby little street rag, and its young editor, Jeremy Byrne, as a despicable long-haired degenerate. It was their strongly held opinion that Winifred Byrne's dissolute eldest son had no business installing a muck-raking fish-wrap at his late mother's elegant Rennie Street address.

But Alexandria Park learned to live with both the publication and its gaudy, street-side emblem, and now the *Star* was a glossy and well-respected magazine of current affairs, sport and the arts. Each month's new edition was read not only in Alexandria Park, but right through the city and out into the suburbs on the other side. Although Justine's job was somewhere beneath the very lowest rung of the ladder, there would still have been any number of other bright young journalism graduates who might have seriously considered kneecapping her in order to take her place.

On her first day on the job, Justine had been given a tour of the premises by Jeremy Byrne himself, no longer long-haired but quite bald, and these days a good deal more patrician than peacenik. He had stood her beneath the crazy yellow bulk of the star.

"I want you to think of it as a talisman of the fearless, fiercely non-partisan journalistic principles upon which our brave little publication was founded," he had told her, and Justine had tried not to find it weird and embarrassing when he had spoken about the star's "inspirational rays," and even mimed them raining down onto her head.

The *Star* was a great place to work, just as its editor had promised. The staff were hardworking, but not above having some fun. The Christmas parties were Bacchanalian feats of catering, and the quality of reporting in the magazine was high. The trouble for Justine was that the *Star* was such a great place to work that none of the journalists ever resigned. There were currently three staff writers in the office, and one in Canberra, and they'd all been in their jobs for a decade or more. The copy-runner before Justine had waited three years for a reporter position before giving up and taking a job in public relations.

On that day when Justine had stood pink-cheeked beneath the star with Jeremy Byrne, she had been convinced that her predecessor had done all the waiting for her. A real job, surely, had to be just around the corner. But two years had gone by with no sign of advancement in sight and Justine was beginning to think that her first byline at the *Star* would not come until one of the current crew died of old age.

Justine hurried along the lavender-lined path, restacking her jumble of cardboard cups so she had a hand free to collect up a bundle of mail lying on the flagstones. At the top of a low flight of steps, she pushed open the front door with her hip. Even before the door had swung closed behind her, a sugar-dusted voice drifted out into the hallway.

"Justine? Is that you?"

The voice belonged to Barbel Weiss, the advertising manager, who had transformed one of the *Star*'s two beautiful, bay-windowed front parlors into a space as well groomed and feminine as she was. When Justine stepped into this office, Barbel—in a dusky pink pants suit, and with her blonde hair twisted into an arrangement that looked like it belonged in a German bakery—didn't get up from her desk, only waved a brochure in the air.

"Darling, take this down to the art department, will you? Tell them the font I want for the Brassington advertisement is this one. Here. I've circled it."

"No problem," Justine said, maneuvering herself to the side of the desk so Barbel could add the brochure to her load.

"Oh," said Barbel, registering Justine's arsenal of coffee cups, and allowing her brow to furrow just a smidge, "you're only just back from Rafaello's. But you won't mind popping down there again, will you? I have a client in twenty minutes, and I thought macarons would be nice. Let's have . . . raspberry. Thanks, Justine. You're a cherub."

The parlor on the opposite side of the hallway belonged to the editor, but his office was utterly unlike Barbel's. It resembled rather the living room of a hoarder, with knee-high piles of foreign newspapers and bookshelves crammed with legal textbooks, political biographies, *Wisden Almanacks* and books of true crime. Jeremy, wearing a shirt that was mostly businesslike but somehow managed to retain the slightest hint of kaftan, was talking on the phone. When Justine ducked in to deliver his soy-milk chai, he held up an open hand to her in a way that meant *come back in five minutes.* Justine gave an eager smile and nodded.

The next room along the corridor was occupied by the staff writers. At the sound of Justine's footfall, Roma Sharples turned from her computer screen and peered over the top of her electric blue–framed spectacles. Famous for being crabby and imperious, she had to be pushing seventy, yet she was showing no signs of retiring.

"Thank you," said Roma, accepting her long black coffee. She peeled a sticky note off the pad on her desk and held it out to Justine. "Give this address to Radoslaw, and tell him we have to be there at eleven sharp. And Justine? Bring the car around to the front, will you?"

Justine set down a quarter-strength latte at the empty workstation beside Roma's. This desk belonged to Jenna Rae, who had presumably been called out on an assignment, and who—being only in her late thirties—offered Justine virtually no hope at all.

The *Star*'s sports specialist was Martin Oliver, who was in his fifties and probably Justine's best prospect, given his personal habits. Martin was on the phone and giving off his usual miasma of booze and nicotine as Justine handed him a heavily sugared double-strength cappuccino. He tapped her on the elbow. On the pad on his desk, he wrote, *Paper jam in p/copier.* And then, *Computer won't print PDFs again. Get Anwen.*

"Yeah, well, the selectors are morons. Wouldn't know a spin bowler from a bowler hat," he said into the phone, while underlining the word *again* so hard that he made a deep gouge in the paper. Justine took up his pen and drew a smiley face beneath his message.

Next along the passageway was a narrow office space that might once have been a closet. Behind the desk sat Natsue Kobayashi, the contributions manager. Natsue was blessed with exquisite taste in clothes and an age-defying complexion that made people surprised to learn that she was old enough to have three grandchildren. Each day, she took precisely forty-five minutes for lunch, and spent the time knitting in luxury yarns—merino, alpaca, possum, camel—for these beloved grandchildren, who lived in Sweden. Natsue also had a preternatural ability to multitask.

Without pausing from transcribing the letter that was clipped to the document holder beside her computer, she said, "Good morning, Justine. Oh, your dress! So cu-u-ute! Kawaii!"

The dress was genuine vintage—it had belonged to Justine's grandmother.

"One flat white," Justine announced.

Natsue, still typing, said, "Bless you. And I see you have the mail? I would be grateful if I could have mine just as soon as you have done the sorting."

"Of course," Justine said.

Justine found the art room mercifully empty of anyone who could add anything more to her to-do list, so she left the designers a hurried note along with Barbel's brochure, then made good her escape. Across the corridor in the IT department, the *Star*'s resident tech angel, Anwen Corbett, appeared to be asleep.

Anwen was partly nocturnal, often coming into the office late at night to tinker with the computers when nobody needed to use them. Now her dreadlocked head, pillowed by a thick computer manual, rested on a desk that was mostly a cluttered disaster of cables, circuit boards and *Star Wars* action figures.

"Anwen," Justine said. "An!"

Anwen jolted her head upright, though her eyes remained closed. "Yup, yup. All good. All here."

"Martin's computer's not printing PDFs again. He wants you to take a look," Justine said.

Anwen let her head fall back to her makeshift pillow and groaned. "Tell him it's a PICNIC."

PICNIC was Anwen's favorite acronym. Problem In Chair Not In Computer.

"I have coffee," Justine wheedled.

"You do?" Anwen said, blinking with puffy eyelids.

"Long macchiato. Available from my desk just as soon as you've taken a look at Martin's computer."

"That's just cruel."

Justine grinned. "But effective."

The photography department was the next stop along the hallway. Justine leaned on the door frame and said, "Morning, Radoslaw. Roma said to say that she needs you for an eleven o'clock job. Here's the address."

Like a prizefighting bantam, the *Star*'s photographer leaped up from behind his vast computer monitor, a can of Red Bull in his hand, and a short-sleeve checked shirt buttoned high under his tidy black beard. Justine glanced at the wastepaper basket, where there were already two blue-and-white cans, spent.

It was because of Radoslaw's driving, Justine knew, that Roma had asked her to bring the company car around to the front of the building. Thanks to him, both sides of the Camry were scratched, and white Duco could be found in several places along the side-alley fence. Nevertheless, Radoslaw always insisted that he drive to assignments. Not even Roma had been able to overpower him on this point.

"Well, you can tell Roma to fuck off," he said, and he made no attempt to keep his voice down. "I've got a job at the racetrack with Martin this morning. Can't they fucken talk to each other? Jesus fucken Christ. They work in the same fucken room. Fuck."

And since this was a fairly normal way for Radoslaw to respond to a message, it was perhaps fortunate that he had never in his life taken a bad picture.

At last, Justine made it to her desk, which was located in a lean-to at the back of the old home. The room's walls were unlined, though they had been roughly painted. Propped against one of these walls was a bicycle that Martin Oliver had probably last used about seven months ago, which was also the last time he'd felt moved to get some exercise at lunchtime, rather than head down to the Strumpet and Pickle. From between the wheels of the bike there emerged a stained white furry muzzle, then a pair of weepy, deep-brown eyes. These belonged to a small and shaggy Maltese terrier, who was dragging a leopard-print leash.

"Falafel," she said. "What are you doing here?"

The dog only wagged his tail, but the answer to Justine's question was on her desk in the form of a note from the *Star*'s art director. In his rather overconfident hand, Glynn had written: *Don't suppose you can take F. to the grooming parlor? Due there at 10 a.m. Groomers will have a fit if he's late again. Thanks! G.*

Falafel trotted up to Justine's ankles and yapped at her impatiently.

"Don't you start," she told him.

For a few seconds, Justine stood and breathed, deliberately. There was no point feeling overwhelmed, she told herself. When everyone wanted everything immediately, you simply had to prioritize. She reasoned that even if Jeremy had asked for her in five minutes' time, and even if he was the boss, he was also a hopeless time fantasist. Five minutes in Jeremy's world could mean anything from ten minutes to six hours. Therefore, she would sort the mail and deliver Natsue's at the very least, then duck back to Rafaello's for Barbel's biscuits, returning via the grooming parlor where she would drop off Falafel. Then she would fix the paper jam in the photocopier, back the Camry down the driveway and start a fight between Martin and Roma by passing on the general gist, though not the precise wording, of Radoslaw's message to Roma. Then she—

"Jus-*tine!*"

Oh, fuck.

It was Jeremy, his voice booming cheerfully down the hallway. "Be good," she said to Falafel. "*Good.*"

Just outside Jeremy's office, Justine slowed and smoothed her dress. *Professional, capable, unflappable,* she told herself, then stepped inside.

"Darl!" said Jeremy. He smiled, and broken capillaries jostled across his cheeks and nose. "Have a seat, have a seat."

Jeremy was big on the *paterfamilias* thing, and Justine knew he felt it was his responsibility, as the editor and her self-appointed mentor, to schedule in some regular little chats. He liked to tell her war stories from his glorious and dangerous past, and to orate on subjects such as ethics, due process, jurisprudence and the delicate machinery of the Westminster system.

"Darl," he said, leaning forward to launch into today's randomly chosen topic, "what do you know about the separation of powers?"

"Well . . ." Justine began, and that was a mistake. When conversing with Jeremy, it was foolish to begin with a word of extraneous fill.

"We thank the French Enlightenment," he interrupted, "for the concept of the separation of powers, which holds that the three branches of government—the executive, the legislative and the judicial . . ."

And so, Justine sat across the desk from Jeremy as he monologued for quite some time. Hands in her polka-dot lap, she tried to look as if she were, in fact, listening intently, and learning. And not as if she were thinking of macarons, and the width of the side alley, and Martin's printing problem, and whether or not Falafel had eaten the packed lunch that was in the bag she'd left, unprotected, near her workstation.

At length, Jeremy's phone rang and he snatched it up. "Harvey!" he exclaimed. "Hold on just a mo, me old chum."

He put his hand over the receiver and gave Justine a rueful smile. "To be continued."

Dismissed, Justine stepped into the hallway. Immediately, from the noise, she could tell that Radoslaw had not waited for Justine to pass his message on to Roma.

Martin was also yelling. "Jus-*tine*! I need to print something out! This year!"

Justine checked her watch. Falafel was already late for the groomer's.

Barbel leaned around the door of her office, her beautifully made-up brow creased with anxiety. "Where are my macarons?" she asked, but Justine could offer her nothing more than a weak smile.

It was going to be quite a day.

$$\text{H}$$

By the time Justine finished work that evening, it was half past six. Her hair fell in lank waves around her face, her skin felt gray and—thanks to the glitchy printer—there was a spray of ink down one side of her dress. She was hungry, too, for although Falafel had not precisely eaten her chicken curry wrap, he had toyed with it enough to make it inedible, and there'd been no time to seek out a replacement lunch.

As she passed beneath the mosaic star at the gatepost, she glanced up at it resentfully.

"Inspirational rays," she muttered, then stepped out onto Rennie Street.

Justine walked three blocks and turned left into Dufrene Street, where the after-work drinkers were spilling out of the Strumpet and Pickle onto the sidewalk. She crossed to the other side of the road, and was just about to pass through the eastern gate of Alexandria Park when she stopped in her tracks, turned around and looked back at the series of glamorized warehouses on the other side of the road that made up the markets.

It's difficult to know what caused her to do this, precisely at that moment. Perhaps the sun was working an angle on her from its current position in Pisces, or the moon and Venus together were tugging on her consciousness from their love seat in Aquarius. Or maybe Jupiter had sent down some kind of vibe from where it was stomping about in Virgo. Or perhaps it was only that Justine's subconscious had subtly suggested that there was a way to delay the inevitable moment when she would walk in through the door of her empty apartment, queue up the next episode of the BBC's latest *Emma*, think vaguely about calling best-pal Tara, but instead collapse on the couch with a helping of Vegemite toast for dinner.

Justine stood poised, at the very edge of the sidewalk, and considered. Was there time? The markets didn't close until seven. She checked her watch. Oh, yes, there was time.

She glanced inside the basket-weave bag that she carried in the crook of her arm, and was happy to see that her black Sharpie pen was indeed there, lying in wait, in its own special pocket. She lowered her sunglasses from the top of her head and approached.

Alexandria Park Markets was a place Justine only rarely went to buy food. More often, she entered its cool, high-ceilinged space in the same spirit as she would an art gallery. She liked to check out the strange and exotic blooms that filled the enormous Mason jars at the florist's, and to pass by the fishmonger's to admire the gleaming sea creatures on their beds of ice.

She made her way past the florist's, past the butcher's and the baker's, toward the fruit and vegetable corner. She sidled up to a timber crate full of watermelons, lifted her sunglasses and looked over to the display of Hass avocados. And there it was, perched on a plastic stalk above the fruits. The offending sign.

ADVOCADOS.

Would the man *never* learn? Here was a fruit seller who was clearly competent. No, he was more than competent. He could stack pomegranates so that they looked like the crown jewels of some far-flung, exotic nation. He could select apples of invariable perfection and keep grapes misted with water so that they looked appetizing all day long. It made no sense that he would stubbornly and consistently continue to misspell "avocados." And yet he did. Week in and week out, Justine corrected his error, and the grocer responded by throwing away the amended signs and replacing them with yet another one for ADVO-bloody-CADOS. It was infuriating. But Justine was determined not to be beaten.

She waited until the assistant behind the counter was distracted, then whipped out her Sharpie. Swiftly, she struck out the extraneous D. AVOCADOS. Ah, yes. This was good.

Satisfied that the world was now restored to rightness, Justine spun around, intending to make a dash for the markets' Dufrene Street exit. But she had only taken a few paces when she ran into a giant fish.

It was hard to tell what kind of fish it was, exactly. It was silver-gray with lips rimmed in pink satin ribbon. Its eyes were enormous, yellow and convex, like the painted halves of a Ping-Pong ball. A very upright dorsal fin began at the back of the creature's head and ran in spiked waves down the length of its spine. The fish had large silver gloves for pectorals, and it said, "Should you be doing that?"

She was just about to get argumentative, when she recognized the human face that was framed by a cut-out oval of silvery fish-fabric.

"Nick Jordan?" Justine said, incredulous.

"Bloody hell. Jus*tine*?"

"Hello!"

"Hello to you too."

"Oh my God. You haven't even changed," Justine said, stunned and smiling.

Nick made a doubtful face and glanced down at his fish suit. "Thanks, I think."

"It must have been, what?"

"Years," Nick agreed, and as he nodded the silver lamé expanse of the suit quivered all over.

"Eleven? Twelve?" Justine offered, as if she were guessing.

"It couldn't have been that long," he said.

But it was. It was twelve years, one month, and three weeks. And Justine knew this, precisely.

♓

Somewhere in a shoe box, or perhaps an album, there existed photographs of Justine Carmichael as a weeks-old baby, pink and tiny as a skinned rabbit, lying on a rug next to ten-month-old Nicholas Jordan, who looked in comparison like a sumo wrestler in a Winnie the Pooh playsuit.

As toddlers, in the sandbox at family day care, Justine and Nick had shared both their Vegemite sandwiches and the traumatic experience of being dethroned by younger siblings. Justine had got off easier than Nick on that front. Her parents had produced a boy—Austin—on their second try, and called it quits. But after having Nick's younger brother, Jimmy, Jo and Mark had gone back for a third throw of the dice, hoping for a girl. And along came Piper.

By the time Justine and Nick graduated to kindergarten at Eden Valley Primary, Nick had been going through a monkey phase and had refused to go to school, even in summer, wearing anything other than a full-length onesie lemur costume. So Justine spent her mornings sitting loyally beside him on the mat while he sucked on his striped tail during story time, and at the end of lunch she would help him to brush the bark chips from the playground out of his fur.

In the early years of primary school, Nick took up the habit of playing soccer during breaks, while Justine climbed trees, or drifted in and out of the imaginative games of the girls, which usually seemed to involve someone lying on the ground, wailing, pretending to be a baby. But outside school, Nick and Justine played together for all of the endless hours that their mothers chatted together over cups of tea or glasses of wine, and the two kids knew that Jo and Mandy's occasional shouts of "five-minute warning!" could almost always be safely ignored. Justine had known precisely where in the Jordans' pantry to find the chocolate biscuits, and Nick had his own toothbrush at the Carmichaels'.

There had once been a VHS tape of the two of them as seven-year-olds: Nick wreaking havoc on the nylon strings of an old acoustic guitar, and Justine, in a pair of sunglasses with heart-shaped frames, crooning into the microphone of a Little Mermaid karaoke set. They'd sung "Big Yellow Taxi," which hadn't been too bad, and "Yellow Submarine," which hadn't been entirely dreadful, but then they'd launched into an innocently raunchy version of Racey's "Some Girls." At some point during that song, Justine and Nick had realized that their audience, made up exclusively of their parents, was laughing uncontrollably. At them. It would be quite a few years before Justine would realize precisely what it was, in that song, that some girls did, and some girls didn't. But on the night of the living-room concert, she didn't need to know the details in order to know that she was being laughed at.

For Nick, the experience had been exhilarating. Shortly after the night of the concert, he'd entered his first Eden Valley Drama Eisteddfod, only to discover the intoxicating fact that the arts could be a blood sport every bit as competitive as a game of Aussie Rules. Trophies accumulated.

Nick didn't speak to Justine for a full three days after she upstaged him by appearing on national television for that famous spelling contest of hers. On the fourth day, however, he'd been unable to help himself and had come out of his sulk to punch Jasper Bellamy, who'd been calling Justine a nerd. After that, things between the two old friends had returned, effortlessly, to normal.

But when Justine was ten, and Nick was just about to turn eleven, everything changed. Mark Jordan took a job on the far side of the country, so the Jordans sold up and left town. Despite everybody's best intentions to stay in touch, the late-night phone calls between Mandy and Jo became less and less frequent, and correspondence dwindled to the obligatory Christmas letter tucked inside a card featuring Santa at the beach in his budgie-smugglers.

The families didn't completely lose touch, though. Because there had been that Australia Day long weekend, in the January of the year that Nick and Justine would each turn fifteen. The Carmichaels had gone west, and the Jordans had come east, for a midpoint reunion in the baking heat of a beachside holiday park in South Australia. Despite the fact that Justine had spent the entire stuffy car trip to their destination playing out in her mind the film-worthy scene in which she was reunited with her childhood best friend, she had, upon seeing him, seized up like a terrified cat in the presence of a dog.

Nick, she saw immediately, had stopped being a slightly goofy boy and had morphed into a young man, almost absurdly good-looking—one of the kind that Justine knew from experience it was safest to avoid if one did not wish to suffer the excruciating embarrassment of rejection. So for all of the Saturday, and all of the Sunday, she had skulked about moodily, thrashing on her Sony Walkman the *So Fresh* compilation she'd got for Christmas and pissing everyone off by locking the bathroom door so she could moon about in privacy, changing her earrings and trying different shades of eye shadow. Nick had been equally aloof, setting off on long runs down the beach, or hanging out at the pool.

And then, on the Sunday night, their parents had pulled rank and dragged the two of them, sullen and resentful, up the beach to a pop-up amusement park. Maybe it was the nostalgic smells of hot dogs and cotton candy that broke them back down into the kids they really were. Or perhaps it was the jarring collisions in the bumper car arena that jerked them out of their self-consciousness. Whichever it was, they had ended up on the beach together late at night, alone, feeling the disco beat of the amusement park music as it throbbed through the sand.

The following morning, Justine was still in bed when the Jordans came over, en masse, to say their farewells. Through the cardboard-thin walls of the holiday cabin, Justine heard everything that was going on—her brother Aussie tearing around with Jimmy, Piper bawling about being left out, Mandy's and Jo's voices going up and down like scales on a violin, Drew's and Mark's voices providing the bass notes.

She heard her mother say, "I'm sure she'll be up in a minute, Nick, love. I know she'll want to say goodbye."

But even when Mandy came into the bedroom and reached up to the top bunk to shake her daughter's shoulder, Justine had only hunkered down further beneath the covers. She was too overcome with embarrassment even to show her face. Because she was sure that everyone in her family, and Nick's, would be able to see how her lips were swollen from all that kissing, how her cheeks had been rubbed raw by the rasp of Nick's faintly stubbled cheek. And, even worse, she felt sure that everybody else would be able to see on the outside of her what she could feel on the inside: something new and worrying, delicious and mortifying, intoxicating and weird. It was as if something had burst open, like multicolored popcorn. She didn't think she would ever again be able to cram it back down to size.

♓

He probably doesn't even remember, Justine's brain said to her. Then it said the same thing over again, just in case she hadn't heard the first time.

Brain: *He probably doesn't even remember.*

Justine: *Will you be quiet?*

Brain: *Why would he remember? All those pages of your diary that you filled, while he probably just went home and forgot all about it.*

But even while Justine was holding a silent dialogue with her brain, she was also managing to keep up her end of a perfectly polite conversation.

"And how's your mum?" she asked.

"No different," Nick said. "She doesn't even seem to age."

"I can imagine." Justine pictured the lovely Jo, with her big white smile and her long brown hair that always smelled of caramel. Jo had been Justine's first hairdresser. She would sit Justine on her kitchen bench and bribe her with jelly beans to sit still through the fringe-trimming part. "Wurls"—that's what Jo had called Justine's unpredictable, weather-sensitive blend of waves and curls. Jo had also been the one to talk Mandy into letting Justine watch *Star Wars* when she was seven years old, even though it was rated PG. And Jo who had defended Justine when she had got in big trouble for calling her grade three teacher a bitch. Justine had overheard Jo telling Mandy, "Ease up on her, Mands. You have to give a girl points for accuracy."

"And Jimmy?" Justine asked.

"Professional tap dancer, believe it or not. It's Piper who followed in Dad's footsteps."

"Oh?"

"Fullback for Carlton in the AFLW. She's a wall of muscle—I wouldn't take her on anymore. What about your folks?" Nick asked.

"In Edenvale, same as ever."

"Don't tell me your mum's still the weather girl?"

"No, these days she's the general manager at the local council. I cannot tell you how much she loves being the boss. Dad's retired, though. He bought himself a Cessna Skycatcher but all he does is fly about and look at crops. Old habits die hard."

"And you? You live near here?"

"On the other side of the park. Nan left her old city bolt-hole to my dad, bless her. You?"

"I'm kind of between addresses, but yeah, this is a good city. I'd say it's home."

Justine peered critically at Nick's silver lamé fish suit. "So, what exactly is the story with the outfit?"

"It's all to do with the oysters," he said, glancing over at the fishmonger's ice-filled cabinets. "There's a special promotion, as part of which I walk around saying things like: *World's your proverbial, buddy. Hey, mate, French kiss a mermaid, you know you want to.*"

Justine winced. "I heard you went to drama school."

Nick explained to her how hard it was to make a living as an actor, how he supplemented his erratic wages with stints as a barista, waiter, catalogue delivery boy, school holiday drama tutor, brickie's laborer.

"That's a lot harder work than being a fish," he said, "but less humiliating. And you? You, what? Patrol the fruit and vegetable signs of the city for correctness? That's a career path, is it? For kids who win television spelling contests?"

He remembers the spelling contest, Justine said, somewhat smugly, to her brain.

"I work at the *Alexandria Park Star.*"

"You write for the *Star*? I love the *Star.* Would I have read anything you've written?"

"Well, I haven't really—" Justine began. "I'm only . . ."

Justine searched for the right words, but before she could find them, Nick said, "Hey, it's actually kind of weird having this conversation from inside a fish suit. I'm finishing up in ten minutes, though. We could, you know, if you weren't busy . . . we could grab some fish and chips, head over to the park? Catch up on the rest of the news? But, you know, no pressure—just if you're not expected anywhere, or anything."

She was hungry, and fish and chips would hit the spot. Even so, Justine managed to pause. She tilted her head and let him see her think.

"If it's not a good time, or . . ."

She smiled.

"I'm not expected anywhere."

$$\mathcal{H}$$

A crisp evening breeze made a Mexican wave through the upper leaves of Alexandria Park's grand old trees as Justine and Nick passed between the wrought-iron pillars of the eastern gate. Nick pushed a beaten-up bicycle with one hand, and though he was out of the fish suit by now, a marine whiff clung to his shorts, his *Where the Wild Things Are* T-shirt, and his skin.

After-work joggers pounded the park's thoroughfares and small dogs with expensive collars chased balls across the grass. Nick picked a spot on a gently sloping bank that gave a view down over the city, and where the grass was coppery in the falling sunlight. He set his bike against a planter box full of frilly, ornamental cabbages, and stretched out on the grass. Propped on one elbow, he unceremoniously tore open the white paper parcel of their meal and took a huge handful of steaming chips.

"Sorry, not very restrained, I know. But I haven't had fish and chips for *years*," Nick said, his mouth half full.

Sitting across from him, Justine took a chip and tested the end of it with her teeth. She was famished and the chip was perfect—crisp and light brown on the outside, all white and fluffy in the middle.

Nick was on to his second handful of chips when he said, "So, the *Star*, hey? What's it like working there? What was your last big story?"

Justine sighed. "No big stories. Yet. At this point in history, I'm just the copy-runner."

"Isn't that like . . . ?"

"Yes, it's exactly like. I am, officially, the shit-kicker. I'd hoped that a real job would have come along by now, but . . ."

"Speaking of the *Star*, isn't it about time the new edition was out?"

"In stores tomorrow," Justine said, in her best advertising voice. "Although, it's occasionally possible to get hold of an advance copy."

She pointed to her bag, out of the top of which poked a brand-new, rolled-up magazine. Nick's eyes widened in genuine, childlike delight.

"Can I?" he asked.

"Be my guest."

Absentmindedly, he cleaned his greasy fingers on his T-shirt before reaching for the magazine. He opened it from the back and thumbed through the pages to land—quite expertly, Justine thought—at the horoscopes. With a smile, she remembered his teenage obsession with astrology: the one that she'd assumed he would outgrow, just as he had done his lemur suit.

It was strange, Justine reflected. On the one hand, she felt entirely comfortable with Nick, as if she'd known him forever. Which, in a way, she had. But on the other hand, he was virtually a stranger to her. He was perhaps only a little taller than she remembered him to be, and only a little less gangly. But his face. His face was different. *How?* she asked herself, as if she had a pen in her hand and it was her job to capture precisely the subtle differences in this new, older Nick Jordan.

At first, she thought of a set of nested Russian dolls. Perhaps looking at this Nick was like looking at the biggest doll in a set, when you were familiar with the slightly smaller, slightly different one that was hidden away inside. But no, Justine thought. It wasn't quite like that. Rather, it was as if older-Nick had pushed out through the fabric of younger-Nick—jawbones, cheekbones and brow bones becoming more obvious and defined. His eyes were still wide and blue, his features still mobile and expressive, his smile still slightly sideways on his face.

He read intently, his dark eyebrows shuffling together in concentration. At last, he closed the magazine and tapped his fingers on its back cover. He looked puzzled, then shook his head slightly, as if to clear his thoughts.

"What's he like?" he asked Justine.

She was lost. "He, who?"

"Leo Thornbury," Nick said, as if this was beyond obvious.

It took a few seconds for Justine to register. When reading the *Star*, she tended to skip over the regular features she found pointless, like the gardening column. And the horoscopes. Which were written by the supposedly eminent astrologer Leo Thornbury.

Justine knew only three things about Leo Thornbury. One was the way he looked in the black-and-white thumbnail picture that topped his column, which hadn't to the best of her knowledge ever been updated. It showed him with a sweep of silver hair and a prominent brow over deep-set eyes, looking—she had once decided—like a cross between George Clooney and Frankenstein's monster. She also knew that he had a special fondness for including in his horoscopes quotations from famous writers, philosophers and wits. The third and final thing she knew about Leo Thornbury was that he was a notorious recluse.

"I've never met him," she said. "I don't think any of us has."

"What? *Never*? None of you?"

"Well, maybe Jeremy. Back in the day. He's the editor. But the rest of us, no. Leo Thornbury doesn't even come to the Christmas party. And that is the most suspicious thing of all. The food at the *Star* Christmas party is so good that even the gardening writer gets over her social anxiety once a year. Apparently, Leo lives on an island, but I don't think we're supposed to know where exactly."

"But what about the phone? Someone must speak to him, at least."

"I don't think so," Justine said. "I've never heard anyone say that they did. To tell you the absolute truth, I'm not certain he's exactly . . . real. Perhaps Leo Thornbury isn't so much a man as, maybe, a machine. A computer in a room somewhere, spitting out random phrases."

"Oh, you cynic."

"Cynic? I thought I was a Sagittarius."

Nick thought for a minute. "So you are. Born on the twenty-fourth of November," he said.

He remembered her birthday. He *remembered* her birthday. *Hey, did you hear that?* Justine said, even more smugly this time, to her brain. *He remembered my birthday.* Feeling a prickle of warmth rising up her neck and into her cheeks, she gave silent thanks that the day's light had dwindled into dusk, and Nick wouldn't be able to tell that she was blushing.

Nick flipped back through the *Star* to the horoscopes. The low light made it more difficult for him to read. But then some invisible switch, somewhere, was flicked, and the lights of Alexandria Park—frosted spheres held high above the pathways on wrought-iron poles—began to glow.

"Ah, thank you very much," Nick said. "Where are we, where are we? Libra, Scorpio . . . Sagittarius. Here we go. *Brace yourself, archers. Throughout this year, Saturn in your sign continues to set off seismic activity deep in your belief systems; be prepared, this month, to experience minor tremors. Late March is auspicious for career advancement, but it is likely that workplace change will continue to be a theme throughout the coming months.*"

Nick looked over at Justine and nodded, as if impressed with her achievements.

"So?" she asked.

"Well, that's good, isn't it? I'd have thought it's very good."

Justine snorted. "Seismic activity in my belief systems . . . what's that supposed to mean?"

"No, I mean the career advancement. The workplace change."

"Nothing changes at the *Star*. Nothing. Except maybe that Jeremy surprises us by coming to work wearing a tie."

"Well, Leo says workplace change. And Leo knows everything,"

Nick said, and although there was a hint of self-mockery in the smile, Justine got the distinct impression that he was, at least in part, serious.

"So, what profundities did Leo have for you this month?"

"Yeah, I don't really know what he's trying to say," Nick admitted. "It says: *Aquarius. 'What a frightening thing is the human,' wrote Steinbeck, 'a mass of gauges and dials and registers, and we can only read a few and those perhaps not accurately.' For water bearers, this is a month of readjustment in which you recognize that it is not only the inner workings of others that can be mysterious, but also the machinations of the self. In quiet moments of watchfulness, you may recalibrate your understanding of what it is that truly drives you.* What do you think that means?"

Justine shrugged. "Um . . . that Leo Thornbury's quote generator is up to S for Steinbeck."

"No, what do you think it means in my life?" Nick asked, but Justine did not think this was a question that was genuinely directed at her.

Then, just before she could launch into a small monologue about the generic nature of astrological predictions, and how the art of them was in making up sentences that applied to just about any person, in any kind of situation, she saw a thought arrive in Nick's mind: it showed up on his face like the notification of an incoming email.

"Hang on," he said.

Nick fished his phone out of his pocket, and Justine watched as he thumbed a query into Google and scrolled down the results at speed.

"Yes, yes, *yes!*" he said. "I've got it. I know what Leo's trying to tell me!"

"Well?"

"He's telling me to play Romeo!"

Justine frowned. "Romeo?"

"Yes, Romeo," said Nick. "Leo wants me to play Romeo."

"I'm sorry? You figure that how, exactly?"

"The quote. The quote!"

"The quote is from Steinbeck," Justine reminded him.

"Yes, yes. But," Nick said, and here he tapped the screen of his phone with vigor. "Not just *any* Steinbeck. It's from *The Winter of Our Discontent.*"

Justine thought, then shook her head. "Sorry."

"Winter of our *discontent*. *Winter* of our discontent. You know where that comes from, right?"

"If memory serves . . . it comes from *Richard III*."

"And?" Nick asked.

"And what?"

"Who wrote *Richard III*? *Shakespeare* wrote *Richard III*." Nick was getting excited, as well as actorish in his delivery. "Do you see? You must be able to see."

"Ah . . . struggling here."

"So, I have this choice. There's a production of *Romeo and Juliet* coming up. They've let me know that if I want it, Romeo's mine. But the show . . . it's not with a big company or anything. It's not even fully professional. But, then, I've never played Romeo. And the director has already lined up a few pretty impressive professional actors for some of the other major roles. There's so little work around."

"So, you want to do it?" Justine said.

"Well, it's a role I've always wanted. But the money will be shit. Or nonexistent. The show's being done on a profit-share basis, which usually means we can afford a cask of wine for the closing-night party."

There was a small silence. Then Nick said, "Leo's horoscopes are always spookily accurate. If he's saying go the Shakespeare, then there will be a good reason. Leo just knows things. Whenever I follow his advice, things go well. Things lead on to . . . you know . . . things."

Justine stared. "This is really how you make important life choices?"

Nick shrugged. "Oftentimes, yes."

"Wasn't it also Steinbeck who said something about only wanting advice if it agrees with what you wanted to do anyway?" Justine said.

Nick shook his head, disbelieving but impressed. "That's right, I remember that freaky memory of yours. You are the only person I know who would be able to produce a fact like that out of thin air."

Justine shrugged away the compliment. "I just think that if you want to play Romeo, you should play Romeo. You don't have to twist the words of some stargazing nut to give yourself permission."

"Leo Thornbury is not a stargazing nut. He's a god." Suddenly energized, Nick leaped up from the grass; the grassy bank became his stage. "Shakespeare was a Taurus. Earthy, lusty. But Romeo . . . now he, he was a Pisces."

"*What?* Did you just claim to know Romeo's star sign?"

"I did."

"And his birth date is mentioned where, precisely, in the text?"

"You can just tell. He's a dreamer, a beautiful dreamer. And nobody's more into self-sacrifice than a Pisces."

"You spent too long in that fish suit today."

"But, soft! What light through yonder window breaks? It is the east, and Juliet is the sun . . ."

"Maybe you should play Romeo," Justine said, and laughed. "Decision making isn't exactly his strong suit, either."

"You may mock, but Leo says this is right. Leo says this is what I have to do. And Leo will have his reasons."

Nick, without warning, sprang up onto the edge of the nearby planter box, placing his feet carefully on the sides so as not to squash any of the cabbages within. With the *Star* coiled into the silhouette of an unlit torch in his hand, he struck a heroic pose against the sky. Justine shook her head, smiling.

"He, that hath the steerage of my course, direct my sail!" Nick called out.

cusp

Toward the end of March, the sun on its great Monopoly board in the cosmos advanced one square from Pisces to Aries, thus concluding a full pass of the zodiac and without pause beginning another. Just after the clock had struck twelve on the night that separated the fish from the rams, a young woman stepped out the back door of her rented two-bedroom unit into a tiny courtyard garden.

Turning her face to the night sky, she allowed her soul to do a slow 180-degree flip inside her body, so that she felt herself to be hanging from the surface of the Earth: a human chandelier anchored by her feet to a ceiling of ugly interlocking paving bricks that there was, now, no longer any reason to look at. She let her gaze travel among the stars.

Most of the time she was Nicole Pitt—Aquarius, freelance gel nail technician, single mother of two and determined avoider of (any more) shiftless men, and the unimpressed provider for her drug-addicted neighbor's skinny cat, whom she had to assume was actually named Shithead. Inside the unit, Nicole's two boys slept on foam mattresses on the floor, their soft little limbs flung out from under their covers.

Her kitchen table—hell, her *only* table—was strewn with a constellation of crap that neatly mirrored the disparateness and disorganization of her life: her older boy's ADHD medication, several near-empty bottles of popular shades of nail varnish that had long needed replenishing, splayed astrological almanacs, a boxy old laptop with a cracked screen, and the latest edition of the *Alexandria Park Star*, lying open at the horoscopes.

But out here, hanging with her head in the stars at this peaceful, stolen hour, she was not Nicole Pitt at all, but Davina Divine—boutique private astrologer, mother to nobody at all, luxury bed linen connoisseur, occupier of a lavish Balinese-inspired home, distant and desultory inamorata to a retinue of charming and occasional beaux. Remote, tranquil and beautifully groomed, she was a trusted tour guide to the many pathways that were dot-to-dotted across the starry sky, a Delphic oracle who knew by instinct as much as training how the swirling forces of the heavens could be expected to push or pull.

As if, she thought.

The truth was that since the day her Diploma of Astrology certificate had arrived in the mail—and this was a few years ago, now—she'd spent vastly more time dreaming about becoming a famous astrologer than she had making any serious attempt to build up a clientele.

In quiet moments of watchfulness, you may recalibrate your understanding of what it is that truly drives you. That's what Leo Thornbury had written to Aquarians in the pages of the *Alexandria Park Star.* He'd foretold that, for the water bearers of the zodiac, the coming month would be one of readjustment: a time to contemplate the machinations of the self. And, when it came to Leo, Davina was an unashamed fan-girl.

It was time, Leo was telling her, to get real. But how? Well, for one thing, she could enroll in the Advanced Diploma of Astrology, and start advertising for some clients. She could put some flyers on the pinboard at her local supermarket. She could do some free natal charts for friends and family, then ask them to spread the word. Having formed this plan, Davina's mind began to drift into a fantasy of what it might be like to meet Leo Thornbury in person. But then an alien yowling broke into her thoughts, and it was loud enough to jerk her head out of the stars and force her soul to swivel back to its workaday orientation.

To her disappointment, she found herself standing in a tiny, miserable courtyard whose brick paving sprouted nothing but a cheap rotary clothesline. To her even greater disappointment, she was—once again—nobody else but Nicole Pitt. The yowling was coming from the narrow length of vertebrae and gingery fur that was weaving around her ankles. With a hand whose nails were painted a greenish purple shot-silk shade of varnish called Mermaid Dreams, Nicole scratched the cat between its tatty ears.

"Hey, Shithead," she said. "I suppose you're hungry."

$$+$$

As Nicole Pitt was spooning out a measure of the cut-price cat food that she'd taken to adding to her supermarket cart each week, Nick Jordan was walking an inner-city street with a duffel bag full of clothes that smelled—like everything in his world seemed currently to smell—of fish.

Nick knew all about the power of the olfactory sense, and how some smells could return you, instantly and reliably, to certain moments of your life. There was a particular brand of shampoo whose scent took him back to the first, thrilling time he'd ever taken a morning-after shower with a girl. And there was an unavoidable link between the whiff of a kerosene lamp and the camping holidays he'd loved as a kid. So he knew that, henceforth, the smell of fish was likely to bring him back to this particular phase of his life: these heartsick but delicately hopeful months that lay in the aftermath of his breakup with Laura Mitchell.

Today had been Nick's last in the employ of the fishmonger at the markets. Tomorrow would be his first day at a new job waiting tables for an upmarket Alexandria Park bistro, and it was this fact that had occasioned the late-night date with his laundry.

The laundromat's tall, empty windows glowed brightly in the dark street, and when Nick stepped through the door he registered with vague disappointment that the place was empty. Although one of the tumble dryers was humming industriously, there were no other customers sitting on the laundromat's benches, or leafing through its dog-eared magazines: nobody with whom he might strike up a casual conversation that would make this a slightly less depressing place to be.

Nick upended the contents of his duffel bag onto a bench and went through all his pockets, the way his mother always insisted that he should. And a good thing, too, for here—lurking in the back pocket of his best black pants—was a paper napkin of the sort that could easily confetti itself across an entire load of washing.

There was something written on it.

Still round the corner there may wait
A new road or a secret gate

The quote was from Tolkien, and Nick had copied it out with a dodgy biro that had bled blobs of blue ink into the napkin's soft surface. It had been part of Leo Thornbury's January horoscope for Aquarius: *With Venus in the spiritual sign of Pisces, you find yourself contemplating the thorny issue of self-worth. But go quietly, Aquarius. Mercury in retrograde brings with it a spirit of chaos that makes traveling unwise. Use these early weeks of the year to catch up on your sleep and practice your intuition, remembering that, as Tolkien tells us, "Still round the corner there may wait a new road or a secret gate."*

Of course, Leo had been right. He always was. It *had* been a bad time to travel, but the trip had been arranged long before January. And so, on New Year's Day, Nick had gone with Laura to far north Queensland to play the role of handbag while she'd been busy with a shoot for some new perfume. Although the resort where they had stayed had been beautiful, and although the water in the resort pool was a temperature that made it the perfect counterpoint to the humid air and although the piña coladas at the poolside bar were both exquisite and on the house, the trip—for Nick—had been miserable.

"It might be time to face it," Laura had said, one frangipani-scented night in their hotel room. He didn't think he would ever forget how beautiful she looked as she spoke, standing there at the foot of the bed with her cream silk robe untied and nothing underneath. "If you haven't made it by now . . . well, what I mean to say is, it might be time for Plan B."

She hadn't said it unkindly. And she hadn't said anything that he hadn't thought for himself. In February, he would be twenty-seven years old, and Hollywood was as far away as it had ever been. Forget Hollywood. Even the local professional theater companies were still in an unreachable stratosphere. Over the previous year, the only significant paying gigs he'd had were a walk-on part in a television soap, a gig at a healthy-eating expo in which he'd played a capsicum in a huge inflatable suit and a role in a rural tour of a puppet show about germs and the importance of washing one's hands. Nick had operated the puppet called Booger, and brought the house down at several school assembly halls with the superb timing of his nose-picking jokes.

"Especially if," Laura had added meaningfully, "we're going to get more serious about each other. Which I hope we are."

But, Nick had thought to himself, while lying there between the sheets of the resort's ultra-king-sized bed, *Still round the corner there may wait a new road or a secret gate.*

"I'm not ready to give up," he'd said. To Laura the lovely, Laura the lithe, Laura of the long, long, long legs. Laura Mitchell the Capricorn, who at the age of twenty-six already had several lump-sum deposits, a share portfolio and income protection insurance.

She'd said, "I don't want to lose you, Nick. But if we're going to be together, it's time for you to be more . . . well, you have to realize that you're not a teenager anymore. You can't eat two-minute noodles and ride a bicycle forever."

"What if I don't mind the bicycle? And the two-minute noodles?"

"Then we've got a problem," Laura said sadly.

Breaking up with Laura hadn't been easy. Not at all. But Nick had done it, and Laura had been poised and dignified in response. For the whole flight home, Nick had wanted nothing more than to soothe her, to soothe himself. *Still round the corner there may wait a new road or a secret gate,* he had told himself, and that had been enough to help him to hold the line.

Nick shoved his clothes into the washing machine, fed some coins into the slot and calculated that he was nearing the four-month mark of his post-Laura life. He was still in a provisional phase, not yet having found a home of his own. For the time being, he was housesitting for an artist who'd gone to Cuba seeking inspiration for a new exhibition. The artist's apartment was groovy, if comfortless. It had few appliances, the bed was a futon that may well have been stuffed with concrete, and every wall in the place was densely hung with the artist's own canvases, many of which featured animals being decapitated. Some mornings Nick found it hard to eat his Weetabix for all the spurting carotid arteries.

Every day of the last few months, for Nick, had been a walk along a tightrope. On one side was the knowledge that Laura was right—that it was time to grow up, give up, get a real job. But on the other side there remained the tingling possibility that his dream future still existed.

The director of *Romeo and Juliet* had been gratifyingly thrilled when Nick had phoned to accept the lead role. It was hard to imagine that the Alexandria Park Repertory Theater production would be attended by any theatrical luminaries who might, after seeing Nick perform, feel compelled to provide him with the break he so desperately needed. But Nick had learned to trust Leo Thornbury. If he followed the astrologer's advice, things worked out.

It had been the director who, pleased with Nick's decision to play Romeo, had tipped him off about the job opening at Cornucopia, a bistro that was conveniently close to the Alexandria Park Repertory's rehearsal rooms, and notable for paying higher-than-average wages. But there was something else in the mix that had Nick puzzled. The bistro was owned by Dermot Hampshire, the food writer at the *Alexandria Park Star*, where Justine Carmichael worked. First, he'd run into her at the markets; now this. What did it *mean*? he wondered.

In the twelve years since he'd seen her, she'd hardly changed at all. Her body was still slight, her hazel eyes still full of mischief. She was whip-smart as ever, too, in a way that made him think about—perhaps even overthink—every word he said. And those eyebrows: they hadn't changed either. Although thick and straight, they were capable of all kinds of dexterous maneuvers that made him wonder if she was privately mocking him.

For the whole evening in Alexandria Park, Nick had waited for an opening, for an invitation to reminisce about that night they'd spent, as fourteen-year-olds, on a South Australian beach. They talked about plenty of other things: about her work and their families, about astrology and Shakespeare. When he'd asked for her phone number, she'd given it to him willingly enough, but he'd been a little taken aback when she hadn't asked for his in return. Neither had she given him even the slightest hint that she wanted to talk about that long-ago night.

He'd thought perhaps they'd be able to laugh together about how the pair of them had slipped away from their parents and found a bottle shop on a street bordering the amusement park. And how Justine—who'd been very obviously younger than eighteen—had hovered nervously outside while Nick, who was tall for his age and could do a persuasively deep voice, had gone inside and managed to procure a bottle of Stone's Green Ginger Wine. They'd shared the better part of the bottle as they talked, gradually loosening up to the point where Nick was showing off all the accents he could mimic, and Justine was reciting poetry.

Nick blushed to think about what kind of gormless dickhead he'd been, back then. So young and so inexperienced. When they'd kissed, he'd probably mauled her half to death without knowing any better. It was no wonder she'd hidden away the next morning and refused to come out to say goodbye. He'd tried several times, once he was back at home, to write to her. But every sentiment he'd managed to get down on the page sounded stupid. Plus, he'd been terrified of misspelling a word.

Seeing Justine again had unsettled him. It'd had the effect of joining him up, circling him back, to a much younger version of himself—and while it had felt good to be reminded of all the energy and confidence of that younger self, it had also felt uncomfortable, as if she'd caught him out for failing to live up to the promise and potential of that self. She had reminded him of parts of himself that were, what . . . receding?

Nick took out his phone, and wasn't sure if he was relieved or disappointed that the screen wasn't showing any more missed calls from Laura. In recent weeks, she'd phoned several times, and left messages saying that she wanted to talk. To see if there was any room for compromise. But Nick kept reminding himself that, for Laura, compromise really meant him being convinced to change his mind to match hers.

Nick scrolled through his contacts until he reached "Justine Carmichael" and tapped on the screen so that the letters of her name glowed, large and clear. Then he paused. It was very late; too late to call. But it wasn't out of the question to send her a text.

Great to see you the other night . . . he began, then deleted the words. "Boring," he muttered.

Justine was someone who could effortlessly pull entire poems out of her mind, who remembered quotes from Steinbeck as if they were song lyrics. If he was going to write to her, he'd have to write something that was at least half interesting.

I was just thinking about . . . he began again. Deleted every word. Sighed.

What was he doing? he asked himself, and was embarrassed to have to acknowledge that he was sitting in a lonely laundromat and composing a text, at midnight, to a girl who hadn't asked for his phone number, and who most likely had a perfectly nice life without him in it. And so, to the soundtrack of the washing machine's rhythmic *swish, swish, swish,* Nick put his phone back into his pocket.

Aries

MARCH 21–APRIL 19

L ate summer drifted into autumn. Things ended, and things began. But in the life of Justine Carmichael, things went on pretty much the same as before. In the mornings, she woke and went to work at the *Star*, and in the evenings, she came home and went to sleep. But no matter how often she looked at her phone and willed it to ring, Nick Jordan did not call.

Home, for Justine, was an apartment on the twelfth and uppermost floor of Evelyn Towers, an Alexandria Park apartment block with classic, wedding-cake curves and mint green trimmings, original leadlight windows and a lobby with a parquetry floor. That Justine could afford to live in such a sought-after address was almost entirely thanks to her paternal grandmother. Fleur Carmichael, knowing that the family's Eden Valley farm would pass to her eldest son, had endeavored to ensure that her two younger children would also inherit something of value after her death. In the case of Justine's father, Drew, the something had been an elegant, city-edge investment property.

Drew and Mandy let Justine have the apartment for little more than a peppercorn rent, although the downside to this arrangement came in the form of fairly frequent, and fairly frequently unannounced, visits from family members who were in the city for the theater, Aussie Rules

football, the tennis, a decent restaurant or dentist. It was usually irritating to be suddenly infested with relatives, but on this particular
Wednesday evening, Justine would actually have been quite grateful
for some company.

She tugged the curtains closed across a pair of French doors that
opened out onto a semicircular balcony, and tried not to look at the
view. Once, the windows and balconies on three sides of Evelyn Towers
had overlooked the nearby park. But in the 1970s, a brown-brick apartment block had been inserted into the narrow space between Evelyn
Towers and its neighboring twin. Justine's view was therefore taken up
by the ugly facade of the next-door block, and her balcony was only a
few meters away from the rusted railing of her neighbor's tiny porch.
She had a clear view into the living room beyond that porch, and, more
disturbingly, through the bathroom window as well. The current oc-
cupant of the flat was a middle-aged man with a massive AC/DC tattoo
on one buttock, and no shower curtain.

Justine dumped her bag on the kitchen counter and fished out her
phone. There were no missed calls, nobody demanding her attention,
and no messages that might have provided a distraction from the nothing that she really needed to do.

It had been two months since best-pal Tara had traded in a city-
based current affairs radio job to become the only full-time reporter at
one of the ABC's more distant rural outposts. In those months, Justine
had begun to discover just how much of her social life was generated
by the engine of Tara's boundless, extrovert energy. Without Tara to
turn up at the *Star* at the end of a working day and drag her off to the
pub, or to arrive unannounced at Evelyn Towers on her way to a party
that Justine simply *had to* come along to, Justine was prone to working
longer hours and spending her downtime with the friends she found
inside the covers of books and DVD box sets.

Justine and Tara had been friends since their first year at university. That they were both journalism majors was one of the very few
things they had in common. While Justine actually liked to study, Tara
put the majority of her energy into volunteering for the campus radio
station and making sure she never missed an event that involved free
beer. This didn't prevent her, however, from acing every subject.

In those university years, Tara—raised in the inner suburbs—had been Justine's guide to the big city, while Justine had been Tara's ticket to experiencing the kind of country life that had featured in her childhood fantasies. Some weekends they stayed in town and on others they drove out to Edenvale, where Tara spent as much time as she could on Justine's uncle's farm, learning to drive all the machinery and trying to get her Blundstone boots authentically trashed.

Unlike Justine, who'd steadfastly held on to an increasingly old-fashioned desire to work in print, Tara had been keen on digital media from the start. In recent years, she'd been offered plum television current affairs jobs in several of the nation's capital cities, and also in an impressive range of overseas bureaus, but she'd turned them all down in favor of this multiplatform reporting position in the country. Now, every time Justine heard her friend on the television or radio, she was talking about fracking or live cattle exports, regional internet speeds or the never-ending drought.

Justine dialed Tara's number, and the phone rang, and rang. Probably, thought Justine, it had been abandoned on the dusty seat of a ute while Tara was interviewing a farmer. Or it might have been left lying on the bar at the local pub while she took her shot at pool.

If you really can't text, said Tara's recorded voice at last, *leave a message.*

The tone wasn't exasperated, just blunt. And that was Tara all over. In all the years she and Justine had known each other, Justine had never had to wonder for a minute what Tara was really thinking.

Resigning herself to an evening of solitude, Justine did the breakfast dishes, hung out a load of washing and scraped the bottom of the Vegemite jar in order to make dinner. Then she took a bath and went to bed early with the handsome Arden edition of *Romeo and Juliet*, which had in recent days taken up residence on her bedside table. She flicked the book open to the marked page and began to read.

Juliet was whining.

The clock struck nine when I did send the nurse, Justine read. *In half an hour, she promised to return. Perchance she cannot meet him. That's not so. Oh, she is lame! Love's heralds should be thoughts, which ten times faster glide than the sun's beams.*

It must indeed have sucked, Justine thought, having to rely on a servant to come back with a message from your beloved. What Juliet would have given for a smartphone!

Justine glanced at her phone, propped against the stack of books on the bedside table. For all the good it did. What was the use of owning a device that could herald love faster than a sunbeam if nobody bothered to avail themselves of the technology?

Brain: *It's been ten days.*

As if she didn't already know.

Justine tried to refocus on the words on the page in front of her, Shakespeare's words. *Is thy news good, or bad? Answer to that; Say either, and I'll stay the circumstance: Let me be satisfied, is't good or bad?*

Brain: *Remind me again why we came home without his phone number?*

Justine: *Because, as you well know, I'm impulsive. By now, I definitely would have called him.*

Brain: *And?*

Justine: *Then I would never have known what I know now. That he had no intention of calling me.*

"Darl," said Jeremy Byrne, the following morning.

It was very early and Justine was dressed for speed in three-quarter black pants and a shirt printed with leaping hares. She had barely set foot in the hallway of the *Star* offices, when the editor's sudden materialization at his office doorway startled her—as did the tenor of his voice, which was unusually low and somewhat conspiratorial.

"Got a mo?" he asked.

"Of course," she said, and as she followed Jeremy into his den of papery clutter, she did a quick poke around in her conscience to see if there was anything troubling her there. Oversights? Conflicts? Misdemeanors? Nope. Nothing. So, what did he want to discuss with her?

"Darl," Jeremy said, sitting heavily in his chair on the far side of his desk, then leaning forward to rest his chin on steepled fingers. "It has been a joy and a privilege having you as our copy-girl. And although I had hoped to have better news for you today, it seems . . ."

Justine's heart was hit by a bolt of adrenaline. What? Was this bad news? She started to speak, but Jeremy sailed blithely onward.

". . . that the changes I have in mind are not entirely, shall we say, perfect? Should you be amenable to the idea, we *could*—as I say, if you were amenable to the idea—call you our contributions manager, which of course is not quite the position that we have in mind for you. Eventually. In the long run. But still, let us consider this another step closer, and in fact, let us hope that in the fullness of time, in due course, an opening will become . . ."

Jeremy's delivery was speeding up and down, so that some words, like "contributions manager," were lost on Justine's ears, while others, like "in the fullness of time," came out so slowly that they seemed unduly important.

"I'm sorry," Justine interrupted. "I'm not following."

"Oh," Jeremy said, and paused for a moment to find a different angle. "Ah, well. Natsue is leaving us. Going to Europe to live with her, ah, family. And I am wondering if perhaps you would wish to replace her in the role of contributions manager. Of course, it's not quite the usual route to a reporter's job, and you could, if you wished, forgo this step and continue to wait for a genuine opening in the newsroom. Believe me, nothing would bring me greater happiness than to be offering you a cub reporter position today. Our goal after all is to have you writing for the *Star*, but the role of contributions manager would offer certain opportunities to make your mark on the publication. Selecting the Letters to the Editor. Proofreading my editorial, hey? Chopping Dermot's column to size. And speaking to our rather rambunctious gourmand on the phone afterward. Hm. Well. You can learn from Natsue, there. The, um, best way to proceed."

Justine tried to keep herself steady as two distinctly different feelings began to unfurl in her chest.

"Natsue's leaving?" she said, with a sad frown.

He's offering me a chance to step up, she thought, with an internal squeal of joy.

"Indeed, indeed. Natsue has been our oasis of calm, and we will miss her very much. And she will leave us very soon. Friday next, in fact. She was willing to stay on longer, but I suggested to her that if her heart is in fact in Sweden, then so too must she be. So, what do you think, hm?"

"I'm ready . . . very ready . . . for a new challenge," Justine said.

"Excellent, excellent. Thought as much," Jeremy said, beaming.

"I'd still be next in line for reporter?"

"Indubitably," Jeremy said.

"Then, yes!" Justine said. "Yes, please!"

"Good, good, very good," said Jeremy, sinking back into his chair, and Justine tried—not entirely successfully—to keep her celebratory dance moves on the inside.

Jeremy continued, "Well then, it seems I will spend the rest of my day in search of your replacement. And let us hope that I am able to locate someone almost as marvelous as you have been. It can be a trial, I know, all the fetching and carrying. Did I ever tell you about the time when I was a copy-boy at the *New York Times* and . . ."

But Justine could not even have claimed to have been half listening. She was one-eighth listening, at best. What was it that Nick had read to her from Leo's column? *Late March is auspicious for career advancement.* Justine remembered that Leo had also written, *workplace change will continue to be a theme throughout the coming months.* Perhaps her long-awaited reporter's job wasn't so very far away after all. Perhaps she would soon be writing for the *Star*. She imagined her first byline, her first cover story, her first Walkley Award–winning . . . whoa, whoa, whoa. Wait a minute, she counseled herself. She had just been promoted to contributions manager of the *Alexandria Park Star*. In her new role, she would be professional, capable and logical. It wasn't as if, for heaven's sake, she was about to start believing in the *stars*.

By Friday afternoon of the following week, Justine had three-quarters-filled a notebook with facts about her new job. Even so, Natsue was still meting out small but important details.

"Don't forget Dermot expects to receive five copies of each new edition," Natsue said. "This is because he likes to have his column on display in all of his venues: at Cornucopia, at the cafe at the cheese factory and at the demonstration kitchen."

The whole time she spoke, her hands were moving efficiently over a keyboard as she transcribed a hard-copy letter that was pegged to a document holder beside her screen.

"That doesn't add up," Justine said, with a frown.

"The fourth copy," said Natsue, without ceasing the allegro music of her typing, "is for Dermot's own private records, and the fifth must go—this is important, Justine, unless you wish to receive several anxious phone calls—to Dermot's mother in the Holy Rosary nursing home in Leederwood."

Justine could hardly believe that this skylit cube of an office was to be hers. On Monday. She loved its compact tidiness, and the way Natsue had arranged the objects on the desk. They were quite usual things— just a computer, in-box, document holder, document spike, a slimline fax machine, a jar of sharpened pencils, a potted fern—but Natsue had created a composition that was somehow pleasing and relaxing.

"Do you know what caused the greatest number of complaints ever in the history of the *Star*?" Natsue asked.

Justine did not.

"It was a problem with the cryptic crossword puzzle. The clues were inadvertently matched to the wrong grid," Natsue said. "Chaos!"

The second most grievous episode in the magazine's history was when the "Down" and "Across" clues were accidentally transposed. And, Natsue said, although these events were now more than a decade in the past, for Doc Millar, the cryptic crossword setter, the pain was both fresh and enduring.

"So, be sure to email the final layout of the crossword for Doc's approval," Natsue said. "And don't be surprised if he drops in to the office to check the setting in person, just to be on the safe side. He takes his coffee strong and black, with three sugars."

Justine continued to make notes as Natsue talked her through the peccadillos of the *Star*'s finance writer and the paranoia of its agony aunt.

"Only two contributors," Natsue continued, "are yet to participate in the email revolution."

They were, she went on, Lesley-Ann Stone, the gardening writer, and Leo Thornbury, the astrologer. Lesley-Ann was an anti-fluoridation campaigner and breeder of vintage daffodils whose monthly contribution came thriftily composed in blunt pencil on the backs of used envelopes and the insides of torn-open seed packets, often with a free sprinkling of certified organic earth.

"In the case of Lesley-Ann, and Leo, our task is essentially one of data entry," Natsue told Justine. "Neither invites further correspondence, and each prefers not to accept contributor copies. Lesley-Ann because she thinks publishing is a waste of the earth's resources, and Leo because he is not interested in earthly affairs. He owns no telephone, apparently. But he does, at least, have a fax machine."

From her in-box, Natsue plucked out a fax and handed it to Justine, who immediately saw that it was a neat and closely spaced page of text that appeared originally to have been typed on an old-fashioned typewriter.

"This is how Leo's stars come to us?" Justine asked, incredulous. "By fax?"

Natsue nodded. "Usually overnight."

Justine handed back the fax and Natsue clipped it to her document holder. As she began to transcribe it at a fearsome speed, there came the sound of a champagne cork popping in the hallway, followed by some general shouts of delight. Jeremy came to Natsue's doorway, unleashing a stream of bubbly into a glass.

"Kobayashi-san," he said, with a bow. "You are hereby summoned to the tearoom for libations. This instant!"

Natsue glanced up at her computer clock, which read 4:05 p.m.

"But, Jeremy, the stars . . ." Natsue said. "Five minutes more, please."

"Absolutely not," Jeremy said, holding out the champagne flute invitingly.

"I'll do the stars, Natsue," Justine offered. "It's no problem. You go."

Justine saw the tension in Natsue, pulled between demands.

"Really, go on," Justine urged. "It'll be good for me, you know, to get the hang of it."

"If you're absolutely sure?" Natsue said.

"Quite sure."

With that, Natsue got up from her office chair for what would be the very last time. Justine waited a moment, then slid happily into her new place behind the desk.

Aries, she read. According to Leo, Arians were going to be affected by Lilith in their relationship sector. Though, what the hell was Lilith? Apparently—thanks to Venus going direct on the fifteenth, whatever *that* meant—Taureans would experience a surge in romantic possibilities. Justine made a mental note to tell this to Tara, who was a proud Taurean. Although it was probably old news, since Tara seemed to live in a perpetual surge of romantic possibility.

Geminis, said Leo, were breaking free of the influence of a series of troublesome eclipses, and experiencing a sense of fresh air and liberation. It was, Justine thought wryly, exactly the sort of one-size-fits-all nonsense that her mother, the Gemini, would get a shiver of pleasure from reading. *Fresh air and liberation*, Mandy Carmichael would read, before spending a day or two noticing how good—how free!—she felt when she breathed deeply.

And here was the entry for Sagittarius: *Beset by restless thoughts, Sagittarians may be feeling the urge for change, but with Venus in retrograde for most of the coming month, now is not a good time to make changes to your appearance. Delay until May any temptation to alter the color of your hair or overhaul your wardrobe. Intuitive archers may sense the impact of stellar activity now taking place in their twelfth house of secrets and desires.*

Nothing more about workplace change, alas. Or about old flames leaping back into her life. She sighed, and looked down the page to the entry for Aquarius. *This month sees you reaping the benefits of the difficult decisions that you have made in recent times. Tread your new path with determination, Aquarius, remembering that temptations to turn back will be amplified by Venus in retrograde, which can bring up wistful, nostalgic thoughts. For water bearers seeking new homes, or considering significant changes to existing environments, the final days of the month will provide favorable cosmic conditions for choosing well.*

What would Nick make of this? she wondered. Perhaps it would appear to him as a subliminal message that he really ought to play Hamlet. Or Henry IV. She shook her head at the thought of Nick's illogical trust in the stars. But she also had a thought. An interesting thought.

If there was anyone who could prompt Nick to pick up his phone and call her, then it was probably Leo Thornbury.

The Wednesday before Good Friday was deadline day at the *Star*—Justine's first as contributions manager. The cover shot for the new edition was an arresting close-up of the troubled face of Tariq Lafayette, the young film director who'd recently won an award for the latest of his hard-hitting documentaries on asylum seekers. The editorial, which referenced Lafayette's work and called on the nation's leaders to show moral leadership, had been written not by Jeremy, but by the *Star*'s Canberra correspondent, Daniel Griffin, and Justine had agonized over the edits. She'd also sunk hours into the food page, trying to compress Dermot Hampshire's column on the pleasures of autumnal food to make room for his recipe for lamb rack and beetroot salsa. Apparently, it was a good sign that he'd hung up on her only once during their protracted negotiations.

Justine spent the early hours of the day going over every column centimeter of the sections for which she was responsible. She wanted them polished to a high gleam before Jeremy dispatched the files at close of business. Late in the morning she was visited, just as Natsue had predicted, by the cryptic crossword setter, Doc Millar. He stood at Justine's shoulder and fixed his watery, doleful eyes on her computer screen, checking, double-checking and triple-checking every last detail of the setting, all the while slurping coffee through the scrubbing-brush bristles of his gray mustache.

Doc had only just departed, having gloomily pronounced the crossword to be satisfactory, when the desk phone rang.

Not again, Justine thought, sure that this was yet another call from Dermot Hampshire, who would want to argue and complain about her edits. As she reached for the receiver, she prepared to go back into battle: *calm, professional battle*, she told herself.

"Hello," she said, trying to sound firm from the outset.

"Justine?"

It wasn't Dermot.

"Yes?" Justine said.

"Hi. It's Daniel. Daniel Griffin. In Canberra."

"Oh," said Justine uselessly. Her brain, meanwhile, helpfully dredged up an image of the *Star*'s chief political reporter and placed it front and center of her mind. It was cobbled together from Daniel's rather suave byline picture and the impressions Justine had formed at the last two office Christmas parties. Although she had been introduced to him, she didn't feel that she had ever really *met* him. She had him pegged as the sort of person who looked over your shoulder while talking to you, just in case there was someone more important on the other side of the room.

Why was he calling her? Perhaps he'd rung to complain as well. Maybe she'd cut his copy too aggressively. Had he been insulted by the number of times she'd taken out a slightly pretentious phrase and replaced it with a simpler one?

She braced.

"Look, just a quick call," Daniel said, ending a too-long silence. "I just wanted to say thanks. For the job you did on that editorial of mine. It was really thorough. The attention to detail . . . you really made the piece sing."

"Oh," Justine said, utterly wrong-footed. "Thank you."

"And while I've got you on the phone—congratulations on the promotion. I did my years as a copy-runner at the *Star* too, and I can tell you there were times when I thought I was going to go gray on the job. I know contributions manager isn't exactly a reporter, but at least it's a step in the right direction."

"Yes, absolutely. A step in the right direction," Justine managed. God, she sounded like a parrot.

"See you next time I'm in town, okay?"

"Okay."

Justine put the phone down and leaned back in her chair. She rubbed her dry, screen-sore eyes as she processed what had just happened. Daniel Griffin had called her to thank her. He had appreciated her work and bothered to call her up to say so.

Brain: *Maybe he's not so up himself, after all.*

Justine: *You don't think?*

Brain: *I can't think. Not without food.*

Justine grabbed her coffee mug, fished her lunch out of her bag and headed for the tearoom. Still glowing from Daniel's compliment, she was just about to toast her cheese sandwich when Jeremy appeared, shrugging on his suit jacket.

"There you are! There you are! Excellent," Jeremy said, and waved a hand at her sandwich. "Heavens! Put *that* away. We have been summoned."

"Summoned?" Justine said.

"To lunch. At Cornucopia. Dermot wants to meet you," Jeremy explained. "Apparently, you've made something of an impression on him over the phone. And so he is offering us lunch. On the house."

Although it was broad daylight when Justine and Jeremy arrived at the Dufrene Street bistro, the dark interior of the establishment cultivated the intimate atmosphere of evening. Huge light globes hung from the dark timbered ceiling, their dim orange filaments glowing like swing sets for fairy folk.

"Mr. Byrne? Miss Carmichael?" said a waitress. She had a long, unstructured ponytail of pale curls, and prominent piercings in the cartilage of both ears. She led the way through a busy maze of tables and chairs to a booth at the very back of the dining room.

The bistro's decor was all about rustic, raw timber and hard edges, but as Justine slid into her booth seat, she discovered the bench was plushly covered in sheepskin.

"Dermot says not to worry about ordering," said the waitress, pouring icy water from a jug into Jeremy's and Justine's glasses. "He's taken care of everything."

When she was gone, Jeremy asked, "So, how have you been managing? With Dermot? Hm?"

"I think we're reaching an understanding," Justine said. "Although, I wouldn't say it's been a simple process."

"Ah," said Jeremy, nodding apologetically. "I am afraid to say that talent does not discriminate against arrogance. Indeed, the two—in my experience—seem to have something of a rapport."

It was not in dispute that Dermot Hampshire was a talented chef, and for Justine and Jeremy he put on a virtuoso rendition of his skills, sending out from the kitchen a steady stream of tapas plates and bowls. There was a rich, spicy broth that was thick with pearl barley, breaded lamb cutlets with elegantly wilted greenery, and small and tempting displays of meats and vegetables and skewers.

The waitress kept appearing out of the gloom, bringing food, taking plates, filling glasses with both water and wine. Before long, Justine was feeling the effects of the excellent, full-bodied Cornucopia house pinot. Her cheeks were warm, and she had a sense of her internal firewalls being softened and pulled down. Realizing that in this state she might say, or do, something ill advised, she resolved to drink only water for the rest of lunch.

Justine was raising her wineglass to her lips for one last sip—just *one*, she told herself—when Dermot Hampshire himself appeared, bearing a large platter of cheeses and a bottle of tawny port. The cheeses were slightly luminous and waxy, beautifully arranged with wedges of fig paste and sliced pear. As well as being the proprietor of Cornucopia, Dermot had founded the Un-ewes-ually Good cheese factory in a small rural town not far from Edenvale.

"Jezza," Dermot said loudly to Jeremy. "Great to see you, mate."

Jezza, Justine mentally repeated. *Jezza?*

"Ah, my good man," Jeremy said. "An excellent repast. Truly excellent."

Dermot inclined his head with mock modesty and expertly cleared a space on the table in order to set down the platter. Then he landed his own intimidating bulk on the bench seat, forcing Justine to shuffle over.

"How did you like the stones?" he asked her.

She was bewildered. "Sorry?"

"The stones," he repeated, picking up a knife and tapping its blade on a plate that now held nothing but crumbs.

The things on the plate had been delicious. Little nuggets of some kind of meat—a bit chewy, perhaps, but not in a bad way.

"They were delicious," Justine said.

"They were lambs' balls," Dermot announced, clearly very pleased with himself.

First, Justine blanched. Then blood hurtled back into her cheeks in a rush.

Dermot chortled. "Why don't you have some more, since you liked them so much?" He snapped his fingers loudly. "Dolly! Hey, Doll! More stones!"

"Thank you, Dermot, but please don't—"

"I insist. And, listen, don't do the polite crap here. If someone offers you more, you take it. You know that thing people say? Less is more? What a crock of shit! In my book, the only thing that's more is *more*. Take my column, for example. I think I'm worth two pages. But the editor, here—he's cramping my style keeping me at one. You tell him, Justine. Tell him I need more room. Room to move."

Justine waited for Jeremy to intervene, but he only looked on with amused interest.

There was the click of china on timber as a serving of "stones" appeared at her elbow, but this time it was not the waitress with the fair curls who made the delivery. It was a young man. With dark hair, blue eyes and a smile that sat ever so slightly sideways on his face.

"Nick!" Justine said. Oh God, she thought, her cheeks reddening— had that come out as a squeak? She hurried on, "You're working *here* now? What happened to the fish gig?"

"They let me off the hook," he said, and Justine laughed, though perhaps a little more than the joke deserved.

Dermot leaned back and put an arm along the top of the seat back, so that his hand rested just behind Justine's neck. He was a big man in any case, but this expansive gesture seemed engineered to make him appear bigger still.

"Know each other, do you?" he said.

"Indeed we do," Nick said, collecting up some empty glasses on the table and stacking them in the crook of his arm.

Dermot, trying to lean even further back, said, "And are you acquainted with Jeremy here, too?"

Nick smiled professionally. "No, I—"

Dermot made a regal gesture. "Jeremy Byrne, editor of the *Alexandria Park Star*, this is Nick, one of my newest recruits."

"A pleasure," Jeremy said.

"Likewise," Nick responded. "And can I just congratulate you on having the good sense to employ Justine. She always was destined to be a writer. Even before the spelling competition, there were signs."

"Spelling competition?" Jeremy asked.

"You mean you don't know?" Nick teased, though his face remained mostly deadpan. "Has she been keeping her true identity a secret?"

Dermot raised his eyebrows in Justine's direction as Nick continued, "You are in the presence of someone who was once the under-ten televised spelling bee champion of the nation."

"Is that so?" Dermot drawled.

"I can't say I'm surprised," Jeremy said.

"She was always one of those scarily clever girls, you know? All the boys at school were terrified of her."

I was? thought Justine. *They were?*

She observed that Nick was affecting a slightly formal demeanor—treading a fine line, in Dermot's presence, between subservience and self-assurance.

"Nick's an actor," Justine said, in the hope of changing the topic. Then she wondered if that statement had been tactless, so she added, "As well as a waiter, of course. If I'm not mistaken, he's about to play Romeo?"

"At your service," he said, taking a half step backward and making the slightest of bows.

Dermot weighed in. "Well, Justine here has recently been promoted. The lucky girl's been given the job of keeping me in line."

Nick's smile was carefully neutral as he collected up an empty tapas plate and Jeremy's crumpled napkin.

"Promoted," Nick said, nodding that he was impressed, although as he straightened up and turned toward the kitchen, Justine saw one of his eyebrows twitch into an unspoken *I told you so.* "So, I'll see you around?"

Justine, feeling Dermot's and Jeremy's eyes on her, shrugged as carelessly as she could manage. "You have my number."

Brain: *Well, that was about as warm and encouraging as a blanket made of icicles.*

Justine: *Shit.*

After a moment, Dermot forked one of the crumbed stones and grinned at Justine. "Did I detect a certain, shall we say . . . *frisson* . . . in the air?"

Justine flushed.

"You've got taste, Justine. I'll say that for you. He's a good-looking kid. But then, all my waitstaff are good-looking kids. So, you and young Nick, are you . . . you know?" Dermot made his eyebrows wriggle.

Justine looked at Jeremy meaningfully, but Jeremy was absorbed in pouring himself another glass of port.

"It's getting late. We should probably—" Justine began.

"Ah, so you'd like to be, but you're not. *Yet,*" Dermot said.

"Jeremy?" Justine said beseechingly.

Dermot leaned in close to her. "You should call him."

"I don't think—"

"Grow a set, lambkin! Call him. *Call* him."

Justine took a steadying breath and smiled as confidently as she could manage. "It's a beautiful place you have here. Almost perfect."

"What do you mean *almost*?" he asked.

She picked up a menu, laid it in front of Dermot, and tapped her finger on the description of a particularly lavish pasta dish.

" 'Fetuccine' wants a double 't'—*fettuccine*—as well as the double 'c.' I felt sure you would want to know."

Dermot peered closely, disbelievingly, at the menu.

Justine went on, "And, for future reference, Dermot, we women already have a set. We just don't hang 'em out where everyone can see them."

Jeremy let out a delighted chuckle. Dermot scrutinized Justine for a moment, and then he laughed, too—a huge guffaw that showed all his super-white teeth.

"I like you, Justine. I like you," he said.

Great, thought Justine, as Dermot poured a generous measure of port into a fresh glass in front of her. Despite her earlier resolution, she took a long slug.

It was well past four o'clock by the time Justine and Jeremy returned to the office, both of them rosy-cheeked and somewhat fuzzy around the edges. After fixing a strong coffee, Justine retreated to her office. She had lost several hours to Dermot's hospitality; there were now less than forty-five minutes until deadline. But where would the remaining time be best spent?

"What's the worst thing that could happen?" she murmured to herself, then clicked open the page that contained Doc Millar's crossword.

It was hard to believe that this dull and generic page—unenlivened by color of any kind, with the horoscopes laid out above the two crossword puzzles, the cryptic and the quick—could cause so much trouble out there in Readerland. And yet, so Natsue had warned, this boring black-and-white page had the power to unleash a tsunami of consequences.

Justine read through Doc's clues forward, then backward. Having found no errors, she read through them forward, just one more time for good luck. Satisfied that she had taken scrupulous care, she was about to close the page for the last time when it occurred to her that she really ought to check over the horoscopes as well. Leo Thornbury in his thumbnail picture stared out at Justine from the screen, mystically, his eyes dark under the silver coif of his hair.

Brain: *This Nick . . .*

Justine: *Yes?*

Brain: *I think you like him. Quite a bit.*

This was probably true. But it was no excuse to tinker with Leo's copy.

Brain: *But who would ever know?*

Justine considered. Leo's original fax was on the document spike on the desk, placed there by Justine, just as Natsue had instructed. But it was well buried now, lying somewhere beneath Lesley-Ann's gardening column and a selection of Letters to the Editor. Furthermore, Leo didn't read the *Star*. And nobody at the *Star* had seen Leo's April fax. Except for Justine and Natsue. And Natsue was by now in Sweden. Even if somebody did send Natsue a copy of the April *Star*, would she bother to read the horoscopes? And, if she did read them, would she remember the text for Aquarius? Word for word? Having done no more than glance at it before Justine took over the transcription?

But, what if Leo were to pick up the magazine, just this one time?

Brain: *He won't.*

Justine: *How do you know?*

Brain: *And anyway, it's not as if the horoscopes are . . . real. They're all just rubbish. What's one random phrase compared to another? What harm could it do?*

The texture of the air in Justine's office seemed to gather a new charge of possibility. She stared at the page layout on the computer screen for so long that it seemed to shimmer and pixelate before her eyes.

Brain: *Go on . . .*

Justine: *No. I'm closing the page now.*

Brain: *But tomorrow the files will be gone and it will be too late. If you're going to do it, you're going to have to do it now.*

Without yet having any definite intent—and without having committed to any course of action—Justine selected the copy for Aquarius. 389 characters. Provided her changes didn't make the entry fall much short of that number, or greatly exceed it, there would be no impact on the page setting.

She could write, *Aquarius—Something or someone from the past will be important in your life this month . . .*

No, too obvious. Justine had seen for herself the way Nick read his horoscope: looking between the lines, searching for hidden messages. She needed to remind him of herself, but not too directly. She could mention a spelling competition? No, too specific. And anyway, how would you work something like that into a horoscope?

Then an idea popped into Justine's head.

Joni Mitchell's "Big Yellow Taxi," she thought, remembering her Little Mermaid karaoke machine. Nick would remember their famous living-room rock concert, surely.

Her fingers flew over the keys. *Were we not beseeched by songbird Joni Mitchell, at the beginning of the Age of Aquarius, to leave our apples spotted and our Paradise unpaved? This month, you experience a power-ful surge of nostalgia for what once was, which also doubles as an intu-ition of what yet might be.*

Justine smiled. Writing hog-shit was surprisingly good fun. But at 276 characters, the entry was too short. She thought back over Leo's copy. It was probably wise to include at least something from the origi-nal. So she added, *In further news, a change of abode may be on the cards, or at the very least a modest makeover chez water bearer.*

That bulked it out to 390 characters. Perfect. Justine read over the copy one more time, jiggled the computer mouse and clicked . . . Save.

"Darl," came a sudden voice at the door, and Justine jumped slightly.

It was Jeremy, still rather rosy from their lunchtime excesses. Hop-ing that she did not look like a child caught with her hand deep in the biscuit tin, Justine smiled widely, and closed the page on her computer screen.

"Everything all right?" Jeremy asked. "Anything I can do? Hm?"

"Ah, no. Everything's fine. I just want my first edition to be, well, perfect," Justine said.

"Very good, very good to be careful," Jeremy said, putting on his jacket and fishing out his shirt collar. "But I would caution against perfection as a goal. As the Italians say—he that will have a perfect brother must resign himself to remain brotherless. And, I would quite like, if you are amenable to the idea, to, ah, send the files off now?"

"Oh, Jeremy, I'm so sorry. I was just going over Doc's crossword one last time."

"Yes, indeed. Very wise, very wise indeed," Jeremy said, nodding. "But you're done?"

"Oh, yes. Absolutely. Completely finished. Good timing, actually."

"Excellent," said Jeremy, taking a step backward into the corridor. "Then I shall send our new edition away into the ether. Next to be seen in glorious Technicolor, between covers."

Had she really just done what she thought she'd just done?

She had.

As Jeremy walked away down the hall, Justine heard him call out, in a rich, singsong voice, "For such is the magic of publishing!"

cusp

It was over onions, of all things. How to dice bloody onions.

Gary's way of doing it was to cut each onion lengthways, then put the halves on a board, flat side down, slice each half vertically, then laterally, and . . . voila! . . . onion pieces of a fairly uniform size. Although this was obviously, objectively, the best way to dice onions, Nola insisted on chopping onions into fat, uneven rings, piling the rings up and hacking at them randomly. Which resulted, of course, in random-sized pieces.

"Just admit it," he'd said, in the kitchen, five weeks ago. "My way's better."

"There's nothing wrong with this way," she'd said, each *chop* of her knife causing a little tremor in the loose underskin of her upper arm.

"Except that it's not the *best* way."

"They're only onions," she'd said.

"Yeah, but the way you do it, it's so, so . . . Rokeville," he'd said.

He'd only been joking, but she stopped chopping. "What did you say?"

"I said, it's so Rokeville."

They were both from Rokeville, originally.

The knife was still in her hand, little triangles of onion clinging to its blade.

"Are you saying that I cut onions like a bogan?"

"Hey . . ."

"You fucking *snob*," she'd said, and the blade's point had entered the timber of the kitchen counter, a millimeter from his index finger.

"Jesus! You could have had my bloody finger off!"

"Get fucked," she'd said.

Then the fight was on in earnest. Now Gary Direen—Aquarius, public service middle manager and round one *MasterChef* reject, a fifty-two-year-old man who was not afraid to wear salmon pink shirts but who had long regretted the youthful decision to have a large pho-torealist image of AC/DC (circa January 1980) tattooed on his left bum cheek—was living alone, with next to no furniture, in a one-bedroom kennel on the twelfth floor of the ugliest apartment block in Alexandria Park. While Nola, his partner of four years, was living further out of the city, in the tidy little duplex they'd bought, together, off the plan.

Like most relationships, Gary and Nola's had its own Pandora's box of unspoken gripes and politely suppressed truths. The onion fight blew the lid clean off it. Nola told Gary that half of Australia had nearly puked watching him do his weepy *MasterChef* backstory segment about growing up with a single mother who didn't know there was a culinary world beyond fish fingers. It was hardly the stuff of tragedy, she'd said. He'd come off like a whiny little brat. So Gary told Nola that he'd snipped the size tags off the lingerie he'd bought her for Valentine's Day to save her facing the reality that she was an eighteen in the arse. Which provoked Nola to tell Gary that the only way for her to orgasm during sex with him was by thinking about Liam Hemsworth.

So Gary, seething with righteous pissed-offedness, packed his bags and checked in to a motel. He maintained his rage for as long as it took to inspect a handful of uninspiring rentals, sign the lease on the least dodgy one, buy a cleanish single mattress from a charity shop, and borrow from his sister's camping crate a plastic plate, bowl and cup, some bent cutlery and an aluminum saucepan.

But by the time the real estate agent gave Gary the keys to his moldy little dog box, his fury was just slightly off the boil. He woke up on his first morning at the apartment, uncomfortable on his second(or more)hand mattress, and cold under a cheap and gutless polyester comforter.

"Onions," he muttered, shaking his head.

Five weeks later, on a chilly overcast April morning, Gary stood pouring milk over his cereal and thinking about Nola, who would about now be taking tea and toast in the climate-controlled ambience of the breakfast nook back home. She'd be all sleep-creased and warm, and wearing that white cotton robe of hers that she tied in a way that showed off the gentle heave of her magnificent breasts.

No, he told himself. He must not think comforting thoughts about Nola. He was angry, he reminded himself. And he had to remain angry. He had to stay angry until Nola called him and begged him to come home.

The bathroom of his apartment was, bizarrely, carpeted; it smelled of wet nylon and mildew. The shower gave out alternate spurts of scalding and freezing water. But Gary stepped in, grimly, and reminded himself he needed to get around to buying a shower curtain.

By remembering some old fights, Gary managed to keep himself modestly angry until lunchtime. Alone in the tearoom with a cafeteria-grade curried egg sandwich, Gary checked the messages on his phone. Nothing. He checked his email. Nothing. But at least Nola hadn't unfriended him on Facebook, or changed her relationship status. And she hadn't, like many women in her situation would, started sharing inspirational quotes, or taking pictures of ice cream tubs next to DVD box sets of *Gilmore Girls*. But equally, she hadn't posted anything that even hinted she was lonely or sad.

Gary took a bite of his sandwich and reached for a copy of the *Alexandria Park Star*, which somebody had left lying on the table. He glanced at the cover with its close-up of a young dark-skinned guy with a scary-looking scar across his forehead, and skimmed over a tut-tutting opinion piece about the arrogance of the Australian cricket team.

"At least they win," Gary mumbled, to nobody.

Then, finding nothing else he especially wanted to read, he turned to the horoscopes. It wasn't as if he was into horoscopes. But at least a horoscope was, in a way, personal. And what Gary Direen wanted and needed, on this day, was a message that felt like it was addressed at least partially to him.

Aquarius, he read. *Were we not beseeched by songbird Joni Mitchell, at the beginning of the Age of Aquarius, to leave our apples spotted and our Paradise unpaved? This month, you experience a powerful surge of nostalgia for what once was...*

If, inside Gary Direen, there was an hourglass that had been filled with anger, then this was the moment that the very last acid yellow grain of it ricocheted down through the bottleneck and landed on the "spent" pile. Now all he could feel was regret, embarrassment and an urgent desire to have everything back the way it was. Deep in the sound library of his memory, he could hear Joni Mitchell singing the chorus of "Big Yellow Taxi." It did indeed seem that Gary Direen hadn't known what he'd got, until he'd thrown it away.

Nola loved Joni Mitchell. Gary loved Nola. He really did. He loved her.

"What the hell have I done?" he whispered.

Two seconds later, the tearoom was empty of humanity, and half a curried egg sandwich lay abandoned on the table.

Margie McGee—Aquarius, writer of haiku, bird-watcher and wildlife warrior, regular blood donor (AB negative) and long-serving Greens political adviser—had over recent months been experiencing a curious phenomenon. It was as if the main content of her mind had shifted just a little way over to the right, and a new, narrow panel had sprung up down the left. There was nothing on this new panel but churning columns of numbers. There were projections, multiplications, calculations for compound interest, best- and worst-case scenarios, all of them depending on stock market movements, interest rates and the CPI. But try as she might, Margie could find no little cross to click in order to close the panel. There was no way, it seemed, to banish her preoccupation with these complex formulae for when she would be able to retire. In five years? Ten? Fifteen?

On a squally Friday morning in late April, Margie was driving Senator Dave Gregson—the sartorially notable champion of renewable energy—back to his city office after a press stunt about global warming. It had been Dave's idea to hold the event at a wind farm in the outer, outer suburbs; he had wanted to stand before a backdrop of frantically spinning turbines and wind-whipped wattles. And this might have been a stroke of illustrative genius, with the visuals reinforcing his near-biblical warnings about the likelihood of future catastrophic weather events.

But in the end, there had been no visuals at all, because every single one of the television networks had stayed away, deciding that a predictable spiel by a minor party senator was hardly worth the drive out of town, and the sole journalist who had turned up—a girl from the local give-away paper—had come without a photographer.

Margie tapped the steering wheel with bitten-down fingernails. Dave, meanwhile, sat in the back, using a stack of unread estimates committee papers as a resting pad for a copy of the *Alexandria Park Star*.

In the rearview mirror, she could see that Dave had done his best to smooth down his wind-buffeted hair, and that he'd loosened his tie— the one they had settled on after a forty-five-minute debate. Hot pink, they'd decided in the end, as a gesture of support for families affected by breast cancer. Not that any such families would ever see or interpret the silk-coded message, Margie thought, with a twinge of frustration.

Flicking through the FM stations on the stereo, she wondered if all of them were playing the same song.

"What star sign are you, Marg?" Dave asked.

She had to think for a minute before answering, "Aquarius."

Dave gave a mild snort of laughter.

"What?"

"It figures."

"What do you mean by that?"

"You know. That kinda Woodstock vibe of yours," Dave said. "Do you want to hear your stars?"

"Go on, then," Margie said.

Dave began to read: *"Were we not beseeched by songbird Joni Mitchell, at the beginning of the Age of Aquarius, to leave our apples spotted and our Paradise unpaved?"*

When he'd finished reading the horoscope, he burst, falteringly, into song. As he reached the last line of the chorus of "Big Yellow Taxi," Margie joined in. Together, they filled the car with the final, dropping note.

There followed a small silence. Margie's eyes flicked from the road, to Dave's pink tie, to the narrow, left-hand number panel in her mind. It was going crazy; inside their racing columns, numbers were appearing, disappearing, reversing, imploding. She gave her head a little shake, wishing it would stop, and tried her best to ignore it.

"'Big Yellow Taxi.' Now there was a song," Margie said, by way of distraction.

As Dave sang a little more, Margie remembered Joni's chords being plucked on an acoustic guitar at someone's backyard barbecue, back in the bell-bottomed days of her youth. Oh Joni, Joni.

Catching sight of her deeply lined face in the rearview mirror, Margie's mind flashed up an image of a much younger self, with dirt on her cheeks and hair like a messy angel's. Her wrists were chained to the front grille of a dozer, her legs in the mud. Yes, that had been her. Almost as fair and fey as Joni herself.

So how, exactly, had pure-hearted forest protester Margie McGee become a woman who read stock market reports to help her make important decisions about her life? When, exactly, had her job turned into advising greenies on which tie to wear to their press conferences? And when, for that matter, had greenies become the kind of people who wore *ties*? It was time to get out. Time to get out of the office and chain herself to a dozer again. Camp up a tree. Get real. And if her retirement savings didn't hold out, she'd go on the pension. And if that meant eating dog food, well, she'd eat dog food until she couldn't take it anymore and then look up a recipe for a pill to end it all. She looked into her mind just in time to see the left-hand panel minimizing itself into nonexistence. She had decided.

"Dave?"

"Yes, Marg."

"I quit."

"You *what*?"

She grinned at him via the rearview mirror. "I quit! I completely and utterly quit."

Not next year. Not in five years or ten years. Now. Right now.

Dave, in the mirror, looked utterly startled.

As Margie sang the boppy little refrain of "Big Yellow Taxi," she felt younger than she had done in years.

✦

Nick Jordan, perched on a stool in the front window of Rafaello's, tried unsuccessfully to eke another sip from the cappuccino he'd finished about a quarter of an hour earlier. Out on the street, Saturday afternoon passersby huddled themselves deeper into their coats, or struggled along behind umbrellas that seemed to have their own ideas about which way to go.

In front of Nick were several newspapers—all of them open to the To Let pages—and also a copy of the *Alexandria Park Star*. The magazine was looking dog-eared and water-rumpled, because for over a week Nick had been carrying it around with him, trying to understand. But he didn't get it, no matter how many times he read and re-read Leo's words.

Aquarius. Were we not beseeched by songbird Joni Mitchell, at the beginning of the Age of Aquarius, to leave our apples spotted and our Paradise unpaved? This month, you experience a powerful surge of nostalgia for what once was, which also doubles as an intuition of what yet might be. In further news, a change of abode may be on the cards, or at the very least a modest makeover chez water bearer.

At least the last sentence was clear. In just over a week Nick's housesitting gig would come to an end and he would be homeless. So, yes, a change of abode was on the cards. But, as for the rest of the horoscope? It didn't make sense. He stared into Leo's deep-set eyes. *Really?* he asked, silently. *You really want me to go back there?*

It was true that Nick's Laura-less days had often been lonely and despondent. But he'd also enjoyed not having to worry about keeping up

Vogue styling standards. He'd fished out a pair of tracksuit pants that he'd almost forgotten he owned, and eaten a scandalous amount of food that registered at the wrong end of the glycemic index.

Nick stared at Leo. *But now you want me to go back? To Laura?*

Was it nuts to make a decision like this based on the stars? Justine would certainly have said so. Justine, he thought. What was going on with *her*? Having not seen her even once for over a decade, he'd now seen her twice in a month. It wasn't possible, was it, that Leo's *powerful surge of nostalgia* referred to Justine, and not to Laura?

No, it wasn't, Nick realized. Because Leo had also chosen to hammer this sentiment home via the words of Joni *Mitchell*. It really did seem that Leo was telling him, even after everything he'd been through, to call Laura Mitchell and give it another chance.

Nick dropped his head to the cafe counter and banged his brow to the timber three times. Quite hard. On the third bang, he left his forehead touching the magazine. A woman sitting further along the bar looked at him with a mixture of concern and alarm.

"I'm fine," he said. Without lifting his head, he offered her a crooked smile. "Totally fine."

To Leo, he said silently: *You know what, old mate? I think the world of you, and it's not that I don't trust you, but before I call Laura, I reckon I might just wait to see what you have to say for yourself next month. Okay?*

Taurus

APRIL 20—MAY 20

For the first few days after the *Star* hit the newsstands, Justine had counseled herself to keep her expectations low. Nick would need time, after all, to realize that the new copy was on sale. Then he would need not only to read Leo's column, but also to weigh up the possible meanings and interpretations of Leo's words, remember that famous rendition of "Big Yellow Taxi," think for a while and decide on a course of action.

But by the time a week had passed, Justine's patient hopefulness had ebbed away. Although workdays were busy and full, weekends felt long and empty. On Saturday, Justine killed some time by sleeping late, then a bit more by watching the first few episodes of the classic BBC *Pride and Prejudice*, again. She ate packet-mix macaroni cheese for lunch and set the leftovers aside for dinner, promising herself that for the evening version she would add some peas.

Why hadn't he called? Had her reference to "Big Yellow Taxi" been too obscure? Did he not remember that long-ago concert at Curlew Court? Or was there another reason? He hadn't seemed, during the evening they had spent together in the park, like a man who was already in a relationship. There had been a freedom about him, a lack of constraint. The Nick she remembered was such an honest soul, far too constant to behave this way if his heart was tied up elsewhere. Oh God, she sounded like Lizzie Bennet. Maybe she was just kidding herself that she knew anything about Nick Jordan at all.

And what had she been thinking, tinkering with the horoscopes? What if Leo had found out? What if he wrote to Jeremy? What would happen if she got busted? And exactly how crap would it be to be sprung for taking a risk that had, as it transpired, returned precisely nothing? There were so many questions, but one thing was certain: her career as an astrologer, brief as it had been, was over.

In the early evening, just as Lizzie Bennet was giving Lady Catherine de Bourgh her famously eloquent serve in the garden, Justine became peripherally aware that something out of the ordinary was going on in the flat next door. She pressed Pause on Lady Catherine's contorted face, tiptoed over to one side of the French doors that led out to her balcony and twitched back the curtain. Through the window of the neighboring apartment, Justine could see that AC/DC man was not, for once, alone. He was with a woman: a generously proportioned woman in jeans and a flannel shirt.

AC/DC man and the woman were packing up all his belongings, Justine realized. And they were laughing. Perhaps there was music on in the background, considering how AC/DC man was swaying slightly as he taped up a cardboard carton. The woman's mouth was moving, her lipstick pink and bright. Maybe she was singing along as she folded clothes into a suitcase.

Definitely, there was music playing, Justine decided, as AC/DC man grooved his way across the living room and took the woman in his arms. He danced her around the half-packed-up living room. And then they were kissing, and the flannel shirt was getting unbuttoned, and . . . Justine let the curtain fall and slumped against the wall. She was even being outdone in the romance stakes by a middle-aged man with a paunch and a bad tattoo.

♉

On Monday morning, Justine dressed carefully in a preppy combination of pleated skirt, button-up shirt and argyle vest, and looked her mirror self squarely in the eye. *Nick Jordan*, she told herself, *is a childhood friend, and nothing more.* She laced her boots tightly and set out for work through the park.

Reaching Soapbox Corner, Justine came upon a blackboard on an easel. Presumably it had been set out by the odd-looking man who stood close by, wearing a grave expression, and holding a fan of photocopied pamphlets about asteroid collisions and the imminent ending of the Earth.

Justine altered her course slightly and slowed her step. When the man turned away, she knew she had a fleeting chance. Only barely breaking her stride, she swept past the blackboard and erased the stray apostrophe and unnecessary E in YOU'RE SILENCE IS YOUR COMPLICITY. As she continued on her way, she dusted off her chalky fingers with all the satisfaction of a cowboy blowing across the lip of a smoking pistol.

Arriving at the office, Justine found Jeremy standing beneath the mosaic star alongside a crisp-looking young man with neatly combed hair. The packing creases were still visible down the front of his royal blue shirt.

"Darl," said Jeremy, beaming at the sight of Justine, "please meet Henry Ashbolt. Henry, this is Justine, your immediate—ah, let's not say predecessor, as that sounds rather morbid. Let us say instead that it is from Justine's fair hand that you grasp the copy-runner's baton."

"Hi," said Henry, giving Justine a knuckle-crushing handshake.

"Hello, Henry," Justine said. "Welcome."

"Thanks," said Henry, and looked back to Jeremy, in a way that reminded her of a dog gazing at its beloved owner.

"So," Justine persisted, "where have you come to us from?"

It was her own university that he named, but Justine had a powerful sense that this fact would not interest Henry Ashbolt. He continued, "I graduated with a double major in political science and journalism, with honors. First class."

Justine bit her tongue before she could say, *I'm impressed.*

"Ah, Justine," said Jeremy, apparently sensing the slight bite of frost in the air, "go into my office, will you, darl? And have a look on my desk. There's a cartoon, just come in from Ruthless. Of the PM. But I want your opinion on whether it would be too, ah, *much*. For the cover, you know?"

Ruthless Hawker was a freelance cartoonist and professional alcoholic who occasionally bestowed the fruits of his caustic wit on the *Alexandria Park Star*.

Jeremy continued, "Though I'm expecting Henry to keep that little morsel of information to himself, eh Henry?"

Justine looked at Henry questioningly.

"The PM's my sister's godfather," he explained. "He went to school with our dad."

"Well," said Justine, now slightly loosening the reins on her tone of voice, "you must be very proud."

Henry shrugged casually, but Justine caught the small twist of amusement at the corner of Jeremy's mouth.

"Nice to meet you, Henry," Justine said, and she continued on up the path. She looked forward to seeing how well Henry Ashbolt coped with delivering mail, fixing paper jams, taking dogs to the groomer's, and trotting backward and forward to Rafaello's six times a day. For *years*.

On Jeremy's desk was a large printout of a fiendishly good caricature of the prime minister. He wore a Gestapo uniform and preened himself in a magical mirror—its frame inscribed with the words BORDER PROTECTION. The mirror reflected him in a snappy suit and bright blue tie, celebrating an electoral victory.

When Jeremy followed Justine into his office, Henry was no longer with him.

"So, what do you think, hm?" Jeremy asked, coming to the desk. He scratched his chin.

"People would talk," Justine said. "Letters to the Editor would be . . . abundant."

"But is it too much?"

"An editor of my acquaintance once told me that fortune favors the bold," Justine said.

Jeremy nodded. "Ah, yes. A beneficial side effect of giving advice is that sometimes people give it back to you, just when you need it. Thank you."

"You're welcome," Justine said, and headed for the door.

"Oh, before you go," Jeremy said, and dropped his voice low, "tell me—what did you make of Henry? Hm?"

Justine considered, then said, "I didn't know you could actually buy Young Conservative as a cologne."

Jeremy chuckled. "I think it's working out spectacularly well with you as contributions manager. The publication is all the better for your, ah, sharpness. Our latest edition looked very polished indeed. The new job suits you."

Although she gave him a smile of thanks, as Justine walked the corridor to her office, she heard the distant chimes of warning bells. Henry Ashbolt was clearly a very ambitious young man. She wondered if she should quietly remind Jeremy that the next reporter's job to come up was supposed to be hers, no matter how well she was doing in Natsue's old chair.

She had just slid into that very chair when she heard her phone ringing from somewhere deep in her bag. When at last she found it, she felt a prickle of anticipation run over the backs of her hands; the number on the display was not one that she knew. Could it be Nick?

Brain: *Hey! Don't forget to smile as you answer the phone. Smiles are audible in people's voices, remember?*

"Hello?" she said.

"Hey, Town Mouse! It's me."

All of Justine's anticipation died away. For it was best-pal Tara. And then Justine didn't know which was worse—the sting of disappointment that it was her best friend on the end of the phone, or the flush of guilt for having felt disappointed that it was her best friend on the end of the phone.

"Well, hello, Country Mouse," Justine said, trying to sound bright. "What's with the new number?"

"I finally ditched Telstra," Tara said. "And you know how long that's been coming for. Arseholes. For some obscure reason that was going to take another seven hundred 'on hold' hours to fix, they couldn't stop billing me for my old plan *and* my new one. So I pissed them off altogether. Yay! But listen, I'm on my way out to a fracking protest. Can't talk long. I only rang to say I'm coming your way this weekend. The BCA have invited me to this gala thing on Saturday night—"

"The BCA?"

"Beef Cattle Australia," Tara said. "And God bless the ABC! They've said I can compromise my integrity by attending, just so long as I come back with a corking story or three, and don't expect them to pay for accommodation."

"My house is your house, as ever," Justine said.

"Thanks, honey. So, what do you say . . . will you be my date for the ball? We might find ourselves sitting with some gorgeous young beef moguls wearing very large hats. And even if we don't, we still have your new job to celebrate. Among other things."

"What other—" Justine began, then stopped herself, realizing. Between now and Saturday lay the auspicious date of May the fourth, which was not only Star Wars Day, but also— "Your birthday!"

"So, you'll come with me?" Tara pressed.

"Come to the ball I shall," Justine agreed.

♉

It was not difficult for Justine to find the particular part of the large and glitzy hotel where the BCA ball was being held. All she needed to do was follow the hat-wearing men and the matrons in pleated chiffon who were making their way by escalator to a first-floor lobby. There, a pianist in rhinestone-studded Converse sneakers was playing Carole King on a shining baby grand.

Justine was wearing one of her grandmother's dresses, a black 1960s sheath which had a lace overlay and an uncompromising zipper that did wonders for her posture. She stood, trying not to sing along to Carole, until at last she saw Tara—beamy and bosomy in one of her signature fit-and-flare cocktail dresses—coming up the escalator.

"Happy birthday for yesterday!" Justine said. "Was the force with you?"

"Always," Tara said, hugging her friend. It wasn't a polite squeeze, but a genuine embrace that caused a little wave of emotion to rise up in Justine.

"Hey," Tara said. "You all right?"

"Of course. Yes. Fine. It's just . . . God, I miss having you around."

They hugged each other again, then Tara said, "Enough of the sappy stuff. Let's get something to drink."

She caught the eye of a roving waiter, lifted two champagne flutes from his tray and handed one to Justine. "And don't go away just yet," she told him.

Tara downed her champagne at an alarming speed, put the empty glass back on the tray and took two more. Justine tried to remember whether or not she was stocked up on aspirin.

"Don't pull that face, my girl," Tara said. "We're celebrating."

Justine was feeling quite light-headed by the time the guests were summoned into the ballroom proper, where the centerpiece of the buffet was a towering, life-sized ice sculpture of a bull. Justine and Tara made their way to their table, but it was disappointingly free of men who were either young or single. Tara introduced herself to the silver-haired gentleman beside her, and before long was engaged in conversation about an unpleasant-sounding bovine condition called campylobacter.

Justine read the menu. The entrée choices were a kingfish tataki or a tart made with goats cheese, no apostrophe. Presumably, she thought, the menu writer had not been able to decide whether the term ought to be shown as *goat's cheese* (cheese coming from the milk of a single goat), or as *goats' cheese* (cheese coming from the milk of more than one goat). As it happened, Justine had encountered this problem before. She reached into her clutch purse, brought out a mechanical pencil and circled the offending phrase. She began to scribble a note in the margin of the menu.

I've always found that a better solution, her note said, *than leaving the apostrophe out is to remove the "s," and show the term as "goat cheese." Then you don't have to worry about specifying whether one or more goats contributed to the—*

"Honey, what are you *doing*?" Tara asked. Evidently, the campylobacter conversation had exhausted its possibilities.

"I'm just fixing up—"

"You're not. Please tell me that you are not editing the menu."

"I'm just—"

"Sweetheart," Tara said, without lowering her voice, "how long is it since you got laid?"

The silver-haired man gave a bemused smile and glanced at Justine, who blushed deeply.

"I'm serious," Tara went on. "Have you had any? At all? Don't tell me you've been on a drought since *Tom*. But that's terrible! The last person you had sex with probably talked about flying primate theory during foreplay."

"Oh, ease up," Justine said. "He wasn't that bad."

"Hello, I'm Tom Cracknell," Tara mocked, "and I'm doing a PhD on the motor cortex and the corticospinal—"

"Tract of the flying fox," Justine finished.

It was true that Tom, at the time of his relationship with Justine, had been rather enamored of his PhD topic. He was the kind of guy who could name the entire sequence of television *Dr. Who* actors, and enumerate pi out to several hundred decimal places. He'd taken Justine to remote rivers to go kayaking, and to indoor climbing centers to scale walls, and to a bunch of other places that were outside her comfort zone. And it had been fun. But when Tom had been offered a postdoctoral position on the Atlantic coast of the USA, it had broken nobody's heart.

"So, it's been what? Eight *months*? And, what—nothing? Nothing?"

"No," said Justine quietly.

"No wonder you're proofreading everything in sight."

"Hey, come on. I am performing a . . . a valuable community service."

"Not a sniff? Not a whisper? Anything on the horizon? A blip even?" Tara said, pinning Justine with her investigative journalist's gaze.

Justine shook her head.

"Ah!" Tara said. "You're leaving something out. I can tell."

"Well, it's not a blip," Justine argued. "I don't think it even counts as a semi-blip."

Tara took a deep gulp of her wine. "I'll take a hemi-demi-semi-blip over nothing at all. Now, tell me everything."

So Justine told Tara about Nick Jordan. About the market, and the fish suit, and lunch at Cornucopia, and about how Nick had always been an actor and was about to play Romeo. She even dished about the fleeting moment of teenage passion on a South Australian beach. But in telling all of this, she found that she was—without exactly deciding to—holding back the part about the stars.

"Okay then," Tara said, as if she might have been rolling up her sleeves. "So, what's your plan now?"

"Plan?" Justine asked innocently.

"You must have a plan," Tara said. "And please tell me it's a better one than waiting to see if he calls."

"Is that really so terrible?"

"It's pathetic."

"But I don't have his number. I couldn't contact him even if I wanted to."

"Rubbish," Tara said shortly. "Honey, sometimes you just have to take the bull by the horns. Facebook him, track down his parents, turn up at that restaurant at lunchtime . . . whatever, but promise me that you will, in some way, shape or form, make contact with that man. Promise?"

"We-e-ell," said Justine. It couldn't be long, now, until Leo's stars arrived ready to be transcribed for the new edition. Maybe, just maybe, she could give the stars one more shot? "There *might* be a way."

♉

Around midnight, at the offices of the *Star*, all was quiet and still. Computers slept behind darkened screens, their green standby hearts steadily beating, while in the hallway, the temperamental old photocopier slumbered beneath its vinyl dust cover. Amid the chaos of Anwen's workstation, a set of *Star Wars* figures stood draped in colorful streamers from a packet of party poppers that had been exploded in honor of May the fourth.

The leaves of the potted fern on Justine's desk quivered slightly in the barely moving air, as did the wispy halo of an angora cardigan slung over the back of the chair. Through the skylight above the desk, nothing could be seen but the murky dark orange of the city's night sky. But was it possible that, at a few minutes past twelve, a silver beam of starlight pierced the glass panel above the desk? Did a single glittering filament spear down into the quiet of the office and spark the fax machine into life?

The machine whirred, readying itself for action, and then its printer head took off, zooming left to right, right to left, across a page. With each pass, it left a swipe of half words in its wake.

Pixel by pixel, predictions and advice were spelled out for each of the signs of the zodiac in turn. Reaching the eleventh sign, the fax machine inscribed the following: *Aquarius: "Contradiction," advised Pascal, "is not a sign of falsity, nor the lack of contradiction a sign of truth." In short, Aquarius, there is nothing for it this month but for you to sit with the prevailing push-and-pull influences of Mars and Neptune. While Mars orders boldness and aggression, Neptune advises caution and reserve. It would be wise to attain clarity before making any major decisions.*

Seconds later, the communiqué was complete, and a single page shot out of the machine and floated down to rest in the out-tray, where Justine—on Monday morning—would find it awaiting her attention.

cusp

I n a dimly lit airplane cabin high above the equatorial zone, the little
girl's forehead was hot under the cool palm of Zadie O'Hare.

"Mummy?" the little girl asked, but now was no time to be cor-
recting her.

Instead, Zadie—Aquarius, art school dropout turned Qantas flight
attendant, collector and proficient wearer of vertiginous high-heeled
shoes, bottle-black younger sister to strawberry-blonde pharmacy
graduate Larissa O'Hare—swung swiftly, but almost silently, into
action.

With her right hand, she performed a decisive act of reverse ori-
gami on a sick bag and whipped it into position beneath the chin of
this little girl, whose mother had declared, not two minutes earlier, that
she was *not* about to hurl. Then, with her left hand, Zadie caught up the
child's sleep-mussed hair into a rough ponytail. It was diamond-cut
timing. The puke pouring into the bag was frothy and brown, like a
chunky Coca-Cola, and it was in no short supply. Zadie could feel the
warmth of it through the paper against her palm.

The little girl's mother, jerked out of the deluded optimism that had
come to her via several mini-bottles of cabernet merlot, was suddenly

in action, all zippered pockets and wet wipes, sympathy and remorse. Zadie straightened up and brushed a tiny globule of spew off the skirt of her uniform. She folded the lip of the white bag, tidy as an envelope.

"You're amazing," the mother had the good grace to say. "How did you know?"

Zadie, composed and competent, flashed the woman an entirely professional wink. "Let's just say, it's not my first rodeo," she said, then strode off down the aisle in her solid navy pumps, as if traversing the marble concourse of a gleaming airport, albeit with a soggy sick bag held between manicured fingertips.

She had almost reached the curtain that cordoned off the rear galley when she realized she was in trouble. She pushed her way through the folding doors of a bathroom cubicle and hurriedly shot home the bolt that intensified the light into a vicious platinum. Vomit pulsed up her own throat and splashed into the toilet bowl: livid orange, like the unholy love child of an airplane curry and a rogue carrot.

The carrot in this image, Zadie recognized with a wry grimace, was a lanky New Zealander called Stuart. Stuart who? Stuart what? Zadie didn't know. Back at the beginning of April—had it actually *been* April Fool's Day?—she'd found herself sitting beside him on a high stool in the air-conditioned cool of a Singapore bar. She'd gone there with her colleague Leni-Jane, who'd been characteristically efficient in going upstairs with a lonesome German businessman with a capacious suite. Zadie, left alone so early in the evening, had known herself to be mildly drunk, dangerously bored and quite pretty in a killer pair of Fluevogs and a pale blue halter-neck dress. And so it wasn't hard for this Stuart, gin by gin, anecdote by anecdote, to gradually insinuate a denim-clad knee between Zadie's thighs.

Here, again, it wasn't her first rodeo, and Zadie recognized in Stuart's oversized brown eyes, thinning sun-crisped hair and finely wrinkled skin the anxiety of a boy, good-looking from birth, who'd relatively recently cottoned on to the fact that he wasn't Peter Pan after all.

Zadie woke in her hotel bed the following dawn with her usually smooth jet-black hair tangled into a classic Medusa, and with her parched tongue all swollen and useless in her mouth. It took a few seconds for her saliva glands to kick in, and also for her mind to register the salient facts: where she was, why she felt raw between the legs, how many different and unusual positions they'd tried, and that she was the only person in the bed, or indeed in the room. Perhaps he was in the bathroom? She swung herself out of bed and peeped around the door. But no. Stuart was gone.

Zadie cracked open a bottle of water from the bar fridge and downed most of it in one slug. She was relieved, she decided. Yes, relieved. As she cast her eyes about, she realized that in the whole beige-on-beige hotel room, the only visible sign of her tryst with Stuart—other than the rumpled bedsheets—was the condom that was lying like a worm casing on the plush carpet. And now that she looked at it, she could quite clearly see that it was split down the side. Shit.

Zadie pressed Flush, and the violent, sucking rush of the airplane toilet's evacuation made her clutch an instinctive hand to her stomach. In her nightmares, this was how it was going to sound, on Thursday at noon, when she presented herself for the *procedure*. That was what the woman on the phone had called it. They were good at euphemisms, down there at the "fertility control clinic."

In what was surely the world's least forgiving mirror, Zadie checked herself out. Her hair was okay, but her skin was shitty, with determined pustules pushing up through the foundation she'd slathered on her forehead and chin. And there was no hiding the way the bodice of her dress was straining over her swollen, tender breasts. Last week, she'd had to cancel lunch with Larissa, because if anyone was going to be alert to sudden and alarming changes to your physiology, it would be your highly observant and academically brilliant sister. The one who would never find herself standing in an airplane bathroom, inconveniently pregnant at the age of twenty-three, trying to weigh up which of two whacking great big evils was supposed to be the lesser.

This would never have happened to Larissa, because Larissa would have been on the pill. Because as well as being on the pill, Larissa would have been carrying a supply of superstrength, steel-reinforced, antimicrobial condoms in her purse. For their whole lives, Larissa had been careful, and Zadie had been curious. But this, their mother Patricia was fond of saying, was only right. Larissa, after all, was a Capricorn, which accounted for her calculating and sure-footed cleverness, while

Zadie was an Aquarian, destined for travel and adventure, exploration and experimentation.

But where was this haphazard Aquarian quest of hers leading her now? With her peripatetic job, she couldn't even have a bloody cat, let alone a baby. She had nothing to fall back on: the only items of any value that she owned were a Kia hatchback, thirty-six pairs of beloved high heels and a first-generation iPad. A single mother, unemployed and without prospects, stuck in the arse end of a cul-de-sac in the far reaches of Nowheresville: that's who she'd be if she chose to have the baby. But the only other option available to her was the fertility control clinic at noon on Thursday. And that, as a destination, felt at least equally terminal.

Zadie's thoughts were broken open by urgent tapping on the cubicle door. Fucking passengers. Couldn't they read? *Occupied*, she wanted to yell. *Ock-you-pied.*

"You 'right, doll?" It was Leni-Jane. Who must have seen Zadie's dash into the bathroom. Who didn't miss a trick. Who, while sweet and hilarious and fun to party with, was potentially the least discreet human alive. Shit.

"Yes, hon. Out in a minute," Zadie said.

Zadie made an effort to pull herself together and straighten up the bathroom. The little girl's sick bag was still sitting soggily beside the basin. With great care, Zadie wedged it down into the bathroom trash, then washed her hands with way too much soap. To mask the smell of spew, she sprayed her face with something labeled "freshening mist." When at last she stepped out of the cubicle, it was within a personal cloud of chemically rendered lavender.

Leni-Jane was waiting for her in the galley, leaning against the storage units with eyebrows raised. Short and plump, with bird-bright eyes and an accent that could have been nicked from Cilla Black, she studied Zadie carefully.

"You sure you're 'right? Look like death warmed up, you do. Come on in 'ere and sit yourself down."

Zadie allowed Leni-Jane to settle her into a fold-down seat and cover her with a blanket. She gratefully accepted a plastic cup of soda water and a peppermint. She was tired, so tired. Tired in a way she'd never felt in her entire life. It was as if her soul had suddenly turned to lead, or her own personal gravity had quadrupled. She imagined herself falling, like a medicine ball, through the fold-down seat, through the floor of the plane, to earth. Making a crater in it.

"Now, what's going on, then?" asked Leni-Jane, her head on one side. With her shoes shucked off and arms crossed, she seemed especially short and wide, like a mother hen on high alert.

"I'm fine, thanks, hon. Truly. It's just that when that little girl chucked, it completely turned my stomach," Zadie said, with a stretched smile. "I'll be 'right."

"Ri-i-i-ght," echoed Leni-Jane, with a suspicious furrowing of the eyebrows. "Hmmmm. You just tuck yourself in there for a harf hour, and we'll see if you're feeling better then."

Leni-Jane crammed her small, wide feet into her shoes and shook back her shag of fair hair. Before setting off into the low light of the cabin, she dropped a magazine onto Zadie's lap.

"Here. It'll take yer mind off things," she advised, with a piercing look that was a little too knowing for Zadie's liking.

What happened next Zadie would later remember with absolute clarity. She would remember the weighty feel of the high-quality stock on which the magazine was printed, and the bright red caricatured nose of the cartoon prime minister on the cover. Zadie would also remember other random things: the color of the red dirt in a Jeep advertisement, the weird retro font used for the headline DIVORCE IS THE NEW BLACK, the black-and-white picture of the magazine's craggy-faced astrologer.

Astrology was not, particularly, Zadie's thing. It was more her mother's thing. Patricia O'Hare did not follow astrology in a mystical way, but rather in a practical, straightforward fashion. Her sign was a fact, like the color of her hair, eyes and skin, and she believed that her Virgo-ness neatly explained everything from how she folded fitted sheets (she did it just like Martha Stewart on that YouTube clip) to the well-equipped first aid kit she carried in her handbag.

Right now, what Zadie would have liked most in the world was for her mother to be here beside her, handing over a steaming facecloth and giving her a stern, loving talking to. But in the absence of Patricia O'Hare, Zadie had to settle for Leo Thornbury and one pithy paragraph of star-divined advice.

Aquarius: This month is auspicious for Aquarians at the beginning of new creative endeavors. This sense of rightness and flow extends into all spheres of your life, triggering seemingly coincidental meetings and events. But, for Einstein, coincidence was merely God's way of remaining anonymous. When the universe sends you a message in the language of chance, it is wiser to open the door than to close it.

Zadie, reading these words, felt her head begin to spin. *Mummy?* that little girl had said, like it was a question. And then there was the mail-order mix-up that meant she'd received a box containing half a dozen bamboo cotton baby suits instead of the push-up bras that she'd ordered. This had happened on the same day that she'd received in the mail a prospectus from her old school, with a covering letter outlining the process for putting your baby on their waiting list. But all these were just coincidences, surely? They didn't mean anything. Did they?

Zadie closed her eyes to steady herself, and it was as if she had somehow rotated her eyeballs inward, to look upon a whole new world. She appeared to be hollow, like a massive geode with distant walls of glittering crystal. But this interior of hers was vast, truly vast, as if she might in fact hold the entire universe within the shimmering walls of her private cavern.

The universe sends you a message . . . The words drifted through Zadie's internal cosmos as if skywritten in stardust. Shimmering, kaleidoscopic, they formed and re-formed themselves, diminished and then magnified. *The universe sends you a message.* And that was when Zadie felt it, deep in the pit of her stomach. It wasn't only that she imagined feeling it, but that she actually felt it: an explosion of potential, a detonating firework of existence, a personal Big Bang. And it was in that moment, and no other—she would later think—that her child's life truly began.

+

Charlotte Juniper—Leo, graduate in law and political science, former student union dictator (largely benevolent), proud owner of a crowning glory of waist-length auburn hair, childhood gymnast, occasional wearer of no underpants to nightclubs—stood naked in a nighttime kitchen that was not her own. She opened the cupboard in which she would have stored the drinking glasses had this been *her* vintage 1950s-decorated loft apartment. But she found only a dismembered food processor. She tried another cupboard but it turned out to be full of tea and coffee supplies. Then another. Booze.

"Ugh," she said with a shudder.

Charlotte had been woken at around 1:30 a.m. by a throbbing in her temples that was the harbinger of a hangover, and by the crush of the future inside her head. Her skin oozed with the aniseed tang of sambuca and her drying sweat gave off the salted scent of celebratory sex. Today Charlotte had been offered, and had accepted, a job. A real job, a grown-up's job. A job that was rare and wonderful and *hers*.

Everyone else she knew who'd entered the job market with a degree in politics or law had soon discovered that they had to be the bad guy if they wanted to make money. The jobs with ideals came with commensurate pay cuts. And yet, an opening had presented itself, due to the early retirement of Margie McGee. Very unexpectedly, the dedicated Margie had quit her job with the Greens to go back to frontline environmental activism. She was planning an epic tree-sit in Tasmania, so Charlotte had heard. Whatever. Thanks to Margie's surprise change of heart, Charlotte now had one of those rare jobs in which she would be handsomely paid to be the good guy. She would have enough money to buy some grown-up clothes, and maybe even drink wine out of bottles.

Charlotte Juniper, adviser to the Greens. Specifically, to Senator Dave Gregson. Dave Gregson, the rockabilly sideburn–sporting activist-turned-politician. Dave Gregson, a former musician and current partner of country and western singer Blessed Jones, who was right at this moment in New Zealand touring her new album. Dave Gregson: upstairs in his bedroom sleeping off the sambuca and the sex. Dave Gregson, who—unbeknownst to Charlotte—had left his phone on silent in his jacket pocket, where it had for several hours now been steadily collecting texts and voice messages from Blessed Jones, who'd come down with the flu, canceled the tail end of her tour, and was coming home on the late-night flight. The same Dave Gregson who clearly didn't keep drinking glasses in any sensible part of his kitchen.

Charlotte jerked open the fridge door, filling the room with chilled fluorescence. A blast of cold, dry air instantly evaporated the tiny patches of sweat nestling in the curves of her clavicles and beneath her heavy, blue-veined breasts. She took a swig of orange juice straight from the bottle. And that was when she heard the unmistakable sound of a key turning in a lock.

The door of the apartment swung open to reveal the petite, backlit outline of Blessed Jones. She looked just like she might have done on an album cover, wearing a nipped-waist dress with a fulsome skirt, dainty ankle boots, a trilby perched on the wild nest of her tightly curling hair, a guitar case in one hand, and all of her haloed by spears of amber light. Charlotte lowered the orange juice bottle down over her pubes. Her nipples pulled tight from the shock.

The silhouette of Blessed Jones made a small noise, a sharp intake of breath.

"You're Blessed Jones," Charlotte said helplessly. "I love your songs."

+

Bricks and planks—Price? Delivery?
Picture hooks (stick on)
Clothes airer (small)
Sink plug (55 mm)
Light globes (bayonet)
Shower curtain

Nick Jordan, riding his bike to the hardware store, tried to imagine what a reasonable person would make of his list, if they happened to find it blowing about on a street, or crumpled up by their feet on the bus. Might they mistake it for an experimental poem? Or, if they accepted it at face value, might they be able to reconstruct the personal circumstances of the list maker?

Would the finder of the list surmise that it had been made by someone who'd just moved into a rental property, which—like every other
rental property of his life—had not a single picture hook on the walls?
Would they be able to imagine the stark smell of damp white paint?
But also the undertone of mold? Would they be able to imagine the
living room with its murky green carpet, still slightly damp from the
steam cleaner, and his block-mounted production posters all leaning
up against the walls at knee height? Would they imagine the stacks
of books, CDs and magazines with nowhere to go? And the list maker's bank balance, too—the size of which would mean that bricks and
planks would have to do, yet again, in place of actual shelves?

"Balcony," the ad for the flat had said. But it wasn't really a balcony.
It was a concrete ledge with a rusted metal railing, only big enough to
hold a planter box full of tomatoes, or the clothes airer that Nick was
shortly to buy, but not both. It was hard to know why the architect had
even bothered with balconies, if "architect" was the right term for the
person who designed the towering toilet block where Nick now lived.
The building had been put up so close to the art deco apartments next
door that Nick would easily be able to spit a cherry pip through the
window opposite his own.

The ad had said the kitchen was "galley-style," which Nick now
knew to be code for ridiculously small. The stove was old and dirty,
with solid heating elements that would probably take a century to
warm up; the bedroom was tiny, and it was best, Nick decided, not to
think about the bathroom, which had been fitted out during the incredibly brief period of human history in which carpet on bathroom
floors had seemed like a good idea.

Nick cruised over a junction, dodging around a retinue of dachs-
hunds who were out for a stroll on a Hydra-headed leash. Reaching the
far side of the road, he paused his bike for long enough to wedge in his
earbuds and dial a number on his phone. Now that Daylight Saving
had ended, his folks were once again only two hours behind, and while
he was pedaling along the quiet Sunday morning streets was as good a
time as any to have the chat he needed to have with his mum.

The phone rang four times. He imagined Jo Jordan picking up
her mobile from her kitchen counter on the other side of the country,

opening its expensive leather cover. He could smell the salted air, and imagine the view from his parents' kitchen window, out over the cluttered coastline and the vivid blue of the Indian Ocean.

"Sweetheart!" she said.

"Hey, Mum. Sorry about the wind noise."

"Where are you?"

"On my bike."

"I do wish you wouldn't talk and ride."

"Mu-u-um."

"Okay, okay. How's the new place?"

"Grim. Grimy. Grotty. Many other things starting with G. Speaking of which," Nick said, taking a breath and preparing to dive in. "Girlfriend."

"Oh, you've met someone," she said. "How exciting!"

"Actually, I am not so sure you're going to like this."

He felt the instant freeze, as if someone had just pumped liquid nitrogen up the phone line. But he went on, "Laura and I are going to give it another shot."

In the silence that followed, he could perfectly imagine the expression on his mother's face. He fancied that he could hear her chewing her bottom lip.

"I mean," he continued, "we're not moving back in together, not right away. We're going to take it from the top. From the very beginning. You know, start dating. One step at a time."

Still, his mother said nothing.

"She's agreed to ease up on the pressure. And I've agreed to have a really good think about my career direction. It's a compromise thing. I mean, maybe it is time that I started to . . . I mean, you know, Dad's always said . . . even *you've* sometimes said . . . I never thought acting was going to be easy, but maybe I didn't know it was going to be this hard. I guess I can't go on being this broke forever. Mum?"

He could hear her breathing. Thinking.

"Mum?"

"You have to chart your own path, Nicko. Girlfriend, career. All of it. It all has to be what you choose. Not what I choose."

"She's—"

"I know, sweetheart. I know. Three years is a long time, and you've invested a lot. I can understand you wanting to hold on. But, once a relationship has failed once . . . I mean, as you grow older, life throws a lot of challenges at you, Nick. You have to be really sure the person you choose is the right one. And every time we've spoken over the last few months, you've seemed so convinced that it was over for good. What's happened?"

Now it was Nick's turn to fall silent.

A *sense of rightness and flow*, Leo had written, and *seemingly coincidental meetings and events.* Was it God's way of remaining anonymous when he put Laura's face everywhere, so that she was there no matter where Nick looked? It seemed that every time he turned a corner, she was right there, in his face, blown up to mega-proportions on billboards or in shop windows.

She was currently in the window display at Country Road, a great deal larger than life: all racehorse hip bones, smoky makeup and flowing bronze silk. Her long, straight dark hair shone and her expression was . . . what? He supposed Country Road wanted her to look languorous and untouchable, as if their brand's clothing were a passport to a place entirely free of the kinds of concerns that could wrinkle your consciousness, your face or your clothes. She wasn't only the clotheshorse for Country Road, but also the eyes of Ophelia spectacles. There was a picture of her in magenta glasses, her hair slightly curled and drifting out around her shoulders in a carefully orchestrated breeze, which was plastered down the sides of half the city's buses.

In the *Alexandria Park Star* itself, one page over from Leo's horoscopes, was a full-page advertisement for Chance sparkling wines, and in it, posed against a rustic backdrop of wine barrels, wearing jeans that rose over her slender hips to an impossibly narrow waist, was Laura Mitchell. Her rose-colored blouse was demurely buttoned, but very tight. Her pale and perfect lips were curled into a come-hitherish expression, and she held, between manicured fingertips, the stem of a champagne flute. The pale golden liquid in the glass glowed with all the promise of a wedding band, a strategic star of light sparking off its surface. *Take a chance*, the advertisement had read, in a huge curling font.

When the universe sends you a message in the language of chance, it is wiser to open the door than to close it.

Nick could hear his mother waiting for his answer.

"I just think that this is . . . right. You know?" he said.

"Nicko?"

"Yes, Mum?"

"You do have a little tendency to see only the best in people. And that's lovely, but . . . just be careful with that heart of yours."

"Hey," Nick said, remembering something else he needed to report to his mum, "you'll never guess who I ran into. Twice. Justine Carmichael."

"Justine? Oh my goodness. Really? How's she going? What's she doing?"

"She's working for a magazine."

"Of course she is," his mum said with a happy sigh. "It was always going to be something wordy, wasn't it?"

Nick found himself telling his mother all about the dinner he and Justine had shared in the park, and then how he'd seen her at Cornucopia, and how she wasn't any different, and he realized that he was blathering on. Maybe even oversharing, as if he'd been bottling up a desire to talk to somebody. About Justine.

"You two were such good friends," Nick's mother said. "You know, Mandy and I, we used to have this little dream that you and Justine . . . well, that was all a long time ago. I do miss Mandy."

There was a pause.

"I sometimes wonder what our lives would have been like if we'd never left Edenvale," Jo said wistfully.

Nick had reached the hardware store. "Got to go, Mum."

"Love you, darling," she said. "If you see Justine again, be sure to tell her I say hello."

Gemini

MAY 21–JUNE 20

On a Friday afternoon in late May, Jeremy Byrne assembled the staff of the *Alexandria Park Star*, at short notice, in the tearoom. He stood at the head of the table, his expression serious.

"What's this all about?" Justine asked, taking a seat beside Anwen.

"Doesn't look good," Anwen said.

"Did someone . . . do something wrong?" Justine asked, but Anwen only shrugged.

Justine looked around at the faces of her colleagues. Barbel hovered in the doorway, and it was clear she was annoyed at the unscheduled interruption to her afternoon. Henry the new copy-runner was perched attentively at Jeremy's right flank. Justine had privately nicknamed him the Hulk, for although he was small and taut, Justine feared that if his ambition got loose it would turn him to the shade of blue favored by the nation's political conservatives, then cause him to swell up and split the seams of his Rodd & Gunn shirt.

Jeremy cleared his throat. Roma and Radoslaw, he reported, had gone that morning, in the Camry, on an assignment to the far side of the city, where they had been involved in a car accident.

"What the hell?" Martin Oliver said, clenching his fists like he was planning to punch someone.

Justine watched Jeremy's face closely, trying not to think the worst. Not, at least, before it was absolutely necessary to do so.

"But are they all right?" Barbel asked, at the same time as Anwen said, "Oh my God."

They were both in the hospital, Jeremy said, and although the collision had taken place on the highway, and at considerable speed, the injuries to both were relatively—mercifully—minor.

"I have come just now from the hospital, where I was able to see each of them," Jeremy assured his staff, going on to say that Roma would this afternoon undergo surgery on a badly broken ankle and wrist. Radoslaw, meanwhile, had been treated for whiplash and shock, and would most likely be discharged in the morning.

"Though the bump he has on his forehead is spectacular," Jeremy added. "He's looking rather like a beluga whale."

The driver of an erstwhile Holden Gemini—still on her restricted license—was also mostly unhurt, Jeremy said, though it was possible she had a pair of soiled pants, since Radoslaw had been amped on adrenaline when he'd leaped out of the Camry to give her an unexpurgated opinion of her driving skills. A few knowing glances were exchanged, but although Justine presumed everybody was thinking much the same thing she was, nobody said anything.

"Of course," Jeremy continued, "this news will unsettle us all. But we are, when push comes to shove, professionals. And our own little show must go on. So, I have already called in Kim Westlake to keep the wheels turning in the photography department. As for Roma's appointments, we will all need to pitch in."

Jeremy announced that he, himself, would be taking over Roma's ongoing coverage of the court case concerning the State Attorney-General and the stand-up comic who was alleged to have defamed her. The other two staff writers were quick to volunteer: Martin Oliver put his hand up for a profile on an award-winning Chilean novelist, and Jenna Rae offered to finish Roma's piece on the impact of funding cuts to the National Ballet.

"That leaves, ah, one more assignment," Jeremy said, "a short profile piece on a talented young performer. Verdi, Verdi . . . Highsmith. Thankfully, Radoslaw already has the images in the can for this one. Ms. Highsmith is just fifteen years old, but I'm reliably informed that she's a face to watch. She's been cast in *Romeo and Juliet* for Alexandria Park Rep."

Justine thought, *Romeo and Juliet*? It had to be Nick's production. Surely.

Martin made a scoffing noise at the back of his throat.

"Yes, I know, I know," Jeremy said. "Try us as they do with their endless drawing-room comedies, the good folk of the Alexandria Park Rep are our very own neighborhood troubadours, and love them we must. And if Ms. Highsmith does indeed turn out to be the real deal, obviously the *Alexandria Park Star* wants to be part of her journey from the very beginning. Any takers for the profile piece?"

Brain: *He might be there. At the assignment.*

Justine: *Who?*

Brain: *Don't be cute. Just put your hand up.*

"I'll do it," Justine said.

"Excellent notion. Thank you, Justine," Jeremy said. "And with that, we are all . . . covered. Good work, troops."

"Um, Jeremy? When's the interview?" Justine asked.

The editor looked at his notes. "Three o'clock. At the Gaiety."

"Today?"

Jeremy checked his notes. "Indeed. Today."

It was already half past two.

♊

Justine arrived at the Gaiety with a new ballpoint pen in one pocket of her coat, a fresh notebook in the other, and two minutes to spare. She wouldn't have been able to say when was the last time she had been to the Gaiety, a fussy, old-fashioned little theater that was the pride and joy of the Alexandria Park Heritage Society. But as soon as she stepped into the foyer, her nostrils filled with a distinctive musty smell that took her immediately back to being eight years old, wearing her best overcoat and too-tight patent leather shoes. She recalled

Christmastime *Nutcracker Suites*, twee Alexandria Park Youth The-ater productions of *Peter Pan* and never-ending performances of *Lady Windermere's Fan*.

In the foyer was a young man, very kempt, in a fashionably floral shirt and exaggeratedly pointed shoes. He introduced himself as the theater's manager, though Justine knew this was code for "the theater's only permanent employee."

Justine said, "I'm Justine Carmichael, reporter for the *Star*." Al-though she had not quite known that she was going to say this, she liked the sound of it.

"They're running a little over time, but let me take you up to the dress circle. They shouldn't be too much longer. Verdi will join you when they break," the manager said, briskly leading the way to a red-carpeted staircase. "As you know, the production doesn't move into the theater for quite some time yet. Today is just to grab some moving images for promotion and so on."

In the upstairs lobby was a tiny, ornate bar and a pair of double doors that opened into the comparative gloom of the dress circle. The manager put a finger to his lips in a shushing gesture, then ushered Justine inside.

Once her eyes had adjusted, she saw that if the theater's velvet seats had been reupholstered since her childhood, then it was in the very same shade of red. The walls were unchanged, too—still a murky duck-egg blue—and the Grecian figures in the murals around the pro-scenium hadn't moved an inch. Above the seating banks, dust motes swirled in the shafts of light that poured from the ceiling rig onto the chalky blackness of the undressed stage. Cameramen stood behind tri-pods near the wings, and a third photographer roamed in bare feet.

Center stage, in a pool of limelight, there stood a young woman in dusty blacks, script in hand. Her hair was a rich chestnut, shaped into an elegant pixie cut. As her wide, flawless face caught the full impact of the light, Justine was momentarily stunned.

"What man art thou that thus bescreened in night so stumblest on my counsel?" the girl said, and her warm, slightly husky voice effort-lessly filled the theater.

Oh, thought Justine, recognizing the words immediately as part of the balcony scene. Into the light there stepped a second actor, script in hand, also wearing black. "By a name I know not how to tell thee who I am," he said. "My name, dear saint, is hateful to myself, because it is an enemy to thee. Had I it written, I would tear the word."

It was Nick. And his face, too, under the lights, was smoothed to its most important elements. His eyes looked larger than ever, his mouth more sensuous. His cheeks were slightly hollowed in a way that suited a tortured young lover.

"I'll leave you now," said the manager. "Enjoy."

"Thank you," Justine whispered, and on the stage the girl who must be Verdi Highsmith went on, "My ears have yet not drunk a hundred words of thy tongue stuttering—"

And with that, the spell was broken. Verdi giggled, and suddenly she was a regular fifteen-year-old girl. Juliet had left the building.

"Tongue's uttering. Not tongue stuttering," she said. "Tongue's uttering, tongue's uttering, tongue's uttering." She giggled again, and made a crazy face to the roaming cameraman.

"Just keep going," Nick suggested.

Verdi closed her eyes, breathed in through her nose, and . . . Juliet was back.

"Art thou not Romeo, and a Montague?"

"Neither, fair maid," Nick said tenderly, "if either thee dislike."

Justine slid quietly into one of the red velvet chairs at the back of the dress circle, where she hoped she would remain out of sight.

The actors were reading from scripts, still getting their mouths around the Shakespearean diction, and there wasn't a shred of costume or scenery to be seen. And yet something was being created—a spell was being woven from word and gesture and intention.

As Nick and Verdi spoke their lines, they moved. This wasn't the scene as the director would block it. The actors were just circling each other slowly, letting their own bodies dictate their movements. It was as if, Justine thought, they were making the stage into a whirlpool, and the swirling dust was gathering charge with each new line. Watching Nick on stage, Justine remembered, had always been like watching a seal plunge into water: an ungainly animal suddenly making sense. The stage was Nick Jordan's element.

"With love's light wings did I o'erperch these walls," said Nick. "For stony limits cannot hold love out . . ."

Justine, in the stuffy, velvety air of the dress circle, realized that she could hardly remember what it felt like to be inside those early days of falling in love and having that love returned. In fact, right at this moment it seemed almost inconceivable that it would ever happen to her again. Because love like this wasn't something you could make happen. It was a magic spark, and you just had to hope that somehow, somewhere, sometime, you would be there when the match struck the flint.

"Good night, good night! Parting is such sweet sorrow, that I shall say good night till it be morrow," said Verdi, and when the scene came to an end, Justine sat quite still, not wanting the world of the play to disappear.

She saw the manager come to the edge of the stage and whisper a few words to Verdi, who jumped down into the auditorium. The cameramen powered down their equipment, and before long Nick was alone on the stage. Justine might have stood up then and called out to him. But she only watched him as he studied the open page, his face shifting into various expressions as he read. After a time, he closed his script and walked into the blackness of the wings.

Behind Justine, the door to the dress circle opened noisily, letting in a wedge of dusty light.

"Um . . . hi," said Verdi, who had clearly just run up the stairs. She gave Justine a strange little wave, her elbow tight to her body, and it was more the gesture of a nervous teenager than of the confident, self-possessed young actor Justine had just been watching.

"I'm Justine," Justine said, holding out her hand. "From the *Star*."

Fumblingly, awkwardly, Verdi took her hand and shook it. She said, "I've never really done an interview before."

And Justine, not wanting to let Verdi know that this was her first proper interview too, said, "I saw just a few minutes of your rehearsal. You two were working so well together. It's going to be a beautiful performance."

"Oh, yeah, Nick's amazing," Verdi said.

Justine's heart was still full of Shakespeare, otherwise she might not have said anything. But as it was, she couldn't help wanting to claim something for herself. "I know Nick, actually. We went to school together."

Verdi looked intrigued. She leaned in, eyes widening. "Really? What was he like?"

"Always the performer," said Justine fondly. "You should ask him about his Toad of Toad Hall. Everyone in Edenvale remembers it."

"So, you went right through high school together, and everything?"

Justine fancied that she could detect signs of Verdi concocting some kind of narrative, making a story for herself out of these shreds of information.

"No," said Justine, "Nick's family went away before he and I got to high school."

At this, Verdi's sparkling curiosity morphed effortlessly into sadness. This girl's face, Justine saw, was like an Etch A Sketch. She had the capacity to wipe it clean of its expression and replace it with another.

"Oh," she said, as if she really were heartbroken on Justine's behalf. "Did you miss him?"

Justine's breath caught. Were they tears, prickling just inside her lower lids? *Stop it, stop it, stop it,* she told herself. This is what actors did. They made you laugh, they made you cry, they used their faces and their voices and their hands and their movements and they made you feel things. That was their job.

Now Verdi's face was doing something new. She looked all of a sudden slightly gleeful, like a mad inventor, or a possessed chef.

"So," she said, and she actually put her outspread fingers together in front of her face, and tapped the index fingers together. "Are you two still in touch?"

"We see each other around from time to time," Justine said lightly, wondering if this was stretching the facts.

"Have you met his girlfriend?"

The words hit Justine hard. Actually, it was just the one word. Girlfriend. She felt her heart sinking.

"She's a model," Verdi explained, quite accurately taking Justine's silence as a no. "You might have seen her—she's on all the ads for Chance wines. And Ophelia glasses. You know the one?"

Justine did not know, but she nevertheless felt her heart drop down through another few fathoms of blue.

"I've known her for a while because when I was, like, twelve, I played the young Laura in a television ad for St. Guinevere's *Ladies College*," Verdi said, raising an eyebrow. "I was, you know, the work in progress, and she was the finished product. But, the amazing thing about Laura is that she actually looks like that—they hardly even have to airbrush her, or anything."

And Justine knew that if her heart sank any further it would burn, because it would be at the molten core of the Earth.

"But it's kind of weird, I think. I mean, you could sell Nick and Laura as a matched pair—they look so much alike. You know, the dark hair, the blue eyes. It's like the way, in cartoons, there's the boy mouse or raccoon or whatever, and then there's the girl one and you know she's a girl because of the eyelashes and the bow. That's Nick and Laura. Don't you think it's weird how some people go for partners who look just like themselves?" Verdi said, barely drawing breath.

"But do you think they're happy?" Justine prompted, feeling guilty even as she did so. Verdi was only fifteen; it was hardly fair to pump her for information.

"Well, it's been a bit on-again, off-again," Verdi admitted.

"Because?"

"You know about Narcissus, right?"

"I do."

"Well, in my opinion," Verdi said, affecting a maturity beyond her years, "Nick might turn out to be the pool."

♊

In the week that followed, Justine worked on her profile on Verdi Highsmith until she had learned it by heart. By the time she turned it in, she had also learned the five locations between Evelyn Towers and the offices of the *Star* where she could study the face of Nick Jordan's girlfriend, the model, Laura Mitchell.

It was so tempting to think, Justine considered—early one morning as she paused in front of a large poster in the window of the local optometrist—that blessings must be evenly distributed, and that since this Laura was so favored with thick hair and symmetrical features, she must therefore be commensurately less well endowed in some other area. Intelligence, perhaps. Or charm, wit or kindness. But Justine knew—and would fiercely have argued the point—that this kind of thinking was unfair.

Brain: *Verdi said she's a bit vacuous.*

Justine: *No, Brain, Verdi did not say that. Not precisely.*

Brain: *Okay, okay, she intimated it. Same thing.*

Justine: *That is sloppy thinking, Brain. It's not the same thing at all.*

Brain: *So, what are you going to do now? Hm? Just going to give up, are you? You don't think Leo might have a little something to say on surfaces and depths, on true love and false?*

Justine: *On the basis of what? The opinion of a gossipy teenager? I think it's better that we just leave things well alone.*

So Justine turned away from the poster of the beautiful girl in the optometrist's window and continued on her way. As she walked, she called her mother, who would—Justine imagined—be collecting up the last of her belongings before heading out the door to work.

"Mandy Carmichael."

"Happy birthday, Mumma Bear."

"Oh, it's my beautiful girl! How are you, darling? You wouldn't believe what your father got me for my birthday. He went and organized, all by himself, for us to go to this cooking retreat in the Blue Mountains. Very exclusive. The focus is on tarts, apparently. Your father thinks this is hilarious. He's going to fly us there in the Skycatcher, and we'll have a night at that old art deco hotel, and then we'll fly back the next day. I mean, it's hardly sensible to learn to cook beautiful tarts when all they are is more bloody calories and I spend half my life . . ." Talking to her mother on the phone could be quite a passive activity, Justine remembered, as she walked and listened. All that was required of her was the occasional *hm-mm* and *ah-ha*. ". . . must go, my treasure. Can't be late. I've got bloody performance management meetings all day today. Love you, sweetheart. Mwah, mwah."

♊

"Got a mo, darl?" Jeremy said, finding Justine at the photocopier just after lunch. "My office?"

It was four days to deadline.

"Of course," said Justine, and there it was again: that little surge of guilt. As she followed Jeremy along the hallway, she thought nervously of the original copies of Leo's horoscopes on the document spike on her desk.

Passing the open door of the staff writers' room, Justine caught a glimpse of the spot where Roma usually worked. Her computer screen was dark, and the flowers in the vase beside her keyboard had wilted.

Jeremy's office was perhaps even a little more chaotic than usual. It looked as if he had been sorting through his books; there were empty spaces on the shelves, and large teetering stacks in various places around the room. The editor sat behind his desk, and it was with some anxiety that Justine took the seat opposite him. But when she looked up, she saw to her relief that he was smiling. Perhaps this was going to be good news, after all. Had Roma's accident, by any chance, triggered her to have thoughts of retirement?

"As you know, we had in mind a protest image for the cover of this next edition," the editor said. "And, as you also know, I do like a good protest picture. Angry faces! Chanting! Raised fists! Yes, I enjoy seeing the populace rise up and make its voice heard."

Justine had seen the picture, a photograph taken on the waterfront, of a rally against live animal export, angry people holding placards doused in red paint that dribbled like blood. She had also seen Glynn's design for the cover: the image enclosed in a border of matching blood red, just a few cover lines and all of them presented in a compressed font at the bottom where they least interrupted the power of the central scene.

"But after the brouhaha about the Ruthless cartoon last month, I have decided, upon reflection, to go with something a little lighter, a little more joyous, a little less divisive."

Jeremy held up a mock-up of his proposed new cover. Where Justine had been picturing red, her first impression was now a cooling green. The magazine's cover was split horizontally into two panes, each of them filled with an image of the face of Verdi Highsmith against a plain, mint green backdrop. As in the classic drama masks, she was both tragedy and comedy: her mouth in the top image was downturned in misery, and in the bottom image it curved upward for joy. The cover lines were now in a mixture of fonts and pastel colors, whimsical and playful. It was gorgeous.

Justine's hands flew to her face.

"So you see—"

"Oh my goodness," Justine said. "The cover story? I've got the cover story?"

"It's a lovely piece you've written. Descriptive, but not overwritten. Perceptive, witty, engaging. I love it, and I think all our readers will, too. And I haven't forgotten that you had the extra challenge of taking on the assignment at the very last minute."

"Thank you," Justine said.

"I'm also aware that you spent quite a lot of time on the Highsmith piece, and that this might be why, er, with, um, four days until—"

Justine interrupted. "I know what you're going to say. I'm so sorry, Jeremy, that I'm a bit behind with the contributions, but I—"

"No, no. No apologies required. I was only going to suggest that it might be best, over the next few days, if we were to flick some of your more—as it were—menial tasks to, ah, Henry. Hm? Perhaps we could have him transcribe Lesley-Ann's column—I notice that's not yet in the can. And I think there are still the book reviews to come? They just need a tweak, of course, but I think Henry's up for that. And maybe he could input the stars as well? Hm? What do you think?"

"That's all . . . fine," Justine said. "I mean, except for the stars . . . they're—"

Her mind raced. Although she had told herself—had come very close to promising herself—that she would leave Leo's column well alone, she now felt panicked. Even if she didn't precisely intend to tinker with Leo's copy, she also didn't want Henry touching it. The stars were, she had begun to feel, in some sense *hers*.

"I mean to say that the stars are on my screen right now, almost done," Justine lied.

"Excellent," Jeremy said. "Excellent. The rest we shall delegate. The stars, I shall leave in your ever-so-capable hands."

Half an hour later, Leo's latest fax was skewered to the document spike in Justine's office, and the month's horoscopes had been submitted for layout. And if, in the process of transcription, the entry for Aquarius had been slightly transformed, well, Justine considered, the risk was minimal. Twice now she'd got away with her little sleight of hand. And, if Nick Jordan's relationship with his beautiful, lookalike girlfriend was entirely watertight and secure, then the horoscope could have no meaning for him. What harm, then, could a few minor alterations possibly do?

cusp

Tansy Brinklow—Aquarius, oncologist, ex-wife of urologist Jonathan Brinklow and mother to teenagers Saskia, Genevieve and Ava, admirer of Diana Rigg (in her *Avengers* phase) and closet conservative voter—lunched each month with her old friends Jane Asten and Hillary Ellsworth. As was often the case, the restaurant that had been chosen for their June get-together was inconsiderately far from Tansy's consulting rooms, for neither Jane nor Hillary ever had to worry about how to fit lunch into a workday.

For all of lunch so far, Tansy had managed to keep her left hand under the table. The soup had posed no impediment to this, and neither had the bruschetta. But then Jane had suggested a cheese plate in place of dessert, and agreeing to that had been a thoughtless mistake on Tansy's part, she now realized, as there was no subtle way of getting blue Brie onto a cracker single-handed. Sitting with her left hand tucked under her thigh, Tansy was acutely aware of the outline of the brand-new ring on her finger. She had no idea whether Hillary and Jane would like it, or hate it. It was made by an art jeweler, and very different: a huge smoky brown tourmaline, checker-cut and rectangular, set in a confection of rose and white gold. Tansy wasn't sure if it was the most beautiful thing she had ever seen, or if it just wasn't her at all. She had told Simon that it was the most beautiful thing she had ever seen. After all, her manners were impeccable.

If you were to be allowed only one word to describe Dr. Tansy Brinklow, it would be "polite." And if you were permitted a second word, it would be "terribly." Her parents, more British than the British, regarded politeness as a cardinal virtue. Others were tidiness, modesty and good pronunciation (there had been private elocution lessons to protect little Tansy from the lazy vowels of her schoolmates). And although Tansy's debutante ball was now a very long time ago, there were ways in which the white satin gloves (with pearl buttons to the elbow) had never quite come off.

Tansy's polite, undemanding smile and her polite, understanding nod were so essential to her demeanor that they had—some six years ago—been her first, instinctive reaction to the surprising news that she was about to be divorced. Jonathan had dropped it on her just after they had buckled into their airplane seats, when they were heading off to Fiji for a two-week family holiday, and the girls were safely plugged in to the airplane's entertainment system.

"Darling," he said, taking Tansy's hand. "I thought perhaps I should tell you now, to give you some time to get used to the idea. When we get back, I'll be moving out. I'm leaving you."

He had thought everything through, he said, and reminded her that when they had bought their new home a few years ago, the ownership had been vested solely in her name. It was obviously easiest and most sensible if she were to keep the family home, while he would retain the inner-city flat and the holiday house on the coast—though she and the girls were welcome to use the beach house at any time, provided she gave two weeks' notice. As for the liquid assets—and these were substantial—he thought a 60/40 split in Tansy's favor would be reasonable, given the years she'd forgone an income in order to raise their children. Did she have any questions?

Questions? They swam and boiled like goldfish in a whirlpool. How long had he been planning this? Putting the house in her name— hadn't that been a tax thing? Or had he known back then that he was going to leave? Was there another woman? Oh God, was there another *man*? Was *that* why they hadn't had sex for four months? What the *hell*? He was *leaving* her? *Why*? But she couldn't catch hold of any one of these questions for long enough to get it out of her mouth, and in any case, this was business class and here was the hostess standing close by in the aisle, smiling brightly, holding a tray of flutes full of preflight Buck's fizz.

"Bubbles?" she asked.

And Tansy had forced a bright smile. "Thank you," she had said.

During the entire Fiji holiday, Tansy had felt what she imagined it was to be concussed. She spent long, stunned days on postcard-white sand, watching her girls squeal in the postcard-blue shallows. In the evenings she drank piña coladas and smoked clove cigarettes, neither of which she had ever been partial to, either before or since. And then she had packed everybody's bags with her usual efficiency and they had all come home, her husband had moved out and Hillary's GP husband had prescribed something to take the edge off it all. Only it wasn't the edge that went; it was the depth. In those years after her divorce, Tansy had lived—she later realized—in something like a lenticular puzzle, a strange place where the third dimension always turned out to be an illusion. It was really only in the last six months, since she had met Simon Pierce, that she was beginning to feel things stirring down in the depths she had forgotten were hers.

Simon was a nurse. A midwife, to be precise. In his uniform of blue shirt and blue pants, with a newborn baby slung over his forearm, he was a heady mix of manly and sensitive. Fifteen years her junior, he owned no house, but lived in a tiny, groovy rented apartment that was walking distance from his favorite bookshop and the city's best art-house cinema, the Orion. He owned no car, but got about on a Vespa, which, he had confessed, he was still paying off. Tansy was still apt to giggle in shock when she recalled the fact that Simon's only real asset was a top-of-the-range Italian coffee machine.

Hillary and Jane had met Simon on a number of occasions and been faultlessly cordial to him on every one of them. Tansy had been quite open, told her friends all about him: how she had met him at the bain-marie window in the hospital cafeteria, and how he had suggested she and he have lunch at a cafe rather than put themselves through a plate of gluey rice and crusted-over green chicken curry. But she had not told either Hillary or Jane that it was on this makeshift first date that Simon had, without any prompting at all, correctly identified that Tansy bore a remarkable resemblance to Diana Rigg in her *Avengers* phase. And although Tansy had allowed Jane and Hillary to understand that the sex was plentiful, she had not gone on about it. Jane's husband's virility had been a short-lived little thing, and Hillary's husband's attentions had for over two decades been diverted to his secretary. It could only have been seen as rubbing it in if Tansy had disclosed that one of Simon's first gifts to her was a pair of close-fitting, black leather driving gloves which she had, more than once, worn in the bedroom.

Tansy took a deep breath and landed her left hand on the white linen tablecloth, beside the cheese platter. The low, curving profile of the gem shimmered in the afternoon sun that streamed in through the restaurant's waterside windows. Hillary froze, a crumb of cheese clinging to her lunch-smudged lipstick. Jane's eyebrows shot up under cover of her thick, russet fringe.

"Simon's asked me to marry him," Tansy announced. She knew her color was high, and that she was likely going all blotchy in the décolletage.

"*Marry* him?" Hillary asked.

Jane looked at the ring and reared back a little. "Oh my God, what is that? Quartz?"

"Tourmaline," said Tansy.

"Virtually the same thing," Hillary said, then took out her glasses and leaned in for a good look. "There's a lot of work in it. It probably wasn't cheap."

"Well, that's a relief," Tansy said, with a smile.

A small look passed, then, between Hillary and Jane, and Tansy caught a distinct whiff of premeditation.

It was Jane who went first. "You do realize, Tansy, that even if it was expensive, it's a small investment. Considering what he stands to gain."

For just the briefest second, Tansy took this as a compliment. Then her eyes narrowed. "What are you trying to say?"

Hillary said, "Put it this way. If there was a wealthy male doctor, a specialist, and he was targeted by a pretty, penniless little nurse, fifteen years younger than he, what would you think? That she was dazzled by his lovely personality?"

"No," Tansy said, with a laugh. "Simon's not—"

Jane held out a hand and enumerated on her fingers. "No car, no house, staring down the prospect of turning thirty-five with nothing behind him, and here's this older doctor, single, worth a mint . . ."

She trailed off. Tansy's mouth moved like a guppy's.

"What I don't understand is what he's been doing with his life," said Hillary. "I mean, *why* doesn't he have any money? He works, doesn't he? Why doesn't he even have a car?"

Jane looked at Tansy sharply. "The other day"—she paused—"you said you were thinking of trading the Volvo, that you were going to test-drive something. Did he suggest that?"

"Yes. Yes, I suppose he did, but—"

"What kind of car?" Jane asked. The look on her face suggested that everything hinged on the answer.

"An Alfa Romeo Spider," Tansy whispered.

Hillary tittered. "Oh, Tansy. An Alfa Romeo? That's so not you."

"He said I deserved it. That I work hard. That I should have what I want."

"But who wants it, really? You? Or him?" Jane said, as she drained what was left of the white wine into Tansy's glass and motioned to the waiter for a second bottle. There was a brief and crowded silence.

"I still can't work out what he's been doing with his money," Hillary ruminated.

"He has traveled," Tansy offered.

"It could be gambling," Hillary said, then her eyes widened. "Or . . . maintenance. Where did you say he was from?"

Tansy told them. Jane's mouth puckered.

"I think you have to admit, Tansy. He's just NLU," she said.

Tansy didn't recognize this acronym. She looked in puzzlement from one of her friends to the other.

"Not Like Us," Hillary said.

"Another way to put it would be"—and here Jane paused for effect—"gold digger."

For a girl born and raised in a prospecting town, this was a power-ful word, and Tansy's reaction was violently physiological. The blush she experienced seemed to have its epicenter in her solar plexus; it was a flood of shame so excruciating that it made her throat burn and her cheeks flame, her nose throb and the backs of her hands prickle.

"Oh, oh, I've just remembered." Hillary riffled through her capa-cious leather handbag to extract a copy of the *Star*. She laid it on the table as if it were a crucial piece of evidence in a court case.

"Who's *she*?" asked Jane, tapping an immaculate gel nail on the cover. "Do we know her?"

"She's the granddaughter of that woman who used to run the dress shop behind the Alexandria Park Markets. Daughter of the youngest son, the one who married that . . . I don't know. What was she? Greek? Macedonian? Anyway, I think it's ridiculous. She's only fifteen and they're letting her play Juliet at the Gaiety. I can't imagine what that would do to a child's studies," Hillary said.

"She's beautiful," Tansy said.

"Of course she is," said Jane. "She's fifteen. Every girl in the world is beautiful at fifteen. Unless she isn't."

"Anyway, the point is," Hillary said loudly, "I just read this yester-day. And I thought of you when I saw it. It's amazingly apt. Oh God, I adore Leo Thornbury. He's always on the money. Just wait until you hear this. Where are we? Aquarius, Aquarius. Here. Listen. *You come this month, water bearers, to a crossroad of the heart. But which direc-tion should you take? The stars urge you to be wary of disingenuous love. 'If only,' mused Katherine Mansfield, 'one could tell true love from false love as one can tell mushrooms from toadstools.' You would do well to listen closely to the whisperings of your secret heart, and seek out the counsel of those you trust most.*"

Jane raised her eyebrows as if in the presence of profundity. Nod-ding grimly, she gave her verdict on Simon Pierce: "Toadstool."

Tansy felt as if she had been punched in the stomach. *Those you trust most.* Hillary and Jane had been her bridesmaids, her daughters' godmothers. They would never lie to her.

"Have I been that blind?" she said, her voice low and strained.

"Well, here's a question," Jane said coolly. "Has he ever asked you for money?"

"I did pay off his credit card debt," Tansy admitted.

"Did he ask you to, or did you offer?" Hillary asked.

Tansy couldn't really remember. Not precisely. He had been talking about how it didn't seem sensible for him to be paying all that interest if there was another option. But she had invited that comment of his, surely. *Don't worry about money*, she had said, *I've got more than I know what to do with*. Oh God, how *had* it happened?

"Who suggested it is irrelevant, Hill. Just the fact that he told her he had a credit card debt is enough for me."

"I just don't think he could . . . pretend," Tansy said. "He's not like that."

She remembered how, the first time she had politely faked an orgasm with Simon, he had stopped, regarded her with a cheeky smile, and said, "Wouldn't a real one be better?"

"I'm sure he feels for me," Tansy insisted. "I'm sure he does."

"That's the trouble with you, dear heart," Hillary said. "You're just so trusting. You never saw it coming with Jonathan, either, did you?"

How *had* it happened? She didn't know. But she did know she'd just gone into the bank, all glowing and postorgasmic on Simon's arm. Primed. She'd been *primed*. And she'd made a bank transfer of thousands of dollars. Oh God, she was a total idiot. She thought of those women on television, their faces blacked out and their voices altered, who weepily confessed to having been stupid enough to hand over their life's savings to Nigerian internet love rats.

Tansy twisted the ugly ring off her finger as if it was burning her and set it on a linen napkin. The three women regarded it, a tiny little catastrophic car crash at a safe distance.

"Oh my goodness," Tansy said. "I have to end it, don't I?"

Hillary said, "Poor you."

"Make sure you invoice him," Jane said. "For everything."

And Tansy Brinklow smiled politely.

+

Len Magellan—Aquarius, curmudgeon, resident of the Holy Rosary nursing home, fundamentalist atheist, sufferer of Parkinson's disease, father of three and grandfather of seven, lover of spicy pickled onions— was dying. Death was inside him, seeping out of his pores and discoloring his skin in lifeless shades of brownish purple and green. He could smell death in his own breath as he leaned a quivering hip against the basin in his en suite bathroom and tried to apply a toothbrush only to his teeth, and not to his nose and chin. He did not believe in an afterlife, or that there would be any reckoning for his mistakes (he would never have used the word "sins"). He did not believe he would be reunited with his dead wife, or that he and Della would sit with their rocking chairs perched side by side on the edge of a cloud where they could peer benevolently down on the earthly doings of their children and grandchildren. He believed his consciousness would simply cease and his body would rot in a box.

Each Tuesday, a volunteer came to sit with Len. She came to him not because he asked for her, but because the nuns who ghosted the corridors had noticed the infrequency of visits from his family. The volunteer was a middle-aged woman with thinning hair and a name badge that said GRACE. He was tempted to remark that having a name badge that said grace would be quite handy at dinnertime, but he couldn't be bothered.

Len was repelled by how easy it was to see Grace's pink, scaly headskin through her graying curls. The fact that he could see how she had tried—with backcombing and hairspray—to cover up her scalp was for Len too personal a thing to have to notice each Tuesday at 11 a.m. The hair thing was almost more repellent to him than the benign pity in her unremarkable gray-blue eyes. But he figured that since he pitied her for her hairlessness, for her taupe lace-up shoes, for her sexless figure and plain face, her pity and his effectively canceled each other out.

It was Len's habit to screen Grace out with the television. To show her just how little he wanted her there, he would grip the remote control and force his convulsing thumb to select the shopping channel. Vacuous Americans trying to sell him acne cures and abdominal muscle crunchers, he would have Grace know, were actually preferable to him than her pious small talk. Although to be fair, he didn't know that she'd actually make pious small talk, since he'd never conversed with her at all. She would just come each week, and sit, for half an hour, while he watched television. And she would smile, as if she believed her mere presence was somehow doing him good.

On this particular Tuesday, however, Len's strategy was flummoxed by the remote control. It failed to respond. And this was all the fault of his daughter, Mariangela. Cheap useless batteries she'd bought. Len scrabbled in the top drawer of the cabinet for replacements, but found none.

"Jesus," he muttered, hoping to offend Grace.

Batteries, like whisky, and spicy pickled onions, were things he had to rely on relatives to bring in for him. It was like being in an Indonesian bloody prison, only there was no black market. It didn't matter that he was loaded—he hadn't managed to find a bent nun willing to duck out to the Bottle-O for him.

"Perhaps I could read to you from the newspaper? Or a magazine? Mrs. Mills down the hall always likes that," Grace suggested.

"Fuck Mrs. Mills," Len muttered.

"Sorry?"

"Nothing."

So Grace took a copy of the daily paper from her bag and began, primly, to read.

"Why don't you piss off and read Bible stories to some illiterate natives or something?" Len suggested, but Grace only kept reading.

It seemed to him that she was choosing carefully what she read to him. There were no crimes, no car accidents, no deaths in her newspaper, only stolen miniature ponies reunited with their owners and celebrities shaving their heads for charity. Len pretended to nap. Through a quarter-opened eye he watched Grace fold the newspaper and put it back in her bag. But she wasn't done. She also had a copy of the *Star*.

"What's your star sign, Len?"

Len faked a snore.

"Len!"

There was a hint of unexpected spirit in her voice that made him snap his eyes open.

"I asked what sign you were born under."

"Don't go in for that hocus-pocus."

"Well, when's your birthday?"

"Can't remember."

"Oh, rubbish," she said.

Len grunted.

"I can find out, Len."

He cocked his eyebrow, daring her. So she peacefully reached for the medication chart in the wall-holder by the side of his bed. *Christ on a crutch.* He hadn't thought of that. Grace flipped open the chart and giggled.

"What?"

"Len is short for Va*len*tine? Born, let me guess . . . February the fourteenth? Oh yes."

Grace giggled some more and Len clutched at the remote control, hoping against reason that it would fire up the television and fill the room with testimonials for a diet pill or a remedy for erectile dysfunction. Fuck it. And fuck his spoiled kids and the three kidneys' worth of private school education that had failed to teach any of them that it was a false economy to spend money on cheap fucking batteries. Grace, meanwhile, cleared her throat.

"*Aquarius,*" she began.

Later that day, some hours after Grace had gone off to read to Mrs. Mills and whoever else was on her list, the words of the horoscope were still circling Len's brain. Mushrooms, toadstools. Disingenuous love. Not one of his bloody children loved him half as much as they loved the prospect of carving up the spoils on the lid of his rosewood coffin. A collective sense of entitlement the size of the bloody Taj Mahal. That was their problem. Which was also his.

The trouble was—and Len could see this clearly now—that he'd been too equitable, and too open. His current will set down that upon his death, his assets (nicely diversified among stocks, shares, bonds and property) would be liquidated and the final sum divided equally between his three children. His children, knowing this, had no incentive to suck up. Had he played his cards closer to his chest, he might've been able to set up some kind of bidding war of sycophantic behavior.

Too late for that now. But not too late to teach those indulged and ungrateful little toadstools a lesson.

Should he, or shouldn't he?

What was it that the hocus-pocus column had said? *Those you trust most.*

Len reached for his cordless phone, and—with a great deal of effort—punched in his solicitor's number.

✢

Nick Jordan was sitting on the floor of the rehearsal room, an open script on his lap and a half-eaten sushi roll in his hand, when Verdi got back from her lunch break in a tizz of excitement.

"Look!" she said, sitting down beside Nick and thrusting something right under his nose. It took him a moment to realize that what she was showing him was the cover of the latest edition of the *Alexandria Park Star*. "It's me, it's me! It's both of me."

"Hey!" Nick said. "You look amazing."

"Don't I?"

She did. The cover of the *Star* was entirely taken up with her mirrored faces. Flicking to an inside page, Nick saw a third and more neutral version of Verdi, full length this time. She wore a green shirt over gray leggings and sat back to front on a bentwood chair, her feet bare, her chin resting on folded arms. Her gaze was direct, slightly flirtatious, utterly unafraid. The headline read: A FACE TO WATCH. And beneath it was the byline: JUSTINE CARMICHAEL.

From just the first two paragraphs of the story, Nick could see that Justine had captured his co-star perfectly, giving the reader a subtle glimpse of the young actor's innocent arrogance, but leaving them in no doubt about her promising talent.

Being around Verdi was a mind-fuck for Nick. One minute she was almost freakishly mature, but the next moment her self-possession would evaporate and she'd be like an eight-year-old child after a sugar hit. It was just as their director, Hamilton, had described: as if someone had squeezed Minnie Mouse and Helen of Troy into the body of one fifteen-year-old schoolgirl.

"She's a really good writer," Verdi said.

"Always was," Nick said, with an unaccountable little flush of pride.

When he was only halfway through the article, Verdi tugged the magazine out of his hands.

"What, I can't finish it?" he asked.

She sighed. "Well, can you, like, do it really quickly? I want to show the others."

"All right, all right," he said. "I'll read the article later. But, before you take it away, can I at least read my stars?"

"Your *stars*?"

"My stars."

"*You* want to read your stars?" Verdi said, hugging the magazine to her chest.

"I do."

Verdi chewed her gum noisily as she weighed the situation up.

"If you can guess what sign I am, first go, then yes," she said.

Nick thought, but not for very long. She was changeable, versatile and energetic—it was nothing for her to come to rehearsals after hip-hop dance class, and then dash off to swim training when it was over. And after she'd been interviewed for the *Star*, she'd loved bringing back to the whole cast the gossip that the journalist was an old friend of Nick's. He remembered the way she'd laced the word "friend" with subtext, and also the way this had annoyed and pleased him, in equal measure.

"Gemini," he said, already quite certain that he was right. "The messenger."

"Wow," she said.

Nick, smugly, held out his hand for the magazine.

"I'll read it to you," Verdi decided, flopping down on the stage next to him. "What sign?"

"What, you can't guess?" Nick challenged. "I picked yours."

Verdi thought. There was more noisy chewing.

"Part of me wants to say Aries. But you're too weird for an Aries. No offense. A-a-nd, part of me wants to say Pisces. But you're not quite weird enough for that. Which makes me think that you're probably . . . Aquarian?"

Nick blinked, disbelieving.

"I'm right, aren't I?"

Nick said, "Too weird for Aries, and not weird enough for Pisces—that's how you worked it out?"

"Yeah, and, well, you know—you're a bit clueless about emotions. That's part of it, too."

"Excuse me?"

"You know," said Verdi. "You're kind of oblivious sometimes."

"Oblivious?" Nick said. "Oblivious, how? Oblivious, when?"

"Like with Laura."

"What about Laura?" Nick said.

Verdi made a *see what I mean* face. "She doesn't *remind* you of anyone?"

"What are you trying to say?"

"Oh God, you're hopeless," Verdi said.

Nick bristled. But then, Verdi was just a kid. What did she know?

"I thought you were reading me my stars," he said, pushing his irritation away.

"Oh, yeah. I was."

Verdi made up a character on the spot—a dreamy, ditsy stargazer with the faintest hint of a lisp—and began to read.

Nick listened closely, and felt a small uprising of goose bumps on his forearms at the mention of a *crossroad of the heart*. Leo was urging him to be wary of disingenuous love, and to be certain that he knew his toadstools from his mushrooms.

"So," said Verdi, letting the magazine fall closed on her lap and looking at Nick with a glint in her eye, "how much do you know about fungi?"

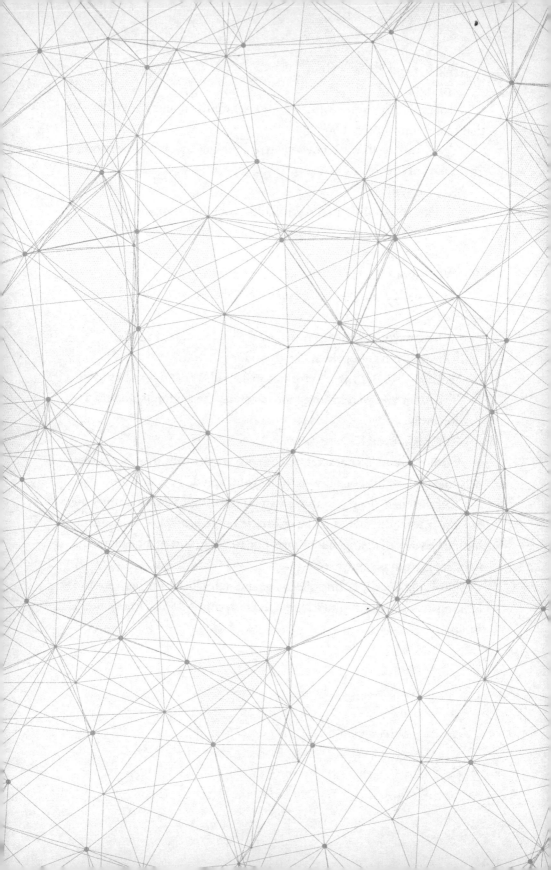

Cancer

JUNE 21–JULY 22

In late June, as a distant northerly sun hovered over the Tropic of Cancer, the southern hemisphere shivered through the shortest day of the year. Wine mulled quietly on stove tops, smelling of cinnamon, star anise, nutmeg and cloves; fire twirlers warmed up, and candles were lit, as humans in tune with the rhythms of the year sought out flickering flames to warm them through the longest night.

The sun had long gone from above the rooftop of Evelyn Towers, and Justine—wearing slippers and a house cardigan—was folding a load of laundry that she had dumped on the dining table. From somewhere beneath the mound of crumpled clothing her phone began to chime. It rang several times before she could find it among the socks and underpants, pajama pants and bras, and she only just caught the call in time.

"Hello?"

"Turn around," someone said. Someone male.

Justine frowned. "Austin? Is that you?"

It was just the sort of thing her brother would do.

"Just trust me," the caller said. It wasn't her brother, though. Justine was now fairly sure of that. "And turn around."

Justine didn't like to obey the voice; nevertheless, she did.

She turned around. But all she saw was her living room—cream couch, folded throw rug, cushions angled just so, books on the coffee table, television off.

"Excellent. Very good. Now walk toward your balcony."

"Seriously?" said Justine. "Who *is* this?"

"Will you please just walk toward your balcony?"

Brain: *Justine, have you ever seen a horror movie?*

Justine: *Yeah, I know. But who do you think it is? Aren't you dying to know?*

Brain: *You know the stupid girl in the diaphanous frock who moves inexorably toward the fluttering curtains? Right now, that's you.*

Justine: *Will you shut up?*

Brain: *Only trying to look out for you, my friend . . .*

"Sorry, *who's* this?"

"Look."

Beyond the glass of her French doors, beyond the molded-concrete rim of her balcony, across a narrow gap, and standing on the porch of the apartment opposite her own, was Nick Jordan.

Justine opened the French doors and stepped out into the cold of the year's longest night, and when she laughed, the sound easily jumped the span between the two buildings.

Without thinking, she said, "What man art thou that thus be-screened in night so stumblest on my counsel?"

Nick, catching on immediately, said, "By a name I know not how to tell thee who I am. My name dear saint, is hateful to myself, because it is an enemy to thee. Had I it written, I would tear the word."

He was wearing baggy tracksuit pants, a slouchy jumper and a pair of sheepskin boots, and Justine could imagine him on a couch on a winter Sunday. She could imagine resting her head against his chest, on a couch on a winter Sunday.

"My ears have yet not drunk a hundred words of thy tongue's uttering, yet I know the sound. Art thou not Romeo, and a Montague?"

"Neither, fair maid, if either thee dislike."

Justine put her hands on her hips and, no longer just reciting, demanded to know, "How cam'st thou hither, tell me, and wherefore?"

"Well, I live here," Nick said.

"*You're* my new next-door neighbor?"

"It would appear so."

Justine had known that someone had taken the apartment; over the past weeks, in her occasional glimpses out of the window, she'd seen signs of life. A scant few items of furniture had gathered together in the living room, and a clothes airer had appeared on the porch. Best of all, Justine noted, this new tenant had invested immediately in a shower curtain. But until now, she had never seen anyone at home.

Nick said, "At first I thought, wow, that girl looks like Justine. And then I thought, shit, that girl *is* Justine."

"You know, these coincidences . . . they're getting a little bit weird," Justine said, even though she felt she was taking a risk in echoing Leo's word—"coincidence." She made a mental note not to say "mushrooms" or "toadstools," or demonstrate any close knowledge of *The Collected Works of Katherine Mansfield.*

"How much of *Romeo and Juliet* do you know, by the way?" Nick asked.

"Bits here and there."

"That's rubbish, isn't it?"

"Maybe," Justine admitted.

"Do you ever forget anything?"

"Nothing important," she said.

There was a small silence. The moon was somewhere behind the thick city atmosphere, not a definite shape in the sky, but a vague diffusion of light.

"Hey, great piece on Verdi," Nick said.

"You saw it?"

"Of course. She said you were at the theater when we were doing the promo footage."

"I was," Justine said. She pulled her cardigan tight around herself.

"But you didn't come and say hello," Nick said. "To me."

"Well, I . . . you were busy."

"But not too busy, you know," he said. "For you."

Brain: *Hey, was that, maybe, just a bit flirty?*

Justine: *It couldn't be. He's got a girlfriend.*

Brain: *Whatever you reckon, but I'm not so sure.*

Not knowing how else to respond, Justine changed the subject. "So, how do you like your view?"

They both looked sideways down the tunnel of the two buildings in the direction of Alexandria Park. In the narrow gap at the far end was a streetlight, and a tiny section of the park's wrought-iron fence. Beyond that were some trees with fairy lights twinkling in their bare branches.

"This flat is expensive enough as it is," Nick said. "I don't even want to think about what it would cost to live around on the street side."

"There *are* views, though, and cheap ones, too," Justine said. "If you know where to look."

"And you *do* know?"

"I can show you sometime, if you like."

At a sudden and familiar sound, Justine looked down at the phone in her hand. It wasn't hers that was ringing, though, but Nick's.

Apologetically, he said, "I should take this."

"Of course."

"Maybe . . . I don't suppose you'd run lines with me sometime?" Nick asked, as his phone continued to chime. "You know, balcony to balcony?"

"I'd love to," Justine said. "Any time. You know where I am."

"See you around, neighbor."

"Good night, good night."

But Nick did not say that parting was such sweet sorrow. He just stepped back inside his living room, leaving Justine standing beneath a dismal, city-bound moon.

♋

It took until seven o'clock the following morning for Justine to fully comprehend that there were going to be certain problems with having Nick Jordan as a next-door neighbor. But as she stood in the semidark of her living room, hands on hips, Justine understood that, henceforth, her curtains were going to be an issue.

The curtains in question, pale green and damask, were a relic of Fleur Carmichael's occupancy of the Evelyn Towers apartment, and although Justine knew that she should just fling them open—in the normal, careless way that she always did at around this time on a week-day morning—she found that it just wasn't that simple anymore. What if Nick thought she was looking in on him, or inviting a conversation? Maybe she should wait, until, say, seven thirty?

Evenings were going to be equally problematic. To close, or not to close? When to close? And then there were the weekends. If she shut her curtains at an unusual time, Nick might think she was doing something weird behind them. But if she didn't close her curtains, he might think that she wanted him to see whatever she was doing—weird or not. Justine wondered if there was, set out in a reference book somewhere, a standard opening and closing protocol for curtains: some kind of code, the adherence to which would ensure that her curtain behavior could be in no way construed as strange or inappropriate.

She was still contemplating the curtain problem, midmorning, at work, when Jeremy came to the doorway of her office, looking harassed.

"Problem," he announced.

"What problem?" said Justine, guiltily clicking closed an internet quiz titled *Are you a curtain twitcher?*

"You can't hear that?"

Once Justine retuned her ears to the world beyond her office, she realized that she could in fact hear something. It was Roma's voice rising and falling, but more often rising. Although Justine caught only the occasional word with any degree of clarity—"bigot," for instance, and "ignorant," "privilege" and "fabric softener"—it was obvious that somebody was copping the fierce side of the formidable Ms. Sharples.

"Who's she ranting at?" Justine asked.

"Young Henry," Jeremy admitted. "She hates him."

"And this was not something you had anticipated?"

"I thought she would regard him as an ant, or a flea, or some other very small thing beyond her notice or concern," Jeremy said. "But I'm a little worried about her swatting him with her crutches."

"What did he say to her?" Justine said, struggling not to find the situation amusing.

"It might have been something about the crackdown on welfare overpayments."

"Oops."

"But, the *problem*," Jeremy said, with a deep sigh, "is that he's supposed to be driving her today. To the Tidepool, for a lunch interview."

Roma's broken ankle meant that she was unable to drive herself. And when Jeremy had arranged for the purchase of the new Corolla to replace the smashed-up Camry, he'd also made the decision that Radoslaw would never again be allowed to assume the driver's seat in a vehicle owned by the *Star*.

"She couldn't take a taxi?" Justine asked.

"She *could*," Jeremy said. "But since she still has the crutches, I'd rather she had someone with her, to—you know—help."

"You're asking me?" Justine said, suddenly understanding.

"I know, darl, it's a job for a copy-runner. And I wouldn't ask if I didn't think it was serious. I don't know if I'm more worried about poor Henry being scarred for life, or Roma blowing a head gasket."

"The Tidepool, you said?" Justine asked, pulling a face.

"It has new owners," Jeremy wheedled. "And excellent chowder. It would also be an opportunity for you to watch Roma in action. Watch and learn, hm? We could chalk it up to professional development. What do you say?"

"Who's she interviewing?"

"Alison Tarf."

"The theater director?"

"The same," Jeremy confirmed.

"About what?"

"Her new theater company."

Justine considered, then stood up and reached for her scarf and coat. "Deal," she said.

The Tidepool was located in a semi-industrial district near the harbor, on the top floor of a low-rise building, squat and circular, with Colosseum-esque arches on the ground floor and a coating of pink-brown plaster. The view from the curved windows was of sheds and bollards, shipping containers and boats, all set against the backdrop of a wintry sea. Lunchtime custom was steady, but far from hectic.

Alison Tarf was a tall woman of roughly the same age as Roma, with sun-damaged skin and white, flyaway hair that retained a vague hint of the beehive that had been so much a part of her look when she had burst onto the acting scene in the 1960s. Justine knew Alison best—well, pretty much everyone in the world knew Alison best—from her portrayal of Eliza, the feisty young convict woman in the classic Australian shipwreck film *Asunder*. But it had been many years now since Alison had acted, either on stage or screen, and nor was she likely to accept any roles in the near future. Directing was now her primary passion, she said, and the work of establishing a new theater company was consuming all of her available energy.

"Sideways Shakespeare?" Roma asked, without warmth. Her plastered wrist looked strangely disembodied where it lay on the table beside her open notebook. "Why call it that?"

Alison Tarf neatly nipped off a piece of her dinner roll.

"Because we will come at Shakespeare's plays from new and unexpected angles," she said, equally coolly.

Roma entered a smattering of shorthand in her notebook. "But why more Shakespeare?" she pressed. "He's been dead for four hundred years. What about the work of new Australian playwrights?"

These questions were deliberately combative but Justine, wedged between the two women, didn't know whether they came from any genuine anti-Shakespeare sentiment on Roma's behalf, or if she was just trying to provoke a response.

"The production of theater is not a zero-sum game," Alison said. "Just because a play is staged, it does not follow that it has taken the place of another. Sideways Shakespeare sees itself in the business of growing audiences. Not stealing them."

"So, you're planning to debut this coming December, I see. With which play? A history? A comedy?"

"We're starting out with *Romeo and Juliet*," Alison said.

Roma Sharples raised her eyebrows. "It's my understanding that Alexandria Park Rep already has that covered this year."

"Our production would obviously be very different," Alison said.

Perhaps it was the resultant tension at the table that made Justine do it. Or she may just have taken temporary leave of her senses.

Whichever was the case, Justine was as surprised as either Roma or Alison when she heard her own voice saying, "Romeo is a Pisces, apparently."

Roma swiveled in her chair and stared at Justine, incredulous.

"What utter claptrap," Roma said, and Justine felt herself shrivel with humiliation.

"Sorry," Justine murmured. Her cheeks were burning. Not only had she interrupted Roma's interview, but she had done so with the weirdest, least professional comment that she could possibly have invented.

"Romeo," Roma said imperiously, "is a Cancer, if ever there was one."

Alison Tarf's serious expression transformed into something like delight. "Do you know," she said, "I've always thought so too! And, I know this is controversial, but I actually think Juliet is a Cancer as well."

"Controversial?" Roma asked, genuinely surprised. "I would have thought it was obvious. Emotional, moody, the pair of them."

"Not to mention clingy," added Alison.

Justine was stunned. Was this really happening?

It was.

"But loyal," Roma went on. "We Cancerians are nothing if not loyal."

Alison grinned, and gestured to Roma's plaster. "You're even wearing your shell. Foolishly, I left mine at home."

Roma's eyes sparkled. "When are you?"

"Third of July," Alison said.

"But so am I!" Roma said.

The two women laughed, lifted their glasses and clinked them together above the tabletop. Then they were off, reminiscing about a third of July, long ago, when snow—which was rare to nonexistent in this part of the world—had settled in the streets of the city.

"That was my twelfth birthday," Roma said. "My mother let me stay home from school."

"It was my tenth," Alison said. "I made a snow mouse in the front yard. There wasn't enough for a man." She continued, "We share our birthday with Julian Assange, did you know?"

"A typical Cancer if there ever was one," Roma said.

"Tom Cruise not so much," Alison said.

"But we have Kafka! And he's more our style, don't you think?" Roma asked.

Alison nodded. "Elusive, mysterious, creative."

And on it went, for quite some time, with Justine feeling like a tennis spectator, until Alison and Roma's tribal affiliations had been explored and confirmed, and a small and contented silence had settled on the table.

At last, Justine ventured to say, "You know, Roma, I'm a little surprised. I wouldn't have picked you as somebody who was into astrology."

Roma smiled and shared a conspiratorial glance with Alison, as if the two of them had not, ten minutes earlier, been in a tense standoff about the contemporary value of Renaissance drama.

"I think you'll find most people have a guilty pleasure," Roma said.

"Reading romance novels?" Alison suggested.

"Stealing fairy bread at children's parties?" Roma said.

"Listening to the Carpenters?" Alison said, and Justine had the sneaking suspicion that this particular choice may not have been entirely random.

"Mine is just a little harmless predilection for the stars," Roma said, and Justine could hardly have been more surprised if her famously ferocious colleague had revealed that her weekend hobby was Morris dancing.

Justine said, "But astrology is so . . ."

"Unscientific?" Roma suggested.

"Illogical?" Alison said.

"Well, yes."

"Perhaps it's to do with a desire," Alison said dreamily, "to enter a different space. A place with different rules."

Roma said, "For me, it's a way of acknowledging that there are forces acting upon us, every day, every hour, that could make our choices auspicious, or doom our plans to failure. That we decide, and act, and react, from within a great web of competing powers."

"But—" Justine started.

"Astrology provides the comforting illusion that these external forces can be known," Alison said. "While at the same time reminding us that they are far beyond us, and far greater than us."

"It's a mystery," Roma added.

"With just a hint," Alison said, "of magic."

Driving back to the *Star* that afternoon, Justine had the sense that she was piloting a capsule of daydreams through the streets of the city. The inside of the car was warm and quiet, and Roma, in the passenger seat, seemed lost in thought.

In the notebook that lay closed on Roma's lap was a record of all that had been said during her second and much more successful attempt at interviewing Alison Tarf.

"What I am after is a wild convergence of theatrical styles and traditions," Alison had said passionately, once she had warmed to her subject. "I want anyone and everyone who can bring something to this endeavor to get involved—everyone from opera singers to musical theater stars. There's a Japanese Noh actor that I have my heart set on wooing. Doesn't speak a word of English! I want television actors, rock stars, puppeteers, rappers . . ."

Maybe even actual actors, Justine had thought, and before lunch came to an end, she engineered a moment to speak to the director alone.

Now, she smiled to herself as she imagined the look on Nick's face when she handed him one of Alison Tarf's business cards and said, "She's expecting your call."

In the days that followed, Justine—having failed to track down an externally mandated curtain protocol—developed her own set of window-covering guidelines. They prescribed that on weekdays curtains were to be opened at 7:15 a.m., and closed at whatever time Justine got home in the evenings. On the weekends, curtains were to be opened at whatever time she got up, and closed at 5:25 p.m. This, Justine realized, would most likely turn out to be her Eastern Standard Time protocol. Come Daylight Saving, she would need to adjust.

It became obvious to Justine, however, that Nick had no correspondingly clear pattern; he seemed hardly to close his curtains at all, night or day. Most evenings when Justine—inadvertently, of course—glanced through her French doors and into his apartment, she found the place all in darkness. Occasionally, she would see the rooms lit up, but no sign of anybody within them.

One evening, while accidentally catching a glimpse into the next-door apartment, Justine saw a slender dark-haired woman showing two delivery men where to position a new and very comfortable-looking two-seater couch—a woman Justine recognized instantly. She stepped sideways so that she was concealed by the green damask, and twitched back a section of the fabric so she could peer between its edge and the window frame.

Verdi had been right. Even when wearing nothing more exciting than a pair of dark blue jeans and a bat-wing T-shirt, and even with her hair pulled into a messy bun and her face apparently au naturel, Laura Mitchell was stunningly beautiful.

Guiltily, compulsively, Justine watched as the delivery men took their leave and Laura kneeled down on the floor to cut away the plastic from a tightly rolled floor rug. She gave it a shove and the rug unfurled—wheat-colored and plush—to meet up with the edge of the new couch. There was no sign of Nick in the apartment.

When Laura disappeared out of the frame of the window, Justine knew that this was the perfect moment to close the curtains and stop snooping. Instead, she hovered for long enough to see Laura return with an armful of cushions in elegantly neutral shades, which she placed on the sofa, trying out several different formations. When she was satisfied with the cushions, Laura smoothed the pile of the rug with her bare feet. Then she reached up and let her dark hair out of its bun so that it fell down around her shoulders, and Justine watched as Laura stretched herself out on the couch, arranging her limbs every bit as artfully as she'd arranged the cushions.

Justine knew that she should look away, but before she could make a move Laura got up and walked to the window, as if Justine's presence had somehow made itself felt. Laura peered through the glass and across the gap. Justine froze.

Justine: *Shit! Can she see me?*

Brain: *Well, if you close your eyes, it's going to be hard for me to tell, isn't it?*

Had Nick mentioned to Laura, Justine wondered, that his next-door neighbor was someone he knew? Had Nick ever mentioned Justine to Laura at all? And, if he had, would Justine's existence bother Laura in the slightest? Justine doubted it. For another few seconds she stood still and held her breath, then watched with relief as Laura closed the curtains, concealing herself from view.

Soon, Justine supposed, Nick would arrive home to this surprise: new couch, new rug, new cushions, exquisite girlfriend. Justine further supposed—and experienced a little spike of envy at the thought—that the plush new floor rug would obviate any need for Nick and Laura to venture as far as the bedroom. And she knew, with a sinking heart, that all the horoscopes, mushrooms, toadstools and Katherine Mansfield in the world were going to fail in the face of *that*.

Another week passed and for all that time Alison Tarf's business card waited, propped against a coffee jar on Justine's kitchen counter. Then came a squally evening when Justine arrived at the twelfth-floor landing of Evelyn Towers having walked through the park without an umbrella. Her damp hair straggled over her forehead, and her feet squelched slightly in her low-heeled pumps. It was, she thought as she searched out her keys, one of those nights when she most wished she was coming home not to a cold and empty apartment, but to a warm house, a cooked meal and signs of life.

It was, therefore, slightly magical when she opened the door of her apartment to find that the lights were on and the air was full of the rich smell of braising. The scent was unmistakable: her mother's famous Moroccan lamb shanks. Further, there was a huge bunch of white roses in a vase on the dining-room table, and the sound of laughter coming from the kitchen.

"Mum?"

"Oh, she's back," Justine heard. And then, "Hi, honey!"

Mandy Carmichael, short and beaming, appeared at the kitchen door in stockinged feet and a cloud of recently applied perfume. A tea towel was tucked apron-wise into the waistband of her glittery evening skirt, and she had a flute of sparkling wine in her hand.

"Oh my Lord, you're drenched," she said.

One-handed, she tugged Justine's wet coat from her shoulders and tousled her daughter's hair. Satisfied that she had made an improvement, Mandy kissed Justine on the cheek. "Shit, I've lippied you," she said, then rubbed vigorously at Justine's skin with a practiced maternal thumb. "Now, come and see who's here. I can't believe you didn't *tell* me, you rat. Living right next door!"

And there, in Justine's kitchen, leaning against the counter, also with a glass of sparkling wine, was Nick Jordan.

"Hey," Nick said. He was wearing his slouchy jumper.

Mandy, while searching out a third wineglass, filling it and handing it to Justine, said, "Can you imagine? I went out onto the balcony to water that poor bloody fern you've got dying out there, and who should I see, right there on the balcony opposite, but Nicholas Mark Jordan! I held this boy in my arms the day he was born. Now look at the size of him."

"Hi, neighbor," Justine said.

"I'm so sorry, kids," Mandy went on, slipping her feet into a pair of shiny high heels. "I'm meeting some girlfriends for dinner, and if I don't get my skates on, I'm going to be late. Darling, I've made lamb shanks for you. Give them another half hour, though." She stabbed at an earlobe with the hook of a dangly jet earring. "There's couscous in the pantry. Why don't you see if Nick'll stay and eat with you? There's enough here for an army. I have to watch her, you know, Nick. She hardly ever eats. She can go all day and outright forget to eat at all." She subtracted the tea-towel apron from her outfit and fluffed her hair. "That never happens to me, worse luck." She patted her rump to illustrate the point. "So sorry, Nick, love, but I have to go. Next time we're in town"—Mandy paused briefly to swipe on an extra coat of lipstick, and squiggle her lips together sideways—"let's have dinner. Hm?"

Nick opened his mouth to reply, but Mandy said, "Drew would so love to see you. And I want to hear all the news. Do give my love to your mother, won't you?"

Nick tried to squeeze in a response, but only ended up looking like a goldfish. Justine smirked; perfect timing was required if you were going to get into a gap in a Mandy Carmichael monologue, and Nick was out of form.

"You know, I couldn't count the times I've thought I must ring Jo, and then I think this is a terrible time, and so I think I'll do it later, but of course later is always just as terrible. Tell her I'm sorry for being such a rotten friend, will you?"

Nick settled for a nod.

"It is so good to see you, Nick. You look wonderful," Mandy said. "Really wonderful. I can't believe it. Right next door! And she didn't even tell me. Makes me wonder what else she's hiding, hm? Right. I'm off."

She kissed Justine goodbye, leaving another lipstick mark, and stretched up to land a smooch on Nick's cheek.

"I won't be back until late, so I most likely won't see you until the morning, girly-bird. I'll make breakfast, all right? I tell you, Nick, the girl never eats. Seriously, I've got to go. Bye!"

The kitchen, once Mandy had left, felt to Justine like a patch of desert in the wake of a whirlwind's passing. She could imagine disturbed leaves and twigs twirling back down to the ground in the suddenly still air, leaving an empty, awkward silence.

"She hasn't changed," Nick offered.

"That is so," Justine said.

And when that opening didn't go anywhere, Nick said, "So, how's work? Any more big stories in the pipeline?"

"Not this month," Justine said, and then silence fell over the kitchen again.

"Shocking day," Nick tried.

"I think the rain's over, though."

"At least your place is warm. Mine's like the inside of an Esky."

Justine ventured, "You really would be very welcome. To stay for dinner."

"I'd love to," Nick said. "I really would. But I have rehearsals start-ing in half an hour. It's one of the drawbacks of semiprofessional shows, all these weekend and nighttime rehearsals."

Ah, Justine thought, *of course.* That was why he was so rarely at home.

"Speaking of the theater," Justine said, picking up Alison Tarf's business card. "I have something for you."

Nick took it. Squinted at the fine print. "Alison Tarf? *The* Alison Tarf?"

"Yes," Justine said. "I met her last week. Through work."

"And . . . ?"

"And she's launching a new company. Called Sideways Shake-speare. In the next few months, she'll be looking for her core troupe. I hope you don't mind, but I told her. About your Romeo. She said, and I quote, 'I'll expect a call.' "

Justine had played out this moment in her mind numerous times, but now that she was in the middle of it, she felt slightly exposed and embarrassed, as if she had overstepped some kind of invisible mark.

Nick didn't say anything. He just looked at the card in his hand.

"I mean, if you don't . . ." Justine began. "If it's not your . . . I just thought it might . . ."

"Look, it was a really nice thought. An amazing thought," he said. "And Alison Tarf—wow. I'd love to work with Alison Tarf, but . . ."

"But?"

Nick took a deep breath.

"I promised, you see. I promised my girlfriend. I promised her that once *Romeo and Juliet* was done, I'd look for more steady work."

"Oh," said Justine.

"Laura's a Capricorn. And her rising sign is Leo. So you can imag-ine what kind of taste she has. In clothes, in wine, in jewelry."

In floor rugs, thought Justine. *And couches.*

"I'm sorry, Justine," Nick said. "I am really grateful that you both-ered. With Alison Tarf, I mean. I should be so lucky as to audition for her."

Justine nodded, and turned away from him in case her disappoint-ment showed on her face. She slipped her hand into an oven glove and took the lid off Mandy's huge Le Creuset casserole dish. Inside, thick juices were simmering, giving off a mouthwatering smell.

"I understand," Justine said, poking ineffectually at the lamb shanks with a wooden spoon. "You made a promise."

"Speaking of promises," Nick said. "You promised to show me your mystery view. Can I see it?"

"What . . . now?"

"I don't have to leave for, oh, quarter of an hour?"

Justine replaced the pot lid and thought for a second. "It might be a bit breezy."

"Please?" he said, and the smile he gave her was vintage Nick Jordan. It could easily have been straight out of grade two: the sort he would deploy when she still had a Freddo frog in her lunch box and all he had left was a bundle of carrot sticks.

♋

It seemed implausible that Fleur Carmichael had not known about the rooftop, but in all of the childhood summers that Justine had visited at Evelyn Towers, her grandmother had never once taken her there.

The door that led to the rooftop was not an obvious one. It was hidden in an alcove on the twelfth-floor landing, painted the same cream as the walls, and had only a small keyhole—no handle. Justine supposed that she had always assumed it was the kind of door that hid nothing more exciting than mop buckets, brooms and broken ladders.

When Justine had moved in to the apartment, her father had given her quite a large bunch of keys. There was the key that opened the front door to the apartment block, the one that opened her own front door, and the one for the French doors, but the purpose of the rest was a mystery. Then, on an idle Sunday, Justine had discovered that one of them opened the door on the landing, and that behind the door was a steep metal staircase.

The air in the stairwell this night was cold and still, but as Justine opened the door at the top, she was hit by a gust of freezing wind. Neither her shirtsleeves nor the thin knit vest she was wearing offered much in the way of insulation.

"Holy shit," Nick said, following Justine out onto the rooftop. "This is awesome."

In fact, the rooftop was nothing more prepossessing than a square of concrete, slick and shining from the evening rain, and furnished with a tilting clothes line, two empty planter boxes and a floodlight with a shattered bulb. Much more impressive was the view, which took in the city, the river and even the twinkling lights of the distant hills.

"I usually come up here for the fireworks on New Year's Eve," Justine said. "And it's a pretty good place to watch the Alexandria Park film festival, too, just quietly."

She had long intended to zhoosh the place up, she told him—get some outdoor furniture, put some herbs and flowers in the planter boxes. But so far, she hadn't even managed to replace the bulb in the floodlight.

Standing at the roof edge, Justine shivered. Almost absentmindedly, Nick pulled his jumper, neckband first, over his head, and passed it in her direction. Underneath, he was wearing only a T-shirt, and Justine saw the skin of his arms immediately pucker into goose bumps from the shock of the cold.

"No, don't," Justine protested. "I'm fine, really."

"Don't be silly. You're cold," Nick said.

The jumper was of soft gray wool, still warm from Nick's body, and it smelled faintly of sandalwood.

"Who else comes up here?" Nick asked, pacing the park-side length of the rooftop.

"I've never seen anybody else," Justine said. "Just the occasional bird."

"There's so much you could do with it," Nick said.

She watched him test the handle of the clothes line, and tug experimentally at its slack lengths of wire. He squatted down by the floodlight, investigating its workings, and Justine—feeling that she was at a safe distance to say something that was possibly too close for comfort—took a breath.

"Nick, you know that promise you made? To your girlfriend? Look, I watched you on stage with Verdi the other day. I used to watch you on stage when we were kids, too. Back at school, you know . . . you have . . . you just have . . . more candlepower than other people. It's your gift."

He came toward her then, the wrecked remains of the floodlight's bulb in one hand.

"Candlepower," he said, with a small laugh. "How about I get you a new lightbulb? It can be my gift to the rooftop."

"Thanks," she said, but she wasn't quite ready to let the conversation slip away. "But are you actually hearing what I'm saying?"

When Justine looked up at his face, it wore an expression of such vulnerability that it embarrassed her.

"Jus, how do you know . . ." he began, then started again: "I mean, how do you *trust* that it's right to follow your calling? Like you, with your writing. You're a brilliant writer, but you've had to wait. You're still waiting. But how do you keep trusting?"

If it had been anybody else asking, Justine might have been able to say something sage or reassuring. But, since it was Nick who was asking, she found that her brain had been reduced to a mess of misfiring synapses. She shrugged helplessly.

Nick sighed. "Last month, Leo said—"

At the mention of Leo's name, Justine's heart kicked up a gear.

"I know, I know. You're not into the stars," he said, "but just hear me out. He predicted I would come to a crossroad. And he said, wouldn't it be great if it was as easy to tell true love from false as it is to tell mushrooms from toadstools?"

Although Justine could hear her pulse beating fast in her ears, she counseled herself to remain still and quiet, to leave space for Nick to say more. While she waited, her ears filled with the conglomerate sounds of the city's nighttime traffic, and the noise of wind brushing through the branches of the big, old trees in the park across the road.

"Well, I'm freaking scared of mushrooms," he said at last. "I would never in a million years just eat one I found growing in a field. Or a forest. Know what I mean? Because I'm exactly the kind of dickhead who'd eat a toadstool by mistake and end up in hospital getting my stomach pumped. What I want to know is, does someone really love you when all they ever want to do is change you into something that you're not?"

It had worked, Justine realized. Her horoscope had absolutely worked.

Cocooned inside Nick's oversized woolen jumper, she was hardly able to believe that it had really, actually, properly worked to set off some doubts that were already there, lurking in his mind. Justine breathed the sweet-but-not-too-sweet smell of the sandalwood jumper, and silently blessed Katherine Mansfield, and all the toadstools and mushrooms of the world as well.

"Laura's amazing," Nick said. "She's such an achiever. All polish and organization and rigor. Always. Believe me when I say she doesn't take weekends off from being good at every bloody thing there is to be good at."

"But there's something you're really good at, too," Justine said. "And, speaking as your old friend, I'm telling you that I really, really think you ought to call Alison Tarf."

"But—"

"Calling her doesn't commit you to anything," Justine argued. "It doesn't mean you've broken any promises."

"That sounds a bit like a technicality," Nick said, looking doubtful.

Justine shrugged. "It's just a phone call."

"Just a phone call," Nick echoed, and Justine watched the corner of his mouth twitch until at last he gave in and smiled properly.

On the morning that Justine came into her office to find that Leo's newest batch of horoscopes had arrived, she sat for a moment and stared at the page that lay, facedown and inscrutable, on the fax machine's out-tray. She had no idea how she intended to proceed. But perhaps, she thought, her own stars might offer a clue.

Sagittarius, she read. *With Venus in Cancer, and Mercury in Virgo, this coming month brings conditions perfect for the flowering of the career success that has been budding throughout the year. At the same time, you find yourself at a peak of personal attractiveness, though it remains to be seen whether the attention you attract is of the kind that you wish to encourage.*

"Ha!" said Justine aloud. *Personal attractiveness* . . . what a crock of shit. Compared with Laura Mitchell, she was about as attractive as a peahen.

Skipping over Capricorn, she landed on Aquarius. *With Mars in Leo,* the entry said, *you may wish to put off provoking any major confrontations, but this same astro-energy will bring developments in your romantic life into sharper focus. Later in the month, Venus opposite Saturn urges you toward careful husbandry of your assets: time and money being the greatest of these. It would not hurt, at this juncture, to carefully take stock of your financial position.*

Justine frowned as she clipped the fax to the document holder. She transcribed each of the entries from Aries through to Capricorn, but when she came once again to Aquarius, she paused.

What to do, what to do? Perhaps she and Katherine Mansfield had already made enough of an impact. Maybe even more than enough. Perhaps it was time to stop meddling and let destiny simply unfold.

With Mars in Leo, she typed, faithfully.

Brain: *Chicken.*

Justine: *What did you say?*

Brain: *You heard.*

Justine: *He's already in a relationship. And I don't think it's particularly honorable to mess with that. There's a thing called the sisterhood, you know?*

Brain: *Ri-i-ight. And would this sisterhood have Lizzie Bennet leave Darcy to wimpy old Anne de Bourgh? Have Maria deliver the captain into the hands of the Baroness von Schräder? Have Juliet tell Romeo to piss off back to Rosaline?*

Justine: *I don't even know Laura. I don't want to make an enemy of her.*

Brain: *But you don't have to be Laura's enemy in order to be a friend to Nick's career. Just restrict your comments—to the professional.*

This was a good point. What if . . . ? Justine wondered. What if, in much the same way as she had come up with a protocol for opening and closing her curtains, she could make up her own rules? An ethics of horoscope adjustment? A set of guidelines that would permit advice in relation to career matters, but rule out any mention of affairs of the heart?

"That could work," she whispered to herself. Then she pressed the delete button, and Leo's words were returned to the void.

Justine thought for a moment, riffled through her memory bank, then began to type.

"All we have to decide," wrote Tolkien, *"is what to do with the time that is given us."*

♋

While the curtain protocol required that, on weekend mornings, Justine open the curtains at whatever time she got up, it was usually the case that she did a good many things first. On this particular Saturday, she:

- had a shower,
- got dressed in skinny jeans, fitted paisley shirt (a Fleur Carmichael 1960s vintage original), and cropped orange cardigan,
- laced up her red boots,
- applied mascara and lip gloss,
- changed the paisley shirt and cardigan for a cobalt blue shirt with bell sleeves,
- unlaced her red boots,
- zipped up her fur-lined tan boots,
- blow-dried her hair,
- plumped her couch cushions,
- folded her throw rug,
- reapplied her lip gloss,
- slid a Joni Mitchell CD into the stereo,
- pressed Play.

It wasn't as if she expected, the minute she opened her curtains, to see Nick Jordan sitting on a chair on his balcony with a pair of opera glasses. Nor did she think he would particularly care about the placement of her throw rug, or be especially impressed by the color of her boots. It was just . . . well, it was just a touch of window dressing.

When she did at last fling back her curtains, she saw—fixed with clothespins to the airer on Nick's balcony—a sheet of white paper bearing a message. At the top of the page was the letter J and in the middle of the page was a sketch of a lightbulb. Under the lightbulb sketch were the words *Give me a shout*.

Justine stepped out into the cold, trying to work out what, exactly, she ought to shout. *Hello? Nick? Coo-ee?* But before she had made up her mind, Nick stepped out through the sliding door wearing rumpled pajama pants and a soft-looking T-shirt. His dark hair was sleep-mussed and shaving had clearly not been part of his life for several days.

"Morning, neighbor," he said.

"Morning."

"For you." In Nick's hand was a small box—a lightbulb box. "For the rooftop. It's definitely the right fitting, and it was the brightest one I could find."

Justine was impressed. He'd said he was going to get her a new lightbulb, but he'd actually gone and done it.

"Hey, that is so nice of you," she said. "I don't know when I would ever have got around to it. And I have something for you, too." She ducked back inside her apartment to pick up a copy of the newest edition of the *Star*.

"It only came out yesterday," she said, holding it up to show him the cover: a black-and-white head shot of the country's most famous coal magnate, her brutal features incongruous with the delicate diamond-bow necklace she wore at her throat.

So there stood Nick, with the bulb. And there stood Justine, with the magazine. And there, between them, between the buildings, was the gap.

"I don't think I should throw this," Nick said.

"Probably not," Justine agreed.

Nick suddenly held the box to the top of his sleepy-head hair. "Lightbulb moment! We need a little basket, like in *The Lighthouse Keeper's Lunch*."

"Oh my God. I haven't thought of that book for years."

"How many times did we read it?"

"Well, I know that during our year, the kindergarten had to replace its copy at least once."

It had been such a simple idea, but such an irresistible one: that tubby little picnic basket, filled with food, being snapped onto a wire and sent out over the sea to the lighthouse keeper.

"A mixed seafood salad," Nick quoted, in a faintly piratical accent.

"Iced sea biscuits!" Justine returned.

"Peach surprise!"

"Could we really have one?" Justine said, half seriously.

Nick raised his eyebrows in amusement, and Justine braced herself to be mocked. But instead, he said, "I've got string."

"I've got a basket. Mum keeps cotton balls in it," Justine said.

By means of some moderately accurate throwing of the basket, some semicoordinated catching of the ball of string and a bit of nifty knot-tying, Nick and Justine rigged a simple string loop that enabled the basket to be transferred to either side of the gap.

And so it came to pass that a lightbulb made the first recorded journey, by basket, to the twelfth-floor balcony of Evelyn Towers from the twelfth-floor balcony of its ugly neighbor, and a copy of the *Alexandria Park Star* made the inaugural journey in the opposite direction. And inside that magazine, running down the gutter edge of a verso page toward the back, were the horoscopes. By Leo Thornbury. Mostly.

cusp

Dorothy Gisborne—Aquarius, Anglophile, longtime resident of Devonshire Street, widow of five years' standing, proud owner of possibly the most extensive collection of commemorative Charles and Diana wedding china in Christendom and fastidious ironer of sheets, tea towels and underpants—typed an address into a Google Maps search field. On her screen, a blue dart appeared in a grid of pale gray that filled out, in fits and starts, into the village of Fritwell in Oxfordshire. It was against the advice of their dating site that she and Rupert Wetherell-Scott had exchanged real-world information so swiftly, but at their age . . . well, there was so little time to lose.

Aware of her quickening breaths, Dorothy clicked Street View. And there it was, his actual house, just as it had looked on a cloudy day sometime in the not-too-distant past when the Google car had crawled down his street. The house was modest: a conjoined and pebble-dashed terrace so unexceptional that almost nobody in the world but Dorothy Gisborne—born in the Australian dust, yet raised on the dewy cowslips, green hedgerows and pert hedgehogs of Beatrix Potter illustrations—would be likely to find it remotely charming. But charmed she was, both by the undemanding coolness of the wintry light, and by the vague hint, in the picture's background, of green fields, dormant bluebells and talking rabbits.

It was 2 p.m. in Dorothy's sunbaked salmon-brick bungalow unit, but it cost her now-practiced mind almost nothing to calculate that it was 5 a.m. in the far-off English summertime. Rupert would still be asleep, his body a single lump under the covers of the double bed that his wife was no longer around to share.

Dorothy's hand, on the mouse, trembled.

"Fool," she told it. "Be still."

Dorothy peered at the house on her screen. She noted the tidy front yard and the letter slot in the front door, the daisy bush in a large stone urn at the side of the narrow steps. If she *were* in fact to go, if indeed she *were* to say yes, then that was the door she would come home to, and *that* was the mat she would wipe her feet upon. And *those* were the daisies that she would pick to put in a vase on the bathroom sink.

She glanced up at the top corner of her screen. 2:05 p.m. 5:05 a.m. Still two hours and fifty-five minutes until she could expect the Skype chimes to come pinging through the ether like a pair of electronic meditation balls in a watery tunnel. Then there he would be, Rupert, the angle of his laptop screen making him appear slightly more jowly than she assumed he really was, and accentuating the cravats he wore, tucked like colorful paper napkins inside his shirt collar.

"Morning, Dorothy," he would say.

And she would say, "Evening, Rupert."

It was a small joke, and not especially funny, but it was a sweet and comforting way to begin their daily exchange.

Now it was 2:12 p.m. 5:12 a.m. Dorothy sighed, and did a slow 360 through the street view. Was that a little bridge down there at the end of the street? Yes, she thought it was. Then they would cross that bridge, she and Rupert, as they walked that street on their way to the old stone village church on a Sunday morning, or to the pub for a shandy on a Friday afternoon. His border collie would follow at his heels, low as a fox, and she, Dorothy, would wear Wellingtons and tweed, and a scarf over her hair, just like the Queen at Balmoral.

"Don't be daft," she muttered, realizing—too late—that she was putting on an ever so slightly British accent. Hot-faced, she closed her browser with a definite click and shoved back her chair.

From beyond her front windows, she heard the zoom and pause of the postman's motorbike. When she stepped outside, her gaze was drawn to the ugly holes in her garden beds where all the daphnes and rhododendrons had toed up from thirst. That would never happen in Fritwell, Dorothy thought, as she wriggled the new edition of the *Alexandria Park Star* out from the slot of her mailbox.

Back indoors, Dorothy arranged upon a tea tray the *Star*, a Charles and Diana one-cup teapot, and a single chocolate biscuit. From a large and laden dresser, she gentled down the gilt-edged Queen Anne china cup in which cameos of Charles and Diana were encircled by gold bands, framed in their turn by Tudor roses and fleur-de-lis. However, she could just as easily have selected the Crown Trent cup, upon which Charles and Diana nestled inside a vibrant red heart beneath a golden lion. Or, for that matter, an Aynsley, a Royal Stafford, a Royal Albert or a Brosnic. Alternatively, a Wedgwood, Royal Doulton or Spode.

Dorothy's Charles and Diana wedding china collection covered the shelves and filled the cupboards of two large dressers in her living room. While it included expected things like cups, plates, vases and jugs, it also incorporated china trivets, thimbles, trinket boxes, candle snuffers, ashtrays and bells. Wedgwood issued commemorative jasperware in several shades, and Dorothy had tracked down every Charles and Diana wedding item in both the blue and lilac colorways (though she elected to pass on the ocher). There were years when Dorothy's chief pastime had been writing away to china collectors in England and America. But then came eBay, and, after Reg died, Dorothy organized for his shed to be lined with shelves that would accommodate the new influx of previously unimagined treasure made in honor of the great nuptials of July 29, 1981.

Dorothy sat down at the round table in the bay window nook that overlooked her backyard. She poured her tea and nibbled her biscuit. On the front cover of the *Star* was that dreadful coal industry heiress. Really, Dorothy thought, you could see in that woman's eyes what the love of money did to a person's soul. She flipped the *Star* over and, for a moment, rested her hand on the back cover as if she could absorb meaning through the paper stock.

"Well, Leo?" she whispered. "What should I do?"

She breathed in, and flicked the magazine open to the stars.

Aquarius: "All we have to decide," wrote Tolkien, "is what to do with the time that is given us." Not even you, Aquarians—the ultimate free spirit of the zodiac, born to the unconstrained element of air—are immune to the seductive pleasures of earthly things and visible successes. But ask yourself, today, on what you truly desire to spend the hours that are given into your care.

In the silence of Dorothy's held breath, the ticking of a small clock grew louder and louder and louder. It was a ceramic Charles and Diana clock, made by Denby. 2:35 p.m. 5:35 a.m. Two hours, twenty-five minutes to go. Tick tock, tick tock. Yesterday, Rupert had worn an orange cravat patterned with slate blue hexagons. He'd told her about how he'd taken Flossie to the vet to have her teeth cleaned, how he'd beaten Nigel at darts for the first time in five years, and how he was thinking about getting the lounge chairs re-covered. And then unexpectedly he'd said: "Come, just come. Come be with me and be my love." Dorothy, stunned, had demurred.

Tick tock, tick tock. Tick, tick, tick. Her life's seconds numbering. And she would spend them on what? On eBay? On commemorative Charles and Di king-sized Royal Worcester egg coddlers? On *things*? Dorothy looked from one teetering, packed dresser to the other. From every shelf, Charles looked down his long nose at her. Diana, demure and lovely, smiled up from under her floppy blonde fringe. And where was Diana now? Dead as a duchess. And one day Dorothy would be, too.

"Oh, Leo," she murmured.

He was right. Tolkien was right. And Dorothy already knew what she must do. She must cast away every plate, cup, vase, trivet and candle snuffer. Every last thimble. And the dressers, too. And all her furniture. And her jewelry, clothes, handbags. She would sell the house.

"Morning, Dorothy," Rupert would say, in two hours and twenty minutes.

"Evening, Rupert," Dorothy would say.

And then, no longer doing anything to prevent those lovely clipped British tones from sneaking into her voice, she'd say: "Well, Rupert, I've made a decision . . ."

+

Blessed Jones—Cancer, celebrated singer-songwriter, clandestine devotee of early Dolly Parton and sucker for the twang of a banjo, owner of a twice-mended and now thrice-broken heart—sat at the dim end of the broad timber bar of the Strumpet and Pickle and silently cursed Margie McGee.

Unlike most of Senator Dave Gregson's other female colleagues, Margie had been safe. Not just because she was older, but because she was too bloody principled. Oh, why had Margie had to go and quit her job? If she hadn't, then that auburn-haired nymphette would never have ended up in the employ of Senator Dave Gregson. And neither, presumably, would she have ended up in the bed that should actually have been shared by Dave Gregson and Blessed Jones herself.

Blessed was subconsciously convinced that the darkness of her sunglasses could in some way prevent everyone else in the pub from observing that it was, indeed, Blessed Jones sitting there with a pint glass of cider before her. The cuffs of her cardigan sleeves were misshapen with crumpled tissues— used ones in the left, clean in the right. At her feet lay a curvaceous guitar case.

From out the sides of her sunglasses, Blessed observed that this Monday night's patrons were hardly the gorgeous, nose-pierced, handholding, tongue-kissing young groovers that filled the joint Thursday through Saturday. The tiny tables that on a Friday would be ringed with laughing, Ned Kelly–bearded hipsters were on this night nothing more than beer coasters for the solitary businessmen who perched on the undersized furniture like lonely giants. Monday night at the Strumpet and Pickle, Blessed realized, was for people who'd finished their day's work but had no place else to hurry off to. And, of course, for the pub's resident conspiracy theorist, who this night had buttonholed some poor bastard over by the fireplace. In healthier times, he'd apparently written a polemical book about the imminent end of the world, but now he was reduced to ranting at open mic nights and making incoherent speeches about asteroid collisions and volcanic ash.

Blessed drew a tissue out of her right sleeve and blew her nose. Then took a slug of her cider. She felt the cold wash of it up behind her forehead and along her cheekbones, but the cider wasn't strong enough to erase the images that kept repeating on the screen of her mind. The big heavy door to the apartment opening. The girl, naked by fridge-light. Maybe that could be the title of a song. *Naked by fridge-light, now nothing is all right, his Fahrenheit appetite, it's relationship dynamite.*

So many times before, Blessed had forgiven Dave. She'd forgiven him the uptight academic who wore black asymmetrical everything, including hair, then a slash of yellow lipstick across her mouth. She'd forgiven him the patchouli-smelling aid worker who'd spent some time advising him and his staff on East Timor. She'd forgiven him the tattoo-covered eighteen-year-old who'd babysat his eight-year-old son, the only child of a marriage that had broken down under the weight of Dave's infidelity.

After each episode, Blessed would ask him: *What did you want? What were you looking for? Why aren't I enough?* But he'd only shrug. Talking to Dave in the aftermath of an affair was like trying to dig through the bottom of a swimming pool, smacking stroke after stroke into ceramic tiles with the edge of a spade. And this time, she didn't have the faith even to try. There was nothing underneath.

"You're a man," she said to the man sitting alone, two stools away from her at the bar, carefully wedging a plastic card back into its slot in his wallet. He was a medical something, in a blue shirt with a logo. Appealing, Blessed decided. Floppy dark hair over one eyebrow and the rim of his glasses. Tasteful glasses. Carnal lips, large teeth. Safely dangerous. Blessed thought: well-mannered wolf.

He made a surprised face and pointed at himself. *Me?*

"Yeah, you," she said, and stuffed the tissue up her left sleeve along with all the others. Maybe some meaningless sex would be good on a lonely Monday night.

"Simon," he said.

"Bronwyn," she said, and although he raised an eyebrow, he said nothing.

"You're a man," she repeated, moving one stool closer to him. "Explain men to me."

On the bar in front of him was a sleek golden laptop. She leaned on an elbow, shamelessly looking at his screen. He had a banking site open. Blessed, squinting in for a better look, caught two words before the man folded his laptop closed. *Tansy. Brinklow.* Blessed remembered the rhythm of that name. *Tansy Brinklow, Tansy Brinklow. Bansy Trinklow.* There had been two chardonnays prior to the cider.

Simon Pierce—Scorpio, midwife and technology geek, hopeless chocoholic, art-house-cinema hound, Vespa driver and owner of a heart every bit as freshly broken as that of Blessed Jones—knew perfectly well who she was, this petite woman sitting beside him, her nose slightly red and her speech just faintly slurred. Further, he knew that the guitar at her diminutive feet was none other than Gypsy Black: a gleaming, buxom acoustic with twin tortoiseshell pick guards and an ornate mother-of-pearl rose inlaid in the headstock. Blessed was pictured with Gypsy Black on the cover of every one of her CDs, every one of which Simon Pierce owned.

He poured Blessed a glass of water from the jug on the bar. And also produced a single-shot Berocca from the man bag that was slung over the seat of his stool.

Oh, thought Blessed, both disappointed and relieved. *No meaningless sex there, then. Tansy Brinklow, Tansy Brinklow, Tansy Brinklow.*

Fuck, thought Blessed, as she found the place in her mind that the name occupied. Tansy Brinklow had been her father's oncologist.

Eyes suddenly wide, she put a hand on Simon's arm. "Are you dying?" she asked.

"What?"

"Dying," she said.

"No! What? I mean"—Simon was bewildered—"no more than the average person."

"Oh. Well, that's good," Blessed said. "A relief, I suppose. No cancer then?"

"Cancer? No."

"Throat, lung, bowel? What's that thing you men have? Not prostrate. Prostate. Oh God, you don't want to tell me about your nads.

I mean, I am a Cancer," Blessed babbled. "Homebody. Sensitive. Easily hurt. What about you?"

"I think I'm a Scorpio."

"Ha!" Blessed burst out. "Isn't that just code for 'Hey, babe, I'm a great fuck'?"

Simon drew back a little, his smile tightening. Blessed reached for her cider. Silence hung around them like a fart.

"Shit, I'm sorry," Blessed said, then added, "Simon."

"I forgive you," he said, then added, "Blessed."

Blessed winced.

"What made you think I was dying?"

"Tansy Brinklow," Blessed said, waving a hand at his closed laptop. "You were paying Tansy Brinklow. Are you in remission or something?"

Simon gave a rueful laugh. "No."

"Then what were you buying?"

He thought for a moment. "Integrity, I think."

Blessed put an elbow on the bar and looked keenly at Simon.

"Go on," she invited.

Two hours passed, then, in which Simon told Blessed about how he had been engaged to Tansy Brinklow and how right they had seemed together and how it had landed on him like a falling building when she ended it because he had suggested she buy an Alfa Romeo, or perhaps only because she was afraid, but in the end the shame of her friends thinking she'd been taken in had been more painful than the love and the leather-gloved sex had been pleasurable and so she had called him a gold digger and sent him an invoice for some money she had loaned to him, but also for some other things, too: restaurant meals, and a weekend at a swank out-of-town resort.

Also in those two hours, Blessed went to the ladies' twice and finished her third pint of cider and Simon refused to buy her a fourth, ordering two hot chocolates instead. And while Blessed spooned the froth off the top in tiny increments, she told Simon about Dave and his policy on renewables, which although it was supposed to be a Green thing she now suspected was just another way of saying that there would always be another girl along in a minute, and how the latest one had fire-red hair and pale breasts that could sink a small Pacific nation and how Blessed had come home early and seen her standing naked by the fridge.

Then Simon told Blessed how he was paying Tansy back, every cent, in installments, and how it would take him a year or more, and how he still had to see her in the corridors of the hospital, and how accustomed he was becoming to the gut-twist of shame, and all because money—to him—was just something that you used when you had it, and lived without when you didn't, while money—to her—was safety, security, success, family, power, armor and, finally, the whole point.

"I thought we'd spend the rest of our lives exploring each other's hidden depths," Simon said. "But she didn't have any. She only had hidden shallows. My mistake."

Blessed sat upright on her stool, her expression suddenly urgent. "Say that again."

"What?"

"Just say it again."

"My mistake."

"No, no," Blessed said, waving her small hands. "Before that."

"She had only hidden shallows?"

Blessed's posture relaxed.

"Hidden shallows," she repeated softly. "Hi-i-dden shallows," she said again, letting the words develop a melody. Then she reached down and snapped open the clasps of her guitar case, lifted and nestled the pretty black guitar into her lap. Gypsy Black was beautiful, and Simon Pierce watched as Blessed began to pluck a halting cascade of bittersweet minor thirds. She closed her eyes and resequenced the chords, beginning softly to hum.

"I turned thirty-five last week, you know," Blessed said, without opening her eyes. "Thirty-five!"

And Simon was about to say *Happy birthday for last week.* But she wasn't with him any longer. He'd been a midwife long enough to know that look—the one women had when they rolled their eyes away from the outside world and inward to the business of birth.

The song spun itself out of her fingers' movements on the brassy strings and before long she was singing, her voice like finest sandpaper and broken birdsong.

I looked for your depths, but all I found were your lies
Learned I could just wade, never swim, in your eyes
You're a skit, not a drama, a bare diorama
A beautiful charmer, no Trench Mariana
I searched but never found in you
Dived but never drowned in you
Now I'm aground on you
You and your hidden shallows

She sang the words once through, then let Gypsy Black loose to sing a verse in fluid fingerpicking shot through with harmonics that seemed to Simon Pierce to be made of mother-of-pearl turned sound. Blessed sang the words again, louder and more plaintive this time, then let the song die on a lingering chord. When she opened her eyes, she had the attention of every soul in the Strumpet and Pickle, even the asteroid guy at the fireplace.

Leo

JULY 23–AUGUST 22

er vestal livery is but sick and green, and none but fools do wear it," recited Nick, and as he delivered his line, he paced the short length of his balcony: four strides in one direction, four in the other. "Cast it off. It is my love; O, it is my lady! O that she knew she were."

"Nope," Justine said across the gap.

It was a Saturday morning in late July, and Justine had taken a dining chair out onto her own balcony and was now sitting cross-legged upon it— the Arden *Romeo and Juliet* open on one knee and a three-quarters-empty box of Maltesers balanced on the other. She wore a thick cable-knit jumper and a beanie, for although it was approaching noon, a thin film of frost still clung to the concrete lip of the balcony, and also to the railing.

"What do you mean 'nope'?"

"You got them the wrong way around. It should be, 'It is my *lady*; O, it is my *love.*'"

"Fuckety, fuck, fuck," Nick said, striding his balcony. Over a pair of dark denim jeans that made his legs look a bit too skinny, he was wearing the jumper Justine had come to think of as the sandalwood jumper.

"Again," Justine instructed, and popped another Malteser into her mouth.

"All right. It is my lady; O, it is my love. It is my lady; O, it is my love. Hey, can I have one of those?"

"Nope," Justine said.

"Just one little ball of malt and chocolate yumminess?" he wheedled.

"Absolutely not. Chocolate must be earned, my friend. You'll need to get through the monologue. Without a single mistake. Twice."

"That's just cruel."

"One must suffer for one's art. Okay. From the top. Enter Juliet, above."

"But, soft! What light through yonder window breaks? It is the east, and Juliet is the sun. Arise, fair sun, and kill the envious moon, who is already sick and pale with grief that thou art more fair than she."

"Neeeeeeeeert," Justine bleeped.

"What?"

"That thou *her maid* art *far* more fair than she," Justine said.

"That thou *her maid* art more fair than she."

"Uh-uh. Feel the rhythm of the line. That thou her maid art *far* more fair than she."

"My God, you are such a pedant!" Nick said, though not unpleasantly. "Do you have your moon in Virgo? Or are you Virgo rising?"

"How should I know?"

"Well, what time were you born?"

"Two o'clock in the morning," Justine said. "What does that have to do with anything?"

"Wait, wait," Nick said. He tapped and scrolled on his phone. "Two o'clock in the morning, on November twenty-fourth, in the year of our birth, means that you are . . . ha! I knew it! Virgo rising."

"What are you looking at?" Justine demanded, laughing.

"It's a site that lets you calculate your rising sign, based on exactly when, and where, you were born."

"That's insane."

"Is that so? Is it? Listen here: *Virgo rising people are highly sensitive to irregularities in their immediate environment, and will instantly recognize when something is off-key or out of place. They will expend a great deal of energy in restoring rightness to their surroundings. In other words, they are precisely the sort of people who keep a special* pen in their handbags for the express purpose of ridding the world of 'advocados.'"

"Well, pedants have their uses," Justine said. "You said yourself that Verdi is already off-book and word-perfect. You want to be shown up by a fifteen-year-old?"

Nick sighed. "You're right. She'd be insufferable."

"Well, then."

"But I don't think I can go on without chocolate. Please? Just one."

"Oh, fine," Justine said. She got up and dropped a Malteser into their lighthouse keeper's basket, and Nick operated the string line to bring it over to his side.

Since its rigging, the basket had enabled a good deal of neighborliness. Though it had not yet conveyed the quintessential cup of sugar, it had carried the DVD of Baz Luhrmann's *Romeo + Juliet* (from Justine to Nick), a Blessed Jones CD (from Nick to Justine), a Band-Aid (from Justine to Nick) and a helping of microwave popcorn (from Nick to Justine).

Now, Nick fished the chocolate bauble out of the basket. "Why, thank you, kind and generous mistress."

"Okay, but no more until the job's done," Justine said. "Enter Juliet, above."

"But, soft! What light through yonder window breaks? It is the east, and Juliet is the sun . . ."

It took half an hour for him to be word-perfect, and Justine had needed to seriously slow her Malteser intake to be sure there would be a few chocolates left for Nick's reward.

"Three?" Nick said, peering into the box he had pulled out of the basket. "Three? *Three?* That's all I get? After all my travail?"

"There would have been more if you'd known your lines."

Nick put all the Maltesers into his mouth at once, and around the edges of them he said, "Thanks, by the way."

"For?"

"Running lines with me."

Justine smiled and closed the book on her knee. "So, did you make that call?"

"To Alison Tarf?"

Justine nodded.

"I did," Nick said. "Well, to her assistant, anyway."

"And?"

"The auditions are being done in a group setting. Lots of improv, apparently. Alison wants to see how people work together, spark off each other, that sort of thing," Nick said.

"When are they on?"

"Not until September. Which is after *Romeo and Juliet* closes, so the timing's—"

"Perfect?" Justine suggested. "Do you have to prepare anything? I could help you rehearse?"

But here, Nick's enthusiasm seemed to ebb away.

"I don't know," he said flatly. "I . . . well, I shouldn't."

"You shouldn't *audition*?" Justine asked. "Why?"

"You know. I promised. Laura and I . . . we went through a rough patch, and split up for a while, but since we got back together, she's just been great. A lot more relaxed. The promise I made—it's important to her, and I want to do the right thing. But then, I'm torn. Because this is Alison Tarf we're talking about. I guess I've got some soul-searching to do."

Hadn't he read his stars? Justine wondered. Hadn't "Leo" already indicated to Aquarians which part of their souls ought to be searched? Justine tried to think of a way to delicately tip one or more of Leo's key words or phrases into their conversation. *Earthly things . . . the hours that are given into your care . . .*

But instead she said, "Auditioning is just auditioning, isn't it? I mean, if you got a spot in the company, there would be nothing to stop you from turning it down. Don't you think you should at least . . . have a go?"

"I don't know, Jus. Maybe it's easier this way."

"Easier?"

Nick dropped his shoulders and sighed. "Maybe it's easier to walk away from it all without ever finding out that you're just not quite good enough. Then you can always imagine what might have been, always having the consolation that you were the one that walked away."

"You don't really believe that, do you?"

Nick gave a wry laugh. "I didn't think I did. But, well, then I read what Leo had to say . . ."

Go on, Justine thought. "Yes?" she prompted.

"Well, Leo said that I should be thinking about how I really want to spend my time. My life. And, you know, maybe I'm not using my time in the best possible way. Maybe I'm wasting my time pursuing an acting career. If it turns out that I'm not good enough, after all, then where will all of these months, these years . . . where will they have gone?"

Ah, thought Justine. So, it was not only a matter of a promise to Laura. It was at least as much a matter of courage and confidence; those old trickster kings.

"But what if you found out that, actually, you *were* good enough?" Justine said. "Isn't that at least a possibility?"

"Shit!" Nick said, looking at his watch. "Rehearsals start in half an hour. I'd better get going."

"Is it really such a scary question that you have to run away from it?" Justine said.

Nick met her gaze, and held it for a moment. "Maybe it is. But I promise I'll think about it. And I really, truly, do have to go."

"Then hie you hence," Justine said.

"Thanks, Nurse," Nick said.

And though that was not the role that would have been Justine's first choice, she supposed it was better than not being cast at all.

♌

Each year, Jeremy Byrne stultified his staff with an event that he called the State of the Nation. If it weren't for the strong coffee the editor made for the occasion, and the Rafaello pastries he ordered in bulk, there would have been little compensation for the hour and a half of her life that Justine sacrificed annually to Jeremy's very detailed roundup of circulation figures and financials, the previous year's successes and his goals for the twelve months ahead.

This year, the State of the Nation was on a Tuesday in early August. During the morning, Justine worked on Lesley-Ann's gardening column. Its subject was the majesty of peonies, but the handwritten copy had arrived in an envelope that also contained a generous sprinkling of potting mix, and Justine had to spend a good quarter of an hour cleaning her keyboard.

When she had finished—both the keyboard cleaning and the editing of the column—Justine found herself, for perhaps the first time since taking over as contributions manager, with an empty in-box. Finance, food, letters, book reviews and gardening were in the can; Doc was yet to send in his crossword, so there was nothing to do on that front.

She tidied up her computer desktop and went through her emails, answering, deleting, filing. She stared at the fax machine as if she might have the power to spur it into action. But it turned out that she did not.

Justine thought.

She picked up a sheet of scrap paper from her recycling pile.

She selected a pen.

Aquarius, she wrote. But what were the magic words? What was the mysterious combination that would make Nick Jordan believe that it was his destiny to audition for Alison Tarf's new theater company?

Justine: *Brain? Any ideas?*

Brain: *Well, I think timing is key.*

Justine: *Oh! The magazine is due to come out right on opening night, isn't it? So, we catch Nick on a tide of enthusiasm for performance . . .*

Brain: *. . . and validate his choice of profession . . .*

Justine: *. . . by making the horoscope read something like a review! A good review.*

Brain: *Now you're thinking.*

Justine's page began to fill with scribbled words and phrases: *applause, acclaim, take a bow, encore.* She had just jotted down the phrase *con brio* when she became aware of someone standing at the door of her office.

He was in his early or midthirties, and his shirtsleeves were pushed up to the elbows, revealing arms that were either naturally olive-skinned or unseasonably tanned. His tarnished-gold tie was loose at his collar and he wore his dark blond hair slightly long. After a second, she remembered.

It was Daniel Griffin. He was not quite as tall as she recalled, she observed now, but there was a sense of solidity in the set of his shoulders, and in the way his chest comfortably took up all the available space inside his shirt. Gym junkie, Justine diagnosed.

"Justine?"

"Daniel?" she asked, looking unsure, though she wasn't in the least.

"That's right."

Daniel took a few steps into the room, which made Justine instinctively lift the page she'd been writing on and flip it facedown on the desk. *Crap*, she thought; that had probably made her look really shifty.

"You've come for the State of the Nation?" she asked.

He inclined his head slightly. "I have."

"Wow. That's dedication to duty."

"I'm nothing if not devoted," he said, hand on his heart. "Hey, that piece you wrote on the young actress? It was good. Very good, actually. You ought to be writing more often. Jeremy's wasting you in this job."

There was a quality of jest to his manner. Was he teasing? She couldn't decide.

"Well, you know what it's like around here. Hard to get an opening when nobody ever resigns," she said. "Or dies."

Daniel twitched his eyebrows upward. "I'll watch my back."

"Wise," Justine said, deadpan.

"See you at the big event, then." And he left her office. Backward.

♌

Arriving at the tearoom—where the catering platters had already been set out amid the usual scattering of newspapers, magazines, photocopied union bulletins, and someone's kid's fund-raising chocolate box, long ago emptied—Justine noticed that Jeremy seemed tense as he plunged a mighty brew of coffee.

Daniel Griffin, meanwhile, was leaning against the counter in a manner that Justine first thought was perhaps a bit too relaxed. But after observing him for a moment, she realized that he was absolutely alert, and watching everyone.

"He is rather nice to look at, isn't he?" Anwen said, bumping her shoulder against Justine's.

But before Justine was forced to respond, Jeremy cleared his throat.

"Thank you. Thank you, ah, everyone. Thank you, for, er, coming along today. And thank you, Daniel, most especially for traveling in order to, ah, be with us today."

In the exhaustive presentation that followed, Jeremy found six different ways of telling his staff that while circulation was just a smidge down from where it had been at the same time the previous year, advertising revenue was holding comfortably steady. The last of the morning slipped slowly around the clock face and most of the staff were half asleep by the time the editor said, "And so we come to the very final item of business for this, ah, State of the Nation bulletin."

Jeremy paused then, and Justine knew—from the faint wobble that she detected at the corner of her boss's mouth, and from the barely perceptible sheen of tears in his blue eyes—that what was coming next was going to be anything but business as usual.

Justine glanced at Daniel, who was studiously looking at nothing at all, and holding his relaxed pose just a little too precisely. And she realized that he knew what was coming too—that he was, in fact, entirely prepared for this moment. He had come here to be part of something very particular. An abdication. And a succession. The first in the *Star*'s entire history.

Roma, too, had worked it out. Shocked, she put her plastered wrist to her chest, and this proved to be a domino-toppling gesture that sent a wave of understanding radiating across the tearoom, just slightly ahead of Jeremy's actual words.

"There have been those who've offered the opinion that the only way I was ever going to leave the *Star* was in a box. But I have decided that—despite all the *Star* has meant to me, and all that it has given to me—I am going to write a different ending for, ah, myself. I have decided . . . that is, I am, ah . . . today I am stepping . . . well, not down. And not up, either, as it happens. Let's just say that I have voted myself the title of Editor Emeritus, a role I propose to conduct largely off-site. Under these new arrangements, I hope to do much more reading, although I know my beloved husband has plans for me to do a great deal more, ah, gardening. In any case, I will be doing a great deal less of the day-to-day, um, grind, as it were.

"Yes, yes, I do see the looks on all your faces, and while I am, of course, gratified by the sentiments I see reflected there, this is, I hasten to add, a day of, ah, celebration. For today, we welcome home from Canberra Daniel Griffin, who has done fine service as our chief political correspondent, and who will be taking over the reins here at the *Star*. As editor. Effective, er, immediately."

Jeremy began to clap. And the sound, for a moment—until his shocked staff took their cue to join in—was too loud, too much. Daniel did not move, only accepted the eventual applause with a casual nod, as if nothing in the world was more natural than for him to be stepping into the shoes of Jeremy Byrne.

As soon as it was practicable to do so, and seemingly from a desire to outpace the rising tide of his own emotions, Jeremy hurried on. "Our darling Jenna Rae has agreed to take over from Daniel, and I am certain that you will all join me in wishing her every success in the nation's capital."

There was more applause, during which Jenna tried to keep her face arranged into a stony mask of professionalism, though everyone could see the delight in her eyes.

"And I'm sure you all understand what *that* means," Jeremy said, and Justine was discomfited to discover that everyone in the room was looking in her direction. She felt a bright flush creeping up both sides of her neck.

"It means that there will be a desk free, here at HQ. And, as part of what is turning into quite the cabinet reshuffle, our dear Justine, who has so very patiently delivered your letters and your lattes, will now be able to take up the reporter's slot that, I hasten to add, she has already unofficially embarked upon, in rather spectacular style, with last month's cover story, no less. I do know, Justine, that this day has been a long time coming. But, come it has! And now we expect great things of you."

There was another burst of clapping as Justine began to register the consequences of Jeremy's announcement. The career she had imagined, planned for, studied for, dogsbodied for, was about to be properly hers. She would move into Jenna's place in the staff writers' room along with Roma and Martin. Her byline would appear in the magazine, not as a fluke, but as a matter of course. She was truly on her way.

Jeremy at this point lurched into a digression about the proposal for the heritage listing of the yellow peril, and Justine used the cover to thumb out a swift text message. *Jeremy has resigned. Daniel Griffin taking the helm. I have my reporting job!* She sent it to her mother, and to Tara. And then, impulsively, to Nick Jordan. Three replies arrived in as many minutes. Her mother wrote: *Wonderful darling clever you must be time to go shopping ill buy you something nice to wear.* This made Justine smile, but she also made a mental note to show her mother, again, how to capitalize letters in text messages, and how to find the punctuation menu. Tara responded: *AWESOMEBALLS!* Nick's reply, the last to arrive, said: *I will bake you some humble pie to celebrate, and while we eat, I will hear your admission that Leo Thornbury does know everything.*

Justine tuned back in to the events in the tearoom just in time to hear Jeremy say, "Which brings us to, ah, Henry."

Henry was blushing so acutely that his whole head seemed in danger of becoming a blood blister. Justine furrowed her eyebrows. Jeremy wouldn't do it, surely. He wouldn't just promote Henry, after only a few months of his being appointed as a copy-runner? What kind of apprenticeship was that? It was nothing! It wouldn't be fair. Justine had grown two years older while carrying the mail and fetching the coffee. It wasn't possible that Henry was going to get out of it after a handful of weeks.

"After a relatively short time here at the *Star*," Jeremy continued, "dear Henry is being promoted to the position of contributions manager, and although this will represent a, ah, steep learning curve, I am sure we will all assist him in whatever way we can as he learns the ropes."

Shit, Justine thought, imagining Henry sitting in her lovely little office, editing the book reviews that she had commissioned. Worse, he would have the task of selecting the Letters to the Editor. Henry! With his conservative take on the universe. And . . . was he really up to the task of checking Doc's cryptic crossword clues? Justine knew that she would have to impress upon him the seriousness of that responsibility.

Another small wave of excitement washed over her. She had her reporting job! She was going to be a writer, a real writer. Implausibly and for a second time, Justine thought, Leo Thornbury had been right on the money about her career success. And hot on the heels of this thought came the realization that it would from now on be Henry's job to transcribe Leo Thornbury's horoscopes; the stars would no longer be hers to command.

Justine's feelings jostled and conflicted, and she wished that she were alone, or at the very least invisible, so that she could sort them out privately. But she was not invisible. She was in the tearoom, in plain sight, and when she looked up from her tangle of thoughts, she became aware that Daniel Griffin's hazel eyes were fixed on her: steady, intelligent and interrogative.

♌

Leaving work that evening, Justine reached the far end of the lavender-lined pathway and paused. After making sure that nobody was behind her to see what she was about to do, she stood right beneath the mosaic star, which hung bright and yellow and shining crazily against the backdrop of the dark and overcast sky. For a moment, Justine allowed herself to feel the warm glow of its inspirational rays raining down—at last—onto her upturned face. Then, smiling at her own stupidity, she swung out through the gate into Rennie Street.

When she was halfway home, her phone chimed the arrival of a text message. From Nick.

So, what time am I expecting you for humble pie?

Justine, slightly flummoxed, responded: *Oh. I had thought the pie to be purely metaphorical.*

Well, Nick responded, *your metaphor is currently in my oven. 7:30?*

I'll be there, Justine wrote, and as she continued on her way, she wondered if it were actually possible that the stars had wheeled themselves into some kind of curiously wonderful alignment.

♌

Justine had never set foot in the brown-brick apartment complex that stood next door to Evelyn Towers. But if she'd ever tried to imagine what the building was like on the inside, she'd have been absolutely correct. The walls and floors of the ground-floor lobby were grimy, and the stairwell was filled with the unmistakable whiff of household refuse.

The smell of Nick's apartment was a relief, for although there was a faintly detectable bass note of mildew, it was mostly smothered by top notes of hot pie and recently sprayed Axe deodorant.

"Congratulations!" said Nick, standing in the doorway wearing a pair of pale jeans and a striped shirt, his arms wide open. When he hugged Justine, it made her feel somewhat short, but also a little bit light-headed.

"I've come to you completely empty-handed," she said. "No wine, no chocolates, no—"

"Oh, shut up," he said, entirely good-naturedly. "Come on in. Wine is this way."

In the narrow hallway, Justine passed a series of hat stands that were cluttered with an insanely eclectic collection: she caught sight of a Tibetan horseman's hat, an English bobby's helmet, a Daniel Boone cap with a genuine raccoon tail and a chef's toque.

In the living room, propped on a rudimentary brick-and-plank bookshelf, was Nick's ukulele collection—one instrument in plain brown, and the others in Hawaiian shades of sunset, warm shallows and guava. Lined up around the base of the walls were posters for plays by Brecht and Chekhov, for *The Tempest* and *As You Like It*, *Henry IV* and *Twelfth Night*. There were posters for *Summer of the Seventeenth Doll* and *Away*, physical theater productions and puppet shows, cabarets and crass-pun pantomimes.

Humble pie, à la Nick Jordan, turned out to be a creamy chicken and leek filling inside a perfect puff pastry case. Because Nick didn't yet have an actual pie dish, he'd baked it in a foil tin from the supermarket, but it had turned out beautifully and he'd served it up with tender spears of asparagus.

Since Nick had nothing resembling a dining suite, they ate with plates on their laps, sitting side by side on the couch that Justine couldn't help but think of as Laura's couch. He'd chosen a crisp white wine to celebrate with, but they drank it out of a pair of sunflower-patterned coffee mugs, since wineglasses remained on his list of things to acquire.

"To you, Lois Lane," Nick said, holding up his cup.

Soon, two scraped-clean plates had been set down on the coffee table, and Nick was opening a second bottle that Justine noticed was significantly less pricey than the first had been. Entirely warm and comfortably tipsy, she had taken her shoes off and was sitting with her feet tucked beneath her.

"Thanks for this, Nick. For dinner . . . for celebrating with me."

"A pleasure," he said. "Don't think I've forgotten, though. Remember, you still have to admit that Leo Thornbury knows everything."

"That's a pretty grand pronouncement," Justine said.

"Well, I'm not going to rush you. Whenever you're ready," he said, mock magisterially, "I shall hear your admission."

Justine laughed. "Okay, then. I suppose now is as good a time as any."

She took a sip of her wine and thought, cleared her throat, and made a serious face. "Leo Thornbury seems to be a rather good astrologer."

"Pah!" Nick said. "Pathetic. Try again."

"Okay, okay. You're right," Justine said. "Ah . . . Leo Thornbury's columns have, for whatever reason, quite accurately foretold the circumstances of my work life this year."

"Those are weasel words," Nick pronounced. "What's this 'for whatever reason' business? The words you're looking for are 'Leo Thornbury knows everything.'"

"Leo Thornbury," Justine began again, and collapsed into giggles.

Brain: *If only he knew, huh?*

Justine: *Did you have to bring that up right now, when I'm having such a good time?*

"Leo Thornbury," Nick prompted.

"Has unusually good insight," Justine finished.

Brain: *Very clever . . .*

But before Nick could argue any further, Justine was surprised—

and she saw that Nick was, too—to hear a key turning in the lock of his front door. Only a few seconds later, Laura Mitchell appeared in the living-room doorway, wearing a shimmery deep green coat that fell almost to the straps of her stupendously high heels. Her hair was fixed in a complicated updo that Justine was fairly certain could only be accomplished by a professional. It was as if Laura had stepped directly off the red carpet, and into a profoundly awkward silence.

"Hey," Nick said, getting immediately to his feet. He kissed Laura on the cheek. "Did I know you were coming over?"

Laura looked from Nick to Justine, and back to Nick. "The advertising thing was at the Westbury, just on the other side of the park," Laura said, gesturing with her small clutch purse as if to indicate the direction from which she'd come, "so I thought I'd call in on my way home. Say . . . hello."

The pause that followed this sentence seemed to stretch, and stretch, and with every passing nanosecond, Justine felt increasingly uncomfortable.

"This is Justine," Nick said, all in a rush.

An expression of perplexity briefly crossed Laura's face, but then Justine observed how quickly and expertly Laura reorganized her features.

"Pleased to meet you, Justine," Laura said, and there was something formal about Laura's practiced good manners that Justine found both enviable and irritating.

"My next-door neighbor," Nick explained.

"Oh," said Laura, the pieces of the puzzle visibly coming together in her mind. "You went to school with Nick. You're the Shakespeare coach, yes?"

"That's me," Justine said, and for some reason her thoughts jumped to the lighthouse keeper's basket. Did Laura know about it? Did it bother her?

Laura took off her coat and hung it on the hook of a hat stand.

"Do you want a glass of wine?" Nick offered.

"Just water, thank you," Laura said. When Nick had gone to the kitchen, Laura took a seat next to Justine and asked, "So, how's he doing with his lines?"

"Beautifully," Justine said. "Really well. Just a little bit of work needed around the final soliloquy. I mean, if there's a part of the play you definitely don't want to stuff up, it's the tomb scene. Can you imagine, there in the crypt, and you've got Juliet in your arms, and you completely dry up and have to call for a prompt? Talk about destroying the mood!"

Brain: *You're babbling.*

Justine: *I know. And see her face? She's trying not to, but she's looking at me like I'm a fuckwit.*

Laura, Justine now understood, was one of *those* women. With all their poise and reserve, they made Justine nervous, and the effect of this on her behavior was positively Pavlovian. Try as she might, when she was in conversation with women like Laura, she couldn't stop herself from lapsing into ridiculously vivacious displays of chattiness.

Justine: *What do I do?*

Brain: *Put your shoes on, buttercup.*

And so, by the time Nick had returned to the living room, Justine had slipped her feet back into her beloved but decidedly unglamorous clogs and buttoned up the duffel coat that had—on her way out of her own apartment—seemed to exude a kind of streetwise chic, but now seemed only childish.

"I should go," she said.

"There's no need to rush off on my account," Laura said, and Justine could see that she was being sincere.

"No, I really should go," Justine said. "I had a big day at work."

At the door, Nick hugged Justine again, but now there was none of the fizzy excitement she'd felt earlier.

"I'm sorry," he said quietly. "That wasn't meant to happen."

And Justine knew that she'd spend the night half awake wondering what *was*.

♌

On the day she officially began as a reporter, Justine found herself at the front door of the *Star* at half past seven in the morning with an Officeworks bag filled with an extravagant selection of black pens, a clutch of classy notebooks, a set of matching desktop containers, some adorable sticky notes, animal-shaped rubber bands, penguin paper clips and novelty erasers.

Nobody else had yet arrived. Justine punched in the code to the electronic lock, and stepped into the half-lit hush of the empty building. At the door to the staff writers' room, Justine paused for a moment, taking in the workstation that had belonged to Jenna Rae. Gone were all the postcards and reminder notes that had been pinned to the felt boards around the computer; the penholder was empty, as was a small bookshelf beside the desk. Justine jiggled the mouse of her new computer in order to wake up the monitor, and found that the computer, too, was invitingly blank, with all of Jenna's personal files removed, and a generic desktop image reinstalled.

Moving desks, she thought, was like a small and uncomplicated version of moving house, and it came with the same mixture of excitement and newness, anticipation and the slight sting of goodbye. But she was glad, now, that she had woken so ridiculously early; she was grateful to have this slice of time in which to set up her new desk unhurriedly, make herself a cup of tea, daydream a little . . . also to duck into her old office to check the fax machine.

And there, in the office that was no longer hers, a single white page lay on the machine's out-tray. Soon, this would all be Henry's. But the fax was here, now. And Justine was here, now.

"Timing, Leo," she whispered, as she picked up the page. "Beautiful timing."

Aquarius, she read. *This month Mars is flexing its muscles in the power zone of your Eighth House. A powerful house, the eighth concerns itself with the greatest mysteries of life—sex and death—but also with rebirth and transformational experience. The eclipse of 21 August brings both revelation and auspicious conditions for relinquishing those things in life that no longer serve you.*

"Un . . . helpful, Mr. Thornbury," Justine whispered.

Brain: *I don't know. Sex and death seem pretty relevant for someone playing Romeo.*

Justine: *Yes, yes. But we don't want him thinking about "relinquishing," do we?*

She checked the time; it was still very early, so she slid in behind the desk. If Henry arrived while she was transcribing the stars, she would be able to tell him, quite truthfully, that she was just helping him out. After all, that was what Jeremy had asked: that everybody pitch in to give Henry a hand.

Justine clipped Leo's fax to the document holder, logged in to the computer and opened up a new file. Fingers flying over the keys, she transcribed the entries for Aries, Taurus, Gemini, Cancer, Leo, Virgo, Libra, Scorpio, Sagittarius, Capricorn and . . .

Aquarius, she typed. *You are on song, water bearers. With Jupiter casting its largesse about in your career sector, you are at last starting to see results for all the many years of hard work you have invested. Enjoy the acknowledgment and acclaim that rightfully come your way. Take a bow, Aquarius!*

Justine had just hit the exclamation point when Daniel Griffin appeared at the office door, making her jump with surprise.

"Sorry," he said. "Didn't mean to alarm you."

"No, no. It's all good," she said. "I didn't think anyone else—"

"I thought you'd be next door."

"I am next door. I mean, I was," Justine babbled. "I just came in to get my last few things and while I was here, I thought I would, um . . ."

Daniel looked at her directly, steadily, slightly amusedly. This only had the effect of making Justine more nervous. He came to the side of her desk, half sat on the edge of it, and peered at the computer screen.

"The stars, hm?"

"Yes."

Justine felt her pulse skyrocket. If Daniel were to look closely enough, he would see that there was a mismatch between the words on the screen and the words on the fax that she was supposedly transcribing. But there was no way, right this minute, of either scrolling the screen so that the entry for Aquarius disappeared from view, or removing the fax from the document holder. At least, not without looking profoundly dodgy. But maybe if she was cool, supercool, he wouldn't notice.

"It's surprising, really, how many people are into the stars," she tried. "Are you? Into the stars?"

"It's hard not to be," he said.

"Oh? Why so?"

"Well, when you're given the best role in the zodiac, it's hard to turn it down."

"Best role?"

"I'm a Leo," he said. "The lion. The sun. The king."

"I see," said Justine, trying not to let her eyebrows shoot up into *you've got to be fucking joking* territory.

"And you?"

It was working: Daniel was looking at her and not at the screen.

"Well, I'm not a Leo," Justine said, perhaps a little too emphatically.

"Gemini?" he guessed.

"Are you trying to say I'm two-faced?"

"Libra?"

"Looking for a diplomatic option that won't offend me, are you?"

"Answering questions with questions? Anyone would think you're a journalist," Daniel said. "But I get it. I'm going to have to work you out, right?"

Justine was not sure this was quite the sort of conversation she wanted to be having with Daniel Griffin on the first day of their new working relationship.

"Something like that," she said.

"Well, why don't you finish up here, then come and see me for an assignment?" he said. "I've got a beauty for you. If I wasn't the editor, I'd want this one myself."

"Oh?"

"Ever heard of Huck Mowbray?"

"The Aussie Rules player?"

"Very good."

"He has that terrible mustache."

Daniel nodded. "And the micro-shorts. At the moment, he's the ruck rover for the Lions, but before moving up to Queensland, he played for a couple of the southern clubs."

"And?"

"Well, he's coming home. To launch a book of poetry. His own book of poetry."

"Huck Mowbray, the footy player, is a poet? Are you serious?"

"Justine, Justine. One should not stereotype. Just because he looks like a grunt doesn't mean he isn't sensitive."

Carefully, while Daniel was speaking, Justine—casually, casually—unclipped Leo's fax from the document holder and folded it—absentmindedly, apparently—in half.

"No need to worry about the deadline. This month's edition's pretty much locked down, and we'll want to keep the Huck Mowbray for the September edition, to coincide with the AFL finals. So, you've got plenty of time. What do you think? You up for it?"

"Does Dolly Parton sleep on her back?" Justine said. Then blushed, and crossed her arms across her own chest, realizing that she had just made a tit joke to her new boss.

Daniel smiled. "I had a press gallery friend who used to say, does Gough Whitlam think it's time?"

"Very Australian," Justine said, chastened.

"Oh, there's more where that came from. Do koala farts smell of cough drops? Does a Tasmanian have two heads? Is Bob Brown?"

Justine would have liked to chime back in, but since the only rhetorical affirmation she had left was "Does a rocking horse have a wooden dick?," she said nothing.

"Right," Daniel said, straightening up. "When you're ready, come by my office and I'll give you all the details."

Once he was gone, Justine leaned back in the office chair and let relief flow through her. That had been a bit too close for comfort.

Justine picked up Leo's fax. Normally, she would have speared it directly onto the document spike. But today she did something different. She tugged off a handful of other documents, skewered Leo's stars, then replaced the other pages on top, burying the fax deep in the pile.

She submitted the stars for layout and logged out of the computer that was, as of today, Henry's. Before she left the office, Justine gave the small white fax machine a friendly little pat.

"Thanks, Leo, old friend. It's been fun," she whispered. "But it's over now."

♌

On the Friday of *Romeo and Juliet*'s opening night, Justine strategically commandeered the office bathroom on the stroke of 4:40 p.m. Behind the locked door, she took off her cute cherry-red Mary Janes and replaced them with a pair of black platform-heeled boots that were both stunning to look at and horribly uncomfortable to walk in.

Over the blank canvas of her little black dress, Justine put on a black evening coat with a deep ruffle at the hem and a frill at the neckline.

At 4:45 p.m., there came a sugary voice from outside the door. "Will you be long, darling?"

"Not long, Barbel," Justine said, and she took out her makeup purse.

Face done, that left only her hair. She couldn't bring herself to go so far as hairspray. It made her sneeze. So she settled for scrunching her light brown waves in her hands and slipping in a sparkly clip at her temple. She surveyed herself in the mirror.

Justine: *So, will I do?*

Brain: *Very nicely indeed.*

The blocks between the office and the Alexandria Park Markets were tough going in the magnificent boots, and this confirmed in Justine's mind that it would be sensible to take a taxi the rest of the way to the theater. But there was first of all an essential errand to be accomplished at the markets. And, this night, it had nothing to do with *advocados*.

The florist's stall at the markets was called Hello Petal, and the woman behind the counter, wearing an apron of vintage ticking, looked like she'd had a long day. Her mascara was smudged beneath her eyelids and her hair seemed tired. Nevertheless, she managed to dredge up a smile for Justine.

"What can I get for you?" she asked.

"I need two bouquets, please," Justine said. "They should match, but one should be a little younger and girlier. The other should be a little older and more masculine."

The florist looked intrigued. She thought for a moment before she began to move around her flower buckets picking one stem here, another there, in what looked like a kind of waltz.

"And, if you wouldn't mind, can you find a way to wrap the second one together with this?" She handed the florist a copy of the new edition of the *Star*, hot off the press.

"Curiouser and curiouser!" said the florist.

♌

Squeezing her way into a seat in the middle of the second row of the dress circle, Justine observed that the gathering audience was made up of a great many silver-haired women with large earrings and vibrant woolen wraps. In general, these women were accompanied by equally silver-haired squires who wore what Justine thought likely to be their second-best suits. The cheap seats at the back were taken up with younger people, many of whom   in their cable-knit cardigans and thick-rimmed spectacles—looked to Justine as if they might be drama students, or university English majors.

Two empty seats in the front row of the dress circle stuck out like the gap in a six-year-old's bottom teeth. But then Laura Mitchell made her way, smiling and apologizing, past the seated patrons toward those seats, followed by a woman with dangling pearl earrings and a plum-colored woolen wrap. This was almost certainly Laura's mother, Justine thought, for the two women had the same expensive-looking jaw structure, the same top-shelf cheekbones, the same thick hair that looked simultaneously sleek and aerated, like something out of a Kérastase advertisement. As she took her seat, Laura caught sight of Justine, and gave a tiny wave, which Justine returned.

The Gaiety was not a theater that was known for cutting-edge performances. And yet, as soon as the curtains parted, Justine could see that this was not going to be a standard *Romeo and Juliet*. Each of the characters wore the same basic costume—a simple long-sleeved black top and three-quarter-length black pants—although the identity of some characters was quickly signaled by headdresses of white or gray. But while the costumes were minimal, the makeup was intense. Every actor's face had been artfully painted to accentuate the mouth and eyes.

The staging was stripped back: a black floor was enclosed by a concave cyclorama that changed with the scenes from pale day to starry,

starry night. As the actors worked the nighttime scenes, the constellations that were projected on this screen rotated in a slow, inexorable reminder of the wheel of time, turning.

As was often the case with semiprofessional theater shows, there were in this production so many things that threatened to unsuspend the audience's disbelief. The young man playing Tybalt had decided to make this Capulet cousin a caricature of evil. Hence, he spent most of his onstage time swishing around his long, crow black hair and demonstrating swordsmanship skills that Justine imagined had been hurriedly gleaned in an adult-education Try Your Hand at Fencing class. Lady Montague delivered her lines with the overblown pomposity of the worst kind of amateur Shakespeare, and while Lord Capulet was okay so long as he stood still to deliver his lines, he tended to lose the plot if he tried to walk and talk at the same time.

But Justine could see that the director had husbanded his varied resources brilliantly. He had lured an experienced, matronly actor into the role of Juliet's nurse, and she rode the knife-edge of comedy and tragedy to perfection. Cast in the role of Friar Laurence was a performer who bore a striking resemblance—in face and voice—to the English actor Simon Callow.

And then there were the lovers themselves. No longer Nick and Verdi, but Romeo and Juliet, with not the least hint of archness in their flirtations. From the start, they portrayed their attraction as soft, sweet and deep, and the poetry of their lines played its proper second fiddle to the emotion. Perhaps the most extraordinary thing about the performances of the four strongest actors was that, together, they almost made Justine believe that a happy ending was possible.

In the tomb, the director toyed with the audience, choosing for Juliet to wake up just a moment after Romeo downed his poison, giving them just enough time for one passionate, living kiss before the poison took effect. Tears squeezed out of the corners of Justine's eyes. She could hardly swallow, her throat was so sore from the effort of not weeping.

"Thus with a kiss I die," Romeo said, and then Justine did cry, hopelessly. Enough to make Laura's mother swivel in her seat. Idiot that she was, Justine hadn't put any tissues into her purse, so she had to make do with the backs of her hands.

Thank the heavens, Justine thought, that the director had cast himself in the role of the prince, so that it was someone with perfect timing who delivered the play's final lines: "For never was a story of more woe than this of Juliet and her Romeo."

The audience applauded loudly. And Justine thought, Shakespeare was a fucking genius. A couplet, as kitsch as a couplet could be, and yet it was enough to fill the heart to overflowing. When the actors took their bows, Justine clapped until her hands hurt.

When the house lights came up, there appeared mysteriously at Justine's right shoulder a handkerchief, newly shaken out of its folds.

"So, now I'm guessing," someone said, "that you're a Cancer."

Justine turned to see, sitting behind her, a person who was definitely Daniel Griffin, although her watery vision made him appear somewhat submerged.

"Oh God. Thanks," Justine said, and she took the handkerchief and wiped her eyes and nose in a way that she would later reflect was probably too hasty. "What are you doing here?"

"You don't think Alexandria Park Rep sends free tickets to the editor of the *Star*?"

Justine noticed, simultaneously, Daniel's use of the word *tickets*, plural, and that the woman sitting next to him was Meera Johannson-Wong, the anchor of the nation's most highbrow television current affairs show. She was famous both for her cutthroat questions and her seriously avant-garde wardrobe, and tonight she was wearing what seemed to be a pinafore pieced together from men's suits. Justine couldn't prevent herself from gawking at Meera, who was twisted around in her seat, talking to a woman in the row behind her, giving Justine a view of the many competing suit collars that rippled down the back of the amazing pinafore.

"That's Meera Johannson-Wong," Justine whispered to Daniel, awestruck.

"Well, thanks for telling me," Daniel said, a little smugly. "We're old friends. I'm glad I haven't been mistaking her for someone else all these years."

Brain: *You caught that, right?*

Justine: *Caught what?*

Brain: *Friends. He said "friends." He's emphasizing to you that they're just friends.*

Justine: *Because?*

Brain: *Honestly, Justine.*

Justine considered. It wasn't such a terrible thought. Daniel was . . . well, he was nice. He'd been nothing but encouraging about her work; he hadn't turned out to be nearly as up himself as she'd first thought. And he was terribly easy on the eye. But he was also, now, her boss.

"So, you're here to check up on Ms. Highsmith's performance?" Daniel said, leaning forward, elbows resting on his knees. "To see if she was equal to what you wrote about her?"

"Well, yes. There was that. But also, Romeo's an old friend of mine."

Brain: *Don't think I missed that.*

Justine: *Oh, go to sleep.*

Daniel scanned his program. "Nick Jordan? He was good. Really good. Both the leads were excellent. So . . . was I right?"

"About what?"

"You're a Cancer?"

Justine gave a mock frown. "Now, why would you say that?"

"Well, you're clearly very emotional. Empathic, sensitive. Easily moved to tears."

"Easily? That's a bit harsh. We just watched one of the most tragic love stories of all time."

"And . . . you're a bit unpredictable, maybe a touch hard on the out-side, but soft on the inside . . . ?"

"All these things may be true. And yet," Justine said, "a Cancer I am not."

Daniel shook his head, bewildered. "You present an unusual chal-lenge, Miss Carmichael."

♌

Backstage, meanwhile, on Verdi Highsmith's dressing table, a bouquet of palest pink roses, mid-pink hyacinths and hot pink gerberas lay in front of her lightbulb-studded mirror, with a note that said, *For Ms. Highsmith, with admiration, from Justine Carmichael.*

Across the hall, in Nick Jordan's dressing room, was an even larger bunch of flowers: white roses, deep blue hyacinths and forget-me-nots. The note said, *For a word-perfect Romeo, from his favorite pedant.* And inside the copy of the *Alexandria Park Star* that peeked mischievously out of the bouquet's wrapping, Leo Thornbury waited to pass on a message.

cusp

G uy Foley—Aquarius, philosopher with mild conspiracy-theorist tendencies, street busker specializing in tin whistles and spoons, occasional but self-justified shoplifter, owner of a canvas swag with sheepskin lining, habitué of a network of backyards, couches and bolt-holes—browsed the tobacconist's shelves with all the unhurried curiosity of a man sheltering from the weather. He whistled through a dark curtain of mustache and studiously did not look at the window that divided the warmth of the shop from the sleety cold of the street. For on the other side of the glass, balancing precariously on Guy's garbage-bag-covered swag, with dreadlocks of wet fur swinging sideways in every bitter gust of wind, stood Brown Houdini-Malarky, his single dark eye full of entreaty.

Brown—street terrier born under the constellation of Canis Major, wearer of a shabby blue bandanna, skilled practitioner in the persuasive art of Voo Dog, lightning-fast thief of park-bench lunches and master-ful demonstrator of an inexhaustible bladder—was not a handsome dog. His shaggy head and long-furred ears were out of all proportion with his skinny body and short legs. His too-long tail was bald, except for a grubby tassel of fur at its tip. An overshot bottom jaw meant that even when Brown's mouth was closed, his stained teeth were clearly visible across his face. From a distance, they resembled a line of clumsy stitches. All things considered, and in no small part because of the sewn-up eyelid on his left side, Brown had the look of a cemetery dog-corpse, recently exhumed.

Brown shivered. Guy had been in the shop for some hours, and it had been raining the whole time. Now Brown was soaked to the point where water was trickling down the runnels of bare skin between the matted clumps of his coat. Although he remained ready to let go a volley of possessive barks in the direction of anyone who so much as looked at the plastic-covered bundle beneath his feet, Brown felt himself in this moment to be very, very close to the raw end of the deal.

It was true that it had been Guy who'd procured this morning's excellent breakfast of bacon rind and toast crusts, and equally true that Brown now owed several weeks' worth of comfortable nights to the sheepskin lining of Guy's swag. But Brown felt that he was more than paying his way. Who, after all, was responsible for Guy's recent busking prosperity? Left to his own devices, Guy would have been lucky to keep himself in Jack Daniel's and Champion Ruby. Even when Guy bagged the prime spot in the railway station, he pulled only the loose change of do-gooders who felt sorry for him and of men who carried wallets and didn't want the weight of coins in their pockets. But with Brown beside him—prancing on hind legs, howling in a crisp, yappy tenor—Guy was seeing some genuine appreciation. Notes! $10 here, $5 there; even uni students would part with a couple of bucks.

Guy and Brown had met on a train, recognizing each other instantly as part of the Brotherhood of the Ticketless. Brown liked trains for the potential of discarded sandwich crusts, and for the occasional one-ride stand. He wasn't above a bit of coochie-coo and scratching behind the ear from time to time, just as long as it ended with him trotting out through the train's open doors and going his own sweet way. But Guy, as well as scratching Brown's ears, had inspected the tatty blue bandanna, reading the words written there in permanent marker.

"Brown Houdini-Malarky," Guy had read, and chuckled. "Well, that's a name and two-thirds."

Guy had pulled out his whistle, and its tinny notes had sparked Brown into song.

"Nice tune, Brother Brown!" Guy had said, and played on, the dog howling in accompaniment. Three train stops and half a hot dog later, the two had struck up an alliance. One that was now, a few weeks down the track, beginning to sour.

Brown shook himself uselessly. He stared through the window at Guy and amped the power of his Voo. *You will leave the shop now. You will leave the shop now. You will leave the shop now.* But Guy merely turned his back, casually slipping a refill bottle of Zippo lighter fluid into the water-stained pocket of his jacket, and Brown made a vile canine cuss against the glass, which appeared to be blocking his thought waves.

One more night, he told himself. Then he was quitting Guy. Brown wouldn't miss the man, but he would miss the man's nice, comfy sheepskin-lined swag. Guy allowed Brown to sleep on a corner of it, and even this small degree of luxury was enough to cause Brown to slip into dreams about having a home of his own: one with devoted humans and a cushion-lined basket, a bowl of bickies on auto-fill and a packet of jerky treats that the humans would bring out in response to the most elementary Voo.

What was he thinking? Bloody hell. The swag was making him soft. One more night. That was all. Then he would turn tail and disappear without notice into some gloomy alleyway, alone again. Independent. Free. For he was Brown Houdini-Malarky—and he was no bastard's watchdog.

Indoors, Guy was inspecting a row of decorative bongs, patiently tolerating the hostile gaze of the shopkeeper and hazing out Brown's Voo. So long as Guy avoided eye contact with the bedraggled dog at the window, he could keep his mind clear of the thought that he should leave the shop and go buy a burger. The shopkeeper had his radio tuned to that crappy community station, and when the announcer's voice burst out of the closing bars of the song, it was like a spurt of warm melted cheese right down the earhole.

"I-I-I-I'm Rrrrrick Rrrrrrevenue," he intoned, his "I" getting the full four-tone treatment, "and tha-a-a-at was Juice Newton with, well, I don't have to tell you, do I? But I do have to tell you that the time is two thirty. The dental hour, as my dear ol' da used to say."

Guy wondered whether or not the radio announcer was going to be able to keep himself from explicating.

"Two thirty? Tooth hurty?" the announcer said, following up with a goofy chuckle.

Nope, Guy thought.

"And now, it's time for the ssstarrrrs, as written by that sssuper ssstar of the celestial sphere, the *Star*'s very own L-l-eo Thornbury."

Guy half heard something about Geminis and chance flirtatious encounters, a snippet of Virgos finding conditions ripe for retail and renovation.

"And to all the fine Aquarians out there, Leo says: You are on song, water bearers. With Jupiter casting its largesse about in your career sector, you are at last starting to see results for all the many years of hard work you have invested. Enjoy the acknowledgment and acclaim that rightfully come your way. Take a bow, Aquarius! And, last of all, for the fish people. Pisces . . ."

But Guy's Aquarian ears had tuned out.

Jupiter casting its largesse about, he pondered. *At last starting to see results for all the many years of hard work you have invested.*

Well, if that wasn't a sign, Guy thought, he didn't know what was. He thought of all that he had lost, over the course of his life, at the blackjack tables at Jupiter's casino in Queensland. But had he lost his money? Or had he, as the astrologer had just suggested, merely *invested* it? *Results*, the astrologer had said.

Jupiter, oh Jupiter! The great sky god was calling him north, and promising him a thunderbolt right into the hip pocket. *On song . . . take a bow, Aquarius!*

Guy glanced at the filthy weather beyond the window and tried to imagine the warmth of the Queensland sun on bare skin, the sensation of toes toasting in the sand instead of turning numb inside boots. What better time to go north than in the heart of a grim southern winter? Well, maybe the *beginning* of a grim southern winter, but that ship had sailed. Anyway, he liked the idea. Liked it a lot. Busking business had been brisk of late and there was enough coin in his pocket for him to buy a razor, even a whizz in the chair at a $10 barber's shop—tidy himself up a bit before he and his thumb hit the roadside—and he'd still have just enough cash in his pocket to sing his little duet with Jupiter.

But if he were to shoot through, Guy considered, what would become of Brown?

Guy turned to meet Brown's gaze, and the instant his two eyes locked with the dog's single one, he found himself thinking: *I will leave the shop now. I will buy a large burger, I will remove the meat from the bun and give it to Brown.* The bells above the door chattered as he passed beneath them, pursued by a disgusted grunt from the shopkeeper.

"Good boy," Guy said, as Brown leaped off the swag, and Brown—doggily hardwired as he was for praise and affection—wagged his tail without meaning to. Guy hefted his swag and looked down at Brown. Guy had grown very fond of his little mate, but he could hardly take him on the road. Who'd pick up a bloke with a grubby one-eyed mutt at heel?

But, Guy decided, he'd be buggered if he'd leave the little chap undefended in the city. So as Guy set off for the railway station burger joint, a plan was forming in his mind.

Half an hour later, warmer and almost dried out, his belly full of beef patty, Brown was sleeping on the floor of a westbound train, his toothy chin resting on his front paws. When he woke, it was with the dreadful sensation of something tight around his neck. It was Guy's belt, fixed as for a collar and leash. Not only that, Brown could smell *that place.*

No, he thought. *No!* But it was unmistakable.

Brown growled, cursing Guy as a bootlicking betrayer, the human equivalent of a steaming pile of cat shit, but the man dragged him easily out through the train's open door onto the platform, where the scents of misery and concentrated dog intensified in his nostrils. And then there were the sounds, drifting through the layers of diamond mesh fencing and over the bare-earthed exercise yards. Brown heard a pack of Staffordshire bull terriers calling each other motherfuckers through the bars. Some border collie was having a psychotic episode, yelling,

"Sheep! Sheep! Sheep!," and a batch of mangy Chihuahua pups were whining for their mother. Brown snarled at Guy's ankle.

"Easy, fella, easy," Guy said soothingly to Brown, even as he dragged the dog across the railway bridge and up a narrow path to the front office of the Dogs Home.

Brown continued to bark, uselessly, between chokes. Did this idiot human not know how many dogs came to this joint only to get the green dream?

Guy opened the door to the office and a woman stepped out from behind the front counter, broad as a battleship in her khaki tunic. She raised an eyebrow and leaned over just slightly—though Brown could see that she was deliberately keeping her flabby face out of reach of even his most desperate lunging attack.

She smiled, cold as charity, and said, "Well, well. You again. Welcome back."

✦

They were having lunch at Medici, and they were getting looks. They always did. And although they studiously ignored the looks they were getting, it could not be denied the two young women had been at least partially deliberate in choosing a table positioned right in front of the restaurant's large picture window. It framed them beautifully.

Charlotte Juniper, media adviser to Greens Senator Dave Gregson, wore an olive green dress with high, high-heeled boots. Her red hair flowed all around her shoulders, and although a light linen scarf was twisted about her throat, there was still plenty of speckled flesh to be seen between the bottom of the scarf and the plunging neckline of her dress.

Opposite her was her friend Laura Mitchell—Capricorn, law graduate and increasingly successful model, disciplined maintainer of a BMI of twenty, connoisseur of imported cheeses and giver of generous and spectacularly apt birthday gifts. It was hard to avoid the word "raven" when it came to Laura's dark, gleaming hair. She was wearing it straight today, and loose. And although the black dress she wore was also loose, it still somehow managed to suggest the small, high breasts and narrow yet shapely hips that lay underneath. Her black shoes were low-cut and flat and her long legs were brown, and bare, even though it was August. The poor waiter had no idea where to look.

"Which cheeses do you want on the platter?" he asked.

"Definitely the Fromager d'Affinois," Laura said.

"And the Leicester," Charlotte said.

Laura and Charlotte sometimes fantasized about opening their own cheese boutique. This would happen, they agreed, once Laura had retired—a millionaire—from modeling, and after Charlotte had saved the world.

Charlotte and Laura's friendship was an unusual one, since it transcended politics, taste and even the normal standards of compatibility. The two women really had only a handful of significant things in common: they enjoyed being beautiful, they took pleasure in lovely clothes, they liked cheese and they each had two ex-stepfathers and were on to their third.

In Charlotte's case, the plethora of stepfathers reflected her mother's full immersion in a nonpossessive, hippie ethic. In Laura's, it stemmed from her mother's openly stated philosophy that a first husband was for genes, a second for money and a third for more money. Laura's mother's fourth husband, Laura's third stepfather, was—Laura's mother had admitted—surplus to requirement, but he was good company, well connected and had a lovely yacht.

Charlotte and Laura had first met when they were in the second year of their degrees, by which time Charlotte had been elected president of the student union, and Laura had been chosen to appear for the university—capped and gowned—in a nationwide advertising campaign. But their friendship was not cemented until one night, in the fourth year of their studies, when a university ball coincided with a period of work placement for each of them.

Charlotte had requested, and got, her placement in the policy department at Bush Heritage. Laura, on the other hand, had been thrilled to get a spot in the legal division of BHP. To the ball, Charlotte had worn a white silk cheongsam, tight and split to the thigh; Laura had worn a strapless black gown with a ballooning brocade skirt. They had made a fetching pair, standing together in the foyer of one of the city's fanciest hotels.

"I can never remember," a hapless, drunk student colleague had said to the pair of them, "which one of you got Bush Heritage and which one of you got BHP?"

"Isn't it obvious?" Charlotte had said. She had gestured first to her gown, and then to Laura's. "See? Good guys, and . . . bad guys."

"Yes, but black doesn't stain," said Laura, just before flinging a full glass of cabernet sauvignon all over Charlotte.

Charlotte had stood there for a moment, dripping and in shock, before Laura had been overcome with remorse. She had taken Charlotte into the hotel bathroom and mopped her up as best she could, then paid for a cab to take them both back to her flat where she lent Charlotte another (black) frock to wear. A few weeks later, she'd bought Charlotte a new and very expensive cheongsam in a deep green that Laura thought would suit her redhead's coloring better than white. They had been friends ever since.

"So," Laura asked, cutting a wedge of the d'Affinois, "how's the handsome senator?"

Charlotte sipped her pinot and gave a cat-cream smile. "I'm moving into his apartment."

"Wonderful news, Lottie," Laura said. "What about the rest of the staff? Do they all know?"

"I supposed you'd call it an open secret," Charlotte said.

"And what about his tendency to wander? How are you going to keep him on the straight and narrow?"

"I have my ways and means," Charlotte said, stabbing a triangle of Leicester. "What about you? How's Nick?"

Laura paused for effect. "We're getting married," she said.

When Charlotte squealed with delight, half the restaurant turned to look at her.

"Not in real life," Laura added. "And not until next year, anyway."

"What do you mean?"

"So, you know the Chance wine campaign?"

Laura had been doing advertisements for Chance for a few years now, and the campaign was developing into something of a narrative about how the Chance girl was growing up, moving through the stages of her life.

"Well," Laura went on, "it seems that this spring, the Chance girl is going to meet a man. Walk through the grape alleys with him, that sort of thing. And next spring, *ta da*! Wedding bells! The year after that, the couple are strolling through the vineyard with a babe in arms. Then comes the handsome dark-haired toddler . . . you get the idea. You would not believe what they're willing to pay us for a five-year contract."

"Wow. But I thought Nick hated modeling," Charlotte said.

"He says he hates it, but he's never really tried it. I mean, as I always tell him, modeling is just acting with a salary. And without all those lines. I think he'll jump at it when he finds out how much they're offering. The people at Chance, the people at the agency—they love his look. They agree we're perfect together. And Nick . . . I think he's starting to realize that acting's never really going to bring home the bacon."

"How was *Romeo and Juliet*?"

"Oh, you know," Laura said, waving a hand about. "Shakespeare-y."

"Heathen."

"I'm not a heathen. I am merely honest."

"So, you've told Nick, then? About the Chance thing?" Charlotte probed.

"Not . . . quite."

Charlotte raised an eyebrow. "Not *quite*? What about Chance? And the agency? You haven't already told them Nick's definitely on board for the campaign. Have you?"

"Look, he's going to say yes," Laura said. "I know he is. It's more money than he's earned in his entire working life so far. It will totally set him up. He'll see that. I just have to present it to him at the right moment."

"Are you thinking leverage before sex?" suggested Charlotte. "Or gratitude after?"

"Oh, stop being such a lawyer. It's really not like that. He'll say yes. I know he will."

"So, when is this 'right moment'?"

"I don't know exactly. Some time after *Romeo and Juliet* finishes."

"Because?"

"Nick's always a little down at the end of a production. He just gets a bit despondent, and doubtful. Opening night, he's always high as a kite. Next stop, Hollywood! But a week or two after closing night, he always comes back down to earth and wonders if he's ever going to get another job. And there I'll be, with just the thing to cheer him up."

"Well, I'll drink to that," Charlotte said, and the two women drained their wineglasses. Almost immediately, their waiter rematerialized.

"Another wine, ladies?" he said. "Perhaps I could recommend the Chance merlot to you?"

Laura let loose a peal of laughter. "Chance? Oh God, I wouldn't drink that shit if you paid me!"

+

On the far, far side of town from the restaurant where Charlotte and Laura were finishing up their lunch date, Davina Divine sat at her kitchen table and drummed her nails—painted a shade called Midnight Forest—on the tabletop. It was already two o'clock, which meant that it was nearly time to set off to collect the boys from school. Only forty-five precious minutes remained of her designated astrology day; tomorrow she would be back in the gel nail business, and everybody she met would think of her not as the amazingly prescient Davina Divine, but as perky little Nicole Pitt.

Davina sighed. Well, she thought, at least she was on her way to her destiny. She had passed her Advanced Diploma of Astrology with flying colors, and, what was more, she had secured some real, live clients. It was true that there were only two, so far, and equally true that she had spent so long on each client's natal chart that her fee had ended up at a fraction of the minimum hourly wage. Everyone had to start somewhere, didn't they? Not even Leo Thornbury had been *born* an astrologer.

But what, in heaven's name, Davina asked the star chart that was spread out across the table, was happening with Leo Thornbury and Aquarius? She knew she was only a beginner, and that Leo must be able to calculate forces and angles that her developing vision was yet to comprehend, but for the past few months, she'd been unable to find even the smallest hint of Leo's Aquarian predictions in the charts. In June, Leo's copy had been all about wariness in love, when Davina had seen Aquarians cruising quite happily through the romantic waters. In July, Leo had made antimaterialism his theme, but the stars Davina saw urged cautious accumulation in financial affairs. And now, in August, Leo was giving Aquarians permission to bask in the sunshine of hard-earned glory, when her reading of the stars was that the water bearers really ought to be hunkering down under a winter-weight Doona while they wrestled with the difficult choices that always arose when Mars came thundering through the Eighth House. What on earth was going on? What, Davina puzzled, was she missing?

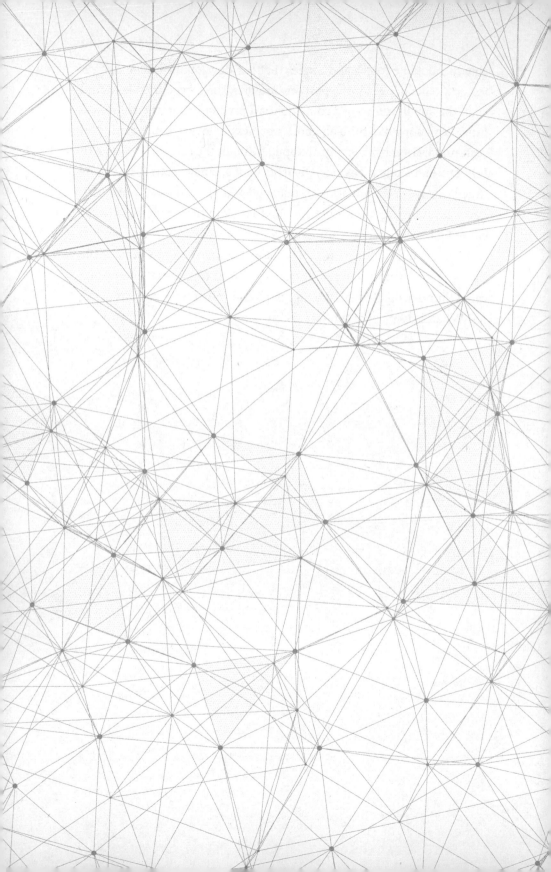

Virgo

AUGUST 23–SEPTEMBER 22

The early days of Justine's reporting career slipped by with alarming speed. She felt as if she were living inside a playback of a sequence of time-lapse photography; no sooner was she getting out of her bed in the morning than she was getting back into it at night, too tired to read more than a few pages before switching off the light.

At the office, she settled into her new desk, pinning up her own selection of postcards and aphorisms on the felt-covered boards around the computer. After her first few days in the staff writers' room, Justine knew she was going to have to teach herself to tune out Martin's swearing and his almost incessant running commentary on his thought processes, but to surreptitiously listen in to Roma's carefully constructed phone interviews, with their elegant, chessboard questioning.

One Friday morning, Justine arrived at the *Star* to find Daniel Griffin at the gatepost beneath the yellow peril, in earnest conversation with a young woman. She wore a pale blue skirt, a beige cardigan and flat shoes, and was doing a lot of nodding and smiling. She also seemed to be trying—by means of dropping one shoulder and bending the opposite knee—not to be any taller than the editor himself.

"Justine, I'd like you to meet Cecilia Triffett."

"Hi, Cecilia," Justine said.

Cecilia's handshake was limp and bony. Her hair, Justine observed, was sleek and light brown, and looked like it would be slippery to manage. Her face was narrow and her lips thin, but her eyes—behind rimless glasses—were a very pretty blue, and her lashes were long and dark.

"Cecilia is our new copy-runner," Daniel explained, and the look on his face suggested to Justine that he was a little amused by Ms. Triffett. "She starts in earnest on Monday, but she wanted to come in today to . . . acclimatize. Justine's a journalist here, but she did her time in your job. I've been telling Cecilia about the history of our magnificent star here, and about how Jeremy brought me out on my first day and stood me underneath it and told me all about the—"

"Inspirational rays," Justine finished, miming their descent.

"He did that for you, too?" Daniel asked.

Justine nodded. "You have to love the yellow peril. It's very . . . unique."

"Well, no," Cecilia said, without pause.

"Sorry?" Justine said.

"You know. Something is either unique, or it's not," Cecilia explained. "It can't be *very* unique."

Justine did know. In fact, this was just the sort of thing that Justine herself would point out to the broadcasters who burbled through the speakers of her kitchen radio. It was exactly the sort of thing she'd chop out, while tut-tutting, from a contributor's column. But just now she had not been writing, nor speaking on radio. She had just been, *bloody hell*, talking. Talking casually enough that she'd said "very unique," and this girl, whose oversized front teeth didn't fit inside her mouth when she closed it, had nitpicked her about it.

"Touché," said Daniel, looking just a little too amused for Justine's liking.

"Cecilia," Justine said, "are you by any chance a Virgo?"

Cecilia seemed both pleased and surprised. "How did you know?"

Justine smiled in what she hoped was an enigmatic way. "Welcome to the *Star*, Cecilia. I can see that you're going to fit right in."

♍

"I've been wondering if, perhaps, it takes one to know one," Daniel said to Justine.

It was midafternoon, in the tearoom, and Justine was hunting through the fridge for a carton of milk that was on the right side of its use-by date, when Daniel arrived to fix himself a fresh plunger of coffee.

"Sorry?"

"Maybe it takes one to know one. I'm going to say that you gave yourself away out the front this morning, with Cecilia. Because you're a Virgo, aren't you?"

"Well," she said, and she stretched out the moment by adding milk to her tea. Stirring. "I'm Virgo rising. Apparently. So, you're close. But so far as sun signs go, still no cigar."

"Virgo *rising*. Shit. I really thought I had it this time."

"Well, take heart. There are only twelve signs. You'll have to get there eventually."

Daniel spooned three sugars into his coffee, shrugged in response to Justine's raised eyebrows and took an experimental sip.

"How was your interview with Huck Mowbray?" he asked. "Is he really as big as he looks on the telly?"

Justine had met with the colossal footballer in the bookshop where his collection of poetry had been launched, mostly to the media, although Justine had recognized in the crowd a handful of off-duty and unshaven AFL players. They had all seemed out of scale to their surroundings, standing about in their twos and threes, arms crossed or hands in pockets, not quite sure what they were supposed to do with themselves.

"Actually, if anything he was even bigger," Justine said.

"And the poetry?"

"Mostly free verse. A few sonnets. A villanelle—called 'The Coliseum,'" Justine reported. "Only a handful of the poems are actually about football, but that's one of them."

"Are they any good?"

Justine felt her eyebrows shoot up into piss-taking territory. "I quite liked 'Hermes at Full Forward,' but 'Grass Warrior' is maybe a little self-consciously heroic."

"And, when he's not writing about football?"

"Then it's love, mostly. Or possibly conquests. I think we can safely read 'The Aftermath of Velvet' as erotica. And 'Victory at Dawn.'"

Daniel made a worried face. "'Victory at Dawn'?"

"I'm afraid so," Justine said. "But, get this. Apparently, instead of trash-talking his opponents when he's on the field, he quotes poetry."

"His own?"

"Not usually, he says. He prefers Yeats, Eliot, Cummings, Hughes," Justine said.

"The big boys, hey?"

"He insists that he's no sexist," Justine said. "He told me Plath and Sexton were particularly potent around the stoppages."

Daniel laughed. "Is that a direct quote?"

"It is."

"Please tell me you've put it in your story."

"What was it your friend used to say: Does Gough Whitlam think it's time?"

Daniel nodded approvingly. "How long's your piece? If it's good—and it sounds like it is—we can let it run."

"Even so, it's way too long at the minute. It was just that I got so much good stuff. The coach gave me some amazing quotes. And the ex-wife? Let's just say she didn't hold back, and also that the velvet probably wasn't hers. I dropped in at the poetry class, as well. The one where young Huck hurled together his first few couplets. The teacher is a real character. He—"

Daniel snapped his fingers. "Capricorn! Not Virgo. Capricorn."

Justine laughed. "Why?"

"Work ethic. You're always at work early, or late, or both. I notice these things, you know. And a lot of people would have stopped at interviewing Mowbray for a profile piece like this. But you've really gone the distance. Sounds like a Capricorn to me."

"An interesting theory," Justine said.

"I'm right, aren't I?"

Justine picked up her teacup and made for the door.

"Alas, Mr. Griffin, you will have to think again. But the good news is that you are now halfway through the zodiac. Only six signs to go!"

♍

The following day was a Saturday, and even before the sun was up, the good people of Alexandria Park were dragging out onto the sidewalks their dead fridges and boxy old television sets, stained sofas and defunct vacuum cleaners. As Justine Carmichael dozed the morning away in her bedroom on the twelfth floor of Evelyn Towers, the neighborhood's verdant verges were being piled up with frayed and badly rolled floor rugs, boxes of *Reader's Digest* magazines, VCR machines, dog beds, enamel fondue sets, broken fan heaters, disgraced bathroom scales, tilting hat stands and ugly standing lamps.

Out in force, too, were barely used appliances and gadgets like doughnut makers and foot spas, cotton candy spinners and cake pop molds. Ordinary families threw out their editions of Twister, Hungry Hungry Hippos and Trivial Pursuit, while more aspirational parents took the opportunity to admit the un-funness of MathMindz, Pizza Fraction Fun and Roll 'n' Spell. For today was the municipal council rubbish collection free-for-all, a once-in-a-year chance to offload domestic crap without having to hire a trailer, pay the scandalously inflated dump entry fee, or get gull shit on one's car.

Justine had had a plan for this particular Saturday morning. It was to wake at around eight o'clock but stay in bed until at least ten reading a novel, or leafing through the new IKEA catalogue. After that, she was going to have a bath and get dressed in something springtime-ish and cheerful, then make her way to Rafaello's, where she would order an almond croissant and a coffee, read the weekend papers, and check that Raf had—as Justine had strenuously recommended—replaced the "half roasted spatchcock" on his lunch menu with a "roasted half spatchcock." There was nothing in the plan, however, about her phone starting to ring, loudly and insistently, at half past six, from somewhere deep inside the handbag she had the previous night flung carelessly on her bedroom floor.

So, when this happened, Justine squeezed her eyes tight shut, waited for the phone to ring out and clung to the idea that she wasn't, actually, awake yet. But when the ringing was done at last, the phone paused for barely five seconds before starting to ring all over again.

"Piss off," muttered Justine.

Brain: *Maybe it's an emergency. Maybe your father's plane has crashed and he's calling you with the last of his battery power, to say his final farewell. Maybe your mother is lying stabbed and bleeding, having been attacked on the streets of Edenvale during her early morning power walk. Justine! Maybe this is that call. The one that you'll rue ignoring for the rest of your days.*

Justine: *Bastard.*

Brain: *You're welcome.*

Predictably, and in accordance with a subsection of Murphy's law, the ringing phone was in the last of the handbag pockets that Justine checked. With half-numb fingers, she swiped at the screen.

Blearily, she said, "Hello?"

"You need to get up and get dressed immediately."

"What?" said Justine.

"No time to dawdle! No time to dilly dally!"

The voice was ludicrously cheerful.

"Nick?"

"Today's the day," he said brightly. "I forgot, too. It's just lucky that I was up so late that I saw it starting. Come on, Jus. You have to hurry."

"Why?"

"Municipal council collection day in Alexandria Park. It's the greatest free garage sale on earth!"

"I'm sleeping."

"Then stop it. Seriously. You should see the stuff, and, hey, early bird catches the worm."

"Consider: second mouse gets the cheese."

"Don't be grouchy. It's trash and treasure Nirvana out here! I'll see you out the front of your place in ten."

Fifteen minutes later, dressed in floordrobe chic, with a kerchief tied over her bed hair and her eyes still feeling slightly gluey, Justine emerged onto Evelyn Street to find Nick waiting for her. He wore a flannel shirt, workman-style shorts and a pair of battered elastic-sided boots. At his side was a supermarket shopping trolley: quite new, its plastic seat and handle still bright green, and all four of its wheels seemingly functional.

"Pinched from Woolworths?"

"Merely on loan," Nick said.

"Truly, you are a professional," Justine observed.

"I've also made us a thermos of coffee. I hope you don't take sugar."

"I don't."

"Excellent. And I've sketched out a route."

A small backpack rode high between Nick's shoulder blades and from the back pocket of his shorts he took out a marked-up copy of a brochure that Justine recognized as the Alexandria Park Heritage Walking Map.

He gripped the trolley handle like he meant business. "Ready?"

♍

By two o'clock that afternoon, the rooftop terrace at Evelyn Towers had been transformed. Spread out in a fetching herringbone pattern over a section of the concrete floor was a quarter of a pallet of moss-green ceramic tiles that were left over from a bathroom renovation in Lanux Court. Resting on the tiles, and angled just so, were two matching wickerwork banana lounges from Austinmer Street, only slightly cat-clawed and frayed.

In addition to this haul, Justine and Nick made a few modest purchases at the local garden center. Fresh, peaty potting mix now filled the roof garden's planter boxes, while inside the earth some tiny seeds—sunflower, basil, parsley, pansy—were just beginning to think about stretching out their little radicles.

Positioned between the planter boxes was Justine and Nick's most impressive free acquisition: a chiminea from the far reaches of Evelyn Street that had been tossed out complete with its wrought-iron tripod stand. Admittedly, the lip of the chimney was chipped, and there were a couple of cracks zigzagging down the side, but the little fireplace seemed otherwise sound. It was going to be perfect for winter nights.

Between the lounges were two small occasional tables (Nick had asked Justine, "What is an occasional table, anyway? A table that's only occasionally a table?") that were topped with star-spangled linoleum and stamped with coffee-colored cup rings. Upon one of the tables now was the mint-condition pewter Battle of Waterloo checkers set that Justine and Nick had scored in the affluent reaches of Kellerman Circle, although not without incident. Nick had been the one to spy the timber box containing Napoleon's French forces, while Justine had located the board underneath a stack of *Healthy Eating* magazines. Another pair of scroungers, however, managed to snaffle the box containing the English army. Debate ensued, and although Justine and Nick had successfully argued that possession of two-thirds of the set was equal to nine-tenths of the right to have the whole shebang, they had been forced to hand over an ostentatious brass candelabra by way of compensation.

Nick, playing with the hard-won English pieces, had triumphed over Justine's Frenchmen in what Nick described as the rooftop's "inaugural" game of checkers. Actually, the game had been a bloodbath, and—unbeknownst to Nick—it was already categorized in Justine's mind as the rooftop's "one and only" game of checkers. About three moves in, while observing the ferociously determined set of her opponent's jaw, Justine had wondered why she hadn't remembered that setting out a board game was a way of stimulating the most primitive center of Nick's brain. One day, she thought, she might even admit to him that it had been she who had suggested to his little brother and sister that it would be a good idea to feed all the money from their family's Monopoly set into Mark Jordan's illegal backyard incinerator.

"That lunch was awesome," Nick said, reaching for the last of the dark chocolate Tim Tam biscuits leaving the empty plastic biscuit tray lying amid the greasy paper bags that had been emptied of their potato cakes, fish cakes and dim sims.

"It was positively gourmet," Justine said.

Reclining in a lounge, she could feel in her arms and shoulders the effects of the day's lifting and carrying. She was also a little bit sunburned, pleasantly sleepy and decidedly in need of a shower.

"If Laura could see this, she'd make me run a marathon in penance," Nick said, his mouth half full of Tim Tam.

"Where is Laura today?" Justine asked, glad to finally have an opportunity to ask this question, which had been playing on her mind.

"Texas, actually."

"Texas?"

"Uh-huh."

"Because?" Justine asked.

"She does this perfume thing, and they're creating a new campaign."

"What's the perfume?"

"Waterlily. And in Texas, there's this big water garden, full of . . . waterlilies."

Justine let out a small burst of laughter, which was complicated by the sip of very fizzy ginger beer she'd just taken. When best-pal Tara wanted to delicately indicate that a person was beautiful on the surface, but didn't have a lot going on underneath, she'd refer to them as "a bit of a waterlily."

Nick handed a spluttering Justine a napkin bearing the logo of the greasy spoon at which they had bought their lunch, and said, "What? What's so funny?"

Justine: *Should we tell him?*

Brain: *You're the card-carrying member of the sisterhood. Not me.*

Justine: *Hm. I think we'll just keep it to ourselves.*

"It's nothing," Justine said, though she was still smiling.

Nick finished the last of his ginger beer. "Well, as much as I'd like to stay and slaughter you and your Corsican Fiend for a second time, I must hie me hence."

"Oh?"

"Curtain call in not so very many hours. And I'm a little underslept. Romeo will need his energy, if he is to woo his Juliet tonight."

"Isn't tonight closing night?"

"Yep."

Nick hauled himself out of his banana lounge.

"Oh," he said, "I meant to tell you."

"Yes?"

"Alison Tarf rang me."

Justine sat up in a rush. "Alison Tarf? She did?"

"She came to the Gaiety. She saw the play," Nick said, pulling a mock modest face. "And she dug out my application and rang me to say she was very much looking forward to my audition."

"Nick, that's amazing. So you *have* to audition now. I mean, if Alison Tarf herself has asked for you, it would just be rude not to show up."

"You know what? I'm thinking that you're right."

Justine, feeling a surge of Lleyton Hewitt–esque energy run through her tired body, thought she might be about to leap out of the banana lounge, shape her hand into a duck's beak and shout, *C'mon!*

Brain: *Remain seated, idiot.*

"You *might*?" she asked.

"Yeah. I'm leaning that way. But I'm just going to hang in and see what Leo's got to say. After all—as you know—Leo Thornbury knows everything."

♍

That night, at about the time Nick Jordan's Romeo was ending the life of a crow-haired, sword-swinging Tybalt, Justine Carmichael was walking softly in sandshoe-clad feet down Rennie Street in the direction of the *Star*. Shards of streetlight caught on the uneven surface of the yellow peril and bounced off at crazy angles as Justine turned in at the gatepost. Thinking invisible thoughts, she made her way up the front steps and unlocked the door. There was, throughout the whole building, no sound but the humming of the fridge in the kitchen.

Now that the small, white office was Henry's, it was no longer a haven of minimalist organization. Piles of magazines and loose papers lay on the desktop and on the floor, and there were scribble-covered sticky notes—orange, hot pink, yellow, blue—stuck all higgledy-piggledy around the frame of the computer monitor. Beside the computer was a framed photograph of a very young Henry, standing—awestruck—

beside the cricketer Shane Warne. Under the desk lay a whiffy pair of running shoes and a bundle of shiny gym garments.

By this point in the month, Justine well knew, Henry would almost certainly have transcribed Leo's stars. To be certain of this, she rummaged through his in-box. Finding no fax from Leo Thornbury there, she moved on to searching the document spike. One by one, she drew the skewered pages off the spike and placed them facedown on the desk. Until she found what she was looking for.

"Ah, there you are, Leo," she murmured, and scanned down the page.

Aquarius: This month sees Venus transitioning from Leo to Virgo, bringing into focus themes of sex, intimacy and trust. Aquarians can expect to be discussing these issues with their romantic partners, but should also anticipate miscommunication in many of their important relationships. When the sun enters your fellow air sign, Libra, you'll find yourself escaping the mire of complication to emerge into a season of freedom and expansion.

She sat down on Henry's office chair, read over the copy again, and thought. Would Leo's words push Nick toward auditioning for Alison Tarf? Or away?

Brain: *What Leo's got to say isn't bad. "Freedom and expansion" might do the trick.*

Justine: *Do you think?*

Brain: *Honestly? No. But even if it isn't, how are we going to do this, exactly?*

Justine drew herself in to Henry's computer and wriggled the mouse to wake up the monitor. A login screen appeared, asking for a username and password. Justine drew a deep breath and entered Henry's username, *hashbolt*. It followed the same formula as her own username, and that of every other staff member at the *Star*.

Brain: *Your pulse is up.*

Justine: *Thanks for pointing that out.*

Brain: *I think you're experiencing guilt and nervousness.*

Justine: *Shhhh . . . I bet it's still here, somewhere.*

The sticky note Justine was looking for was an orange one. One orange note said, *Eloise's birthday*. Another said, *Don't look back, you aren't going that way*.

"Ha! Got you!" Justine said gleefully, finding at last the small orange square upon which Anwen had written Henry's password, along with the instruction *Learn then destroy*. After Justine tapped in the code, a rainbow wheel of doom twirled on the screen for what seemed like a very long time. And then Henry's desktop screen appeared in full Technicolor.

"Yessss!" hissed Justine. Feeling rather pleased with herself, she clicked open a folder called "Current Edition" and scrolled down to the document named "Horoscope."

Brain: *Hey, what do your stars say?*

Sagittarius: *"Let your soul stand cool and composed before a million universes," urged the poet Walt Whitman, and he might easily have been speaking to you, archers, as you embark upon a period of great uncertainty. Mars's energy is strong in your astro-chart in the coming weeks, creating a period during which the risks you take may pay off spectacularly. Or, in your excitement, you may fly just a little too close to the sun, and face the scorching consequences.*

Brain: *And you don't think, maybe . . . ?*

Justine: *What? No, I don't think anything. It's the horoscope. Get a grip.*

Brain: *If you're completely sure . . .*

Justine: *I am. Back to Aquarius. What are we going to do here?*

Brain: *Well, you want Nick thinking about Shakespeare, believing Shakespeare is his destiny . . .*

Justine: *Continue.*

Brain: *So if Leo were to quote the Bard himself . . .*

Justine: *That, actually, is rather clever.*

Flicking open an internet browser window, Justine entered a search for Shakespearean quotes on courage, and scanned through the results.

Once more unto the breach, dear friends . . .

"Nope," Justine said quietly to herself. Nothing from *Henry V*; that Henry was too warlike.

Screw your courage to the sticking place . . .

"Urgh. No thank you, Lady Macbeth."

Cowards die many times before their deaths . . .

No. Not that one, either. Far too grim.

But then, there it was. From *Cymbeline*.

"Boldness be my friend! Arm me, audacity," Justine whispered to herself. "Bingo!"

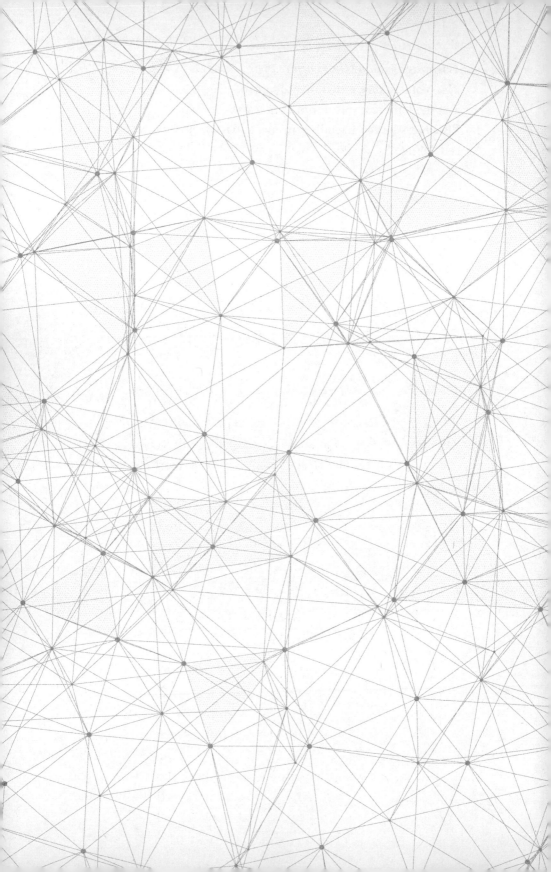

cusp

I n a pink dawn, in a gray inner-city suburb, in a narrow stone terrace house, in a pine-floored bedroom, in an antique brass bed, in
a pair of floral flannel pajamas, Fern Emerson hovered somewhere
between wakefulness and sleep. Today was to be her first day off in
nine months.

Back at the beginning of the year, Fern—Libra, florist, habitual
wearer of a single gerbera behind one ear, stylish reinventor of vintage
dresses, surreptitious smoker of menthol cigarettes and drinker of gin
slings, lover of Brat Pack movies and occasional karaoke diva—had
taken the risky step of shutting down her mobile flower van and re-
opening Hello Petal as a static concern in the Alexandria Park Markets,
with all of the new and alarming overhead costs that this move entailed.

Seven days a week, Fern had risen at a ridiculous hour to secure
the best flowers from her wholesaler. Then, throughout each long
day, she had single-handedly filled the buckets and accepted the orders, cut the stems and folded the tissue paper, arranged the blooms,
tied the ribbons, smiled with the joyful customers, handed tissues to
the weeping ones, enthused with brides and made creative sugges-
tions to wealthy matrons. There were no lunch breaks. Evenings had
been taken up by accounts, tax, quotes, emails, advertising and other

irritating miscellany. She was lucky if she could manage to find a few minutes to cover her red-raw hands with balm and white gloves before collapsing into bed.

All this hard work was paying off, though. Hello Petal's bottom line had tracked steadily upward to the point where Fern had felt ready to take on an assistant. She'd found young, big-eyed Bridie, who—with her wispy hair and apron of faded red and white ticking—looked like something straight out of a sooty Dickensian street. Now, Fern had decided, Bridie was ready to tackle a day's trade on her own. Which meant Fern could take a long-overdue, deliciously exciting, all-to-herself, magnificent day off. She sat up in a froufrou of white bed linen, grabbed at the strong glasses on her bedside table and blinked the room into focus.

What would she do? Oh, there were so many things she longed for. She wanted to sort through her stash of vintage dresses and fabrics, and sew a skirt, or maybe even two. And she wanted to spend the entire day in the bath rereading *I Capture the Castle*, topping up the hot water as many times as she damned well pleased. And she wanted to hop in her classic VW bug and drive to the seaside so she could walk the tideline collecting shells, then finish off the day with a soothing G&T at some nice little pub on the esplanade. But most of all, she decided, she wanted to go on a charity-shop crawl through the entire city and come home with new treasures to revamp. Dresses! Cardigans! Fabrics! Who knew what else?

Fern tore a page out of her current annual journal, unfilled since late January, licked the tip of the blunt pencil that lay beside it and drew herself a rough map of the city. If she was strategic, she could hit three shops before lunch, and two more afterward. And that would still leave time for her to get home, admire her purchases and put *Pretty in Pink* on in the background while she ripped skirts from bodices, or ruffles from necklines. It was going to be a good day. No, it was going to be a great day.

Fern's first stop was a specialty retro charity shop in a deeply hip neighborhood with a main street lined with shops that sold Swedish minimalist furniture, handmade soaps, wooden clogs or obscure fruits. Fern paused to admire the color-coordinated irony of the window display, where a glowing, plug-in statue of the Virgin Mary was surrounded by mannequins dressed in skirts, shirts, cardigans, vests and shoes that covered the spectrum from periwinkle to Prussian. The backdrop was a chrome yellow screen hung with small devotional images of the Madonna, but Fern did not fail to observe that one of the pictures was of Madonna herself, in the "Like a Virgin" phase of her career.

Inside, Fern leafed through the long dresses and the short. In the mirror, she held up against herself a mushroom-colored chiffon dress with a pussy bow at the throat and a skirt of delicate pleats. But although the fabric of the dress was in good condition, the mirror revealed that the color didn't really do much for her. And while it was at it, the mirror also revealed to Fern the proliferation of silver streaks in her dark curls. And, for its final trick, the mirror showed Fern a man hunting through the bins of vinyl records just behind her. She smiled at the way his shoulders pulsed faintly to whatever was playing through his over-ear headphones. He had good hair—nut brown and close cropped. He had nice hands, too: large and tanned. There was an outdoorsy quality to him that made Fern imagine how his worn plaid shirt would smell of fresh loam and eucalyptus smoke.

Stop, stop, stop, stop it, Fern, she told herself as she returned the mushroom-colored dress to its rack.

Behind the counter, a pink-haired girl was pinning gloves together in pairs. Astrid, read her name tag.

"Hello," Fern said, and smiled. "I wonder, have you got any fabric in at the moment?"

Astrid blinked thickly kohl-rimmed eyes, then smiled back. "Um, actually, we *do*. An amazing batch came in the other day. Deceased estate, yeah? Must have been a whole cupboard full. Fifties stuff. Sixties. Seventies. So cool. It's out in the back room, if you can stand the mess."

"I'm not afraid," said Fern.

But once she beheld the mess, she was. It was a hoarder's paradise, a cataclysmic firetrap of discarded stuff. One side of the storage room was piled floor to ceiling with garbage bags full of donations, while the opposite side was a presumptive avalanche of clothing, books and bric-a-brac. The back wall was no better: a teetering stack of cardboard boxes with a dangerous inward lean. A small clearing had been left to allow access to a tiny washbasin, but there was a makeshift shelf over the top of it, stacked to the roof. An electric kettle balanced precariously on the lip of the sink, which was filled with a jumble sale of coffee mugs. Astrid smiled at Fern's evident shock.

"Somewhere behind *that*," she said, indicating the barricade of packing cartons, "is the back door."

"Far out," said Fern.

Astrid tugged some stacks of pressed and folded fabric out of the pile, and Fern had to fight back a nervous urge to cover her head. But delight quickly overcame trepidation, for in the stacks were meters of 1960s pinwale corduroy with tiny geometric prints, generous lengths of gorgeous floral Viyella, delicate slivers of Liberty lawn, wedges of primrose-colored seersucker and embroidered gingham.

"Hey!" yelled Astrid suddenly. "Hey! No! Hey!"

Fern quickly saw the problem. The shop's front door was blocked to chest height by a fortress of large cardboard cartons. Astrid ran to the glass door. Just as she pulled it open, a delivery guy in blue coveralls added another carton to the stack.

"What the fuck do you think you're doing?" Astrid shouted.

"Backlog from central warehousing, love," said the guy, then returned to his van. Fern mentally reran the plan for her glorious day off. Being barricaded into the first shop on the list was definitely not in it.

"You can't be leaving them *there*," Astrid yelled. "This is a fucking shop. People have to be able to get in and out!"

The delivery man gave Astrid an implacable look before heaving another box onto the pile.

"Door to door, love," he said through a gap in the stack. "I picked this lot up from one door, and now they're at yours. That's all I'm paid to do."

"But you're blocking the fucking doorway. What do you expect me to do?"

"Tell someone who cares, sweetheart."

Astrid stormed to the counter to snatch up the telephone, while

Fern stood transfixed by the ever-growing pile of boxes. After a moment, she became aware that the good-looking vinyl hunter had appeared at her side with his earphones now slung about his neck. There were maybe eight or ten albums under his arm. The Pixies, Fern observed. And the Sugarcubes. *Nice.* Together, he and she watched as the last box went onto the top of the stack, fully blocking the doorway from top to bottom. Astrid gesticulated wildly while forcefully explaining the situation to a central warehousing colleague on the other end of the phone. Meanwhile, the delivery guy slammed the back doors of his van and drove away.

"Not good," the vinyl hunter observed.

"No," Fern agreed.

"Should we try the back door?" he asked, pointing with one thumb to the rear of the shop.

Fern gave him a rueful smile. "Much of a muchness out there."

"I guess there's nothing for it but to dig, then."

He put aside his record stash, swept a trio of Cabbage Patch dolls off a low armchair and dragged the chair over to the doorway, to act as a stepladder.

"Holy shit, be careful," Fern said, as he climbed up onto the chair's unevenly sprung seat.

He tried to maneuver the box on the top of the stack, but it was firmly wedged against the top of the outer side of the door frame.

"I reckon I'm going to have to pull out the one directly underneath," he said. "Then work from there. With any luck, they're not too heavy. Give me a hand, just in case?"

Fern climbed up beside him, each of them balancing with one foot on the seat of the chair and one on an armrest. Fern stumbled, and as he steadied her, she became dizzily aware of his sinewy strength. Although she had imagined he would smell earthy, now she was so close to him, she could tell from his lightly chlorinated scent that he'd recently been to the swimming pool. It was a nice smell, all clean and active.

"You 'right?" he said.

Oh God, he was really friendly, too.

"Yep. All good."

Stop, stop, stop, stop, stop it, Fern, she commanded herself. *You are thirty-eight years old, and he's what? Twenty-five? Thirty at a push. Your career in love has been one of disaster after compound disaster, and now you are going gray. And besides, he's almost certainly married. Or at the very least shacked up. With an art theory lecturer, probably. Or the owner of a funky inner-city cider bar.*

Together, Fern and the man worked away, balancing and rebalancing themselves and the weight of the second-top-most box, until at last it jerked free. It was so heavy that Fern almost dropped her side of it. The box that had been above it slammed down onto the stack and tilted sideways. It seemed to hover for a moment before tumbling onto the sidewalk.

"Someone's going to get bloody well hurt," Astrid enunciated into the phone. "What do I want you to do? I want you to get someone over here to help. No, not in an hour. *Now.* I've got two customers here, standing on a dodgy armchair, lifting down a . . . Jesus, they're going to drop it. I have to go."

Astrid rushed to help and, after some negotiation, the three of them managed to lower the box to the floor. Fern, catching her breath, observed the neat labeling that appeared in thick black marker pen, both on the top of the box and on one of its sides.

"*RW 12*," she read. "What do you reckon's in it?"

"Remnant welding-rods?" the man suggested.

"Renaissance wineglasses?" Fern countered.

"Railroad widgets?"

"*What?*" she asked.

"I don't know," he admitted.

"Risqué Wellingtons?" she offered.

"Ruby winkle-pickers?"

And this might have gone on for some pleasurable time, except that Astrid produced a box cutter and sliced through the packing tape with the air of an angry surgeon.

Inside the box, cocooned in bubble wrap, and carefully nested together in layers, were an incomprehensible number of china items that had been made to mark the 1981 wedding of the Prince of Wales and

Lady Diana Spencer. Plates, bowls, saucers, trinket boxes, clocks and cups, cups, cups.

"Bizarre," the man said.

"RW is royal wedding," Astrid decoded, unwrapping a twin-handled Charles and Diana loving cup.

"This box is labeled twelve," Fern pointed out, as a barely plausible thought dawned on her.

The boxes still blocking the doorway—all of which were identical in size and branding to the one in front of them—might have numbered eighteen or twenty. They couldn't all, surely, be filled with more of the same?

"Holy fucking nuptials, Batman," said the man.

"We're going to need a cup of tea," said Astrid.

And so it was that Fern Emerson spent her first day off in nine months wading through a sea of bubble wrap and commemorative china, drinking tasteless tea and eating raspberry shortcake biscuits. It was just after four o'clock when Fern returned home with her amazingly inexpensive haul of vintage fabrics. Opening the front door, she had the strange urge to call out *hello!* into the white-walled hallway, even though she knew that there was nobody there to answer.

It was still a pleasure for Fern to hurry a length of spring-toned Viyella through the washing machine and the tumble dryer, and to lay it flat and press it smooth, and to pin out the pattern pieces for her favorite box-pleated skirt style, and to listen to the *arp, arp, arp* of her fabric shears as they did their work. But the sad truth was that she was not quite as happy as she had hoped to be on the evening of her first day off in nine months. And although she occasionally looked up from her handiwork to see Molly Ringwald biting her rosebud lips, or Andrew McCarthy looking hurt and bewildered, and although she sang along to "If You Leave," her evening was not as sweet or simple as she had wanted it to be. The mere presence of the good-looking man in the charity shop, with his earphones and his LPs and his relaxed good humor, had reminded hardworking Fern Emerson that underneath all her busy-ness she was lonely. And now her heart was hurting. She'd have been better off staying home and reading in the bath.

+

Grace Allenby—Pisces, once-upon-a-time Commonwealth Games backstroker and retired swim instructor, breast cancer survivor and dragon-boat sweep—arrived at the Holy Rosary nursing home at around 10 a.m. each Tuesday.

This particular Tuesday, she began her rounds, as usual, by visiting Mr. Pollard in the Bluegum Wing. He was an elderly farmer who sat for most of his days with a life-sized border collie soft toy beside him in his Tilt-n-Lift bed. After that, Grace visited Mrs. Hampshire in the Acacia Wing, where she would sit for half an hour and hear more about the spectacular success of her talented son, Dermot, the chef.

Next, she set off in the direction of the Myrtle Ward, where she would visit Mr. Magellan, whom she knew would be sitting up in his plush recliner brandishing a remote control and cussing at his television. He would ignore her, of course, but she would read to him anyway. For Len, Grace always chose cheerful, lighthearted snippets of unnewsworthiness that would irritate him, provoking the mildly abusive hostility that Grace knew was one of Len's few remaining pleasures in life. Another was his little secret: the one he'd told to Grace, but not to his own children. Fuck 'em, he'd said. He'd cut them out of his will! All three of them. And he'd left every bloody cent of his money to the Dogs Home.

"Dogs!" Len had said, spluttering with laughter. "Don't even fucken like dogs!"

As she made her way along the hallway of the Myrtle Ward, Grace peeped through the part-open doors into the comfortable, well-appointed, but ultimately sterile suites. She was a few doors short of Mr. Magellan's room when she noted that his door was uncharacteristically wide open. Then she caught the lethal scent of disinfectant. Her heart beat faster and she hurried, marveling that she still did this, every time, even after all these years.

His room was just as she expected to find it: the carpets damp from the steam cleaning, the bathroom's porcelain parts gleaming like freshly bleached teeth, the recliner chair pushed to the center of the room and stacked with neat piles of striped pajamas, chambray shirts and old-man corduroy pants. A toilet bag rested on top of one of the stacks.

Grace sat on the stripped bed and closed her eyes in silent prayer.

After a time, she took out the copy of the *Star* from which she had planned to read to Len. That dreadful footballer with the tight shorts was on the cover, she noted briefly before flicking to the horoscope page. Silently, but with her lips moving, she read the entry for Aquarius.

"Boldness be my friend! Arm me, audacity." Take heed of the Bard's words and ride this month's roller coaster to completion and fulfillment. Now is not a time for timidity. Rather, the moment is right for you to take your endeavors to the next level, to advance to a higher plane. Take the plunge, Aquarius!

Grace made a sad, wry smile and closed the magazine.

"See you around, Len," she whispered. "You old bastard."

Then she stood, took a deep breath, and set off to visit Mrs. Mills.

Mariangela Foster (née Magellan)—Taurus, stay-at-home mother to three sons, compulsive household tidier, eBay shopaholic and uncannily gifted Tetris player—knew what to expect when her phone rang at 6:37 on that Tuesday morning. So too did her husband, Tony. Tony, already in his suit and his paisley shirt with the French cuffs, was standing at the coffee machine, empty mug poised. The phone rang twice, thrice, as he watched his wife compose her face before lifting the receiver. Mariangela's was an oval face with durable olive skin and mobile features of operatic dimensions, and he could see that she was going for a look of dignity and resignation.

"Hello?" she said, in a voice that perfectly matched her expression.

A pause. Then: "Oh, good morning, Sister Clare."

Mariangela listened for a moment, then produced a perfect, muffled sob.

"When?"

Pause.

"Was it . . . peaceful?"

Mariangela listened, and the tear that slithered out of the inside corner of her eye was as fat as a fake pearl. Tony watched it track down the side of her nose and onto her cheek, where she swiped it away with one of her practiced, former-beautician's hands.

"Thank you, Sister. Thank you for letting me know. I'll call my brothers and we'll come by later this morning to see to all his things. I'm sure my father would want me to thank you for all your care . . . no, no, we all appreciate it so much . . . yes, of course. Thank you again. Goodbye."

Mariangela replaced the receiver and turned to Tony, her hands clutched against the bodice of her satin dressing gown.

"Well?" Tony said, setting down his still-empty coffee mug. He did not yet venture the smile that was budding in the muscles of his face.

There followed a moment, a very still moment, in which the kitchen seemed emptied of everything, even air. And then, at last, Mariangela breathed out, and her features collapsed into a reverie of relief.

Tony rushed to embrace his wife, her crocodile tears already being replaced by real ones as the reality dawned that all their troubles were now over, their debts paid, their future secure. No more reminder letters about Luke's overdue school fees, no need to refinance the credit card again, no more trying to convince debt collection agency hounds that they'd got the wrong number, the wrong Fosters, the wrong information. Doubtless it would take a few months to get through the legalities, but after that, well, they were in the money.

"Wooooo!" hooted Tony, and maneuvered Mariangela into a dance hold.

"Wheeeeeeee!" squealed Mariangela, as Tony twirled her across the checkered linoleum.

It was then that their eldest son, Luke, appeared in the kitchen archway, his pajama pants sloping down over one hip and his dense dark hair quiffed upright by sleep. Tony and Mariangela froze.

"What's going on?" Luke asked, his eyes still squinty.

Caught completely and utterly *in flagrante delicto*, his parents hadn't the first idea how they were going to tell him his grandfather had just died.

Libra

SEPTEMBER 23–OCTOBER 22

September 23 not only marked the Spring Equinox, a brief moment at which the Earth hovered with its axis perfectly perpendicular to the sun; it was also the day when the sun shifted—nominally, if not actually—into the sign of Libra, the scales. And, in this particular year, September 23 was the date set for Drew Carmichael's fifty-fifth birthday party.

Night was falling as Justine steered her boxy little Fiat 126 along a westbound highway en route to Edenvale, singing along to the 1980s hits that crackled out of her crappy car radio and reaching every few moments into the bag of jelly beans that lay open on the passenger seat, along with several copies of the Huck Mowbray edition of the *Star*.

Once and once only, Justine had made the mistake of going home with a single copy of a new edition of the magazine stuffed into her luggage. Her father—who had for almost two decades been engaged in a fierce but unrequited battle for supremacy with the *Star*'s crossword setter, Doc Millar—could spend the better part of a weekend on the cryptic. Occasionally he would groan out loud when he unraveled a wordplay, or exclaim something like "You sick bastard!," or "Ha, thought you'd get me with that one, didn't ya, didn't ya?"

When Justine pulled into Curlew Court, she gave thanks that her car was so very small, because the cul-de-sac was already crammed with Range Rovers, Land Rovers and dual-cab utes. Light and sound from the party spilled around the sides of the Carmichael house, and over its low roof. With a smile, Justine identified the deep throb of Pink Floyd's "Obscured by Clouds."

From the street, number seven was a modest and unexceptional brick bungalow. Around the back, however, it became clear just how profoundly Mandy and Drew were committed to parties. The back of the house opened up like a doll's house, its glass doors folding away so that the living room and kitchen segued into the timber deck, where half the population of Edenvale was now gathered. Justine moved through the crowd, kissing cheeks and greeting aunts and uncles, both honorary and actual, until she got to the far end of the deck. Just beyond its edge, out on the grass, Drew Carmichael presided over the spectacularly overengineered rotisserie that he'd built himself in the farm shed of his older brother, Kerry. The heavily carved remains of an unfortunate lamb revolved over a bed of dwindling coals.

"Happy birthday, Daddo."

"That's not? It couldn't be? Not . . . Justine Carmichael, staff writer for the *Alexandria Park Star*?"

Justine was unsurprised to find her father Drew quite drunk, although, to be fair, she knew he got almost as inebriated on the pure fact of having a party as he did from drinking her Uncle Kerry's stout. By the steps that led down from the deck to the back lawn was a claw-foot bath full of crushed ice, and the necks of stubbies poked up out of it like so many bottled messages bobbing about on an Arctic sea.

Drew called out, "Mandy, where are you? Prodigal daughter's home! Time to kill the fatted sheep!" He hugged Justine. "Oh, shit. We already did! And we ate a fair bit of it, too. There's plenty left, though. Kitchen counter, if you're hungry."

Mandy appeared through the crowd with a tray of wineglasses.

"Hey, gorgeous girl! How was the drive? You hungry, love? Red or white?" she asked, teetering in a pair of heeled boots that just about brought her up to Justine's modest height. She leaned in for a kiss and Justine smelled a cocktail of semillon, Miracle perfume and the fake tan Mandy had clearly popped on her exposed, end-of-winter décolletage.

Justine took a glass of red, and Mandy whispered, "Thank God you got here before your father passes out. He started at two when Kerry turned up with the hogget. I think he's forgotten this is his fifty-fifth, not his bloody thirtieth." Then, pulling away, she said, "Your brother's somewhere about. Aussie? Austin? Austin James Carmichael, where are you? And he's brought the girlfriend home with him. About time, too. I like this one. I really do. I think we should be angling to keep her. You'll have to tell me what you think."

Justine had never entirely got used to the idea of her little brother being a man. He was at least a foot taller than she was, and as broad as Uncle Kerry across the shoulders, and yet, to Justine, there was a part of him that was perpetually five years old with grass-stained knees and an endearing lisp.

Under his arm, tonight, was a girl. A pretty girl. She wore a lacy, deep-red cardigan and her curly dark hair was caught up in a clip, though tendrils of it fell down around her open face.

"This is Rose," Austin said, clearly very pleased with himself. "Rose, this is my sister."

"You must be the famous Justine," Rose said, beaming.

Justine held out her hand, but Rose brushed the gesture away and leaned in for a hug. Over Rose's shoulder, Justine tried to make eye contact with Austin to gauge whether he thought this kind of effusiveness was normal, or weird. But if his face said anything at all, it was only that this time he was hopelessly in love. Still in Rose's embrace, Justine felt a surge of sappy, happy-ending emotion that was harder than she expected to swallow back down.

"So," Justine said, trying to get herself under control, "how are you surviving the Carmichaels en masse?"

"Oh, no problem," Rose said.

"She's a wool classer," Aussie said, without taking his eyes off his girlfriend, "so she knows her way around a pack of half-cut farmers. Don't you?"

Rose shrugged off the praise, but before any more could be said, Mandy appeared in their midst. "Come and sort the Pavlovas, will you, girls?"

She led the way to the kitchen, where the light was startlingly bright after the brazier-lit ambience of the deck, and Justine squinted as Mandy whipped the Glad wrap off two vast, white circles of meringue.

"Here you go: blueberries, raspberries, strawberries. And there's a couple of kiwi fruit for you to cut up. A-a-and some bananas. Tin of passionfruit—show Rose where the opener is, Jussy. Knife each, cutting board each. And you're set."

"Remind me why it is that Aussie doesn't have to do the Pav?" Justine asked, only three-quarters in jest.

"Listen to her, would you, Rose?" Mandy said, then put on a whiny brat voice: "It's Aussie's turn to unpack the dishwasher; Aussie never has to fold the socks; it's not fair."

"It's *not* fair," Justine said, now only half in jest.

"Pavlova is secret women's business, my girl. Give up the desserts and the salads, and"—Mandy whacked Justine's bottom lightly with a tea towel—"you'll spend every barbecue turning sausages and smelling like the floor of an abattoir."

And with that piece of sage advice, Mandy was gone, platter of cheeses in hand, back out to the deck, leaving Rose and Justine alone in the kitchen.

"I don't think I've ever seen my brother quite so smitten," Justine offered.

Rose's cheeks colored. "I love him too. I knew straightaway that I would love him. You know? You know how you just . . . *know*?"

But Justine, distributing blueberries in a haphazard fashion, thought that it was all very well to know. What happened when the person you knew about didn't seem to know about you?

Justine didn't want to envy anyone. Not Aussie and Rose for all the fireworks joy that was coming their way; not her mum and her dad, for the way they'd worn grooves into each other over the years; not Kerry and Ray, who were dancing together on the deck in the same predictable, confident way that they bickered about whether or not it was going to rain. But tonight, it was going to be hard not to.

♎

"Something, something, t, something, r, something," Drew said. "Future? Saturn?"

It was early afternoon and although the Carmichaels' fridge was crammed with odd-shaped wedges of cheese, half-drunk bottles of white wine, and a large Tupperware container full of slices of charred lamb, the place showed almost no other signs of having recently been the venue for a large party. The back of the house was once again a wall of glass, the indoor-outdoor furniture on the back deck had been wiped clean and restored to right angles, and the claw-foot bath had been pushed back into storage beneath the deck.

Drew, with rumpled hair and more wrinkles beneath his brown eyes than Justine had properly noticed before, was in his armchair with his copy of the *Star* folded open to the crossword puzzle. Mandy was at the kitchen bar, with her magazine wedged into a recipe holder as she wrote out the ingredients that would be required for Dermot Hampshire's pear and hazelnut tart.

Justine had woken late, assembled an odd outfit from clothes she'd left in the drawers of her old bedroom, given in to her mother's entreaty that she eat a large serve of eggs on toast and taken the family's ancient spaniel, Lucy, for a very, very slow stroll around the neighborhood. On their walk, they had passed the place where Nick Jordan, aged eight, had broken his collarbone falling off his skateboard while showing off to an unimpressed Justine. Half a block from there, Justine and Lucy stopped for a moment in the echoing mouth of the storm drain where Justine and Nick used to practice demonic laughing.

"Mwah, ha, ha, ha, ha," Justine tried, for old times' sake.

Lucy was now lying on the rug beside Drew's chair, and she was so still that it was hard to be certain she wasn't dead. Justine sat beside the old dog, absentmindedly stroking her furry belly and finishing off the last cup of tea she planned to drink before setting off for home.

"Come on, smarty pants," Drew said. "Something, something, t, something, r, something."

Justine had already contributed the words "tesserae" and "gazpacho" to this month's crossword. Now she only shrugged.

Drew sighed. "Meters? Miters? Motors?"

"What's the clue again?"

"Leave! Crazy old fart."

"So, 'Crazy' means there's an anagram."

"Yes, yes. Thank you for that, Einstein. But an anagram of *what*?" said Drew. "This Doc Millar of yours. He's a sadist. You know that, right? He enjoys suffering and pain."

"You're the masochist who does the puzzle," Justine said, draining the last of her tea.

"*Leave! Crazy old* fart,'" Drew tried. Then, "*Leave! Crazy* old *fart*." He shook his head.

"Well, I'll have to leave you to it," Justine said. "For city life calls me away."

"You're going? Already?" Mandy said from the kitchen bar, making a cartoon sad face.

"Things to do, people to see, places to go," Justine lied.

Drew took off his reading glasses, hauled himself out of his chair and said his goodbyes in the living room, but Mandy walked alongside Justine, down the front path to the curb. She watched as Justine loaded her bag into the Fiat, then took hold of her daughter by the shoulders and looked into her eyes.

"You didn't seem altogether yourself last night. Anything I should know?" Mandy asked, and for once, she actually waited for an answer.

"Well, I think I can tell you that you're going to have a lovely new daughter-in-law any tick of the clock," Justine said.

"I was asking about *you*," Mandy said, her brow furrowed with concern.

"It's just that . . . Aussie and Rose. They're so happy, and—" She stopped before the ache in her throat got any worse.

"Darling girl," Mandy said, drawing Justine in for a hug. "Your time'll come."

"I just have to keep believing that, don't I?" Justine said into her mother's shoulder.

"You do," Mandy said. "And it will. You never know what's just around the corner."

⌣

It was evening by the time Justine reached Alexandria Park and backed her tiny Fiat into the worst car space in Evelyn Towers' ridiculously tight parking allotment. There the little car might remain for weeks, or even months—its red Duco continuing to fade to the color of rust, its hood crusting over with wattle blossom and starling shit—until Justine's next trip home. Duffel bag hoisted on her shoulder, Justine fought her way past the unpruned lilac bushes that lined the side path to the street.

When she reached the twelfth-floor landing, she found Nick standing at her front door. It was about now that Justine wished she'd not dressed herself from the ragbag of her Edenvale closet. And she wished that she'd brushed her hair. Or, at the very least, put on a little bit of mascara.

Nick himself was clearly fresh out of the shower, his dark hair all shiny-wet. Under a rather sharp-looking sports jacket, he wore a pair of nicer-than-average jeans and a pale blue print shirt that was bordering on pretty.

"And where are you off to this fine Sunday night, Mr. Jordan, all dressed to kill?"

But Nick seemed distracted. He ran a hand through his wet hair. "How was the party?"

"Great," she said. "It was ... great."

During the drive back, she had been looking forward to telling Nick all the news from home—how their primary school bully had found Buddhism, and how pillar-of-the-community Nora Burnside had got caught shoplifting toothpaste from the supermarket—but now that she was standing here, she could see that this was not the right time.

"So, there's something I need to talk to you about," Nick said.

Justine: *Is this going to be good? Or bad?*

Brain: *Well, we generally don't like the phrase "there's something I need to talk to you about." It's too much like "I hope you won't mind me saying, but . . ."*

"I'm not doing it," Nick said.

Justine knew, immediately, what he meant. Even so, she heard herself ask, "Doing what?"

"I'm not auditioning. I can't."

Inside her chest, Justine felt that sinking feeling again. Down, down, down. Down through layers of blue.

"I thought—"

"I'm really sorry," Nick said. "I know you wanted me to, and I know you went out of your way to give me an in with Alison Tarf. And I wanted to audition. I did. But it turns out I'm going to be traveling for a lot of the summer, and there's no way I can make the scheduling work, and, look, I wanted to tell you in person."

"Traveling? Because?"

"I've got a new job."

"An acting job?" Justine asked hopefully.

"I'm told it's like acting without all the lines," Nick said drily.

"Oh?"

"Laura and I, we're going to be the Chance couple. You know, the winery? They want to sign us for five years to do a series of ads. Television, print, internet. You would not believe what they're willing to pay me to wear an Akubra hat and hold a wineglass."

"Modeling?" Justine said, not trying very hard to hide her disdain. "You are going to be a model?"

"Let me explain," Nick said, looking pained.

Knowing that there were too many emotions leaking out of her, Justine couldn't work out where to look, how to stand, where to be. "You don't have to."

"I need you to understand. I don't know if you've read the horoscopes. Probably not, but you'll never guess who Leo quoted at me this month. Go on. Guess."

Justine shook her head miserably.

"Shakespeare," he said. "*Shakespeare*. Can you believe it?"

She could.

"'Boldness be my friend! Arm me, audacity.' That was the quote. From *Cymbeline*."

Justine considered. Carefully, and even though she knew she was sailing close to the wind, she said, "And this couldn't have meant, for instance, that you should have the courage to audition for Alison Tarf's new, um, *Shakespeare* company?"

Nick sighed. "No, I don't think so. I really don't. Because that wouldn't take real courage. See, that doesn't really frighten me. It doesn't rock me to my very soul. But to give up something that really matters, for the woman I love? That hurts. That takes real fortitude. Actual guts."

Justine waited for him to go on.

"'Boldness be my friend! Arm me, audacity.' That's what Leo said. So I'm going to do the bravest thing I know how to do. I'm going to sacrifice something I want, something I really want, to give Laura something she really wants."

"Which is, what?"

"All of me, Justine," he said, with total sincerity. "Every last bit. Leo said I have to take it to the next level. 'Take the plunge, Aquarius!' That's what he said. So that is what I'm going to do. I'm going to ask her to marry me."

Brain: *I strongly advise that you do not say anything at this point.*

Justine said, "Sagittarians are supposed to be blunt, right?"

Brain: *No, no, no, no. Mouth shut, Justine!*

Nick said, "Well, forthright. Yes."

Brain: *Justine! Shut. Up.*

"Well, let me be forthright. It does not surprise me in the least that Laura is the face of Waterlily perfume. That's just perfect. Actually, it's beyond perfect."

"What are you talking about?"

"All pretty on the surface. Beautiful. Gorgeous. But have you ever turned a waterlily upside down? Nothing but those straggly little roots. Nothing. Going. On. Underneath."

Nick shook his head in disappointment. "You know, I see this all the time. Women always hate Laura. It's because she's beautiful. They hate her, even before they get to know her."

"Excuse me?" Justine said. "I don't *hate* her. And even if I did, it wouldn't be just because she's beautiful. You may be totally obsessed with the way people look, but I'm not."

"Obsessed, am I?"

"Have you ever stopped to consider that what you two really like about each other is that you look just the same?"

Brain: *No, no, no, no. Do not go where you're heading. Abort mission! Abort mission!*

"I mean . . . what's your relationship really all about? Because it's certainly not about what's best for you, Nick. What is it about? Actually? Hm? Some weird desire to reproduce by osmosis?"

"What?"

"Imagine how perfect your children will be!" Justine's voice was dripping with scorn.

"What are you talking about? You don't know the first thing about my relationship with Laura."

"I know it's not right for you. The right relationship for you wouldn't be with someone who thinks you're cut out to be a freaking *model*."

"What do you care, anyway?"

"You know what? I don't. Go marry Miss Waterlily. Advertise cheap wine. Bold and audacious, you are. Truly." Justine had gone beyond the point of being able to rein herself in. Her brain had retreated to its inner quarters—a plush padded cell where it could rock from side to side and mumble incoherently. "Pour your talent down the toilet! Because that's where you'll be *taking the plunge, Aquarius!*"

"I'm not standing here listening to this crap," Nick said. He turned away from her and headed for the stairwell.

"There's nothing more to listen to!" Justine called after him, but there was no answer except the sound of his footsteps on the stairs.

Justine sat, shell-shocked, on her couch, and looked across the gap at the darkened windows of the next-door apartment. When her phone rang a few moments later, she pulled it out of her pocket hopefully, but the screen did not say "Nick Jordan." It said "Dad." She considered not answering, but she knew that this would make her dad worry that she hadn't made it safely back to the city.

"Hi, Dad."

"Your father is a genius," Drew said.

Justine sighed. Inaudibly, she hoped. "Because?"

"*Leave! Crazy old fart.* I have solved it," he crowed. "So, clever daughter of mine: a six-letter synonym for 'leave,' if you please?"

"Too tired, Dad."

"Okay, I'll make it easy on you. A six-letter synonym for 'leave' is . . . depart."

"Excellent," Justine said, slumping further into the couch cushions.

"Now, we must ask ourselves—what are the possible anagrams for depart? And what might any of them have to do with flatulence?"

"I feel sure you're about to tell me."

"Aha! Not only does the Middle French *péter* mean 'to break wind,' it is also the etymological origin of the word 'petard.' And 'petard,' as you—being my daughter—will already have worked out, is an anagram of depart. And there you have it. Your father is a genius. The word is 'petard,' my crossword is complete and Doc Millar can go dip his left eye in hot cockatoo shit."

"Truly, you are a scholar and a gentleman," Justine said.

"Incidentally, do you know what a petard actually *is*? I've always imagined it was a kind of gantry or hangman's gallows. Something one could be 'hoist' by. But, it turns out that a petard was a sixteenth-century war machine used for breaking down walls. Essentially, a kind of bomb. Fart the walls down! So what that expression means, 'hoist by one's own petard,' is that the victim is raised up into the air by being blown up, exploded, by one's own device."

"Well, thank you for the edification, Father."

"You're home safely, then?"

"I am."

"Leave you to it then, chickie. Just wanted you to be able to sleep, safe in the knowledge that there are no blank squares in the crossie. Tell Doc, if you see him, that I will not be beaten."

"'Night, Dad."

Justine, still incapable of standing up, looked again in the direction of her French doors. The windows of the opposite apartment were still dark. Boldly and audaciously, Nick was going to propose to Laura Mitchell.

Hoist by one's own petard, Justine thought.

Ka-boom.

⚓

In the dying days of September, Justine decided that it was time to make a few out-of-session New Year's resolutions. The first of these was that she would leave Leo Thornbury's horoscope column alone. No matter if she arrived at work early one morning and happened to see Leo's fax perched invitingly on the out-tray of the machine in Henry's office; no matter if she stayed at work late one evening and heard the fax machine begin to shudder and print. No matter the time of day, no matter the circumstances, there was no way she was going to tinker with Leo's predictions. Not ever again. Never. For she had proven to herself that she was the worst counterfeit astrologer the world had ever seen.

Her second resolution was to accept the fact that Nick Jordan was destined to be Laura Mitchell's husband, and the Chance wines guy, and that she, Justine, would admire him on billboards and send a set of His and Hers tea bags as a wedding gift.

Her third resolution was to apologize to Nick.

In the week that followed the making of these resolutions, Justine had most success with the first. She did not once, or in any way, interfere with Leo Thornbury's horoscope. She didn't see his fax, go looking for it or enter Henry's office. Ten out of ten. So far, so good.

It was more difficult to measure progress toward meeting her second resolution. How did one know when one had got hold of a hope and totally, completely, utterly and finally extinguished it? Justine wasn't certain, but she knew she was doing her best not to think about Nick in any way that exceeded neighborliness and friendship.

Then there was the third resolution. Justine apologized to Nick in several formats. She called him and sent him a series of apologetic text messages—but Nick neither picked up her calls nor responded to any of her texts. Moving up a gear, she wrote a groveling letter and popped it into his mailbox. But there was no response.

Getting yet more serious, Justine took a pair of sturdy kitchen scissors and walked the streets of Alexandria Park until she found a hedge of young olive trees growing in the front yard of a stately mansion. She cut off a decent-sized branch, took it home and sent it in the lighthouse keeper's basket over to Nick's side of the gap. The next day, however, the olive branch was still in the basket, apparently untouched. And there the branch remained, withering a little more each day, all through the week that followed: the week in which Justine's city was held fast in the ticker-tape grasp of the Australian Rules football grand final.

Throughout the suburbs, flags were affixed to street front windows and fences, cars flew tassels of streamers from their aerials, and people wore their striped footy scarves to work, to the supermarket— anywhere, everywhere—even though the weather was mild.

On the morning of the day before the game, Huck Mowbray phoned Daniel Griffin to offer him the chance to watch the big event from the comfort of a corporate box. But he didn't invite only Daniel Griffin. He invited Daniel Griffin, plus one, and Daniel called Justine into his office to explain that it was only reasonable, since she had done all the hard work on the *Star*'s Huck Mowbray cover story, that she be the one to accompany him.

"Well?" Daniel said. "What do you say?"

He was standing behind his desk with a brightly striped scarf slung about his shoulders. It was in the colors of an AFL team that had been bundled out of the contest in the second qualifying final. Justine's team—which she followed with complete loyalty but a low level of interest—hadn't even made it to the finals, having played disastrously all season.

Justine: *Is he asking me in a date way, or a work way?*

Brain: *Assuming the latter, it could be seen as a good opportunity to network. There could be interesting people in that corporate box.*

Justine: *Assuming the former?*

Brain: *In the context of Resolution Two—to stop thinking about Nick Jordan—this might be just what you need.*

"Thank you, Daniel," Justine said. "I'd love to come."

⌣

As it turned out, the experience of watching a football final from a corporate box was a dismal disappointment to Justine. As a networking experience, it would only have been profitable if she'd been planning to purchase an air-conditioning unit or insure a sports car. Accompanying the air-conditioning salesmen and sports car insurance agents were women who were either pregnant or trying to be, and Justine found that she had very little to contribute to their conversations about episiotomies and folate. To keep herself occupied, she'd eaten too many of the team color jelly beans that were in little bowls on every shelf and table, and then had to spend time in the ladies' room scrubbing the garish colors off her teeth. Really, she'd rather have watched the game from out in the open seating with a tomato-sauce-laden pie and a beer, rather than indoors with the antipasto and chardonnay.

With two minutes left in the game, by which time it was clear that the competition's perennial underdogs had the premiership cup firmly in their grasp, Huck Mowbray—having drunk several liters of premium ale—leaped to his feet, raised his stubby and spouted a snippet of Tennyson's "The Charge of the Light Brigade" in a rousing baritone.

"When can their glory fade?" he intoned. "O the wild charge they made!"

At the final siren, the stadium was a vortex of noise, and Justine imagined that the sudden updraft of cheering might be enough to knock the hovering television network helicopter off its course. Down on the field, the winners leaped into each other's arms, feeling no pain, while the vanquished sat on the muddied turf with their arms about their knees, feeling a double helping of it. The stadium's sound system thundered out the tub-thumping song of the winning team, and Daniel had to lean in close to make himself heard. Justine could feel the warmth of his breath against her ear.

"Shall we sneak off for a quiet drink somewhere?"

Justine laughed. "Where do you propose to find a quiet spot in this city tonight?"

"I know just the place." He grabbed her by the hand, apparently out of a desire not to lose her in the crush. But even when they were well beyond the stadium, making their way through streets crazy with football fever, Daniel still had Justine's hand in his. And she found that she was not, for some reason, making any attempt to retrieve it from him.

"Where are we going?" she asked him.

"Zubeneschamali," he said.

"Say again?"

"Zube-ne-scha-mali," he repeated. "It's a chartreuse bar. Down by the river."

And Justine, not wanting to seem ignorant, kept her next question to herself.

It turned out that a chartreuse bar was a bar specializing in chartreuse, which, up until this evening, Justine had not known to be anything other than a wanky name for a shade of greenish yellow.

Zubeneschamali was indeed down by the river, on the uppermost floor of a warehouse building, and reached by a half-hidden staircase that gave the place the feel of a speakeasy. Inside, while there were one or two striped scarves to be seen, there was no colossal television broadcasting the postgame agonies and ecstasies, and for the first time since Justine and Daniel had left the stadium they could hear nobody at all singing the winning club's song.

Predictably, perhaps, the bar was decorated in shades of chartreuse. The walls were painted thus, the stools were upholstered thus and the booth seating was piled with cushions in all the colors of a jaundiced rainbow. In the glassed-in shelves above the bar were bottles upon bottles, each of them filled with liquids in every possible shade of yellow through to green, while hanging down beneath these shelves were bunches of what looked to Justine to be dried herbs.

Daniel ordered two tasting flights at a price that made Justine's eyes go wide.

"Ever drunk chartreuse before?" he asked, when a series of six shot glasses appeared before each of them.

"Not to the best of my knowledge."

"A herbal concoction. Historically, made by French monks. It's supposed to contain something like a hundred and thirty different botanicals," Daniel explained.

The drink was, to Justine's palette, sweet and syrupy and violently alcoholic. Nevertheless, the contents of all twelve glasses seemed swiftly to evaporate as she and Daniel talked—about Alexandria Park and house prices and good places to eat, about Jeremy Byrne's retirement and Radoslaw's driving, about the *Star* and Daniel's plans for it. When the flights were done, Daniel sent for more of the yellow chartreuse that Justine had liked the best.

"So," Justine said, "are you missing Canberra?"

"Not really. I mean, it's better than it was, but it's still essentially a pretend city in a cow paddock. Quarantine for politicians and their hangers-on."

"Such as press gallery journalists?"

"They're the worst of all," Daniel said, with a self-deprecating grin.

They talked politics and movies, books and music, about whether you could simultaneously be a Brontë person *and* an Austen person (Justine said yes, Daniel no—he was all Brontë, he said). And as they talked they drank more chartreuse, which, just for good measure, they followed with more chartreuse.

"Better to be full of chartreuse than full of shit," Daniel said, taking another slug. "That's what I always say."

"Is that so?" Justine said. "I heard it's pretty well known around the Canberra press gallery that your motto is 'charm to disarm.'"

Justine watched Daniel lose a touch of his composure. "Who told you that?"

It was Tara who'd dropped this little tidbit of information into Justine's lap. Apparently, Daniel had quite a reputation for softening up his prey with charm before delivering the sucker-punch question.

"So, it's true?" she pressed. "'Charm to disarm'? Isn't that a bit manipulative?"

"Oh, do we say manipulative? Or do we say strategic?"

"I say tomayto, you say tomarto?"

"But seriously, who was it? Who told you that?"

Justine laughed. "A good journalist never reveals her sources."

"Fair enough," he said. He took another sip of the bright yellow liqueur, and thought for a moment. "What this does indicate, though, is that . . . you've been checking up on me."

Justine's eyebrows leaped upward in her defense. "I'd hardly say checking up."

"But, you cannot deny that you have been talking about me. Which would seem to indicate some level of interest?"

There was a silence, in which Daniel looked at Justine, very directly. Almost too directly. It gave her an inkling of what it might be like to be a zebra, separated from its pack, out on an African savannah. Daniel moved a little closer to her, his elbow on the table.

"I like you, Justine," he said simply.

Justine blinked.

Was she about to kiss her new boss?

It appeared that she was.

☙

Justine: *Hello?*

Silence.

It was morning. Probably late morning, Justine thought, given the intensity of the light that was seeping through a crack in the curtains. For a moment, she thought she was late for work, until the distant knowledge somehow dawned that this was Sunday.

Justine: *Hello?*

More silence.

Were they her own curtains? she wondered, trying to orient herself in space. Yes, they were. That was a good sign. And, over there, hanging on the wall above a dressing table: it was her very own map of the world, speckled with red pins for all the places she had been, and forested with green pins for all the places she wanted to go. Mongolia, Newfoundland, Norway, Finland, Buenos Aires, the Galapagos Islands, Jersey, Lucknow . . . yes, it was definitely hers.

Justine would have liked to go back to sleep, but she was too thirsty.

Also, her teeth felt as if they were sprouting a coral reef. And she needed to pee, which meant that even though it seemed like a perilous mission, she was going to have to try to get out of bed.

When she sat up, Justine was overcome by an intense feeling of land-sickness, as though she'd been at sea for several years and was now struggling to cope with a world that was not swaying, but holding dangerously, disorientatingly, still. She closed her eyes, but the sensation didn't abate. She opened her eyes, and saw that she was not alone.

Shit.

Daniel Griffin was in her bed. He was lying on his stomach, the bare skin of his shoulders uncovered by the quilt, one olive-skinned arm dangling toward the floor. His hair was thick and lush and messy against the white of her pillowcase, and just in case Justine was in any doubt about how he and she had spent the night, a deluge of images poured forth. This hand, here. That tongue, there.

Justine: *Hello? HELLO?*

But her brain didn't answer. The fucking thing had gone on holiday. To Chartreuseville, presumably.

Justine edged out of bed. From her bedside chair, she snatched up a pair of thick socks that would do for slippers and a long, light cardigan that would work as a makeshift dressing gown. Via the bathroom, she went to the kitchen, still in a state of low-level panic. It was not until she had dissolved and consumed some aspirin that her brain, at long last, made an appearance.

Brain: *Good morning!*

Justine: *Good morning? Good fucking morning?*

Brain: *Um, curtains? They're open.*

Justine: *Shit!*

Clutching at the fronts of her cardigan, Justine crept, crablike, around the walls of her living room and hastily tugged the curtains over the French doors.

Brain: *That's better.*

Justine: *Better? Better than what? Better than the complete fucking disaster we're in the middle of? We were supposed to be going to the grand final, not to bloody bed! What were you thinking? I finally get the reporter's job I've been waiting for—for years, I might add—and I just slept with my new boss? What the hell?*

Brain: *Can we have coffee before we talk about this?*

In the kitchen, Justine clumsily spooned coffee grounds into her gas-top percolator.

Brain: *Ahhhh. That smell. I feel better already.*

Justine: *This is bad, this is bad, this is very, very, very bad. How could we be so stupid?*

But her brain went silent when Daniel arrived in the kitchen and wrapped his bare arms around Justine's middle. His hand, warm and dry, slipped inside her cardigan. She felt skin on skin over solar plexus and it was meltingly nice.

"Good morning," Daniel said softly.

Justine: *Um . . . help?*

But there was no answer from the brain. There was, instead, Daniel's other hand on her thigh. And his lips on the back of her neck. She turned around inside his arms and kissed him properly.

"Scorpio," he whispered into her ear.

"Afraid not," she said.

What did one wear to work on the Monday after a weekend during which one accidentally slept with one's new boss? This was the question Justine pondered as she stood in front of her bedroom mirror wearing nothing but underpants and a bra.

She picked out a black dress and held it up against her body. It was one of those dresses that looked simple, but fitted Justine in a special way that made it an irreplaceable, die-hard favorite. Nevertheless, it was not an option. It had a lace panel at the back, between the shoulders, that might be interpreted as a little bit sexy. So, no. No black dress.

Maybe the gray pants and the cobalt blue shirt with the ruffles and the bell sleeves? Nope. It was an outfit that said casual. It said comfortable. And comfortable said *I'm okay with everything that happened.* And thinking, now, about everything that had happened was enough to make Justine blush. The couch, the rug, the kitchen counter . . . they were never going to seem quite the same to her again.

Daniel had stayed for the better part of the day. He'd kissed her goodbye at the front door, and then, before she could close it behind him, he'd turned back.

"We should probably talk about how it's going to be," he'd said. "At work."

"How is it going to be?"

"We're adults, right? And we're smart people. Work is work, and play is play. We can just keep them . . . separate."

"Of course," Justine had said. "Smart. Separate."

"Hey?"

"Yes?"

"The play part. I liked it. A lot, okay?"

After he'd gone, Justine had gone into the bathroom for a shower, and, throwing off her cardigan, she'd noticed in the mirror the purplish bite mark at the base of her throat.

Brain: *Classy.*

Justine: *Oh, you're back now, are you? Any ideas?*

Brain: *We could always freak out.*

So freak out they did. Tenaciously. For all of Sunday evening, and for most of the night. And now it was Monday morning, Justine was operating on perhaps three hours of sleep, and she had nothing to wear to work. When her wardrobe was half empty, and her bedroom chair lost beneath an avalanche of fabric, she finally settled on a pair of tweedy brown pants, and a burnt-orange jumper with the cuffs, collar and hem of a white shirt peeking out. And she would tie a narrow silk scarf around her neck to hide that mark, just to be on the safe side.

It was still early when she reached the far side of Alexandria Park, but she was feeling too strange and nauseated to enjoy stopping in at Rafaello's, so she wandered in to the markets. Today, it was not with any joy, nor the usual satisfaction of the spelling vigilante, that Justine crossed out the rogue D in ADVOCADOS. Today, she was just irritated. She felt a little stab of pain in her temple, too. She hoped she wasn't coming down with something.

⌢

"Justine?"

Daniel stood in the doorway to the staff writers' room, and although his expression was carefully inscrutable, neither Martin nor Roma looked up from their work to see it.

At last, Justine thought, glancing up at the clock on her computer screen. It was almost five o'clock, and until now Daniel had made no effort to engineer even a moment to be alone with her. And all day, she had been distracted by this fact, even though she knew it ought not surprise her. Work was work, he had said, and play was play. He was only being true to his word.

"Can I see you in my office?" he asked.

Justine nodded, equally inscrutably.

Brain: *See, I told you so. You just had to wait.*

Justine: *Okay, smarty-pants. So, you were right.*

But, having followed Daniel into his office and taken a seat, Justine had the distinct impression that this was not going to be the kind of moment alone that she had been hoping for.

"What do you reckon the chances are," Daniel began, looking serious as he leaned back in the chair that Justine still thought of as Jeremy's, behind the desk that Justine still thought of as Jeremy's, inside the office that was a good deal tidier now that it was no longer Jeremy's, "that 'Davina Divine' is a real name?"

"I'm sorry?"

"This morning I opened a letter from someone calling herself Davina Divine," Daniel said, handing across the desk a sheet of folded letter paper. "I'm interested to know what you make of it."

It was the kind of paper that you'd get in a stationery set: the kind you might buy for a teenage girl when you didn't know what else to get her for Christmas. The page had a thick border of blue, purple and aqua swirls, amid which tiny mermaids frolicked. Justine could see the matching envelope, neatly sliced open, lying on top of a manila folder right in front of Daniel. The letter had been addressed to the editor;

the writing, on the envelope and the letter itself, was in sparkly purple ink, the scented kind. Justine could smell it: sweet but nasty, like half-chewed bubble gum.

"Read it," Daniel urged.

To the Editor,

I am writing to you in the hope that you will send my letter on to your astrologer, Leo Thornbury. I would have written to Mr. Thornbury directly, but for all my trying, I have not been able to find an address for him. I, too, am an astrologer, though of course I am not anywhere near in the league of Mr. Thornbury. I hoped he might be kind enough to explain to me where I am going wrong with the star sign of Aquarius, since for the past few months, his readings for the water bearer have been very different from mine—almost opposite in some cases. I know that I must be getting something wrong, but I don't know what it is, and I earnestly hope that Mr. Thornbury might give me some advice that will help me in my career.

Yours faithfully,
Davina Divine
Dip Astro (FAA), Adv Dip Astro (FAA)

Justine was only about one sentence into the letter when her heart began to trot. Two sentences in, and it was cantering. By the time she reached the sign-off, her pulse was in full gallop. The kitsch mermaid letter paper quivered in her hand.

"So, I'm wondering," Daniel asked, "whether you can offer me any insights into Ms. Divine's inquiry."

From within a rush of adrenaline, Justine tried to evaluate the situation. Daniel had received a letter from a crazy star lady. That was all. That, on its own, couldn't mean anything much. But then Daniel opened the manila folder in front of him, and there, inside, was a stack of papers that Justine recognized only too well. As Daniel fanned out the contents, Justine saw Leo's faxes, most of them a bit crumpled, and all of them speared through somewhere near the middle with small ragged holes. Daniel had been back through the contents of the document spike.

Brain: *Not good.*

Interleaved with the faxes were pages torn from the *Star*. The horoscope pages. On both the faxes and the clippings were hot pink stripes of the kind made by a highlighter pen. Aquarius, Aquarius, Aquarius. The word jumped out at Justine from several places at once.

Brain: *Seriously not good.*

On Leo's faxes, Justine glimpsed the highlighted words "new path with determination" and "prevailing push and pull" and "Saturn urges you." In the clippings, other words—Justine's own words—had taken their places: "Paradise unpaved," "God's way of remaining anonymous," "mushrooms from toadstools," "Boldness be my friend."

Daniel, observing that Justine had seen and registered the contents of the folder, closed it. "Why did you do it?" he asked.

Justine attempted speech, but her tongue felt as if it had been anesthetized. Helplessly, she shrugged.

Daniel continued to watch her, and as he did so, Justine became intensely aware of the kinds of problems one faced after sleeping with one's boss. You could be in the middle of being very badly busted for tinkering with the horoscope column, but remembering how sweetly he'd kissed your nose. Or having the inappropriate thought that you knew exactly what your boss looked like at the moment of orgasm. Which was, in Daniel's case, wide-eyed, like a tawny version of Astro Boy.

"I'd have thrown the letter in the bin," Daniel said. "Except I remembered that morning, right after you were promoted. When I got to the office, you weren't at your new desk. You were at your old desk, typing in the stars. To help Henry, you said."

Justine felt utterly seen-through.

"But I do have a theory," Daniel said, "about why you did it."

He toyed with a pen as he spoke, threading it in and out of his fingers. He looked serious, but slightly pleased with himself, a bit like a detective about to cleverly explicate a whodunit.

"It's only ever been Aquarius. None of the other signs," he said. "Which is what makes me think that you . . . well, let me put it this way.

My theory is that by altering Leo's horoscopes, you were attempting to promote your better self, to quash the more materialistic parts of yourself, perhaps even help yourself recover from a failed love affair, but certainly go after what it is that you really want in life. To chase your dreams. Because you're the Aquarius, aren't you, Justine? And you've been trying, through Leo's column, to change your own fate."

Brain: *Actually, Justine, that's genius.*

Justine: *I know. And way better than the truth.*

Justine fixed her face into a mixture of contrition and admiration.

"Wow," she said to Daniel. "That's amazing. Because you are absolutely right."

And was she imagining it? Or did Daniel's gym junkie chest swell ever so slightly?

"Okay, then," Daniel said. "I'm glad we're getting somewhere."

He didn't exactly smile, but his facial muscles made a gesture in that direction.

"It was deeply stupid of you, though," he said, and Justine let the contrite part of her expression come to the fore. "You probably thought, 'It's only the stars.' And, you know, you'd be right. It is only the stars. But Leo Thornbury is one of our oldest, most distinguished contributors. Because you're smart, you probably calculated that the risk of Leo ever noticing the discrepancies was virtually nil. But, Justine, what if he *had* got a copy of the magazine? What if he had seen the changes you made? What you did was disrespectful in the extreme. Not to mention unethical."

"I know," Justine said. "And I'm sorry. I won't do it again."

"Bloody oath, you won't do it again," Daniel said. "Because if you did, I'd have to send you back to the salt mines of copy-running at the very least. Let you go, at the worst."

Work is work, Justine thought ruefully.

"So, no, you are not going to do this again. And to make sure you're not even tempted, I want you to know that although I'm not going to tell Henry anything about your editing experiment, I am going to tell him that when this month's stars arrive I want him to pay special attention. I'm going to tell him I expect 100 percent accuracy in transcription. And that I may even be checking up."

"Who else knows about this?"

"Just you and me," Daniel said. "And I think it's best if we keep it that way."

"Thank you."

"All right then." Daniel picked up a pen and drew an absentminded line across the page in front of him. "And, Justine?"

"Yes?" she said, longing for him to say something, anything, that would confirm to her that they had actually spent half the weekend in bed together. That he liked her.

"You've got the makings of a really good journo," Daniel said. "Don't do anything dumb like this again, will you?"

The question stung, even though it was entirely fair. She *had* been stupid. She had been stupid to tinker with the stars, and she had been stupid to get involved with Daniel.

"I won't," she said.

"Promise?"

"Promise," she said. And she meant it, too.

Arriving home that evening, Justine felt spaced out and fogged up. Every joint in her body ached and she couldn't tell whether she was hot or cold; her cheeks were burning, but she was shivering. Did she have a fever? No, of course not. Getting sick was just nothing but inconvenient.

She went to close her living-room curtains, and there on the balcony opposite was Nick Jordan wearing his sandalwood jumper and sheepskin boots, and he was taking the olive branch out of their lighthouse keeper's basket. Looking up and seeing Justine, he smiled, put one hand to his heart, and held out the withered branch as if it were a rose.

Justine opened the French doors, and the evening air made her shiver quite violently.

"Was this once an olive branch?" Nick asked.

"It was once a very big sorry."

"I've been away," Nick said, letting the branch fall to his side.

"So far away that you couldn't return any of my phone calls?"

"Maybe not that far. But I needed a bit of time to process that little conversation of ours."

"I really am sorry, Nick. For all the stupid things I said."

"They weren't stupid."

"Yes, they were. And rude. I should not have said the waterlily thing. I lost control of my mouth."

"That happens to Sagittarians."

"I thought you were never going to speak to me again," Justine said miserably. There was a painful lump in her throat.

"Hey, are you all right?"

"Yeah, I'm . . . no, maybe. Look, I don't know," Justine said. "My head. And now, my throat."

"You're sick?"

"No. I hate being sick. It's boring."

Nick shook his head, indicating that he thought she was being hopeless. "Go inside and get warm. I'll be over in a tick."

"I'm fine," Justine insisted, but Nick was already on his way.

It hadn't been that long since Justine had last seen Nick. It was only a matter of weeks, really. And yet there was something about seeing him at her front door—after this lapse of time—that made her want to speak German. *Unheimlich*. That's what Nick was. He was just like himself, only slightly more himself, as if he were too sharply outlined or all his colors were turned up to supersaturated. *Unheimlich*: unfamiliar in a way that could only make sense if whatever was unfamiliar was also, simultaneously, completely familiar. By God, but the Germans had good words.

Justine smelled the sandalwood scent of Nick's jumper and began to worry that she might do something irrational, like throw herself against the warmth of him, and cry, and confess. About Daniel ticking her off. About the stars. About . . .

"You really look like shit," Nick said.

"Thanks," she managed.

"Have you got any lemons?"

"There might be a very sad one at the bottom of the fruit bowl. Why?"

"You, couch. Right now. I'll be back in a minute."

Justine curled up at one end of the couch, and pulled the throw rug over her. From the kitchen, there came the sound of drawers opening and closing, and cutlery clinking on crockery. At last, Nick emerged to hand Justine two painkillers and a mug that was full of hot yellow liquid that looked like it was sprinkled with some of Lesley-Ann Stone's certified organic dirt. Justine sipped at it experimentally and made a face.

"What the hell?"

"Lemon and honey," Nick said, sitting on the ottoman not far from Justine's feet. "The usual suspects. But also crushed garlic and a sprinkle of cayenne pepper. I know, I know. But it'll make you feel better."

She took another sip, but the foul brew had not improved.

And here, Nick did something strange and nice. He reached out and touched Justine by putting the back of his hand to her forehead. It had the odd effect of making tears rush up underneath Justine's eyeballs.

"Drink that brew. And I mean all of it. Take the tablets, and head off to bed, hey?"

And then he took his hand away.

"I really am sorry, Nick. I hated you being angry with me."

"I'm a stubborn bastard, sometimes. Forget it, now."

But Justine wasn't quite done. "If you love Laura, then there must be many good reasons that you do."

"It's okay, Jus. Really. Forget it."

"Your friendship," she said. "It's one of the oldest of my life. I don't want to lose it."

"Me neither."

Justine knew where the conversation needed to go next. She wasn't relishing this part, but it had to be done. "So, when last we spoke, you were about to make a proposal. I trust it went well?"

"Yeah, I think so," Nick said.

"So, it's all official then? When's the big day?"

Nick gave her a bemused look. "Ah, I think you're jumping the gun a bit there. I understand that what Laura and I have is a kind of pre-engagement agreement. Actual engagement, I'm told, doesn't happen until there's a ring."

"I see," said Justine. "And when does the ring happen?"

"I'm led to believe that this can be a lengthy procedure. A stone must be acquired, designs must be vetted, jewelers must have time to do their thing."

Justine winced. "Sounds expensive."

"It is," Nick said, a little grimly. "Look, I should go. You should sleep. Take care of yourself, okay? If you're still feeling rat-shit tomorrow, give me a call and I'll come over and make you another lemon drink."

"Oh, goodie," Justine said, frowning into the mug.

When Nick was gone Justine took one more sip then tipped the mixture down the sink. In her bedroom, she was met by the disappointing discovery that she'd that morning stripped her bed. The sheets, Doona cover and pillowcases were all bundled up on the laundry floor, but right now the effort of applying fresh linen was beyond her. Likewise, getting into pajamas was a bridge too far. She took her clothes off and dumped them on the floor. Wrapped only in her dressing gown, her teeth chattering from cold, she crawled under the uncovered Doona and flicked her electric blanket on to its highest setting.

As she fell into a restless sleep, Justine knew two things for certain. One was that Laura Mitchell was a very lucky woman. The other was that she quite definitely had a fever.

For the next two days, Justine was too sick to go to work, or even to get out of bed. At lunchtime on the third day, she felt sufficiently improved to eat a little bit of canned soup and transfer her sickbed to the couch. There she remained for the rest of the day, watching episodes of *I Dream of Jeannie*, and phasing in and out of wakefulness.

She was in the shallows of sleep when she was woken by a knock at her apartment door. Opening her eyes, she found that it was just a few minutes before six o'clock. By the time she got to the door, the landing was empty except for a huge bunch of cream-colored roses, their petals tipped with pink. They were wrapped up in shiny white paper and affixed with a note that said: *Sick, huh? That's one hell of a way to avoid me. Hope you're doing okay. DG x*

Justine picked up the roses and put them to her nose, but they were of the kind that didn't smell of anything. She took the bouquet inside, filled a vase with water, and thought. Then she scrolled through the contact list on her phone and selected Daniel's name.

"So," he answered. "You got the flowers."

"I did."

"Do you like them?"

"Thank you. They're really beautiful."

"Why do I get the feeling that a 'but' is coming?"

"Because it is," Justine said.

There was a long silence, in which Justine drew up her courage by reminding herself of how she'd felt on Monday while trying to play Daniel's *work is work* game.

"I'm not going to be able to do this, Daniel."

"*You're* upset with *me*? About the astrology thing?"

"No, it's not that. I was entirely wrong, and you were totally fair. It's the whole thing. I know myself, Daniel, and I just know that I'm not going to be able to share a bed on the weekends and then, come Monday morning, pretend we're nothing more than colleagues. It makes me too uncertain. It . . . well, it hurts."

"But, Justine, it's a workplace. It's not like we can—"

"I don't think you're wrong. About the need to behave like that," Justine said. "It's just that I can't do it. You seem fine with it. But I'm not. I'm a heart-on-my-sleeve kind of girl. I'm sorry."

"And there's nothing I can do to talk you out of this?" he asked.

"I don't think so," Justine said.

"Look, I know the situation's not ideal. It would be better if we didn't work at the same place. It would even be better if we were still . . . just colleagues. And I know that we started out fast. Maybe too fast."

"Definitely too fast," Justine said.

"But it was good, right?"

You had to hand it to him, Justine thought. He had confidence.

"It was," she admitted.

"All right then," Daniel said, though Justine had the distinct impression that it wasn't in relation to what she had just said. "I didn't want to have to do this, but you've left me no option."

Justine went cold. "Do what?"

"Leo's stars arrived. I have the fax right here, and I'm going to read you your stars. Ready? *It is spring, Aquarius, the season of renewal.*"

Justine: *Aquarius? Why is he reading Aquarius to me?*

Brain: *Remember your little chat in his office?*

Justine: *Oh shit.*

Daniel went on, "*Those harboring resentments and anger will do well to allow in the strong cleansing tide of grace and forgiveness. This month brings an expansion of the spirit and a surge of generosity toward all creatures, great and small. Does not everyone deserve a second chance? Or even a third?*"

Justine wondered just how many times one could be hoist by the same petard.

"So," Daniel said, after a moment. "Might that surge of Aquarian generosity extend to me? Might I have a second chance?"

Justine thought for a moment. "Work will still have to be work, though, right?"

"Yes, but just give it some time. Give me a chance to show you that it's doable."

"I don't—"

"You know, I've been reading up a bit, about the stars. And I've learned that Aquarians and Leos are polar opposites on the horoscope. Air needs fire. Fire needs air. So the astrologers say."

"Meaning?"

"Give me another chance at this. How about this weekend?"

The Virgo rising part of Justine might have accurately pointed out that there were many discrepancies in the situation in which she now found herself, and all of them pointed to the need to approach this proposition cautiously. But it was not the Virgo rising part of Justine that was responding. It was the impulsive Sagittarian.

"What did you have in mind?" she said.

cusp

They came for Brown Houdini-Malarky under cover of darkness, those whispering women in their khaki tunics and huge suede gloves. One minute he was asleep on the rags at the back of his pen in the distant back blocks of the adoption area, and the next he was struggling and yapping, being manhandled into a transport crate. His world tilted and swayed as they walked him to the main building. Soon he was tumbled out into a fluorescently lit room and pushed into a small indoor pen, its floor lined with newspaper. The door of the pen swung closed. A bolt was shot home. And Brown knew precisely what all of this meant.

Brown was not alone in the bright room. Lori the poodle, with her mange and her buggered cruciate ligaments, had already been locked in the next-door cell. The door opened again and the women were back with the crate. This time it was Fritz that they brought with them, a dachshund-cross with dodgy bowel control. Crate-load by crate-load, the women filled the upper-level pens: Dumpling the pug, her face a muddle of glaucous eyes and slobbery folds; Esther the geriatric sheep-dog who'd outlived her human and was too old for rehoming. Then the lights went out. The next time they came on, Brown knew, it would be tomorrow, and all five dogs would be ready and waiting for the vet.

Shortly after first light, the doomed dogs were each given a little bowl of diced beef for breakfast. Fritz, the eternal optimist, gulped down his meat. But neither Dumpling nor Lori could stop howling long enough to eat theirs. Esther, thick of waist and devout of temperament, calmly chunked down her final breakfast, and lay quietly with her head on her paws, comforted by the stories she'd been told of an afterlife known as the Rainbow Bridge.

Brown had no stomach for food. Having repeatedly cased the cage, he knew it to be impregnable. Curse that bastard Guy. Curse him and his bitch of a mother and every worm-ridden pup that might ever spring from his distempered loins. Bastard! Brown eked out a small amount of pleasure in this cussing, then wondered if it was the last pleasure of his entire life. With all other options closed to him, Brown lay down at the back of his pen, curled into a ball and drifted into shallow sleep.

The vet came at noon. She was Annabel Barwick, a young woman with a soft helmet of ginger hair and a bright new wedding band on her left hand. Brown, watching her through his one good eye, thought it to her credit that she spoke to them in a tone of affectionate despondency, apologizing to each. Assisting her was vet nurse Jesse Yeo, a young man with stovepipe legs, jet black hair and sensitive eyes rimmed with red.

Brown focused his mind and visualized a laser beam of Voo Dog power issuing from his eye. *The one-eyed dog is not supposed to be here,* he Vooed. *The one-eyed dog must be returned to his pen, unharmed.* But the vet and the nurse were preoccupied and he could catch the eye of neither one of them.

Fritz—bless him—still thought there was a chance for charm to work, so he bounded up to the cage front with an upbeat volley of barks. But this only meant that he was first: the nurse held his little chestnut forepaw while the vet grazed off a bit of fur with the clippers, and drove in the needle. Then little Fritz was in a garbage bag on the floor. Brown watched it all. He watched as Lori was injected, and as her cries for someone called Prudence became incoherent, and stopped. He watched Esther close her eyes and slip away to meet her master.

Brown knew who would be next. But he'd be buggered if he'd go gentle into that good night. Having thoroughly studied the room beyond his pen, Brown knew it to be a total bastard of a place, entirely bereft of nooks and crannies. It had an easy-wash floor covering curving up the base of the walls, and there was hardly any furniture. The door that led to the hallway, and to the world beyond, was closed; the place was sealed.

But here was a piece of luck. Just as Jesse the nurse crouched down at the door of Brown's pen, Annabel the vet took several steps toward the main door and reached for the handle. The timing, Brown realized, was going to be perfection. All he had to do was lunge out of the pen, past Jesse, and bolt for the door. Yes! The vet levered down the handle. The door began to open. It was a narrow opportunity, but wide enough for a street terrier of indefatigable enterprise.

Brown sprang, easily evading Jesse's large, grasping hands. His claws struggled for traction on the slippery floor, but there was no sense leaving any effort on the bench. Pedaling his hind legs like a rabbit's, he scrabbled forth. The door was only slightly ajar, but he'd get his head through it, he was sure. And then he'd be gone. Down the hall, out the door. And away!

"Little bugger," Jesse muttered. "Annabel! Shut the door!"

Slam. The latch slid home. The heavy white door was flush with the wall. And Brown was on the wrong side of it. Of course, he ran, leading Annabel and Jesse in a merry dance, once, twice, thrice around the room. But it was hopeless. Soon he was cornered. Jesse lifted him by the scruff of the neck. And now Brown was aloft, squirming and arching and snarling as the nurse carried him toward the table. Meanwhile the vet was drawing green fluid into a syringe.

Fifteen-year-old Luke Foster—Libra, wintertime center half-forward for the Aussie Rules team, summertime wicketkeeper for the cricket squad, habitual smoother of an embarrassing front-and-center cowlick, and die-hard fan of the (original) *Star Wars* movies—reached into the glove compartment of his mother's Saab, drew out an aloe-vera-infused tissue and handed it to her. It was Friday morning and they were parked a few blocks away from the public school that would, as of today, be his alma mater.

He had left St. Gregory's a day ahead of schedule, without any fanfare or farewell. No part of him had wanted to suffer under the pitying glances of boys whose parents were doctors or old money or business owners or abalone divers, and who had financed their sons' education with actual cash money rather than an imaginary inheritance. His private school mates would continue on their blazered, boatered, red-and-blue-necktied way to Head of the River rowing successes, private cello or euphonium lessons, and places at Group of Eight universities. And he would not. He would have to find his way to his destiny in a yellow polo shirt.

"I'm so sorry," sobbed his mother, Mariangela. "Oh, Lukey, we wanted the best for you. We really did."

In the two years that Luke had been at St. Gregory's, he'd never troubled himself with even the idlest curiosity about how his parents could afford the fees. He and his younger brothers, both of whom were still in primary school and safely out of this whole mess, had had their names put down for the exclusive boys' high school before they were even out of diapers, and perhaps this was one of the things that had made him believe that his parents had some kind of plan for paying the fees. And although he'd never really thought about it, if he *had*, he would have thought they'd have a better, more watertight plan than maxing out the credit card and waiting for his grandfather to die. Especially since, now that his grandfather *had* died, all he'd left to Luke's mother was her own mother's wedding ring, some ugly rosewood furniture and an out-of-tune piano.

Part of Luke wanted to ask his mother what the hell she'd been thinking. Why hadn't she just sent him to the local public high school from the start? Today, as he walked into an unfamiliar classroom in his too-clean, too-new, too-stiff yellow polo shirt, the gossip would already be doing the rounds. *That's the kid who got taken away from St. Gregory's.*

Another part of Luke—the part that hated to see his mother with her eyes bloodshot and her nose swollen—wanted to take Mariangela's hand and stroke it, to tell her that everything was all going to be all right, that he'd never really loved St. Gregory's that much; that now she could turn up at school pickup in her Ugg boots and a black puffer jacket instead of designer office wear or yummy mummy gym getup; that the local public school had something that St. Gregory's never would have. Girls. That would make her laugh.

"You going to be all right today, Lukey?" Mariangela asked.

"Course."

Luke pulled down the Saab's sun visor, slid open the little door that hid the vanity mirror and smoothed his cowlick down flat. But, of course, it only sprang back as he juggled himself and his backpack out into the street.

"Bye, Mum," he said.

"Bye, darling," she said, and blew him a miserable, weepy kiss.

"Have a good day," he said.

"I'll try," she sniffled.

In an eerily accurate Yoda voice, Luke said, "Do, or do not. There is no try."

+

Patricia O'Hare—Virgo, career homemaker turned empty nester, mother to adult daughters Larissa and Zadie, grandmother-in-waiting, stock market genius and baker of the lightest passionfruit sponges known to humanity—volunteered each Friday at the Dogs Home. This was just one of the many activities that Patricia had taken up in order to keep herself busy now that her girls were largely independent. Although she had her share portfolio to manage, and much knitting to do now that Zadie was expecting, these pursuits were hardly enough to keep an efficient woman like Patricia away from the slippery slopes of *Dr. Phil* at lunchtime and chardonnay at 4 p.m.

Patricia discovered the Dogs Home when she went there, after a period of mourning for Bonnie the blue heeler, to choose herself a new dog. On her very first visit, as she walked the aisles of pens, she came upon a liver-and-white greyhound sitting demurely on her narrow haunches at the front of the cage, striking a pose that put Patricia in mind of a 1920s showgirl sitting beside her suitcase and waiting for a lift. The dog looked at Patricia as if to say, "Oh, there you are at last." And a good match it had turned out to be, too, with both woman and dog sharing an air of inherent respectability, a love of comfortable couches and appreciation of good grooming.

On her first few Fridays as a volunteer, Patricia walked dogs. With Alsatians, huskies, vizslas, Shelties and shih tzus, she trod the well-worn tracks that traced through the remnant bushlands around the Dogs Home. She had a lovely new sun hat, purpose bought, as well as a pair of new running shoes in a spunky, youthful color scheme. She found the days less enjoyable when it was her turn to shovel dog poo out of pens, but Patricia was under no illusion—if the service were not in some way unpleasant or inconvenient, everyone would be doing it.

It didn't take long, however, for the Dogs Home administration to realize that Patricia had skills that made her invaluable in the office. Within two months of starting out as a volunteer, she was triaging the mail, proofreading the newsletter, doing the banking and coordinating the volunteer database.

Every few months, however, Patricia would wake up and realize that it was not just a Friday, but one of *those* Fridays, and she would wish that she were going anywhere else that day but the Dogs Home. Those Fridays were the ones on which that lovely young vet, Annabel Barwick, cleared the diary at her own inner-city practice and drove out to the Dogs Home for a grim morning of pro bono work.

While Annabel did her work in the surgery down the corridor, Patricia stayed in the office, trying as hard as she could not to think about the contents of the heavy-duty plastic bags that would later that day be slung into the tray of a council ute.

By midmorning on this particular terrible Friday, Patricia's waste-paper basket was overflowing with used tissues. She'd loved that old sheepdog, Esther. She would have taken the dear old girl home with her, if it weren't for the fact that she'd promised Neil that she wouldn't bring home every lost cause that tugged at her heartstrings.

Patricia plucked another tissue from the box and removed the thick rubber band from around the middle of the day's stack of mail. She noticed the letter immediately. It was large and fat, and the envelope was of thick and expensive-looking paper stock: not at all the sort of letter that was usually received by the Dogs Home. It came, she saw, from the venerable law firm Walker, Wicks and Clitheroe.

The first thing Patricia noticed when she opened the letter was that the rather regal signature at the bottom of the page was that of Don Clitheroe himself. Whatever this letter had to say, she reasoned, it must be important. She pushed her glasses higher on her nose and read on. It seemed that a client of Clitheroe's, a gentleman named Len Magellan, had recently died and bequeathed his entire estate to the Dogs Home. His instructions were to liquidate all his assets so that the Dogs Home might have access to the capital in the most immediately useful form. The amount that might be expected to be garnered from the sale of Mr. Magellan's assets was in the vicinity of . . .

"Squeeeeeeeeeeeeeeeee!"

Patricia's scream filled the reception area like a siren. It spread down the corridor, through the tearoom and the toilets, finally penetrating the surgery where Annabel had just drawn up a measure of Lethabarb to be plunged into the leg of a scruffy, one-eyed terrier. The scream left the building to set off the entire canine population of the Dogs Home into a cacophony of barking, yapping, yowling and howling, amid which Patricia stood up and performed some motions that were perhaps distantly related to those of a rain dance. Then her eyes went wide, and she set off at a run down the corridor in her bright-colored sneakers.

"Annabel! Annabel! Annabel!" she yelled. "Stop! Stop! Stop! Don't do any more!"

But Annabel Barwick and Jesse Yeo had already stopped, and were peering nervously out of the surgery door, prompted by the scream to wonder if a gunman, or similar, was on the loose in the Dogs Home. Instead they saw a bright-eyed and tearful Patricia O'Hare coming down the hallway brandishing the sheet of creamy-white paper that would mean the Dogs Home could afford to give Brown Houdini-Malarky— now panting in relieved reprieve on the newspapered floor of his pen— another chance at life.

+

Fifteen-year-old Phoebe Wintergreen—Leo, serial though reluctant favorite of classroom teachers, drinker of lime milkshakes, only child and omnivorous consumer of books, lover of Shakespeare and impassioned bathroom-mirror performer of grand soliloquies—was angry. She'd been angry all afternoon. She'd been angry in maths, where she'd solved quadratic equations with sufficient violence to break three leads in her mechanical pencil, and also in PE, where she'd thrown herself into interval training with the red-faced vigor of a boxer preparing for the revenge bout of their career. She'd turned up to her after-school music lesson flushed and fuming, and attacked her warm-up scales as if her cheap, borrowed saxophone were in fact a dangerous, inflexible snake that she must wrestle into submission.

Phoebe was angry all the tiring way up the steps of the highway overpass, and angry all the way down the other side, her book-filled backpack jouncing painfully on her spine and her sax case knocking against the side of her knee. She was angry as she climbed over the low, broken gate at the front of the ugly, rented brick bungalow where she lived. The cloud of rage that hung almost visibly about Phoebe's form was enough to send Tiggy the cat streaking away to a safe place under a hydrangea bush. Oh, yes, Phoebe Wintergreen was angry.

Alice Wintergreen—Gemini, Woolworths night-shift shelf packer and workplace union organizer, youthful single mother and television cooking show addict—was not angry. She was tired, but only in the way that the bodies of shift workers learn, almost, to accommodate. And she was a little fretful—about the electricity bill, about the suffering of the displaced people on the television news, about the rising price of groceries, about the erratic behavior of the increasingly demented Mr. Spotswood from next door, about global warming and the cost of Phoebe's saxophone lessons and the broken seat belt in the car—but here again, it was only in a way that was now so familiar to her that it was hardly worth remarking upon. Baking helped, and right now Alice was making a batch of candied chili and double chocolate cookies. She was chopping the chocolate and monitoring the finely sliced chilies that simmered in a sugary syrup on the stove, when she heard the front door being wrenched open, then slammed closed.

"Enter, stage left," she whispered to herself, just before her daughter swept in.

"I hate him," Phoebe wailed. She dropped her saxophone case to the floor and flung off her backpack.

"Hello, love," said Alice.

"I hate him! I hate him more than any person, living or dead, has ever hated anybody. In the entire history of hatred, there has been no hatred as great and terrible as mine for that cream-faced loon!"

"Tea?" said Alice.

"I despise him. I loathe, detest, despise, abhor, and . . . um . . . *abominate* him. You should see how he reads Shakespeare. Thinks he's so clever, but he wouldn't know an iambic pentameter if it crawled up between his buttocks and died there. He doesn't even deserve to *live.*"

"Who's this?"

"Luke . . . *Foster,*" Phoebe spat. "That's who."

"Who's he?"

"New boy."

"At this time of year?"

"His parents couldn't afford St. Gregory's anymore, so they pulled him out and inflicted his moronic presence on us. On me! I ask you, I ask the universe: What is it about me that makes whatever deity that sits on high believe that I deserve suffering of this magnitude? For what sin, I ask you, am I being forced to share a drama class with such an ill-favored bolting-hutch of beastliness. Such a swollen parcel of dropsies, a huge bombard of sack, a stuffed cloak-bag of guts . . ."

"What's that from?"

"*Henry IV, Part One,*" Phoebe said in an aside, then continued: "I curse him. And I not only curse him, but his sire and his dam to boot. I curse every single one of his forebears whose lustful stupidity landed this whoreson obscene greasy tallow-catch in *my* drama class! I hope redback spiders lay their hatchlings in his scrotum! I hope he gets a rare and disgusting skin disease that means he has to stay at home and never, ever—"

"I wish you wouldn't check yourself out in the mirror while you're ranting," Alice said.

"What? There isn't even a mirror in here!"

"Honey, I'm not blind. I can see you admiring yourself in this."

Alice tapped a floury knuckle on the dark-glass door of the microwave, leaving a smear like a quotation mark. "It ruins your performance, love. Always did. Even when you were three."

"Mu-u-um. This is *serious*. He ruined my drama exam! Ruined it! And now I'm going to fail. And when I do, it will be entirely because of that loathsome, shriveled dugong's pizzle and his iPhone."

"I thought it was only the internal exam."

"How is that relevant? It's my best subject! I mean, who on earth has 'Bad to the Bone' for a ringtone who is not concurrently a total . . . carbuncle!"

"Hang on. You hate this Luke . . . because his phone rang in the middle of your drama exam?"

"He spoiled her. My beautiful Juliet. You know how hard I've worked! I'd just got to *and shrieks like mandrakes torn out of the earth*, so I was just really winding into it, and then—da da da da *da*, there's this blast of George-arsehole-Thorogood. I completely lost concentration and I just couldn't get it back again."

"Oh, Phoebs," Alice said. "I'm sorry, love."

Under the light touch of her mother's sympathy, Phoebe deflated like an unknotted balloon. She subsided into a chair and her upper body capsized onto the kitchen table. Her light brown curls spread out over the tablecloth.

"I will hate him for*ever*," she said.

And that was when the doorbell rang.

"Oh God," Phoebe said, rolling her eyes. "That'll be Mr. Spotswood, won't it?"

"Probably," said Alice, with a tight smile.

"How many times today?"

"Three already."

"I suppose you want me to get it," Phoebe said.

"Would you? Please?"

"O-*kay*," she said, and hauled herself back onto her feet.

In the years that their elderly neighbor, Mr. Spotswood, had been losing his memory, Phoebe had learned a thing or two about how best to accommodate him in conversation. If Mr. Spotswood confided that he was planning, once again, to vote for Robert Menzies, Phoebe would tell him she was certain this was a good decision. And if Mr. Spotswood remarked upon his surprise that he'd just this day turned on his television set to discover the pictures now appeared in color, Phoebe would simply agree that these new advances in technology were amazing. On her way to the door, Phoebe limbered up her mind in readiness for improvisation. When she opened the door, however, what she saw was not Mr. Spotswood, but Luke Foster.

Phoebe gave a slight shake of her head, as if to displace the obvious hallucination that there was, on her doorstop, a teenage boy with thick, devilish eyebrows and a serious cowlick in the middle of his forehead.

"I, um, asked Maddie where you lived," Luke said, holding out a tall, white milkshake cup bearing the logo of a fancy boutique cafe that Phoebe had heard of but never been to.

Getting no response from the stunned Phoebe, he continued on hurriedly, "She said you liked milkshakes. It's lime-flavored. I hope she wasn't taking the piss."

He tilted the cup slightly, by way of invitation to take it. But Phoebe only continued to blink, unable to get any words to flow mouthward from her racing, cluttered brain.

"It's an apology," Luke said. "For today. I'm so sorry for being such a fuckwit. And not only because you were so angry about it, but because your monologue was the only thing worth listening to all day. You're really talented."

There was no great distance between the front door of the Wintergreen residence and the 1970s electric stove in the kitchen, where Alice Wintergreen stood stirring her candied chillies. So Alice heard most of what passed between Phoebe and Luke. She heard Luke tell Phoebe that *Romeo and Juliet* was going to be performed at the Botanic Gardens in the summer, and that he would get her a ticket, if she liked, as a proper apology, and she heard Phoebe make a stuttering acceptance speech. When Tiggy announced her presence on the kitchen windowsill with a gossipy meow that might almost have said,

You'll never guess who's showed up at the front door, Alice gave the cat a Cheshire-sized grin.

"I do believe, Miss Tiggy," said Alice, changing the direction of her stirring to counterclockwise, "that our girl will henceforth be in need of a good countercurse. Don't you agree?"

scorpio

OCTOBER 23–NOVEMBER 21

When Halloween arrives each year, with the bones of the pagan festival of Samhain still visible through its ragged cloak, it prepares the people of the northern hemisphere to hunker down for the life-and-death test that is winter, and reminds them to make their peace with the dead. But in the southern hemisphere, where Halloween comes just before the start of the cricket season, at a time of year when sunscreen sales are on the up, the night of the dead is really just an opportunity to break out an outrageous costume and concoct brightly colored alcoholic beverages.

For the staff at the *Alexandria Park Star*, Halloween was a big event because the advertising manager, Barbel Weiss, always threw a party—a big party. During her childhood, Barbel's nomadic European parents had settled for a time in Minnesota, where young Barbel had loved the annual festival of pumpkin carving, costumes, scary stories and trick-or-treating. So each October 31, she and her wife, Iris, hosted a Halloween party at their Austinmer Street home, and invited a large circle of friends and colleagues. Year by year, the party's reputation had grown, and the guests took their costumes seriously.

Justine's preparations had involved buying a children's bow and arrow set from a toy shop and digging out from her suitcase of travel memorabilia a Statue of Liberty headdress made of mint green foam. She had dipped the starry headdress into PVC glue and then pressed it into a baking tray spread with silver glitter.

That year, Halloween fell on a Tuesday, and at five o'clock Justine was making her way along Rennie Street in the direction of home, talking to best-pal Tara on the phone.

"Well, it's nice," Justine said.

They were discussing Daniel. More specifically, they were discussing dating Daniel, which Justine had been doing over the past few weeks.

"Nice?" Tara repeated. "Any advance on that?"

"I think I'd be prepared to go so far as 'very nice.'"

Drawing level with the windows of a real estate agency, Justine halted. A large poster in the front window described a bay-windowed mansion as being in a "highly sort-after address." Cradling her phone against her shoulder, she reached into her bag and pulled out her Sharpie. The pen made a squeaking sound as she wrote, straight onto the window glass: *I think you may mean "sought-after."*

"According to every bit of press gallery gossip I've ever heard," Tara continued, oblivious to the fact that the world was, even as she spoke, being saved from homonymic spelling crime, "Daniel Griffin is entirely gorgeous. Also charming, smart, good at his job, funny and totally ripped. You, yourself, said the sex was good. But now you're only drinking expensive wine with him and snogging on the doorstep at the end of a date? I don't understand that. What's really going on, here?"

Justine sighed. "It's such a weird situation. When we're together away from work, we have a really nice time, but then something comes up, like this party tonight. Everyone we work with will be there, so we'll pretend nothing's going on. It makes me really uncomfortable. I suppose there are reasons that it's not considered world's best practice to shag one's workmates."

"Oh, come on," Tara said. "Everybody does it. Everybody's been doing it for as long as everybody's been . . . doing it. I suppose the real question is: why don't you *want* to do it?"

This was a good question.

One night, Daniel had taken her to dinner at Cornucopia (where she had been gratified to see that the fettuccine on the menu now had its full complement of "t"s and "c"s), and she had thought that this was quite lavish enough. But he had surprised her by paying the bill at the end of the main course and taking her to Raspberry Fool for dessert wine and cheesecake. Then he'd commandeered a water taxi to take them on a longer-than-necessary ride on the river that eventually landed them at Clockwork, where they had coffee and chocolate. Daniel hadn't let Justine pay for a thing, not even the coffees, and she knew that the whole night must have cost a bomb.

On a Sunday, he'd driven her out to a seaside vineyard for lunch. The grapevines were greening up nicely, and the whole place smelled sweetly of springtime grass. Daniel and Justine drank a different wine with every course, and spent a few hours after lunch lying on beanbags under shade sails in a sea breeze that was neither too hot nor too cold, too strong nor too flimsy. It was, all of it, just right.

Even so, Justine couldn't shake the feeling that she'd been on the same date numerous times. Each time the food was lovely, the wine was the very best, the conversation was entertaining and Daniel was entirely chivalrous. There was nothing, absolutely nothing, not to like.

"It's hard to explain," Justine said weakly.

"Try," said Tara.

"I feel like there's something missing."

"What?" Tara pressed.

Justine: *What am I trying to say, exactly?*

Brain: *Sorry. No clues up here.*

"Maybe . . ." Justine began. "Maybe I don't know because the thing that's missing is something I've never had before. It might not even exist, for all I know."

Justine heard Tara sigh heavily. "Not content with having Daniel Griffin's affections on a platter, my best pal wants a freaking unicorn to boot."

♏

When Justine's grandmother died, she had left nothing to chance; her will had gone on for pages, and pages, and pages. To Justine, she bequeathed a lovely selection of earrings and pendants, bracelets, rings and items of impossibly fragile Belleek china. But far more than any of these, Justine valued the two other things she'd inherited from Fleur Carmichael, and those were: a wardrobe full of vintage clothes and a petite figure that enabled her to wear them.

Although a very well-dressed woman, Fleur had not believed in fashion, or in buying garments that would last only a season. She had always bought good-quality clothes and expected them to do her a life-time. This was why she had never thrown out her 1960s embroidered gingham sundresses, tailored coats and evening dresses, or her high-waisted pants or Liberty print blouses. Justine liked wearing these clothes, not only because of the way they looked, but also because it felt like carrying around a part of her grandmother with her.

For Barbel's Halloween party, Justine had decided to wear a gar-ment of her grandmother's that she'd never before had the opportunity to take out for a spin: a narrow knee-length dress in sparkling silver Lurex. It was a little scratchy against the skin, but for tonight's pur-poses it was perfect. And it seemed especially appropriate to be wear-ing one of her grandmother's dresses tonight, since October 31 had been Fleur's birthday. Had she still been alive, she'd have been notch-ing up eighty-eight years.

The silver dress was laid out on Justine's bed, along with silver tights, silver ankle boots and the newly silvered Statue of Liberty head-dress, and in the bathroom was a shopping bag full of all the other things Justine needed to complete her look.

First, she painted her face a matte silver and applied highlights of glitter on her lips, cheeks and brow. She fixed stick-on stars in haphaz-ard constellations at the corners of her eyes. Next, she sprayed her hair silver and scattered a palm-full of glitter over her head before the spray dried out, all the while pondering the reality that there would most likely be glitter on her bathroom floor and all over the vanity unit for years to come. She had just put on her clothes and fixed the headdress in place, when she heard her phone announce an incoming message.

It was from Nick. *Are you home?*

With glittery fingers, Justine tapped back a message: *Somewhat.*

Nick: *How can you be somewhat at home?*

Justine: *I mean that it's somewhat me.*

Nick: *Mysterious. Can you come out to the balcony?*

Justine looked in the mirror at her painted face. Nick had to call her . . . *now*? This was a classic case of Murphy's law if there ever was one.

"Murphy," she whispered, "you truly are an arsehole."

Over on his balcony, Nick was looking perfectly normal in jeans and a T-shirt. Justine cloaked her be-silvered awkwardness by being excessively awkward. That is, she struck a gawky *ta da* kind of pose.

Nick raised his eyebrows. "In honor of Halloween, I take it?"

"Twinkle, twinkle."

"So, you're . . . a star?"

"Almost."

Justine went inside and came back with her bow and arrow set.

Nick scrunched his eyebrows together before the lightbulb moment hit. "A shooting star. Even better. Hey, have you got any Tabasco sauce?"

"Bloody Marys, huh?"

Nick nodded. "It is Halloween."

"Hang on."

Justine found a bottle of Tabasco at the back of her fridge and sent it in the basket over to Nick's side of the gap.

"I could make a Bloody Mary for you?" Nick suggested.

"I think I'll be pretty well catered for where I'm going, actually."

"Which is?"

"A party. I have a colleague who is very into Halloween," Justine said. "What about you? You're not trick-or-treating?"

"We were going to a thing. But Laura's away, and there was a mix-up with her plane booking and now she's not going to make it home until tomorrow. I could go on my own, I suppose, but I wouldn't really know anyone. So, alas, my fabulous costume will have to remain unseen."

That gave Justine an idea, one that got out of her mouth before she had taken the time to fully consider its ramifications.

"Unless, of course, you were to come to the party with me?"

♏

At Austinmer Street, Justine and Nick were met by Gloria, who'd been brought out of storage and propped up by the mailbox. She was a full-sized skeleton, and this year she was accessorized with a tatty blonde wig and a red rose between her teeth. In the back courtyard, Barbel approached with a tray of cocktail glasses. Her normally smooth platinum blonde hair was teased out into a fright and streaked with purple and green, and her Day of the Dead makeup was immaculate.

"Oh, my," she said, "if it isn't a little shooting star! You look gorgeous, sweetheart. And this is?"

Justine introduced Nick to Barbel, who looked him up and down, frowning. "Blue. Very blue. But you might need to explain."

Nick was indeed blue. He wore a sleek blue wig, a deep blue shirt spotted with tiny silver stars, and his face and neck were covered in swirls of blue body paint. When he turned around and bent over a little, it was evident that he had cut two ovals out of the seat of his pants, one for each buttock. Each visible bum cheek was painted blue. Barbel threw back her wild head of hair and laughed hysterically.

"A blue moon! I love it! Now, a cocktail?"

Half the drinks on her tray were black and smelled strongly of aniseed, and the other half were a sunrise of yellow through orange with a small plastic eyeball floating in red syrup at the top.

"Sting in the Tail?" Barbel asked, pointing. "Or Zombie Apocalypse?"

Justine chose the Sting in the Tail; Nick the Zombie Apocalypse.

"I'm so glad you could come," Barbel said. "Make yourselves at home, won't you?"

Justine saw that Radoslaw was there, and Anwen, too. Jeremy and his husband, Graeme, were sitting together on a love seat in their matching cowboy outfits, and Glynn was standing at the outdoor barbecue wearing a rubber apron with internal body parts mapped out in relief. It made him look as if he'd been in the middle of his own autopsy before being asked to flip the halloumi.

Justine and Nick were several drinks into the celebration by the time Daniel arrived. He was wearing a suit and tie, and to Justine's eye the only thing about him that looked unusual was that his thick hair was sharply parted and slicked back with some kind of product. But as he approached, she could see that there was a small metal badge on the lapel of his suit jacket. 007.

"Ah," Justine said, understanding. She raised her glass to him. "Greetings, Mr. Bond. Nick, this is Daniel Griffin, editor of the *Star*. Daniel, you remember my friend Nick? Nick Jordan."

"The last time I saw you, you were Romeo," said Daniel. "I have to say you look a little different . . . blue."

There followed an explication of Nick's costume, and Justine's, during which Daniel reached over to adjust a strand of Justine's silver hair. This was a breach, albeit very slight, of the "work is work" agreement, and Justine wondered whether it had been truly absentminded or whether Daniel had been making a point to Nick.

"You'd know Nick's girlfriend, too," Justine said. "Or should I say, fiancée? At least, you'd have seen her."

Daniel looked unconvinced. "I would?"

"She's a model. The one in the Waterlily advertisement."

Justine observed the disbelieving up and down look that Daniel gave Nick, the one that clearly said: *How does a guy like you get a woman like that?*

"So, you're the new editor?" Nick said.

"Yeah. Since August. We've had a lot of changes at the *Star* this year. Probably more than in the magazine's whole twenty-five years."

"Leo predicted it, of course," Nick said, in that self-mocking way that also contained a degree of seriousness.

Brain: *Uh-oh.*

"Leo Thornbury?" Daniel said. "Our eminent stargazer?"

"Yeah, he called it earlier in the year," Nick said. "Justine admits it now, that he was right, but she didn't believe it at the time."

"She didn't? But she takes such a keen interest in the stars." And with this, Daniel gave Justine a gentle nudge: the evening's second breach of the "work is work" policy.

Nick made an expression of incredulity. "Interest in the stars? Justine? This Justine?"

Brain: *Danger! Danger! Avert conversational trajectory! Now!*

Justine said, "Are either of you hungry?"

But neither Nick, nor Daniel, appeared to hear her.

"You know, it took me the longest time to figure out Justine's star sign," Daniel said. "But I got there eventually."

"Really?" Nick asked. "I'd have thought she was just about a perfect type. You know—curious about everything. Never sitting still. Honest." He raised his eyebrows at her. "To a fault, sometimes."

Justine: *Fuck, fuck, fuck, fuck. In a minute, someone is going to say Aquarius, or Sagittarius, for that matter. And then I'm totally fucked.*

Brain: *You're going to have to do a better job at distracting them.*

Justine: *How?*

Brain: *Just say something!*

"*Erklärungsnot!*" said Justine loudly.

"What?" said Nick.

"Do you need a tissue?" Daniel asked.

"No, no. I was just thinking, the other day, you know, about those great German words that have no translation."

"And what was that one?" Nick asked, his eyes looking extra bewildered inside their rims of blue paint.

"*Erklärungsnot.* It means something like 'explanation emergency.' Like when you've got caught out lying, and you don't know how you're going to get out of it."

"O . . . kay," Nick said, and took a long sip of his Zombie Apocalypse.

"What's your cocktail like?" Daniel asked, nodding toward Nick's drink and swirling around the black dregs of his own.

"Totally foul, but very alcoholic," Nick admitted.

"Same," said Daniel.

Nick said, "Would you rather have some wine? I know I would. I saw some inside."

"Please," said Daniel.

"Justine?" Nick asked.

"I'm okay," said Justine, wishing her pulse would slow down. She had slipped out from under the prongs of a closing portcullis. But only just. And Nick's words were echoing in her mind.

Honest. To a fault.

♏

Leo Thornbury—Sagittarius, octogenarian, stargazer and famously reclusive astrologer, best friend to an elderly Portuguese water dog called Venus, beachcomber and habitual drinker of a refreshing four o'clock Tom Collins—made only one concession to the fact that it was Halloween. Instead of making his daily cocktail with Bombay Sapphire, he dipped in to his supply of special-occasion gin, which was distilled in the Black Forest region of Germany, and cost a fortune to have freighted to his extremely remote address.

Leo had lived these last twenty years far from the madding crowd on an island off an island, which was itself, technically speaking, off an island. He chose the location for the clarity of its air and the blackness of its night sky, and he'd had built for himself a house whose centerpiece was an octagonal pavilion with a glass ceiling. Leo's large, bespoke desk was also octagonal, and it was placed so that its midpoint perfectly aligned with that of the ceiling. The desk was topped with midnight-blue leather and also with a fine dusting of the white beach sand that seemed to get into everything, here at the seaside edge of the world.

The sun had set and the sky above Leo's octagonal ceiling was darkening its canvas in readiness for the night. Leo threaded a sheet of paper into his Remington typewriter. *Aries*, he typed. Then he sat back in his leather chair, pressed the knuckles of one hand against his lips, and thought. Surrounding his typewriter were several astrological ephemerides, both open and closed, a number of star maps, rolled and unrolled, well-thumbed reference books, handwritten notes, various drafting dividers and compasses, rulers and #2 pencils.

It was something of a chore, these days, to magic up the horoscopes for the *Alexandria Park Star*, month in, month out. Sometimes Leo idly muttered to himself that he wondered why he did it. But, in truth, he knew. He wrote for the *Star* because he was an admirer of Jeremy Byrne's, and also because Jem was a shameless and highly effective flatterer. It was hard to imagine that young Jem was now of retirement age.

Leo had, for a time, provided his astrological services to Jem's mother, Winifred, a flamboyant Leo, with Aries rising. She had been quite a woman, Leo remembered, and found himself needing to mop

a sudden sheen of sweat on his brow. After tucking away his handkerchief, Leo set his fingers to the typewriter keys. He crafted a paragraph
of prediction and advice for Aries, Taurus, Gemini, Cancer, Leo, Virgo
and Libra. By the time he completed Scorpio, darkness had arrived in
its fullness. Glancing upward, Leo was gratified to see a night sky copi-
ously freckled with silver. Like this, by starlight, was Leo's favorite way
to write his horoscopes, though it must be admitted that he also had
help from the low, pearly light that shone from a small electric lamp on
his desktop.

Sagittarius, Leo typed. By reflex, he consulted the handwritten
notes that he had earlier compiled. But in truth, he had no need to do
so. He knew their troubling contents only too well.

"Come on, Leo," he encouraged himself, and set his fingers to the
typewriter keys.

But still, deep inside himself, he balked. He never particularly liked
writing the horoscope for his own sign, but this night he wanted to do
it even less than usual. He stared at the word *Sagittarius* until it started
to lose its meaning. Then, with a heavy sigh, he scrolled down and left
a blank space on the page. He would have to come back to it later. For
now, he would go on to Capricorn.

So Leo completed the horoscope for the goat people, and then
found himself at Aquarius. He took off his spectacles, rubbed his eyes,
replaced his spectacles and hunted about his desk for the right scrap of
paper.

"Aquarius, Aquarius," he mumbled. "Where are you, my little water
bearers? Ah. There you are."

Leo read over his notes, and thought for a time, his brow furrowed
in concentration. He was fond of Aquarians, those free spirits, those
passionate doers. They were not, perhaps, as emotionally evolved as Pi-
sceans; Aquarians, in Leo's experience, tended toward odd blind spots
when it came to love and even friendship. But who could fail to enjoy
their courage and original thinking? Jules Verne had been an Aquarian, and Virginia Woolf, too. Thomas Edison, Lord Byron, Mozart and
Lewis Carroll. Charles Darwin—now, there was an Aquarian for you.

*Aquarius: "It's a rare gift," wrote Ursula K. Le Guin, "to know where
you need to be, before you've been to all the places you don't need to be."*

And though few of us possess this rare gift, there is no need, Aquarius, to search quite so hard as you have been in the fruitless corners of your reality. This month's stars urge you to stop seeking, but instead to simply see. To stop weaving, and learn what pattern might appear of its own accord.

Leo finished typing and looked back over his words with some satisfaction.

"Yes," he whispered to himself. "Yes, that is right."

Without strain, Leo completed his horoscope for Pisces. Then he scrolled the paper in his typewriter back up to the blank space he had left beside the word *Sagittarius*. But before Leo even began to summon his courage, he caught sight of the brown and imploring eyes of Venus. Though she lay quite still on the floor, her body was tightly sprung, her muscles poised to respond to the slightest word or gesture that might herald a walk on the beach.

"One more sign to go," Leo told her. "Just the archers, my girl. And then I'll be done."

Venus made a small noise of protest, somewhere between a yawn and a whimper, and Leo's resolve melted to nothingness.

"My girl," Leo said, "my dear old girl. As you well know, I can deny you nothing. Come on, then. Let's go."

Venus was on her feet in half a heartbeat, and they set off, out through the glass doors of the pavilion and into the salt-smelling night. The rickety old dog led the way along a well-worn path in the light of a full moon night. As bracken gave way to dune grass, Leo's ears tuned in to the rhythmic lift and collapse of the waves, and the moment the pair reached the edge of the white sand, Venus dashed into the water. This was her element, and the years fell away from her aching limbs. She gave a joyful doggy smile that showed off the worn and stumpy teeth that studded her bottom jaw.

Leo looked up to the stars. The beautiful stars. The divine stars. But troubling stars, too. *Something is coming to an end for you, Sagittarius,* the heavens whispered to Leo, and he knew that when he returned to his desk to complete his horoscope for Sagittarius, those were the words that he ought to type out, there in the blank space he had left on his page. *Something is coming to an end.*

Perhaps, Leo thought hopefully, it was nothing more than his eighty-second year that was reaching its conclusion. But, no. He knew better. He looked to his dog, who stood in the shallows, lime-bright fronds of phosphorescence making whorls around her legs. *But please,* he wished in the general direction of the stars, *not Venus. Not yet.*

Venus's canine senses registered Leo's sudden onset of sadness like a drop in barometric pressure, and she came trotting out of the water toward him to investigate. Perhaps it was the clown in her that made her decide to shake, flinging a fine shower of water and sand over Leo's legs. He laughed, and she widened her doggy grin, and the old man lowered himself down to the sand and sat beside her, scratching her damp ears.

Something is coming to an end, he thought again.

"Well, I'm not going to write those words," he told her, and she tilted her head to listen. "I won't."

♏

On the stroke of midnight, on the night of Halloween, a shooting star and a blue moon were making their way through Alexandria Park. The shooting star walked barefoot and carried a pair of silver ankle boots over her shoulder by their laces, while the blue moon appeared to be melting a little in the uncommonly warm night air. Both of them were carrying toffee apples—purchased from some costumed street vendors who'd set up a late-night Halloween food stall near the main junction of the park's many paths—and from time to time, they took sticky bites as they walked.

Although he was sweating beneath his body paint, and although toffee apples can be frustrating things to bite into, Nick Jordan knew that he was inside a moment that he was likely to remember. He had learned to recognize these moments: the ones in which time seemed to slow and his senses became acute, in which he wasn't wanting anything or rushing anywhere, or thinking forward or backward. He was simply in the moment, and the moment was good. This had something to do with the warm wind that was blowing through the park, and something to do with the zydeco music from the buskers in the bandstand, and quite a bit to do with Justine. In a truly perfect world, he realized, what he would do right now would be to take her hand.

"So, what's the story with you and Daniel?" Nick asked.

"Oh. You noticed."

"Maybe. But I can't say I'm entirely sure that I know what I was noticing," Nick said. Why, Nick wondered, had Daniel seemed so put out that Nick and Justine were leaving the party together? And, if it pissed him off so much, why hadn't Daniel offered to walk Justine home himself? "So, you two are . . . what? Together? Flirting? Over? It was hard to tell."

Justine laughed. "I don't know what we are."

"But, are you dating?" Nick pressed.

Justine's eyebrows hunched down low over her eyes. "Sort of. How can I put this? I like Daniel, but every time we go out, I find myself wondering if he's just a little bit too caviar and roses for me."

"Because you're what?"

"I think I'm a bit more Vegemite and dandelions," Justine said. "He's like a proper grown-up, and I'm . . . not."

Nick laughed. "I know what you mean. You and me, we're just a pair of Edenvale kids at heart, really."

"I missed you a lot, you know," she said. "After you left Edenvale."

"I missed you too," he said.

"You know, I've been wanting to ask you something. Do you remember that time? That Australia Day weekend? In South Australia?"

Justine kept walking while she said this, and Nick noticed how she kept her gaze on the ground, as if what she was doing was less risky that way.

"I was beginning to think we were never going to talk about that," he said. "I thought, maybe, it was a bad memory for you. Or something."

"You *did*?"

"Well, you made it pretty clear that you regretted it. You wouldn't even come out of your room to say goodbye to me."

"Nick!" she said, stopping in the middle of the path and turning to face him. "We were fourteen!"

"Meaning?"

"Meaning that it wasn't that I didn't want to talk to you. It was that I wanted to talk to you *too much*."

Instead of turning away from him, then, and instead of keeping on down the pathway, Justine stayed quite still, looking up into his face, those fierce Carmichael eyebrows of hers pushed together so there was a little furrow of skin between them. Her lips were bright and sugary, and there was a stray shard of crimson toffee on her silver-painted chin. She looked so funny and so vivid that he wanted to laugh.

He reached for her hands.

"That was one of my favorite nights of all time," Nick said, although it wasn't until he heard himself say this aloud that he realized the absolute truth of it. On the beach, with Justine, half drunk on Stone's Green Ginger Wine—it had been another of those perfect snapshot moments that Nick knew he'd never, in his whole life, forget.

"It was?"

Justine looked up at him, and the scattering of stuck-on stars at the corners of her eyes glittered.

"Jus?"

"Yes?"

"When I'm with you, I . . ." he began, and then stopped, because he knew that although there were a great many things he would like to say, inside this moment, there were all kinds of reasons that he could not. It wouldn't be fair. Not to Laura, not to Justine. Because although he wished there were a way of keeping the things he wanted to say in the bubble of this moment, he knew it to be impossible. So he settled for landing a kiss on the top of her silver hair, and said, "I'm so glad you're my friend, Jus. I'm so glad we found each other again."

And then they continued on their way: the blue moon and the shooting star.

♏

At home on the twelfth floor of Evelyn Towers, Justine took a long, cool shower. Runnels of glittery paint and silver stars swirled around her feet like galaxies, then disappeared down the plughole. Justine stood beneath the flowing water until, at last, it ran clear.

Justine: *So, I guess that's really it, then. He's glad I'm his friend.*
Brain: *I guess so.*
Justine: *We gave it our best shot, didn't we?*
Brain: *We did. We absolutely did. And a friend is no small thing.*

♏︎

The day after Halloween was sweltering, and the day after that was hotter still. But this was not a city where the sun shone steadily for days on end from a cloudless sky; this was a place where even a short string of scorchers had to be paid for in thunderstorms and rain. The change came on the Thursday night of that week, with spectacular displays of lightning, and hailstones that pummeled car roofs and hoods. The city's garbage cans were scattered to the four winds, and more than one trampoline took flight. When Friday arrived, it was gray and wet and tepid, and Justine's weather-vane hair frizzed like a merino's fleece.

It was past six o'clock and Justine had spent a good part of the day trying to inject some spark of creativity into a feature story about the Alexandria Park real estate market, a subject that was inexhaustibly fascinating to the magazine's readership. Now there was nobody left in the office but Justine, and Daniel. This seemed to be how they had tacitly decided things were going to work: each of them would stay at the office until everybody else had gone home, and then they would have the privacy to talk for a while, or to make plans.

Tonight, when Daniel came into the staff writers' room, he dragged Martin's chair over to Justine's workstation and sat on it the wrong way round. Leaning over the chairback, he grinned at her in a way that made her imagine what he must have been like as a schoolboy. He sat close enough to her that he could have touched her, but he didn't. In his hand were two tickets, glossy black with red writing.

"They're for the new screen at the cinema," Daniel said, clearly very pleased with himself. "Orion's answer to Gold Class. The manager there is trying to cultivate me as a contact."

Justine had already told Daniel that something she loved to do was to go to the Orion and take potluck with whatever was screening. Her favorite way to see a movie was with no preconceived ideas and no hype. In fact, the less she knew about a film before she sat down to watch it, the better.

"Shall we go see something neither of us has ever heard of? Have dinner at Afterward? Walk in the rain?"

"All that sounds very nice," Justine said. And it did.

"Right you are, then. I'll go get myself organized."

Justine powered down her computer, tidied her desk and shrugged on her coat. She picked up her teacup with the intention of emptying out the dregs in the tearoom sink. But on the way down the hall, she passed the open door to Henry Ashbolt's office and saw a sheet of paper lying in the out-tray of the slender white machine on the desktop.

Brain: *Ahem. Resolution One states that there will be no tampering with the horoscopes.*

Justine: *I don't think it says anything about just reading the horoscopes.*

Brain: *In other words: I'm just going to get the bottle out of the liquor cabinet?*

Justine: *I'm not going to do anything. I just want to see what Leo has to say.*

Brain: *To Nick? Or to you?*

Justine: *Maybe a little of both? Come on. Just a little sneak preview. Please? You're curious, too. I know you are.*

Brain: *A preview, you say?*

Justine: *Yes. Nothing more. I'll take the fax into the tearoom and read it, and when I come back past Henry's office, I'll put the fax right back where it is now.*

Brain: *You promise?*

Justine: *Faithfully.*

Beyond the back window of the tearoom, the purple blooms of a stunted jacaranda tree were drooping under the weight of so many raindrops. Justine set the fax down on the counter beside the sink, so that she could read it while she rinsed out her cup. *Aries, Taurus, Gemini, Cancer, Leo, Virgo, Libra, Scorpio, Sag—*

"Hey," said Daniel, joining Justine at the sink. He had the handles of several coffee mugs threaded through his fingers.

Justine dropped her teacup and it landed with a clang in the sink.

"Oh, shit. Sorry," she said.

Brain: *The fax, Justine! The fax!*

Justine: *I know, I know. What should I do? What should I do?*

Brain: *Fold it up and put it in your pocket before he sees it.*

Justine: *But it will get all creased! I can't put a creased page back on the fax machine!*

Brain: *Good point. Um . . . you can photocopy it later, and put the uncreased version back on the machine.*

"Nice weather for ducks out there," Justine said, nodding toward the window.

Justine: *Oh my God. I'm talking about the weather. Even worse, I'm talking about the weather like my dad's golf mates. Daniel's going to see right through me.*

Brain: *Pocket, Justine! Pocket!*

"You okay?"

"I'm fine. Totally fine," she said, and, smiling as innocently as she could manage, she folded Leo's fax and slipped it into the pocket of her coat.

♏

At 3:47 the following morning, Justine—alone in her bed at Evelyn Towers—woke with a horrible thought at the front and center of her mind. Usually, when she woke with horrible thoughts in her mind, she fairly quickly worked out they were irrational. That the apartment was actually a huge Pringles chip cylinder, and somebody was suffocating her by putting the lid back on was, patently, fairly unlikely. That she had lost the PIN number to her underpants drawer, or forgotten to re-charge her liver were not particularly convincing scenarios, once she'd had a waking moment to think about them. But this morning's horrible thought was not as implausible as her usual 3:47 a.m. thoughts. This one was scarily realistic. Could she really have come home from the cinema without her coat?

Justine got out of bed and looked at the pile of garments on her bed-side chair. No coat. She went out into the living room, but there was no coat slung over the back of a dining chair or crumpled on the kitchen counter. It was not in the bathroom, and she hadn't dropped it by accident on the twelfth-floor landing. And the more she thought about it, the more clearly she could picture herself laying her grandmother's pink-purple coat over the seat of a stool at the Orion cinema bar. Was it possible that, after the tapas and the drinks, Justine had stood up and just left it there?

When the Orion opened its doors at eleven that morning, Justine was already waiting in the street. Although the guy behind the ticket counter initially insisted that he be the one to look through the coats in the cloakroom and check the lost property box, he eventually gave in to Justine's pleas and allowed her to conduct her own search. But although she went through the cloakroom with absolute thoroughness, looking under every other abandoned coat to make sure that hers wasn't hiding beneath it on a hanger, and although she hunted through every cubicle in the ladies' room and in the men's, and although she successfully begged to be allowed back into the fancy new part of the cinema where she and Daniel had watched a crazy Mexican film about a chauvinist dickhead deserted by his long-suffering wife, it was no use. Justine's coat was nowhere, which meant that so too were Leo Thornbury's latest horoscopes.

Justine: *I am up shit creek.*

Brain: *And I'm afraid to say that the paddle count is nil.*

Back at her apartment, Justine made herself a cup of tea and compiled a full and unexpurgated list of all her options. This didn't take long, for the grand total was two. The first was to tell Daniel that she had lost Leo's horoscopes along with her coat, and that someone would need to contact Leo and ask him to send another copy. This course of action had the advantage of being honorable, but the serious disadvantage of Daniel knowing that she had taken the fax in the first place.

The second option was more complicated. It would involve getting hold of a typewriter, and making up the horoscopes for all twelve signs of the zodiac. Then she would have to go into the office late at night, photocopy the typed page so that it looked like a fax, and slip the photocopy onto the machine in Henry's office.

Justine: *Why the hell did you let me pick up that fax?*

Brain: *My control over your impulses is, as you well know, flimsy at*

best. And, by the way, have you considered that Leo's faxes have that
little header showing the number of the sender? Of course, it's in a com-
pletely different style to the typing on the rest of the page . . .

Her brain was right. But, she could find one of Leo's old faxes. And
photocopy that. And snip out the header. It would be a simple matter to glue the number to the top of her typewritten page and photocopy the two things together, but slightly more complicated to make
the lines around the glued piece of paper disappear entirely from the
photocopy. It could probably be done, though, Justine figured, with the
help of Wite-Out and some adjustment to the copy brightness setting
on the photocopier.

But where would she get one of Leo's old faxes? It was unlikely that
she'd find one on Henry's document spike; probably, they were all in
that manila folder of Daniel's. So, in addition to all of the fraudulent
things that option two involved, it also included stealing from Daniel's
office.

Justine bit off a fingernail, took a sip of cold tea, fired up Google,
and typed: *where can I buy an old-fashioned typewriter?*

♏

It was midafternoon on Sunday when Justine arrived home with a
refurbished Olympia SM9 manual typewriter, a ream of paper and a
commensurately depleted bank account. Out of all the machines that
she had seen in the suburban home of a semi-professional typewriter
enthusiast, she had chosen the Olympia SM9 because the typewriter
enthusiast had told her that Don DeLillo had owned one. Apparently,
he had written all of his novels, including *Libra*, on just such a machine; Justine had chosen to take it as a sign.

Although it was ahead of schedule, she closed the living-room curtains. The Olympia SM9 was quite pleasing to look at, with a rounded
pale gray body and shift keys in the same bright green as the cursive
brand name that appeared in the center of the top cover. Justine poured
herself a large glass of wine, and threaded a sheet of paper into the
machine.

How was she going to do this?

She was no astrologer. She'd be hard pushed to put the planets of the solar system in their correct order, let alone know where these celestial bodies were hanging out in the sky, right now. And even if she did know where they were, and how they were positioned in relationship to each other, whether they were direct or retrograde, she wouldn't have the foggiest idea what any of that was supposed to mean. Justine felt like she was standing in the wings, and her cue was any minute, except that she didn't know her lines, or even which play she was supposed to be in.

Brain: *So just don't mention any planets. Keep things . . . vague.*

Then Justine had an idea. She remembered something that best-pal Tara had told her about radio. The secret of radio, Tara had said, was not to think that you were speaking to a whole heap of people out there in Listener Land, but that you were speaking to one person only. That person might be a friend, or a relative, or some kind of invented ideal listener.

"I can work with that," Justine whispered to herself.

All she had to do was think of a person, one for every sign of the zodiac, and write them a message, a personal message. Justine flexed her fingers and began.

For Aries, she thought of Nick's mother, Jo Jordan, and wrote her a message about old friends, and how they never disappeared entirely from your heart. For Taurus, she told Tara that the world was her oyster, and for her mother, the Gemini, she predicted that there would soon be a wedding in the family. Roma Sharples was her Cancerian, and Justine told her that she should definitely continue mentoring the young people in her workplace. She was beginning to enjoy herself, searching up relevant quotations and impersonating Leo's quasi-mystical tone. The keys of the typewriter felt so different from computer keys, but there was something pleasing in the trotting-pony feel of it, and in the extra effort that it took to get the letters evenly inked onto the page.

But then came Leo.

Leo, she typed, and she knew that her model for the lion had to be Daniel Griffin.

But what should she say to him?

She took her hands away from the typewriter keys, and thought for a time.

At last, she wrote: *The British philosopher Bertrand Russell once wrote that real life was, for most people, "a long second-best, a perpetual compromise between the ideal and the possible." But you are a lion, and lions do not compromise. Whether this applies in the workplace or your home, your romantic life or your friendships, it is the season for you to let go of anything that you wish was ideal, but that you know is merely possible.*

This was sad, but also true.

Carriage return, carriage return.

And now she was up to Virgo. Her brother was a Virgo, so here she let it rip on the subject of love, and quoted Elizabeth Barrett Browning. For her Libran father, she wrote that games of skill and tenacity, possibly even word games, would feature prominently in the coming weeks, and although Justine's favorite Scorpio—her grandmother—was no longer living, this didn't mean she couldn't write her a message about how much other people admired those who lived their lives to the full.

Having no Capricorns close at hand, Justine paused for a time at the tenth sign. Then she remembered Nick telling her that Laura Mitchell was a Capricorn, so she wrote a message about how hard work and natural talents would bring success and joy. And that, momentarily, made Justine feel rather honorable. The twelfth sign of the zodiac, Pisces, was far easier, since Jeremy Byrne was a fish person. To him, she wrote about new phases of life and taking pleasure in simple things.

Of course, in composing the horoscope for Sagittarius, she had written to herself: *It can be difficult to know when enough is enough. When something comes to an end for you this month, archers, you may find this challenging, even though you know that to let go is for the best. Remember that when all else fails, a journey is usually a tonic. Perhaps it's time for you to get your suitcase out from beneath your bed and take to heart the words of Susan Sontag, which might as well be the Sagittarian mantra: "I haven't been everywhere, but it's on my list."*

And what she wrote to Aquarians, to Nick—to her good friend, Nick—was also a kind of farewell, a signing-off: *With your Aquarian gaze focused upon the wide world and the future, it can be easy to forget that other source of inspiration and wisdom—yourself. What would happen if, instead of seeking the advice of those around you, and the counsel of those you admire, you were to trust in the murmurings of your own heart? As the great Jane Austen observed: "We have all a better guide in ourselves, if we would attend to it, than any other person can be."*

Then she took the Olympus SM9 down to the basement of Evelyn Towers and threw it into the Dumpster. The typewriter hit the metal floor of the Dumpster, hard, and Justine heard sounds of splitting plastic and twisting metal. Something, indeed—Justine thought—was coming to an end.

cusp

D aniel Griffin—Leo, successful political journalist turned editor of the *Alexandria Park Star*, named in his high school yearbook as the man most likely to have his picture on the cover of *Esquire*, and the cowed-but-unbroken whipping boy of a personal trainer called Sadie—looked up when he heard an unexpected knock at his office door early one November Friday.

Standing in the doorway was a courier—a young guy with shaved, muscular legs poking out of his shiny shorts. In his arms he held what appeared to be a bundle of jacquard fabric.

"Daniel Griffin?"

"Yes?"

"This is compliments of Katie Black, the manager at the Orion. She said to tell you that your girlfriend left her coat in the bar. And because Katie recognized you, she put it aside in her office to be sure it got returned to its owner."

Daniel looked puzzled. "But that was weeks ago."

"She also wanted you to have this," the courier admitted, handing over a press release. "Katie said to tell you they've just finalized the program for the summer film festival. Also that she looks forward to reading the *Star*'s coverage, and that she's available for an interview any time to suit you."

Daniel gave a wry smile. "Thanks, mate. Tell Katie I appreciate her going to the trouble," he said. *And purely out of the goodness of her heart, too.*

Daniel held the coat up by its shoulders, catching a faint whiff of camphor. The fabric was covered with small pink and purple hexagons, the buttons were Bakelite, and the garment had probably last been in fashion in about 1963. Justine did have a bit of a weird, charity-shop thing going on with her fashion sense, but Daniel thought she'd most likely leave that phase behind now that her salary was growing.

The coat was quite small, Daniel noticed. He didn't think of Justine as being small, but the coat was evidence that she must be. And that made him think that if there was one thing that was consistent in his relationship with Justine, it was that he was perpetually getting her wrong. *Relationship?* he asked himself. *What relationship?* If they'd had, or were having, a relationship, then it was almost as if it had been conducted in reverse gear. With every date, things were getting less passionate, not more.

As he hung the coat on a hanger on the back of his office door, Daniel noticed the corner of a folded sheet protruding ever so slightly from one of the pockets. Of course, Daniel knew that the honorable thing to do would be to leave the sheet of paper where it was. But, really, what kind of journalist would he be if he didn't at least have a look? And, when it came to Justine, wasn't he looking for clues?

Immediately that he unfolded the page, he knew what it was. And almost as immediately, he wished that he did not know.

"Fuck," he said.

She'd done it again. Hadn't she? He'd ticked her off and given her a chance. But she'd done it again.

"Fuck," he reiterated.

Then, after breathing a few times, he asked himself what kind of journalist he would be, if he didn't check all the facts. Good journos did not jump to conclusions, he reminded himself.

An hour later, Daniel sat at his desk looking over all the proof that he needed, but wished that he had not found. He felt numb, for it was clear that, this time, Justine had not simply been impulsive. What she had done, she had done with a gobsmacking degree of premeditation. And it wasn't just Aquarius, either.

The text of the entire horoscope column, as it appeared in the most recent edition of the *Star*, was different from the text on the fax from Justine's coat pocket. But, even worse than this, Daniel had found on Henry's document spike a replacement "original" fax that did match the published text. Under close inspection, he'd been able to see the faint, telltale lines of shadow around Leo's fax number at the top of the page: evidence that the document had been doctored.

At a quick glance, Justine's fake fax looked the same as Leo's, but on careful examination, Daniel had recognized that the typeface on the fake was very slightly different from that of all of Leo's other "originals."

"Jesus," Daniel said, rubbing at his forehead.

Justine was, so far as Daniel had been able to determine, a normal, logical, reasonable and intelligent human being. So why would she go to so much trouble to mess around with horoscopes?

And what did it mean that she had written this for his star sign: *The British philosopher Bertrand Russell once wrote that real life was, for most people, "a long second-best, a perpetual compromise between the ideal and the possible." But you are a lion, and lions do not compromise. Whether this applies in the workplace or your home, your romantic life or your friendships, it is the season for you to let go of anything that you wish was ideal, but that you know is merely possible.*

This had to be a message for him, personally. Daniel paced his office floor. He thought, and he thought. Then he noticed someone standing in the hallway outside his office, looking rather lost. He was wearing a *Where the Wild Things Are* T-shirt that looked like it had seen better days, and holding a bike helmet as if it were a bowl. Inside it was what appeared to be, mostly, a bunch of weeds. It was Justine's friend. Romeo. The blue moon. *Nick*. That was it.

"G'day, Nick," Daniel said.

"Yeah. Um . . . Dan?" Nick said.

Daniel did not especially like being called Dan, but he let it ride.

"Sorry to interrupt," Nick said. "I just called in to see Justine, but I don't know which office is hers."

"That one, just there," Daniel said, indicating the door to the staff writers' room. "But I'm pretty sure she's not in yet. Which is odd. She's quite the early bird, usually."

"Oh, right," said Nick. "Okay if I leave these on her desk?"

He held up the bike helmet full of plant material. Daniel saw a few dandelions poking out of an arrangement of grasses and stinging nettles, sow thistles and dock, very freshly picked. In the other hand, Nick held a couple of slices of wholemeal bread wrapped in cling film.

"It's her birthday," Nick explained.

"And you've brought her . . . a bunch of weeds? And a sandwich?"

"Vegemite," Nick elaborated.

"Because?"

Nick looked as if he were about to say something, and then thought better of it. He settled for saying, "It's kind of a joke."

"Right," Daniel said.

"So, I'll just—"

"Nick, are you actually sure her birthday is *today*?"

"Yeah. It's today."

"You're certain?"

"We've known each other since we were born. And as far as I know, she hasn't changed it by deed poll or anything."

"But, right now, we're not in Aquarius. Are we?"

Nick looked puzzled. "No, that's February. Give or take a few days in late January."

"Hey, can you . . . ?" Daniel said, stepping back into his office and gesturing for Nick to follow. "Look, you've known her forever—maybe you can tell me what I need to know. Would you mind having a look at something?"

And so Daniel showed Nick the evidence that was spread out across his desk. From April through to September, Daniel explained, Justine had changed the horoscopes for Aquarius, but spiked Leo's original faxes. But now, and even after Daniel had confronted Justine with this fact in October, she had taken things to a whole new level in November, replacing Leo's actual fax with a fraudulent one, with the text for all of the star signs completely rewritten.

"She promised me she'd stop doing it. But not only has she kept going, she's ramped it up. I suppose I should be furious, but I'm really more bewildered than anything. And disappointed," Daniel admitted. "I suppose this seems pretty funny to you. You're probably thinking, 'It's only the stars—what's the big deal?'"

Nick put down on Daniel's desk the Vegemite sandwich and the bike helmet full of daisies and weeds, and as he started to look through the documents one at a time, carefully, Daniel noticed that Nick did not look even slightly amused. After a while, Daniel began to feel unsettled by the attention Nick was paying to the documents, and by the stony look on his face.

"I probably shouldn't have shared any of this with you. Or with anyone. But I don't understand her. I need some perspective here, because I'm at a complete loss," Daniel said. "Why would she do it? It's bloody disrespectful to Leo. It's unethical in the extreme. It's just plain . . . stupid. And Justine is anything but stupid. So, why would she do it? She told me she was an Aquarius. That she was trying to change her own fate or something. No, hang on. That's not totally accurate. What actually happened is that *I* suggested all of that to her. But she allowed me to believe it. Even though it wasn't true. Was it?"

Nick shook his head.

"So, what's with the Aquarius thing?" Daniel continued, feeling increasingly agitated as he spoke. "What's with Justine and Aquarius? There must be an Aquarian in her life. But who? Do you know?"

"Yep," said Nick. "I do."

"Well?" said Daniel.

Nick ran a hand through his hair. "It's me."

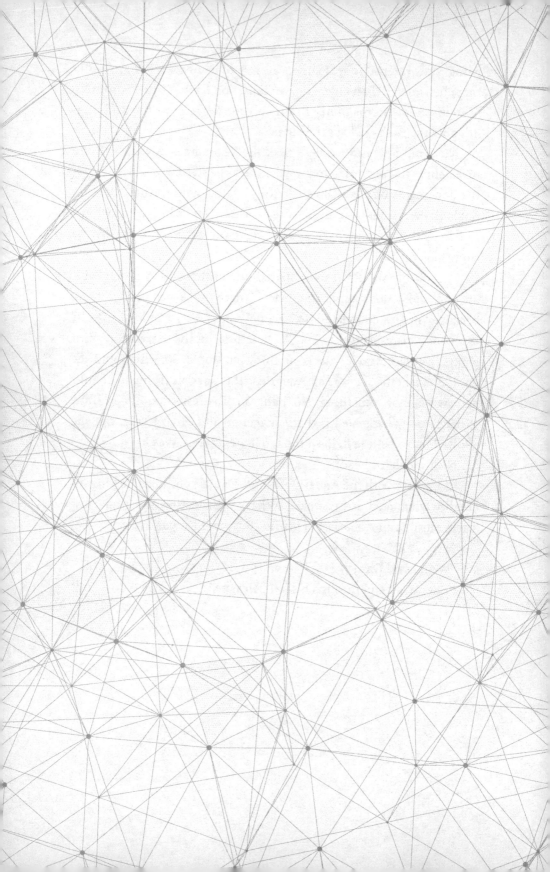

Sagittarius

NOVEMBER 22–DECEMBER 21

A t precisely 7:15 a.m. on Friday, November 24, Justine Carmichael flung open her living-room curtains. She'd not had any particular expectation that Nick Jordan would be standing on his balcony with a party hat perched on his head, and a fistful of helium balloons. Nor had she anticipated that a gift, or even a card, would be nestling in their lighthouse keeper's basket. But when she saw the basket was empty, and that it was over on Nick's side of the divide, and when she observed that there didn't seem to be anyone at home in the next-door apartment, Justine did feel just a little disappointed.

Before long, though, birthday texts and phone calls began to arrive. Mandy called during her drive to work, and yelled the way she seemed to think a person had to if they were talking through a car's speaker phone. Then there came a call from Justine's father, who was somewhere out in the bush chasing brumbies off an airstrip; he sounded out of breath, but cheerful. Justine laughed at the crass joke that arrived via text from her brother, and smiled at the far more civilized text that came from Tara, who promised to phone later in the day for a proper chat.

Then came a call from Auntie Julie, Mandy's sister, who'd never once, not ever, forgotten to call Justine on the morning of her birthday. And surprisingly, right on the dot of 8 a.m., there was a text from Tom. It was lukewarm, even for an ex's text. *Best wishes and many happy returns of the day,* it said, and Justine wondered if Tom had installed some kind of phone app that sent out automatic and standardized birthday messages to everyone on a list, and according to a designated time zone.

Once this little flurry of calls and texts was over, the silence of Justine's empty apartment settled, uncomfortably, all around her. As she put two and a half Weetabix in a bowl, she thought about having no presents to open. As she poured on the milk, she dwelled upon the fact that she had nobody to share a birthday breakfast with. As she ate her cereal, Justine knew that she had not been forgotten by the people who loved her. But, she equally knew that she was not anyone's best beloved.

Birthdays had felt different when she was a child, Justine mused as she walked through Alexandria Park on her way to work. When she was turning seven, eight, nine, she had woken up on the morning of her birthday already knowing that the day was special, that it was *hers*. And the day had kept its specialness all the way through, right until Justine was back in bed at night. Back then, November 24 had been brighter, sharper, sparklier, zingier, than any other day of the year.

Then there had come a period of time, through her teens and early twenties, when Justine experienced her birthday feeling only in occasional waves. November the twenty-fourth would feel mostly normal, except when Justine remembered, out of the blue, that it was in fact her birthday. Then the birthday feeling would fizz up in all the colors of a packet of Fruit Tingles at once. But now that she was turning twenty-seven, all she could feel was the ghost of that hard, bright joyfulness, and she was sad to think that it might yet fade more and more, until one day birthdays might feel like nothing out of the ordinary at all.

To cheer herself up from this gloomy thinking, Justine decided to cut through the markets on her way to work, and strike a blow for the textual dignity of the avocado. Approaching the greengrocer's, Justine caught sight of a gorgeous display of summertime fruits. There were strawberries and raspberries, blackberries and blueberries, red currants and black currants, and a small tub of early cherries, all of them gleaming like clusters of precious gems. It was enough to make Justine think wistfully of the summer puddings and fruit-laden Pavlovas that her mother had made for her childhood birthday parties, and almost enough to make her overlook the extra D in the sign above the avocado stack.

But not quite.

Sharpie at the ready, Justine peeked around a stack of cantaloupes. She looked left, and right, and left again, before striding up to the offending sign and putting a thick, satisfying X through the superfluous consonant.

Perhaps Justine had that day been careless in her reconnaissance, or perhaps she was simply unlucky, but before she could recap her felt pen, she felt a heavy hand land on her shoulder.

The greengrocer was only a little taller than Justine, but he was substantially wider. He had an undershot jaw and prominent canines, and even on a good day these features gave him the look of a bulldog. Right now, though, he looked like an enraged and salivating bulldog. He grabbed the hand of Justine's that was still holding the uncapped pen. He squeezed it until her fingers hurt, and black ink was smearing against her palm. He was so close to Justine that she could see the white mortarlike fill between his teeth, which suggested he hadn't flossed for the longest time. Or, perhaps, ever.

"Get. Out," he said, and though he was not exactly shouting, he was not far off it. "And do not come back here. And do not touch my signs ever again, or so help me."

"But I was only trying to c—"

"Out! Get out!" Now he was shouting.

"But it's 'avocado,' not 'ad'—"

"You are a filthy vandal. Out!"

Shoppers and staff alike watched after Justine as she fled, her cheeks hot with embarrassment and fear. Shaken and flushed, Justine made her way along Dufrene Street in the direction of the *Star*. She was several blocks away from the markets before she realized that she had dropped her Sharpie. Although, for all the good it did her, she still held its lid in one trembling hand.

Rafaello himself was at the counter when Justine swerved in through the open door of his cafe, her cheeks scorching and her hands still shaking. Was it possible, she wondered, that the grocer's angry glare had inflicted some kind of flash burn?

"Ah, just the girl," Rafaello said. "Today, your cafe latte and almond croissant are on the house. And here"—Rafaello put down on the counter a sheet of paper, and a nicely sharpened pencil—"is everything you need to scribble all over my new summer menu. I figured I'd get you to do it now. That way, there'll be no excuse for you to scribble on them once they come back from the printer. Yes?"

Justine gave Raf a weak smile. "Can I just pay for my coffee and croissant?"

Raf reeled backward. "A golden opportunity to proof my menu, and the Apostrophe Queen says no?"

"I promise I won't scribble on your menu," she said earnestly.

"Not even if my twice-baked soufflés are unhyphenated?"

"Not even then."

"Not even if my raspberries are missing a 'p'?"

Justine considered. "Well . . ."

"Ha! You see?"

"I could come by and do it tomorrow? It's just that I'm a little . . . weirded out."

"Okay, lady," Raf said, withdrawing the paper and pencil. "Tomorrow it is."

Justine took a seat in a secluded corner of the cafe, out of sight of the window. It was past nine o'clock, which made her, technically speaking, late for work. But she needed a coffee, and some time for the color in her face to subside.

When at last she felt a little more settled, she made her way to work. At the front gate of the *Star*, she saw that someone had propped a bicycle against the fence. It looked a lot like Nick's. She passed beneath the yellow peril and walked up the front steps.

Cecilia was at the photocopier in the hallway.

"Morning, Cecilia," Justine said.

"Hey, Justine," Cecilia said.

Justine passed the open door to Barbel's office.

"Morning, Barbel," she called.

"Morning, Justine," Barbel called back.

And then Justine came to the open door to Daniel's office. She was about to call out a cheery "Good morning, Daniel," but then she saw that Daniel was not alone. In Daniel's office, wearing Lycra shorts and his *Where the Wild Things Are* T-shirt, was Nick Jordan. His face was serious, and so was Daniel's. On Daniel's desk, filled with what appeared to be a semimangled bunch of dandelions, was Nick's bike helmet. And beneath the helmet was a scattering of pages that Justine recognized immediately.

"Justine," Daniel began.

But Justine had already turned and fled.

Justine: *Being eaten alive by piranhas.*

Brain: *Being burned at the stake.*

Justine: *Being given to Michael Jackson's plastic surgeon as a test dummy.*

Brain: *Tongue-kissing a fistful of human excrement.*

Justine: *Ew!*

Brain: *What's the problem? I thought we were supposed to be making ourselves feel better by making a list of everything we could think of that would be worse than what just happened?*

Justine: *Yes! But there's no need to be revolting about it.*

Brain: *Oh, okay. Um . . . being tickled for forty-eight hours by a tap-dancing five-year-old who sings the Happy Birthday song the whole time, but slightly out of tune.*

Justine: *I don't know . . . I think I might even take that one over what happened this morning. I'm going to lose my job, you realize. And nobody will ever employ me again. At least, not as a journalist. I'll have to go work at McDonald's. Or maybe I'll have to spend my whole life holding up those SLOW and STOP signs on the roads. And Nick's going to hate me now. And so will Daniel.*

Brain: *Was that a knock at the door?*

Justine: *No.*

Brain: *Justine, it was a knock at the door.*

Justine: *Was not.*

Brain: *You know it was, right?*

Justine: *It was a knock at 12B's door.*

Brain: *Ah, nope. Your door.*

Justine: *I don't want to answer the door. I don't want to see another living human. Ever again. For as long as I live. Or even talk to one. That's why I drew the curtains and locked the door and switched off the phone.*

Brain: *You're going to have to open the door, Justine.*

Justine: *Maybe it's just Mormons.*

Brain: *I hate to tell you this, my friend, but you're in denial.*

Justine: *So, who is it then?*

Brain: *Most likely, it's Daniel. Or Nick.*

Justine: *No, no, no! I don't want to see either of them. Which one of them is it?*

Brain: *Which of them would be worse?*

Justine: *Nick.*

Brain: *Then that's who it will be. It's just that kind of day.*

On this occasion, however, Justine's brain was wrong. At the door was Daniel, his shirtsleeves rolled to the wrist, his tie loose at his collar, and his brave face held on with the metaphorical equivalent of dollar store sticky tape. Justine flushed with shame.

"Can I come in?"

Justine nodded and opened the door wider.

Daniel looked around the apartment as if it were the first time he had ever seen it. Or perhaps as if he were trying to see it, and her, anew.

"Can I get you a cup of tea?" Justine ventured.

"No, I'm fine."

"Coffee?"

"No, thanks."

He didn't sit. Instead, he leaned against the edge of her dining table. From the tabletop, he picked up the plastic bow that had been part of Justine's Halloween costume. She watched him as he turned it over in his hands, testing the resistance in its string.

"So," he began, and Justine—perched on the arm of the living-room couch—waited for him to continue. She felt like a prisoner in the dock, waiting for her sentence to be pronounced.

"So . . . you understand that I have to suspend you. From the *Star*."

"Suspend?"

"Far out, Justine. You're lucky I don't—"

"I know, I know. That's what I mean. I mean, you're only going to suspend me? That's amazing. That's more than I deserve. It's—"

"I'm going to suspend you, on half pay, while I decide what to do. It might still be the case that I have to let you go."

"Oh."

"And for what? Over the bloody *stars*? Justine, what the hell were you thinking? I can't believe that a writer with so much promise could be such a . . . dumb arse."

"I'm sorry, Daniel. I'm really sorry."

But Daniel waved her apology away as if there were no longer anything she could say that he would believe.

Justine said, "The last thing I want to do is give you any dog-ate-my-homework excuses. I know that everything I did was just plain wrong. And I'm sorry. But is there anything I could say that would convince you that—"

"Given all the circumstances, I'm the wrong person to make the final decision. I can't think clearly about this one. So, I'm going to delegate to a higher authority."

"Jeremy?" Justine whispered, and the mere thought of her former boss's disappointed expression was enough to bring on a fresh wave of shame.

"Yes. And in the interests of full disclosure, I'll also have to tell him that my relationship with you has been, well, less than professional.

I thought we could do this, Justine. Maybe I'm just a hopeless optimist, but I thought we'd be okay."

"I'm so sorry. I—"

"I'm going to have to talk to Leo Thornbury, too."

"You will? What will you tell him?"

"Just the facts. As I see them."

Justine nodded.

"One other thing," Daniel said, not looking at her. "Not a work-related thing."

"Yes?"

And now he did look at her, very directly.

"How long have you been in love with Nick?"

Justine could see how much it hurt him to ask that question. She understood, too, that it was a privilege to be allowed to know anyone well enough to see their tenderness and pain leaking out around the edges of their brave face. She'd been careless with his feelings, and the least she could do now was to tell him the absolute truth.

"For as long as I can remember, I think," she said.

Daniel held the bow up between his two hands. "Sagittarius, hey?"

"Yes," Justine said.

"Free-spirited."

"Yes."

"Impulsive.

"Often."

"Honest to a fault."

Justine winced. Daniel stood up straight, and set the bow back down on the table.

"I'll be in touch," he said. "And, Justine?"

"Yes?"

"Happy birthday."

In the days that followed, Justine stayed indoors and kept the curtains of her apartment closed. At first, she told herself all that was required for her misery to be complete was for Nick Jordan to come to her door and yell at her. But after a while she began to think she was wrong. If anything, a bit of yelling would come as a welcome relief. At least it would be something. But Nick did not come to her door. And he did not phone.

She would have liked to call best-pal Tara, and to tell her the whole terrible story, but she didn't know if she could bear the disappointment of a single other person whom she loved or admired. So Justine locked herself away at her home, subsisting on the meager offerings in her fridge and pantry.

Soon, the powdered milk supply was exhausted, which made tea and coffee unappealing, and after that the bread in the freezer ran out, which made toast an impossibility. The freezer was empty except for the ice trays, the fridge contained no eggs and no yogurt, and all that remained in the fruit bowl was an orange that was in the process of transforming into a green. Eventually, Justine was forced to confront the reality that it was going to be necessary to leave the apartment in search of provisions.

Her sunglasses were nowhere to be found, and when Justine stepped out onto the street after these days spent in semidarkness, the sudden summer glare was blinding. For quite some time, she stood on the stoop, blinking. When at last her vision cleared, she saw a small removal van parked out the front of the ugly brown-brick apartment block next door, its rear doors thrown wide open. Two men were lifting packing boxes into the van, while a third man formed them into stacks.

Immediately, she knew what was happening. She knew it in her gut even before she saw the familiar two-seater couch being loaded into the back of the van. When she saw Nick coming out of the front door with a suitcase in either hand, Justine felt the impulse to go to him, to talk to him, to explain. But just a little stronger was her impulse to turn in the opposite direction and hurry away up the street.

When Justine returned with her groceries, the van was gone. Upstairs, she pulled back her curtains and saw just what she expected to see: Nick Jordan's apartment was more or less empty. Where the wheat-colored rug had been laid out, there was now nothing but green carpet.

In the bathroom, the shower was once again without a curtain. And lying on the concrete floor of her balcony, as if it had been thrown there, was the lighthouse keeper's basket. The string line that had connected the two apartments was gone. Whether it had been untied—or cut through—Justine didn't know.

cusp

T ansy Brinklow stood in the archway at the edge of her practice's waiting room. In her arms she held a clipboard, and her
glasses were low on her nose as she scanned down her list of
appointments with a lightly furrowed brow.

"Giles Buckley," she announced.

She watched as a tall man stood, adjusting his braces as he did so.
She met his eye and acknowledged him with a facial expression that
was just short of a smile.

"Mind your head on the arch," she said, and then set off down the
hallway toward her consulting room.

Her room was furnished with leather-and-polish gravitas. She was
not the sort to put silver-framed pictures of her daughters on the desktop, or set out a humorous flip-over calendar. She did supply tissues,
but these she kept in a drawer.

At her gesture, her patient sat. She sat, also. She opened a file and
folded her ring-less hands together on top of the papers within.

"Let's get straight to the point, shall we, Mr. Buckley?" she said.
"Your tumor is benign."

"Sorry?"

"It's good news, Mr. Buckley. The tumor is benign. It's only that it's made its home in a rather awkward spot in your lung. Hence the short-ness of breath, the wheezing, the blood when you cough."

She spoke for a time then, about surgery, and surgical risk, and re-covery times, but Tansy could see that Mr. Buckley was not entirely present with her. He sat, staring at the palms of his immense hands. Every now and then he shook his head ever so slightly, as if disturbing an insect that had landed on his hair.

"Mr. Buckley?" she prompted. "Do you have any questions?"

He looked at her, his brow furrowed. "So, what do I do?"

Tansy blinked. It was not every day that she had good news to de-liver, and yet this poor man looked more confused than relieved.

"Do? You mean about the surgery?"

He went on, "No, no. Not that. I mean, what would you do, Doc? If you just found out that you still had the rest of your life? That it was still yours, after all?"

"Oh," said Tansy. "Well. That's hard to say. What do you . . . enjoy, Mr. Buckley?"

He held his hands up and out like he might have been about to start juggling fruit. "If you're given a second chance, then shouldn't you, you know, do something *with it*?"

A lump thickened and expanded in Tansy's throat. Inexplicably, she thought of Simon Pierce's soft hands, as different as a man's hands could be from Giles Buckley's. It was as if she could suddenly feel Si-mon's touch in six different places on her body, all at once.

"What would *you* do, Doc?"

"I would buy an Alfa Romeo. A convertible," Tansy Brinklow said out loud, surprising herself by doing so. Then she closed her mouth firmly before the other part of her response could escape her lips. *And I would marry Simon Pierce.*

+

"Not that one," Laura said, with a little laugh. "This one."

She led the way to the considerably shorter queue—the one for first-class and business-class passengers. But being in the shorter queue didn't change the fact that it was stupidly early in the morning, and Nick was suffering from the slightly cold, creaky, unoiled feeling—of body and soul—that he always felt when he was forced to be awake before dawn. They were heading to South Australia on an early morning flight, to spend several days posing for the cameras amid alleyways of grapevines. He'd emailed to Chance all his measurements so that they could have his tight-fitting moleskin pants at the ready. And an Akubra hat in the right size.

"Are you okay?" Laura asked.

She'd asked him this once already, at the apartment. Although he had officially moved back in with Laura, the cardboard boxes that contained most of his possessions were still piled up in the entrance hall. During the period they'd been apart, Laura had arranged for almost all the picture hooks in the place to be removed and for the walls to be repainted, so Nick's production posters remained stacked against a wall. None of his books, CDs or DVDs had as yet found a home either.

"Why don't we just wait and see what we actually *need*," Laura kept saying, "before we go cluttering the place up again?"

With Christmas just days away, the airline's check-in counters were festooned with scalloped loops of silver tinsel and clusters of red and green baubles. In front of Nick in the queue was a woman in a zebra-print playsuit with aggressively spray-tanned shoulders. Nick could see how the chemicals had rubbed off on the fabric at the shoulder straps

"Nick? Are you okay?" Laura repeated, putting a gentle hand on his arm.

In the time-honored fashion of people who are not yet ready to say why they are not fine, Nick said, "I'm fine."

It didn't make Nick feel good to behave this way, but he felt safest to be locked inside himself for the moment. Even though he didn't know precisely what was wrong with him, he did know that, right now, letting out his thoughts and feelings could do nothing but harm.

"Okay," Laura said, and she shrugged as if to say *suit yourself.*

Nick and Laura reached the front of the queue, and as they stepped forward to check in their bags, the girl behind the counter looked hard at Laura.

Here we go, thought Nick.

"Are you . . . aren't you? It is! You are! You're on the Waterlily ads," the girl said. "Oh my God! Those ads are so amazing."

And Laura—whose shining dark hair was caught back in a simple ponytail, whose makeup was restrained but still perfect, and who didn't in any way look the least bit pre-dawn—smiled winningly.

"I don't suppose?" the girl asked, pulling her iPhone out of the pocket of her airline-issue jacket. "Would you mind?"

It amazed Nick that Laura never did mind this kind of attention. She was always entirely generous and patient when people wanted to take pictures of her, and with her. As the girl came around to the customers' side of the console, grinning and blushing, Nick saw Laura effortlessly switch on her modeling face, which was just ever so slightly different from her everyday face. It was as if she were somehow able to solidify her features, or standardize them. It was her business, Nick supposed, to know precisely what to do with her eyes, her cheeks, her lips, in order to get a completely predictable, gorgeous result.

"Are you sure you're okay?" Laura asked, once she and Nick had reached the far side of the security checkpoint, and taken their seats at their gate lounge.

"Yeah, I'm fine," Nick said again.

"It's just that you seem . . ."

And she was right, of course. He did "seem." Because he was.

"I think I'll go get something to read on the plane," Nick said. "Do you want anything from the shop?"

Laura smiled a little sadly. "Just a more cheerful you."

At the concourse newsagent, Nick picked up a packet of black currant pastilles and the year's final edition of the *Alexandria Park Star*. The cover was a Ruthless Hawker cartoon, and Nick gave a little snort of laughter as he decoded its message. The scene was set in a Christmastime living room. At the hearthside, a small table held a crumb-scattered plate, a near-empty brandy balloon and a nibbled carrot. At the center of the image, dressed in onesie pajamas, was the child version of the nation's prime minister, and he was reacting with unconstrained delight to what he had discovered had been left for him, overnight, on the mantelpiece. For there, strung in loops, just where you would expect the bulging stockings to be hung, were small bouquets made out of the testicles of the nation's five most influential union bosses, each little bundle tied with a red bow and garnished with a sprig of holly.

Nick opened the magazine to the page where Leo Thornbury stared out from beneath his thick, shaggy eyebrows.

Aquarius: Through the ups and downs of the year just gone, water bearers, you have found your way to precisely the place you need to be. Expect good fortune in your career, especially if your job requires you to be in the public eye. And, as the spiritual forces of the universe converge within you, there will emerge a new clarity in which love can blossom. Rest assured that whether or not it is clear to you at this moment, you are on the road to where you need to be.

Since he knew from Daniel Griffin that Justine had been suspended from the *Star*, and that Daniel himself was now personally overseeing the astrology column, Nick was as certain as he could be that these words had been written by Leo Thornbury himself. Even so, holding the magazine in his hands made him feel a cocktail of different emotions—none of them particularly pleasant.

There was some anger in the mix, though not so very much anymore. He no longer wanted to go over to Justine's apartment and dangle her off the balcony by her feet until she explained what the fuck she had been thinking.

She had fooled him. Brilliantly. And for months. She had made him into a fool. Because looking back over everything that "Leo" had written, it should have been obvious to him that a ventriloquist had her hand up Leo's shirt. But what was this little prank of hers really all about? Was it just her way of proving to herself that he was ridiculous to pay attention to his horoscopes? Had she been planning, ever, to reveal this little ruse to him? Or was she just going to keep on laughing at him, privately, forever?

Yes, she had made an idiot of him, but even worse than that, she had taken something from him. She'd spoiled it: his one little sprinkling of magic in an otherwise pragmatic world—a harmless handful of stardust and mystery, once a month, on the page of a magazine.

Now that his anger had subsided, he was left with confusion. He had so many unanswered questions. For example, did it necessarily

294) MINNIE DARKE

follow that if you set your course by a false guide, you would end up at the wrong destination? Or, did fate have complicated ways of making sure that you ended up where you were supposed to be, anyway?

For the better part of the year, it had not been Leo Thornbury's astrological predictions, but Justine Carmichael's false ones, that Nick had taken for his compass. This was the equivalent of mistaking a satellite for a star, or of typing out a whole page of text before realizing that your fingers were resting on the wrong keys. It was like trying to find your way around London using a map of New York. So, *was* it the case—as Leo was now suggesting—that Nick had arrived at precisely the place he needed to be? Or was he in the wrong neighborhood altogether?

He was in a place that any number of other people would want to occupy. He had moved in with, and was almost engaged to, an incredibly beautiful woman; he had a new job and was making good money; he was no longer cavorting around a healthy-eating expo in an inflatable capsicum suit, or doing a job that involved wearing a stinking fish costume. He ought, he knew, to be happy. But he was not.

Nick shoved the copy of the *Star* back into the magazine rack, took out a copy of *GQ* and set that magazine down on the counter with his roll of pastilles.

"That'll be eleven thirty-five," said the young guy behind the counter.

Capricorn

DECEMBER 22–JANUARY 19

The human consensus that the Earth finished its annual lap of the sun on December 31 was nothing more than an accident of history—an arbitrary decision that might just as easily have gone a number of other ways. 364.25 other ways. But it didn't. It went the way of December 31, which meant that this date became for all time synonymous with the idea of ending, which, of course, cannot be separated from the notion of beginning. For even as we say a gleeful goodbye to the blots and blemishes on the messy page of the outgoing year, we look forward to turning over to its blank and omnipotential flip side. Tomorrow.

Like so many other people, though possibly with more reason than most, Justine Carmichael that year woke on the morning of December 31 with a sense of relief hovering somewhere in the outer reaches of her consciousness. The year was very nearly done. And, come midnight, the whole messy mess of it would be sealed off with the tick of a clock. Done. Dusted. Put down to experience, and filed. In a dark and dusty place.

That year, New Year's Eve fell on a Sunday. Justine woke, early, in her childhood bedroom in Edenvale, and the sun was already beating down vehemently when she stepped out onto the back deck. Shading her eyes, she picked up the shape of her mother, out in the garden, with a bucket. It was Mandy's habit to keep this bucket at her feet while she was showering. Now, wearing a short cotton dressing gown, she was distributing the collected runoff to her beloved Red Sensation cordylines and her Big Red kangaroo paws.

Justine responded to her mother's good morning wave, and made a desultory plan to walk Lucy at some point during the day—a day that she otherwise intended to spend running down the clock, sitting on the couch and watching the original *Star Wars* trilogy in her pajamas.

♏

In the lead-up to Christmas, Patricia O'Hare had spent rather a lot of time in shopping malls and supermarkets, and her consequent exposure to high-rotation Christmas songs had left her with a snippet of a tune, like a sugary splinter of candy cane, lodged in her brain. Now it was New Year's Eve, but the embedded tune was showing no signs of dissolving; Patricia found herself humming "It's the Most Wonderful Time of the Year" as she walked the concrete paths of the Dogs Home.

In the traditional post-Christmas rush, the shelter had filled to capacity with expensive Spoodle and Cavoodle puppies who'd made unexpected puddles on even more expensive carpets. This year there were also a good many pug puppies that had seemed a lot cuter before they'd chewed their way through several pairs of shoes. A three-year-old chocolate Labrador had been surrendered after eating the baubles off the Christmas tree, again, and one family had said they'd pick up their aging Alsatian when they got back from Bali, if he was still there.

This was traditionally a tough time of year for the Dogs Home: not only were there more animals than usual, most of the volunteers were on holidays. Although Patricia was considered to be an office specialist, this was no time to be a prima donna. So, in the early afternoon, Patricia and her shit shovel entered the pen of the dog that was perhaps the ugliest in the shelter. He was a street terrier and a Dogs Home recidivist, and the likelihood of him being rehomed was virtually nil. The most recent time that he'd been brought in, he'd been wearing a grubby blue bandanna on which someone had written a name: Brown

Houdini-Malarky. This, therefore, was the name he had become known by, and this was the name that was written in chalk on the small blackboard that hung on the wire front of his pen.

"Hey, Brown," Patricia said.

Brown wagged his scraggy, tassel-topped tail. He knew there was no point being crabby with the help. So he just watched as she scooped up a pile of chocolate-mousse-textured excrement. Then, because he was not by nature a grumpy dog, he added a little howl-harmony to the song she was singing.

"You have a lovely voice, Brown," Patricia told him, and gave him a scratch between the ears.

Brown would have liked to take credit for what happened next. In fact, he would take credit, he decided. In the future, as he strolled the streets of the city, a street terrier back in his natural habitat, he would tell how it was the irresistibility of his Voo that made the woman hurriedly carry the shit shovel and bucket out of his pen. He'd claim that it was his superior mind powers that had caused her to shut the door carelessly, and dash away in her bright-colored shoes, with her telephone against her ear, without so much as a backward glance.

"Zadie's what?" Patricia said into the phone. "In labor? Now?"

Brown watched the woman stop and stand still on the path.

You will not look back, you will not look back.

"Have they broken her waters? . . . Uh-huh."

You will not look back. You will not look back.

It was working, Brown saw. The woman was not looking back. Instead she had tears in her eyes, and seemed oblivious to her actual surroundings.

"It's really happening, isn't it? I'm going to be a grandmother . . . Okay, okay. I'm on my way."

After the woman disappeared from Brown's view, Brown waited a prudent moment or two. Then he nudged at the door to his pen with his snout.

Yes! It swung open easily. Brown put out his head, looked to the right, and then to the left, although his lack of a left eye meant that he had to swivel his head further to get a good look in that direction. Seeing that the pathways were clear, he thanked his lucky stars. When it came to being adopted out, it was a disadvantage to be housed this far back in the compound. But when it came to escape, it was a definite plus to be here in the back blocks where the humans were thinner on the ground.

At a distance down the path, Brown spied a pair of garbage cans pushed up against a span of concrete wall. He judged that because they tapered toward their bases, he'd be able to squeeze into the space behind them. From here it was—for a street terrier of courage and enterprise—only a short dash to the compound's back gates. All Brown needed to do was hide, and wait.

Brown slipped out of his pen. He'd have liked to be able to say that he resisted the unworthy temptation that came upon him as he ran for the bins, but the truth is that he did not. Passing the pen of a yappy little Pomeranian who'd been getting his goat for months, Brown sprayed a hurried message in piss across the wire. *Free at last! I'm Brown Houdini-Malarky, and I'm free at last!*

♐

Caleb Harkness—Sagittarius, weekday landscape architect and week-end underwater hockey captain, unconfirmed bachelor and collector of vinyl records—had not been able to forget the pretty dark-haired woman with the gerbera behind her ear whom he had met at the retro charity shop where he'd also found a mint-condition LP of the Pixies' *Doolittle*. Since the day he had met her, he'd been kicking himself for being a dickhead. Not only had he been too shy to ask for her phone number, he'd been too much of a dill even to ask her name, or find out where she worked.

On that fateful day of the Charles and Diana wedding china, there had been ample time and ample opportunity. While those twenty pack-ing boxes full of china had been blocking the shop's doorway, he could have sought out some kind of useful information. And even once the entrance had been cleared, there had still been plenty of time. Along with the shopgirl, Caleb and the woman with the gerbera behind her ear had opened box after box in an increasingly hysterical mood of incredulity. They'd had to know: just how much Charles and Diana wedding china could one person conceivably own?

During the whole episode, the single fact he had gleaned—and this was only because she had offered it in passing—was that she was a florist. Where? In this city? In which suburb? He hadn't asked. He was a monumental moron.

True, she was most likely married, to some intense and sophisticated abstract painter, probably, or a playwright with sideburns. Or, for that matter, a playwright with exquisite breasts. But what if she wasn't? He'd never had much time for the concept of chemistry, but he was pretty sure he'd been atomized by the way she smelled. Like lilacs after rain. She was slender and dark, with a sexy rasp to her voice. She was witty and had a ready laugh, and above all she was somehow familiar, as if he already knew what it might feel like to wake up with her curly head in the curve of his arm. And this was why he had decided to systematically visit every florist in every suburb of the city until he found her.

But who knew there could be so many? She was nowhere to be seen in the glossy, commercial florist near the hospital, which sold pink and blue teddy bears and foil balloons with sparkly messages. Nor had he found her in any of the classier flower boutiques in the city center. He'd had high hopes on the day he'd gone into the Asian-inspired florist—its window invitingly cluttered with orchids and other tropical blooms—that wasn't far from the charity shop. But she wasn't there either.

He began his search with total optimism, but reached the end of his list without any joy. Now it was New Year's Eve, and it was on Caleb's mind to add "forget pretty florist" to his list of resolutions, which also included "stop wasting whole evenings browsing for records on eBay," "get a better filing system for tax receipts" and "save money by packing weekday lunches."

On this day, the last of the year, Caleb's uber-organized younger sister was hosting a family dinner, and since this sister did not consider her brother capable of making a sufficiently impressive salad or a dessert, she had allocated him the job of bringing the prawns. All he had to do, she'd said, was pick up a couple of kilos on the way.

So there he was, in the Alexandria Park Markets at around 4 p.m.

on New Year's Eve holding a paper-wrapped parcel of raw prawns that were never going to make it to his sister's dinner table. For just across the way was a florist's stall that had not been on his list. It was called Hello Petal and behind the counter, with a bright orange gerbera behind her ear, was his pretty florist. Caleb didn't stop to think. He walked toward her. And by the time he realized that he had no plan for what he was going to say, he was standing less than a meter away from her.

She wore an apron of embroidered gingham and pinned to the strap was a hand-stitched calico name tag. Fern. Her name was Fern. It suited her perfectly. Caleb felt his hands start to sweat as he watched her set a tray of velvety potted pansies onto the counter. She lifted her gaze. And saw him.

He could see that she recognized him.

"Hello again," she said.

He could see that she was pleased.

"Hi," he said. "I've been looking for . . ."

He searched nervously about him for a noun to insert. Roses? *Boring. Obvious.* Lilies? *Funereal.* The gap in his sentence was going on for too long. Caleb blinked. Fern widened her smile. She knew what he was looking for. She was bloody lovely. He might as well just tell the truth.

"I've been looking for you," he said.

♐

It was from inside the lip of a culvert at the side of a busy highway that Brown Houdini-Malarky saw the last of the day's light—which was also the last of the year—ebb from the sky. He had spent several hot, thirsty hours wedged behind those garbage cans, waiting for someone to open the back gate, and toward the end of the working day he had begun to think that it was never going to happen. But at last someone did come, and in a spectacular piece of luck, it was a volunteer with rickety knees and lousy vision; Brown had slipped by him unseen, even though the spaniel that the man held on a leash had barked like crazy.

Now that night had fallen, Brown trotted along the shoulder of the highway until he came to the bright lights and foody smells of a roadhouse. Out the front of the roadhouse's diner was a garbage bin overflowing with delights. Already on the ground were the scraps of a mostly eaten burger. Brown scoffed these down, and then, reaching up and resting his paws on the side of the bin, he used his snout to overbalance a milkshake cup that had been wedged into the mouth. Yellow, banana-flavored milk dribbled down the side of the bin and Brown lapped at it gratefully. This was his first meal in months that wasn't kibble or Pal.

Brown retreated to a safe spot in the shadows and sat on his haunches to watch the road-trains come and go. As a mode of transportation, these trucks were imperfect. Brown knew from experience that they usually skirted the edges of the city, only rarely going smack through the middle. However, road-train drivers were often lonely, which made them a good deal more likely than car drivers to give a lift to a small fellow traveler. If Brown could hitch a lift in a road-train, it would get him at least part of the way back to the streets he knew so well.

The first truckie Brown saw was of the wrong sort. He had a sharp face, a businesslike manner and a gleaming rig, which meant he would almost certainly be intolerant of dog fur. The second truckie looked more accommodating, but he was heading away from town, not toward it. *Third time's a charm*, Brown thought, spying a corpulent, untidy-looking truck driver coming out of the diner with an armload of greasy food and sugary drinks. By the time the driver reached his road-train, Brown was sitting on the ground beside the cab, wagging his tail in a friendly, but not overexuberant, manner.

The truckie saw the small ugly dog and immediately experienced a sequence of very clear thoughts. *I will open the door of my rig*, he thought. *I will let this cute little fella hop in, and I will take him for a ride. Also, I will open the passenger window wide for him, so he can put his head out and smell the breeze.*

Moments later, Brown Houdini-Malarky was speeding toward the city with the wind in his fur and one eye open for his next opportunity.

7

Laura Mitchell wore a knee-length black sheath dress with a subtle lace detail at the neck and hem, and strappy black heels. Her hair fell in carefully constructed waves around her shoulders and while her makeup was not precisely subtle, neither was it in any way over the top.

"You look amazing," Nick said, who—at Laura's insistence—had donned his tux.

They were out the front of their apartment block, waiting for the taxi that would take them to the Galaxy casino. There, they would meet up with two of Laura's colleagues, Eve and Sergei, who had suggested eating at Capretto, the flashiest of the casino's restaurants, where the meals were tiny and the kitchen didn't close until very late. After dinner, the four planned to head up to the ballroom on the top floor for Galaxy's traditional New Year's Eve concert, headlined this year by one of Nick's favorite artists, Blessed Jones.

Laura flashed Nick an exquisite smile. "This will be a night to remember, won't it?"

Nick nodded. He knew what she meant. Both he and Laura knew, but had not openly acknowledged, that at some point tonight Nick would surprise Laura by producing the ring box that was presently in his pocket, and proposing to her.

The design of the ring wasn't any more of a genuine surprise than the timing of its presentation. Laura had been involved in every part of the process—selecting the jeweler, choosing the stone (a deep red ruby), sketching the setting (simple, elegant, white gold), ensuring the correct sizing and sending Nick a text message to let him know the ring was ready to be collected.

It was only practical, Laura had said, for a woman to be involved in selecting her wedding jewelry. After all, she'd told him, if it was going to be forever, it had to be perfect.

♑

Tansy Brinklow put her foot down and her brand-new Alfa Romeo Spider put on yet another burst of exhilarating speed. It was just after 8 p.m. on New Year's Eve, the top was down, "You Sexy Thing" was throbbing through the speakers, and the ends of the silver-gray cash-mere scarf that covered Tansy's hair were blowing in the wind.

Tansy had no particular destination in mind. Right now, all she cared about was passing a road-train that was blocking her view of the road ahead. She indicated briefly and slid into the left lane. As she passed the monster truck, it seemed to her, fleetingly, as if something had flown out of its passenger window—something like a dirty rug, or a mangy soft toy. But when she looked in her rearview mirror, there was nothing lying on the road. Tansy shrugged and drove on toward the city, not realizing that a small brown stowaway was now huddled down on the floor behind the driver's seat, panting with relief.

♏

At around 9 p.m., Nick and Laura's taxi was passing the western edge of the city's Botanic Gardens, and Nick—even though he was periph-erally aware of the tightness of his shirt collar and bow tie—was feel-ing the way he often did when someone else was driving him around, which was pleasantly mesmerized and dreamy.

"What are you thinking about?" Laura asked.

"Hm?" he said, although he'd heard her perfectly well.

"I said, what are you thinking about?"

"I was thinking about my stars," Nick said, and this was mostly true.

And, as the spiritual forces of the universe converge within you, Leo had written, *there will emerge a new clarity in which love can blossom.* But, of course, thinking about the stars, and about Leo Thornbury, in-evitably caused Nick to think of Justine.

"You and your stars," Laura mocked, squeezing his hand.

At that moment, Nick saw a small dog—a terrier of some kind—leap out of a black convertible onto the road. No longer feeling mes-merized, Nick leaned forward to watch the dog weave its way between the cars that were traveling in the same direction as the taxi. He saw it make its way safely to the traffic island, wait for a moment, then bolt—through the oncoming traffic—in the direction of the Botanic

Gardens. For the most part, the dog did an amazing job of dodging the speeding cars. But then it miscalculated and was struck on its left side by a fast-moving car. The dog slid sideways across the asphalt. There was blood on the road; the car didn't stop.

"Holy shit! Did you see that?"

"Yes, yes. That does not look good," the driver said.

"Stop the car," Nick said.

"What's the matter?" Laura asked, peering out into the traffic. "Was there an accident?"

"A dog was hit. I'm going after it." Nick flicked open the latch of his door.

"A dog?" Laura asked, incredulous. "Nick, we've got a dinner reservation."

"You go on. I'll catch you up. Order without me, all right? I'll be there as soon as I can."

"You can't just go running after a dog! Not tonight! It's New Year's Eve, Nick. We've got *plans*."

But Nick had already stepped out into the heavy traffic, and was blowing a kiss to her through the window of the taxi's closed door.

Nick, as the dog had done, made it safely to the traffic island and paused there. Unlike the dog, he had the advantage of being easily seen by the drivers of the cars that sped along the section of road. Holding up both hands in a gesture that was part surrender, part plea, part apology, he made his way through the muddle of swerving vehicles and honking horns to reach the far side of the road, where, on the sidewalk, the dog had left an erratic, spotted trail of blood.

Nick jogged along, following the evidence, until he found the dog huddled into the foliage at the base of a hedge. Through a single dark eye, the dog watched Nick approach, its whole body trembling. There was blood in the dog's fur, and one forepaw appeared to be painfully twisted.

"You poor little bugger," Nick said. "I think we'd better get you some help, hey? Come here, mate. Come on, come here."

Nick crouched low as he continued to move forward, and the noises he made were soft and soothing. Even so, the dog's one eye seemed to grow larger, and darker, from fear, and just when Nick was within pouncing range, the dog got to three of its four legs and dived through a narrow gap in the hedge.

"Shit," said Nick, and he took off at a run, following the hedge and trying to remember how many entrances there were to the gardens, and where the hell they were. After a few minutes, he came to a pair of gates made from tall spears of wrought iron. Affixed to the left-hand gate was a playbill for Sideways Shakespeare's *Romeo and Juliet*.

Nick pushed on the right-hand gate, which swung open. Inside this precinct of greenness and quiet, he surveyed the darkened dips and rises of the lawns, the curving pathways and the black shapes of the trees. The lampposts at the sides of the paths were almost invisible in the dark, and their globes of light seemed to hang in the night, as fuzz-edged as dandelion flowers. Nick searched the scene, until he saw a flash of limping movement at the crest of a rise.

The dog had a good head start on him, and it was many minutes before Nick—running as fast as he could in his shiny, grip-free shoes—reached the place at the top of the slope where he had seen the dog. The rise gave a view down over the Botanic Gardens' famous lily pond, but once again the dog had disappeared from sight.

Oh well, Nick thought, he'd tried his best.

"Hey Siri," he said to his phone. "Call Laura Mitchell."

"I'm sorry," Siri said. "I didn't quite catch that." His Siri was aging, and lately had become quite hard of hearing.

"Call Laura Mitchell," he enunciated to his Siri, but as he did so, Nick sighted the dog laboring up a stretch of lawn on the far side of the water, heading for a stand of tall conifers.

"Which Laura did you want to call?" Siri asked, flashing up options on the screen of his phone, but Nick ignored her.

Which way to go? Nick wondered. Which way was shorter, around the lake to the left side, or the right? Or . . . there was a third option.

Across the middle of the pond was a narrow concrete weir, over which water flowed in a shallow waterfall. If he were to walk across it, he reasoned, he'd barely get his feet wet. He would do it, he decided—he would go straight across the middle of the pond.

The concrete weir was as wide, or even slightly wider, than his footprint; it was hardly a wire strung between skyscrapers. Nevertheless, Nick felt his pulse accelerate as if he were attempting some death-defying feat. Left foot, right foot, left foot, right . . . But then, in his haste, he stepped directly onto a lily leaf rather than carefully edging a toe underneath it. The leaf's surface was slippery. Nick's foot slid sideways. Without thinking, he flung out his arms wide to recapture his balance, and as he did so, he let go of the phone in his hand. It made only the barest splash as it followed gravity all the way to the bottom of the lily pond.

"No!" Nick cried out, for although it was a long way from the newest iPhone in the world, it was still Nick's second most valuable possession, after his bicycle. He stood with hands on hips and looked back at the dark water, floating with leaves. His phone was gone, and there was nothing, he knew, to be done about it. But now it was pretty much compulsory for him to find this dog. If he found the dog, the loss of his phone was noble. If he didn't, it was only stupid.

♑

It seemed to Phoebe Wintergreen that she and Luke were the only two members of the audience who had come to *Romeo and Juliet* without a picnic blanket and a basket full of dips and crackers, wine and plastic glasses. Although Luke had spread out his coat for them to sit on, the heels of Phoebe's hands were numb from being pressed into the dewy grass, and her skirt felt damp all over.

They'd taken turns sipping from the neck of a bottle of Stone's Green Ginger Wine that Phoebe had nicked from the pantry shelf where her mother hid her cooking plonk, but although the evening had begun with such promise, Phoebe was sensing all her hopes fading away. Surely if Luke was going to reach over and take her hand, he'd have done it by now. They were in Act Three, for heaven's sake.

Tybalt—striding across the stage with heavy blades swinging in both hands—was being played by a woman. She was tall and imposing, with auburn hair pulled back tightly into two thick braids, and a costume that suggested her as a Viking shield maiden. Mercutio, already fallen on the ground behind her, wasn't dressed in matching Viking style, but in what might have been Oscar Wilde's velvet smoking jacket.

"Mercutio's soul is but a little way above our heads," said a distraught Romeo, looking up into the sky, "staying for thine to keep him company. Either thou or I, or both, must go with him."

Romeo's costume was of a different style again. He wore a simple white shirt and a pair of rustic, knee-length breeches that made him look like he might have just been out herding goats in an Austrian meadow.

Tybalt, with utter disdain, held a blade tip to Romeo's throat, and the audience took a collective breath as the actress delivered her next line: "Thou wretched boy, that didst consort him here, shalt with him hence."

But Romeo dodged the threat, gripped his own blade tighter and readied himself to fight. "This shall determine that!" Romeo cried, and lunged for Tybalt.

As Romeo and Tybalt dueled, Phoebe caught sight of what seemed to be a dog. It was limping down the right flank of the audience and being pursued by a guy in a tuxedo.

"Look," Phoebe whispered to Luke. "Over there."

"Is it part of the play?" Luke whispered back.

"Not the version I know."

"What's he doing?"

"He wants to catch it, I think."

Phoebe could see that the tuxedo guy was trying to keep low and remain unnoticed, but that he wasn't really succeeding.

When the dog reached the edge of the stage's pool of light, the tuxedo guy pounced. But the dog had no plans to be contained. It yelped and struggled, the blood from his jaw smearing all over the front of the guy's white shirt, then launched itself back to the ground, landing with a yowl of pain. It took off at a limping run, his head half turned back to keep an eye on his pursuer. Phoebe put a hand over her mouth as the dog ran straight into the middle of Romeo and Tybalt's duel.

"What the hell?" yelled Tybalt, suddenly off-book as a flash of grubby fur fled past her feet.

It seemed to Phoebe that the dog was going to run straight through the set and out the other side, but then, catching sight of the arc of Romeo's swinging blade, the animal reversed direction. People in the audience laughed nervously, unsure of what was going on while the poor dog dashed confusedly in this direction and that, getting under the feet of first one of the fighters, then the other, while the tuxedo guy hovered at the edge of the stage light with his arms spread as if he hoped to be able to snare the dog if it bolted in his direction.

Then Alison Tarf herself—the director of the play, and of the company—appeared in her stage-crew blacks, her pale hair flying about as she tried to grab the troublesome canine. But the dog swerved away from her and ran between the legs of Tybalt, who lost her balance and fell heavily into Romeo, her sword fist striking hard against his face. Romeo dropped his sword and let out a cry of distress. Most of the people in the crowd were out of their seats or up on their knees, straining to see what was going on.

"My toof! My toof! I've lost a fucking toof!" Romeo shouted.

"Is this for real?" Luke asked Phoebe.

"I have no idea *what's* happening."

There was blood on Romeo's hands and face, and Mercutio—who had been lying dead on the cobblestones—suddenly sat bolt upright.

"It's my bloody front toof," Romeo cried out.

Tybalt, on her hands and knees, was searching the path. "I've got it! I've got it," she said, holding something up between thumb and forefinger.

Then Alison Tarf managed at last to snatch up the tiring dog by its rib cage. She was still holding the panting animal tightly against her chest as she took center stage. "We do apologize," she said, a little breathlessly, "for this unscheduled interruption to the production. Please talk among yourselves for a moment while we reorganize ourselves."

Phoebe, overhearing snippets of the conversation that followed (*what are we going to do . . . fucking catastrophe . . . no understudy . . . send everyone home! . . . give them back their money . . . where's James? . . . taken him to the emergency dentist*), couldn't believe her bad luck. Why couldn't it have been Juliet who'd needed to be helped off the stage? If it had been Juliet, then she—Phoebe Wintergreen—would have been able to go down and say to Alison Tarf, *I know Juliet. My soul is cousin to her soul! I can be your Juliet.*

☍

Nick, under the withering gaze of Alison Tarf, opened his mouth to speak.

Then stopped himself.

What was he thinking? In his pocket was a very large ruby ring that his girlfriend was expecting him, at some point during this evening, to slip onto her finger. And in Alison Tarf's arms was a bleeding dog—a dog that had become Nick's responsibility. The animal needed the attention of a vet. But Nick also knew Romeo's part. He still knew every word, he realized, thinking of Justine, sitting on her balcony, cross-legged, with his open script on one knee and a box of Maltesers in the other.

"I could—" Nick began.

"You could *what*?" Alison Tarf said tersely.

"I could . . . play Romeo," Nick said. "I know Romeo. I did Romeo just this year. At the Gaiety. I still have all the lines."

Then Alison Tarf looked at him more closely. With refocused vision, she stared at him, hard. "I saw you. I saw that play," she said. "And didn't I call you? About an audition?"

"I'm sorry, I—"

"*Who* is he?" asked Juliet, perplexed.

"He," said Alison Tarf, suddenly lit up with joy and mischief, "is our new Romeo."

Nick stroked the head of the exhausted dog. "See all those people, buddy? They need for the show to go on. Do you reckon you can just hang on through to curtain call? Please? I'll get you to the vet just as soon as I can. All right, mate?"

And was it Nick's imagination, or was there just the glimmer of understanding in the dog's one, dark eye?

"Okay," said Alison, "let's do this thing."

Nick asked the director, "What about costume?"

Alison Tarf took Nick by the shoulders and surveyed him in his tuxedo and blood-splattered shirt. "You'll do just fine as you are."

♑

Annabel Barwick—Cancer, weekday veterinarian and weekend quilting enthusiast, star of wedding photographs that co-starred a cockatiel called Sheila, practical supporter of numerous local animal shelters and founder of a vaccination charity for homeless Nepalese dogs—was working late that New Year's Eve.

She hadn't intended to work late, but a young red-and-tan sheepdog had been brought in, vomiting and listless, and the X-rays had revealed that a squeaker from a soft toy had become firmly lodged in his bowel. The dog was now coming out of its anesthetic with a seam of Annabel's immaculate stitchery down its shaven belly.

Having sent home all of her staff but one nurse, Annabel sat at the front desk of the surgery filling in paperwork relating to the sheepdog's operation. Beyond the glass door that led out into the street, the city was in party mode, and Annabel could sense the pulse of its festivities. When the door opened at around 11:15 p.m., it let in a gasp of noise—the bass beat of music, the shouts of revelers, the irritating mosquito-buzz of vuvuzelas. It also admitted a young and good-looking guy wearing a tuxedo and holding a bloodied terrier in his arms.

No, no, no, no, no, thought Annabel, feeling the last of her hopes of leaving the surgery before midnight evaporate into nothingness. Briefly, she considered telling the man that she couldn't help. That perhaps he could try a different clinic. But then she looked into the eye of the broken dog. It needed help. And now that she looked at the dog more closely, she realized that he had crossed her path before.

"That's Brown Houdini-Malarky," Annabel said, coming around to the other side of the counter.

"You know him?" said the guy in the tuxedo.

"Did you adopt him?" Annabel asked, incredulous.

"What?"

"From the Dogs Home? Did you adopt him?"

"What? No, no. I don't know the first thing about him. He got clipped by a car, not far from the Botanic Gardens. I just happened to see it, so I chased him and got hold of him, and came as soon as I could. Well . . . there was a bit of a delay. Shit. He's not going to die, is he?"

The vet smoothed back the fur that fell down over Brown's one good eye. The dog's breathing was labored, but not disastrously so. There was sticky, clotting blood in his fur, and it was all over the fine white pleats of the man's tuxedo shirt, too.

"Oh, Brown. Did you do a Houdini again?" Annabel asked the dog. And then, to the man, "Can you bring him this way?"

With Brown lying on a consultation room table, it didn't take Annabel long to identify that the dog had a very badly broken leg and a slightly less badly broken jaw. She also suspected there was a bit of internal bleeding in the picture.

"It's not good," Annabel told the man. "I mean to say, I can probably save him, but the question is whether or not I should."

She explained that Brown Houdini-Malarky had been in and out of the Dogs Home for most of his life. He'd been given more than a fair chance of being rehomed, but with his missing eye and . . . well, he wasn't exactly an oil painting . . . nobody had ever opened their heart to him. He'd already been on death row once, she said. That he hadn't been put down already was miraculous. All things considered, if she phoned the Dogs Home to ask them what to do, they'd probably tell her to—

"No."

"No?"

The guy took a deep breath. "Look, I have to get going. I'm already really, really, disastrously late for where I'm supposed to be. But if you can do the surgery, I'll pay."

"You realize we could fix him up, only for him to be put down in six months, or a year? If no one adopts him. And surgery's expensive. I mean, I'll discount it as much as I can, but . . ." Annabel trailed off.

"He really is ugly, isn't he?" the guy said, scratching the dog fondly behind the matted fur of one ear.

"He's a shocker," Annabel confirmed.

At another time, Nick Jordan might have made a different decision.

But right now he was high on applause and full of confidence in himself and the elasticity of his bank account.

The opening-night crowd at the Botanic Gardens, amazed that Sideways Shakespeare had managed to make the show go on with a substitute Romeo, had leaped to its collective feet at the end and given the cast and crew a standing ovation. And not only that, when Nick had stepped forward to take his bow, the applause had intensified yet further. There had been shouts and whistles and fist pumping. He had been a hero. He had been the hero.

"I don't care what it costs. I'll pay," Nick promised.

♉

Nick took the stairs to the front entrance of the Galaxy casino two at a time, and after pushing through a revolving door that seemed to take forever to turn, stepped into the sparkling ambience of the casino's foyer. One wall was taken up with a vast water feature that appeared to drop curtains of diamonds. All around were women in glittering dresses and men in clouds of cologne.

Nick, with his blood-splattered shirt, untied tie and scruffed-up hair, was attracting attention. But he didn't have time to worry about that right now. Patting the pocket of his rumpled jacket, he reassured himself that even though his phone was at the bottom of a lily pond, Laura's engagement ring was still safely in his possession. Nick found an elevator and hammered impatiently on the Up button, and at last the twin doors opened.

The word BALLROOM was etched into the metal beside the topmost button on the control panel. Nick pushed it and he was away. Almost: just before the doors sealed in the center, they halted with a jerk, and slid back open. Nick felt a spike of frustration as a teenage girl and boy hurried into the lift with the air of two kids who'd just found a really good hide-and-seek spot. Seeing that they weren't alone in the lift, they tried to compose themselves, but neither one of them could get the silly grins to disappear entirely from their faces.

They were too young to be here, Nick observed. And they'd had a bit to drink. In fact, Nick was pretty sure that the neck of a bottle was sticking out of the girl's grubby patchwork shoulder bag. She had a bob of dense sandy-colored hair and was pretty in an off-center way that had something to do with her eyes, which were blue-green, and very large.

The girl made a small lurch forward, as if she were going to speak to Nick, then checked herself. Nick remembered that he probably looked a bit alarming in his bloodstained shirt, so he tried to exude a nonimpatient and nonthreatening vibe as he gestured to the control panel and asked the kids, "Which floor?"

"Um . . . ballroom," the boy said.

The elevator's three external walls were made of slightly tinted glass, and as the whole structure slid up over the face of the building, Nick and the lift's two other passengers were treated to an increasingly impressive view. The usually open spaces of the city—the parks and gardens, the civic squares and riverside esplanades—were tonight cluttered with humanity.

Nick checked his watch.

It was 11:55.

There was still time, he thought, to make this a night to remember.

♑

It was Fern Emerson's firmly held view that New Year's Eve was the most anticlimactic, disappointing and bogus celebration ever invented. This was in large part because, back in her early twenties, on three consecutive New Year's Eves, Fern had ended up in hospital.

The first time, she'd gone out for the night wearing brand-new high-heeled shoes that had hurt like hell. It had been well before midnight when she'd admitted defeat, taken the horrible shoes off, and left them on a park bench. But then she'd stepped, in bare feet, on a rather large shard of broken glass that had needed to be removed under local anesthetic.

The following year, Fern had been helping a hopelessly inebriated girlfriend into a taxi when the friend had accidentally kicked out with an uncoordinated foot and sent Fern flying into oncoming traffic, where she collected a decent concussion.

The year after that, in an attempt to break the jinx, Fern had got the hell out of town. With a few friends, she'd gone up the coast to a tropical resort where she planned to see in the New Year with mai tais and a spot of midnight skinny-dipping. That was why Fern had been completely starkers when she had stepped on the venomous spines of a stonefish. She'd been rushed to the local hospital, in agonizing pain and wrapped in a towel, vowing and declaring that she would never again, not ever, under any circumstances, celebrate New Year's Eve.

But this year, she had felt that resolution dissolve into nothingness as Caleb Harkness had looked at her nervously across the Hello Petal counter and said, "I don't mean to be forward. Or maybe that's a lie. Maybe I do mean to be forward. But, what are you doing tonight? I don't suppose there's a snowball's chance in hell you're free. To go out. With me? It's probably a bit late to get tickets to the concert at the Galaxy. But, for those in the know, there's an overspill venue. Very exclusive."

And that was how Fern found herself at 11:45 p.m. on the roof of the Galaxy casino, huddled by the side of a large air-conditioning vent from which poured the gorgeous voice of Blessed Jones. Beyond the edges of the rooftop was a 360-degree view of the pulsing, night-lit city. Everything was perfect. Almost.

Fern shivered. It was an occupational hazard of hers to be always a little bit damp, and the cardigan she'd thrown over her working blacks was only thin.

"You're cold," Caleb observed. He helped her to her feet and led her to a plant room that sat on the rooftop like a recently landed TARDIS. The door was unlocked.

"Is it always this easy?" Fern asked, amazed. Their journey to the roof had taken them in and out of elevators, up flights of stairs and through doors bearing signs that warned of dire consequences. And yet, Fern realized, they'd encountered barely any obstacles.

"Almost always," Caleb said, holding open the plant-room door.

"How do you know this stuff?"

"Misspent youth," Caleb said, with a smile that hinted, truthfully, at his extensive repertoire of funny, crazy, stupid, true stories.

Inside the plant room, the air hummed with electrical noise. All around were mechanical things whose precise functions Fern could not have guessed at. There were levers and pulleys, and large wheels that were turning, wire coiling or uncoiling as they moved. All along one wall were huge metal cupboards, their doors wide open to reveal panels cluttered with switches, knobs and wires.

Caleb shut the door and stood there uncertainly, his hands in his pockets. It seemed to Fern that now they were inside, in this brightly lit space, neither she nor Caleb had any idea what to say, or how to be. She endured a few more seconds of awkwardness, then took a deep breath, and a risk.

"Were you really looking for me?" she asked.

"Absolutely."

"Really?"

"Why so surprised?"

"Things like that don't happen. Not to me."

"They do, actually. Here, look, I can prove it."

From his wallet, Caleb drew out a well-thumbed scrap of paper and handed it to Fern. It was a list of all the florist shops in the city. "Now I'm starting to worry that you'll think I'm a stalker."

Fern read through the list: the Tilted Tulip, the Bloom Room, Mother Earth, Laurel . . . and on, and on it went.

"But your shop wasn't listed in the yellow pages," Caleb said.

"I missed the cut-off date."

"And all for that," Caleb said, "I might never have found you."

"Just think, though," Fern said, her mind boggling. "Someone threw out all that Charles and Diana china. If they hadn't, you'd have just gone out the door with your Pixies LP and we'd never have even talked."

"You remember which LP I bought," Caleb said, grinning.

Fern, her arms still wrapped around her cold shoulders, grinned back.

And there, in the plant room on the rooftop of the Galaxy casino, at 11:55 p.m. on New Year's Eve, Caleb Harkness kissed Fern Emerson for the first time. The kiss began gently, but didn't take long to warm up. Soon Fern was tugging at the buttons on the front of Caleb's shirt, and Caleb was reaching up under Fern's black skirt to discover that her black stockings were held up with garters.

"Oh, man, that's sexy," Caleb said.

Soon Fern and Caleb were a tangle of arms and legs and tongues. They staggered backward and Caleb's foot landed on the head of a broom; the broom handle fell sideways into the open switchboard cupboard. There came a series of rapid, electrical-sounding bangs. Sparks flew, and, unbeknownst to Caleb and Fern, one of the Galaxy casino's glass elevators came to a shuddering halt somewhere between the twenty-third and twenty-fourth floors of the building.

Caleb held Fern protectively to his chest as a faint burning smell wafted through the air of the plant room.

"Fuck," he said.

"Fireworks," said Fern.

♑

Nick felt the elevator pull up short, and then bounce a couple of times like a box on a string.

"That's not good," said the girl with the patchwork bag, looking up at the lift's ceiling.

Nick hammered on the button marked Ballroom, but to no effect. He tried the buttons for G, LG and Mezzanine. Desperately, he pushed a sequence of random numbers, and also the button that was supposed to make the doors of the lift slide open. But the doors did not open. Nor did the lift budge a millimeter. The only thing that happened was that the soothing tones of Ben Lee's "We're All in This Together" continued to seep in through the speaker above the closed doors.

"Fuck!" Nick said.

Then he remembered that his mobile phone was most likely being nibbled on by carp.

"Double fuck!" he yelled, and kicked at the door.

The boy and the girl each took a step closer together, then sprang apart as if they'd given each other an electric shock.

"Oh, shit. Sorry. Look, it's all right. I'm all right. I'm sorry," Nick said. "I've had a pretty strange night, yeah? And, along the way, I lost my phone. We'll have to use one of yours."

The boy and the girl looked at each other.

"Mine's flat," the boy said. "I mean, totally."

"And I don't have one," the girl said.

"Are you serious? What kind of teenagers are you?"

"Impecunious in my case," the girl replied, with a shrug. "Disorganized in his."

"Sorry. Sorry. Shit, I'm sorry. It's just . . . look, I'm several hours late to meet my girlfriend, and I've got this massive ruby in my pocket and she's expecting me to put it on her finger tonight, and I really wanted to see Blessed Jones, and by now the concert's probably all over, and this was supposed to be a really, you know, important night . . ."

"It can't be long, though, can it?" the girl asked, trying a sequence of buttons for herself. "They'll get the lifts moving again soon, won't they?"

"Look," the boy said, pointing.

Further along the face of the building, Nick saw another of the casino's glass lifts trundling upward with ease.

"Triple fuck," Nick said, though not angrily this time.

"Why?" the girl asked.

"Because humans are lazy bastards. If all the lifts in the place were down, someone would notice almost immediately. But one stuck lift? You'd just go get in another one. Wouldn't you? We could be here for a while."

"We could try the emergency phone," the boy said meekly, and Nick felt himself color a little, knowing that he'd so far failed to be the responsible adult in the situation. He located a button showing the symbol of a telephone and after he pressed it, the speaker beside it let out a series of extended beeps. The bleeping went on, and on, and on. And then, abruptly, stopped.

Nick pressed the button again. But for a second time the emergency phone failed to put Nick in contact with anybody who could help.

"It's New Year's Eve," the boy said, with a shrug. "Busy night, maybe?"

A few blocks away from the casino, a bank of electronic billboards—shimmering with images and flashing lights—made a tall peak in the city's skyline. On a square screen in the center was a display of diminishing numbers that Nick presumed to be a countdown of the seconds until midnight. There were 10, 9, 8, 7, 6, 5, 4, 3, 2, 1 . . .

"Well, happy New Year, guys," Nick said glumly, and as he spoke, the sky beyond the bank of billboards filled with the sparkling blooms of fireworks—bright white, pink, red, blue, green.

"Go on," Nick said. "Kiss your girlfriend. I won't look."

The boy blushed beetroot. "She's not, um . . . we're just friends."

And although the boy was too absorbed with his own discomfort to notice for himself, Nick quite clearly saw the heartbroken expression that spread outward, sudden as fireworks, in the girl's blue-green eyes.

♐

Two hours west of the city, in the town of Edenvale, Justine Carmichael sat at the optimal end of her parents' leather couch—the one closest to the coffee table, upon which was a depleted bottle of gin, a small plate of partly dried-out lime slices and a bottle of flat tonic water. She wore what looked like, and in fact were, her pajamas: an oversized pink and white striped T-shirt with the word *Dream* emblazoned in gold letters across the chest, and a pair of black leggings with a large, ragged hole in one knee. As the clock ticked over from 11:59 to 12:00, Justine was alone, except for the gin and tonic in her hand, the snoring spaniel on the living-room rug, and the live footage of the city's fireworks display that was playing on the screen of a muted television.

Earlier in the evening, Mandy Carmichael, wearing a too-short nurse's uniform, and Drew Carmichael, in a pair of aviator goggles and an ancient leather flying jacket, had tried to entice Justine to come with them to their New Year's Eve party. It was being held out in the MacPhersons' shearing shed and the theme was "what you want to be when you grow up."

"I don't have anything to go as," Justine had said, aware that she was failing to prevent herself from sounding petulant.

"But you can just go as anything, darling," Mandy had said. "Anything at all. It's not like I ever wanted to be a nurse. I figured that if all you've got left is nice legs, you might as well show them off, hey?"

"Mac's doing a whole forty-four-gallon drum of his punch," Drew had put in.

Pissed fifty-year-olds, conversations with proud parents about Justine's old school friends and their weddings and babies. Hay dust. Sneezing. The underlying smell of sheep shit and lanolin.

"I don't think I can face it, Daddo. Not tonight."

And now it was midnight, and a new year. Justine took a slug of gin and tonic. On the television, revelers sang and leaped and kissed, and overexcited reporters said things through brightly lipsticked mouths, while potassium nitrate burned all over the sky. The world was going on without her, but Justine didn't need to know. She hit the Off button on the remote, went out onto the back deck, and dragged one of her mother's indoor-outdoor couches closer to the edge of the timber decking where it gave her a better view of the sky.

To the stars, Justine whispered, "Let's try to do better this year, shall we?"

♑

Below the stalled glass elevator on the side of the Galaxy casino, traffic lights turned green, amber, red. Cars accelerated and stopped. A lit-up Ferris wheel wound on and on, conveying each new carload of passengers ten minutes into their futures. Nick pressed the emergency telephone button again, and again, and again, until at last he gave up and sat down.

The girl brought the bottle out of her bag, and—although it appeared to be close to empty—offered it to Nick.

"Stone's Green Ginger Wine?" Nick asked. "Seriously? I can't believe you kids still drink this crap."

Nevertheless, he took a deep slug. The burning sweetness at first made him wince, but then it triggered a small flash of memory. Beach sand, and the distant thump of bass, and a teenage version of Justine leaning against his chest as she pointed up at an indigo sky. What was it that she had said?

"Then there was a star danced," Nick murmured to himself, and the girl smiled at him across the elevator.

"And under that was I born," she returned.

"What did you say?"

"Then there was a star danced," the girl repeated. "And under that was I born."

Nick blinked. "You know it?"

"Of course. It's Beatrice from *Much Ado About Nothing*. And I would have thought you'd have already known that . . . Romeo."

Nick winced. "You two were at the Gardens tonight?"

The pair nodded.

"So you saw the dog? You saw everything?"

"Yup," the girl said. "It was amazing. The way you just stepped into the role, without knowing the blocking or anything. You could hardly even tell that you weren't the real Romeo."

"Thanks," Nick said. "I got the dog to the vet. Right after the show. I think he's going to be all right. I'm Nick, by the way."

"Phoebe. And he's Luke."

"She's an actor, too," Luke said.

"You are?" Nick asked.

Phoebe did a humble face.

"You would not believe how much she loves Shakespeare. She's really amazing," Luke said, and now Phoebe colored. "She knows all these quotes, and soliloquies and everything. Insults, too. She can be really scary when she gets going. Try her out. Go on. I bet she knows anything you can throw at her."

Nick shrugged. There wasn't much else to do.

"O Time," he quoted. "Thou must untangle this, not I . . ."

"It is too hard a knot for me t'untie," she said, without so much as an attempt at humility. "Viola, *Twelfth Night*."

"Fair is foul, and foul is fair," Nick challenged.

"The witches in the Scottish play," Phoebe said, tapping the side of her nose. "Hover through the fog and filthy air."

"See?" said Luke.

"I have a friend just like you," Nick said to Phoebe. "She has a freak-ish memory, too. She only has to see a script once and it's just about burned into her brain. She can be kind of scary, too, but she's great to run lines with. Well, she was."

"Was?" Phoebe asked, her interest piqued.

Nick sighed. "That's a really long story. And, with any luck, we won't be here long enough for you to hear it."

Beyond the glass, on the bank of electronic billboards, the highest and largest of the screens was refreshing itself. A glitzy hot pink and gold promotion for a stage musical gradually pixelated into blackness, and when a new advertisement appeared, Nick realized it was an image that he knew all too well.

There stood Laura, waist deep in a lily pond, her perfect torso covered in a dress whose bodice rose up over her breasts in pink, pointed petals. Her expression was somewhere between meditative and seductive; her hands were held aloft, her wrists curved sensuously outward, the tips of her index fingers touching the tips of her thumbs. In stretched-out capitals at the bottom of the image was the single word: WATERLILY.

Nick made a grim snort of laughter.

"What?" asked Phoebe, confused.

"That's my girlfriend," Nick said.

When Phoebe swiveled her head, her thick curls barely moved. "What? Where?"

"There, on the billboard."

"The Waterlily chick? Are you serious?" said Luke. "Whoa. You're a lucky guy."

Phoebe thought. She frowned. She began to say something. Then stopped. At last she settled for asking Luke, "How do you know?"

"How do I know what?" said Luke, baffled.

"How do you know he's a lucky guy? I mean, I do hate to sound like the token whiny feminist in this elevator, but just because she's beautiful doesn't mean he's lucky."

"No, but—"

Phoebe looked to Nick. "Love looks not with the eyes?"

"But with the mind," Nick answered.

"Therefore?"

"Is winged Cupid painted blind."

"Very good, Nick," Phoebe said, and took a sip of the Green Ginger Wine. "Should we try the emergency phone again?"

"You try," Nick said. "Maybe you've got the magic touch."

After Phoebe pressed the button, the speaker let out several irritating, overlong bleeps. Then there came a voice, although it was hard to tell, at first, if it was being produced by a human or a machine.

"Hello, you have reached CTG Building Management Services. You are speaking with Nashira. How may I assist you?"

♑

At that precise moment, as in every other, the sky's celestial bodies were connected in a unique and momentary web of magnetism. When the world turned—as it always did, for there was no stopping it—that web pulled tight, and a brand-new soul was dredged up out of the darkness into the starlight, sparkling. Long, newborn legs kicked out into sudden mysterious space, and an outraged mouth drew in unavoidable gusts of the strange new lightness of air.

Here was Rafferty O'Hare—Capricorn, future owner of enormous blue eyes, outrageously long eyelashes, mishap-scarred knees and the besotted indulgence of all women who were related to him, and a great many who were not. To tell the truth, he had already—though he was bright red and covered in smears of vernix—taken instant possession of the hearts of his mother, Zadie, lying utterly spent on a hospital bed, his grandmother, Patricia, perched on the bed's edge with tears in her eyes, and his aunt, Larissa, who looked almost as wrecked as her sister.

Over the past hours Zadie had been wrenched, stretched, cracked and forced open, and now she felt a swamping tide of love flooding into all the new spaces inside her. Soon she was overflowing with it, and it had to have somewhere to go. She grabbed at her mother's hand and held it to her cheek.

"Mum?" she said, gasping. "I love you, Mum. I love you so much. Rissy? Riss? God, I love you. You're the best sister anyone could ever have."

Then she turned to the other side of the bed, where Simon Pierce the midwife was wiping his hands on a white towel, watching these four humans fall in love. Always, this was his favorite part. Even though it wasn't his miracle, he was allowed to touch the edges of it.

"Simon," said Zadie passionately. "I love you, Simon. I love you so much."

In one way this was completely true, and in another way it wasn't. Well, not yet, anyway.

☍

By the time the local elevator technicians had made their way through the heaving city streets and climbed the stairs to the plant room on the roof of the Galaxy casino, it was 1:05 a.m. and Fern Emerson and Caleb Harkness were no longer at the scene. They were at Caleb's residence—a tubby little motorboat that he kept moored on an outer arm of a less-than-salubrious marina—where Fern was realizing that not every New Year's Eve was necessarily anticlimactic.

As the technicians inspected the damage, and man-bitched about having drawn the short straw of working on New Year's Eve, Laura Mitchell stood in the neon-lit powder room on the top floor of the Galaxy casino, angrily dialing Nick Jordan's telephone number for perhaps the hundredth time that night. Also for the hundredth time that night, her call went through to Nick's voicemail, and although this didn't surprise Laura in the least, it nevertheless added another pennyweight to the growing mass of her fury.

It didn't take the technicians long to diagnose the problem, and it wasn't a serious one; the broom handle had only tripped a circuit breaker.

When Nick Jordan, Phoebe Wintergreen and Luke Foster felt their elevator jerk back into action, Phoebe jumped up and down, and looked as if she might be about to hug Luke. Luke, missing this cue entirely, slugged the final sip of Green Ginger Wine.

"Well, halle-fucking-lujah," said Nick.

☍

Blessed Jones stood center stage in the Galaxy casino ballroom with Gypsy Black in her arms, her musicians and backup singers arranged in a casual arc behind her. The final set of the concert was almost over and Blessed could feel sweat trickling down between her breasts and dampening her dress between her shoulder blades. Her hair was extra-frizzy from her own perspiration, and her throat was beginning to feel the effects of her hours of singing. And yet, she was entirely happy. For this was where she belonged: here, in this spotlight, on this stage, with this guitar, singing to these hundreds of people whose attention she held on a string made of nothing but breath. Blessed plucked a chord and signaled to the guy at the sound desk for a tiny bit more of Gypsy in the foldback. As she stepped forward to the microphone, she felt the crowd lean in to meet her.

"Here's a song that I wrote when my heart was broken," Blessed said, and that was all she said. Just those words, but they were enough to make the Galaxy ballroom crowd break out into cheers and whistles.

"Oh," said Blessed, with mock surprise. "Do I get the feeling some of you have been waiting for this song?"

The cheers and whistles intensified and a chant broke out. *Hid-den Shallows. Hid-den Shallows. Hid-den Shallows.* In the months since she'd written it, "Hidden Shallows" had accelerated up the charts and boosted Blessed Jones's popularity to stratospheric heights.

Hid-den Shallows. Hid-den Shallows. Hid-den Shallows. Everyone in the crowd—including those who'd never before seen Blessed Jones perform live, and those who owned none of her albums, and those who'd never even heard of her six months earlier—was aching to hear this song.

"You know, it's strange," Blessed said to the crowd, and paused, feeling the power of being able to pause like this and have everyone wait for whatever it was that she would say or do next. "It's a mystery. How things arrive in our lives. Because I got the words to this song from a guy in a bar . . ."

She was half singing by now.

"A guy whose heart was broken just like mine, and wherever that guy is tonight, I want him to know that my heart is mended now and I hope that his is all better too."

The crowd cheered and chanted. *Hid-den Shallows. Hid-den Shal-lows. Hid-den Shallows.* And Blessed began to pick the opening strains on Gypsy's strings.

"You're really sure this is the tune you want?"

Hid-den Shallows. Hid-den Shallows. Hid-den Shallows.

"All right then."

The crowd gave one last cheer before quieting down to listen to Blessed's fingerpicking, to her silk-and-sandpaper voice. As Blessed sang she felt herself travel backward in time, to the shock of the naked girl by the fridge, and the ache that came after the sucker punch of betrayal, and it was out of that pain that she sang.

Standing in her bright pool of light, Blessed couldn't see the entirety of the room, but she could see the spotlit faces of the people swaying on the dance floor at her feet. And she could see, over by a lighting rig, a guy standing on a chair in a tux, his bow tie untied, and the bib of his white shirt covered in what might have been blood. He was young and he was beautiful, with dark hair and an open face, and he was staring at her with a look of such recognition that Blessed knew that, this night, she was singing this song for him above everyone else. She turned her body just a little toward him. As she shifted into the third repetition of the chorus, she met his gaze and sang.

𝄉

Nick Jordan didn't know how music worked. He only knew that it did. He knew it wasn't only the words, and he knew it wasn't only the tune. He knew it wasn't only the small woman with the big crazy hair and the bittersweet voice, and he knew that it wasn't only the gleaming black guitar with the ornate mother-of-pearl detailing. He knew it was all of these things together—and something else as well—that was swelling up his heart so that it hurt in the best possible way.

Standing on a chair—a chair he had climbed upon for its view of the room, in order that he might catch a glimpse of Laura Mitchell—Nick Jordan had found himself in the spotlight of Blessed Jones's heartbroken gaze, captured by the peach skin of her voice. She was singing her most famous song. To him.

I looked for your depths, but all I found were your lies
Learned I could just wade, never swim, in your eyes

You're a skit, not a drama, a bare diorama
A beautiful charmer, no Trench Mariana
I searched but never found in you
Dived but never drowned in you
Now I'm aground on you
You and your hidden shallows

As her words went in through his ears and down through his mind and soaked into the deep red sponge of his heart, Nick knew that it wasn't Laura Mitchell who was the waterlily, and it never had been. It wasn't Laura who had nothing going on underneath but straggly, sickly roots. It was he, himself. And Justine had known it all along. In the person of Leo Thornbury, she had tried every which way she could to tell him to look deeper, dig deeper, go deeper. Be deeper.

Justine.

Blessed Jones and her stage band played a long, instrumental interlude that conjured a montage of memories in Nick's mind. There was Justine, dwarfed in his jumper on a cold night on her rooftop, its too-long sleeves flapping like a pair of boneless wings. And Justine on the twelfth-floor landing, yelling like a shrew that he was flushing his talent down the toilet. And Justine with her eyebrows formidably fixed as she wrestled the Battle of Waterloo checkers from a rival trash and treasure hunter. Justine in smeary silver makeup, with her lips all sticky and red from a toffee apple, raising her face to Nick's. Justine standing outside Evelyn Towers looking heartbrokenly into the open back of the removal van while he stood with suitcases in his hands, pretending not to see her.

Justine hadn't messed with his horoscopes to fool him, or to laugh at him. She'd done it because she was trying to tell him something that he ought to have known for a hundred other reasons: *she* was the one for him.

Blessed Jones sang the chorus one last time and closed her eyes to sing the final, soaring, bittersweet notes, and when the song came at last to its very end, she opened her eyes to look straight at Nick once again.

"Thank you," he mouthed, and Blessed Jones nodded her frizzy head in a barely perceptible gesture of *you're welcome* before the New Year's Eve crowd went wild for her.

♑

There were many women in the world who didn't know how to walk properly in high-heeled shoes, but Laura Mitchell was not one of them. When Nick looked away from Blessed Jones to see Laura walking in through the door of the Galaxy ballroom, his first thought was that she walked so elegantly in those strappy black heels that they might almost be part of her actual legs.

Nick leaped down from the chair and pushed his way toward the door through a steamy crowd that smelled of sweat, tequila and jubilation. When he was close enough, he called to her, "Laura! Laura!"

As she registered several things in quick succession—that he was here, that he was coming toward her, that he was a mess in a bloodied shirt and a rumpled tuxedo—her face reminded Nick of a squally day that had everything from sun showers through to thunder and hail. By the time he reached her, though, she had settled her features into permafrost.

"You're alive then," she said.

"I'm so sorry. I would have called. I wanted to call, but I dropped my phone in a pond," Nick said. "I've been trying to get here. For hours. Laura, I'm so sorry."

Nick reached into the pocket of his tuxedo and pulled out the ring box.

"Here?" Laura said, looking around her, incredulous. "Now? Are you serious?"

Nick flicked open the ring box, and he saw Laura try not to look at the ruby within.

"Not *now*," she said. "This isn't right. You've completely fucked New Year's Eve. Now we're going to have to wait until Valentine's Day."

"No," said Nick. "I think now is perfect."

He took her hand, but he didn't turn it over the way you might if you were going to slip a ring onto someone's finger. He gently turned her hand upward and placed the ring, box and all, on her palm, and Nick saw the weather on her face flicker once again between sunshine and rain.

"I want you to have this ring. As a farewell present."

"What? What are you talking about?"

"Laura, you are the most beautiful woman I have ever seen. You are perhaps the most beautiful woman I will ever see in real life. For all my life, I will see you on the billboards of the world and wonder at your beauty. When you are one of those silver-haired women advertising age-defying skin cream, I will look at you and be grateful that I ever had the chance to admire you at close range.

"You are also one of the strongest and most hardworking people I know. You will be an extraordinary success, and as I watch that success from afar, I will admire it and applaud you. But, I'm not going to marry you."

"You're breaking up with me? With a ring?"

"Listen, Laura. I'm never going to be who you want. I'm never going to be what you want. I can't promise that I won't be riding a bike and eating two-minute noodles when I'm sixty. I'm sorry, Laura, but I'm not right for you. But somewhere out there"—Nick gestured vaguely in the direction of the city, the country, the world—"is the person who *is*. I want you to go find them."

Nick leaned in to kiss Laura's cheek. "Make sure Eve and Sergei see you home safely, yeah?"

"I don't believe this. Where are you going?"

Nick didn't answer. He just stepped away, giving Laura a fond salute.

And then he left the building.

Via the stairs.

♑

Because it was a blood-temperature night, Justine slept quite comfortably on the back deck under the stars. Peacefully, too, since it was one of the few blessings of the perpetual drought that Edenvale's night air was free of mosquitoes.

At around 3 a.m., Justine woke to the sounds of her parents arriving home from their party: Mandy making coochie-coo noises to Lucy, while Drew clattered about in the kitchen fixing himself an aspirin. Before long, the house lights were extinguished again, and Justine drifted back to sleep listening to the creaking of insects inside the dry earth of the garden.

Perhaps it got colder in the dark hour just before the dawn, and perhaps that was what woke her. Or perhaps it was a kind of sixth sense that there was somebody close by, watching her as she slept. Whatever it was, Justine opened her eyes to see Nick Jordan sitting a couple of meters away from her in a bloodstained shirt, with a black jacket draped across his lap. She sat up and stared.

"Nick?"

"Question," he said. "Why did you do it?"

"What are you doing here?"

Nick leaned forward, his forearms resting on his knees. "I need to know. Why you did it."

"But how did you even know I was here?"

From the Galaxy casino, Nick had jogged across town to Evelyn Towers, where Aussie Carmichael had opened the door of Justine's apartment in a pair of Road Runner boxer shorts and a pungent haze of marijuana smoke.

"Your brother told me," Nick said.

Justine looked at her watch-less wrist, and then at the moon. "It must be, what?"

"It's half past four."

"How the hell did you get here?"

That part had not been easy. By the time Nick knew he was bound for Edenvale, the trains had all stopped for the night. He'd have ridden his bike, if that had been required, but it would have been an eight-hour ride, and he didn't feel like he had eight hours to spare. He'd have paid for a taxi, if that had been necessary, but on this night he'd already given away a ring worth more money than he'd earned in the past eighteen months, and written a blank check in the name of a damaged, one-eyed mutt.

"The short answer is that I hitched," he said.

"And the long one?"

"I'll tell you in a minute. But first I want you to tell me. Why you did it."

Justine bit her lip. "I'm so sorry, Nick. I never meant for—"

Nick shook his head impatiently. "Not an apology. That's not what I want. I want to understand."

"You really don't know?"

"I think I might know, but I don't want to guess," Nick said.

She started to say something, and then stopped. Started again. Stopped.

At last, she said, "I did it because I didn't want you to stop being you. I did it because I didn't want you to give up everything you are. I still don't . . . want you to do that."

"But that's not all of it, is it?" Nick pressed. "I mean, why should you care so much? Why would you care enough to risk your job?"

"It was really stupid. And wrong."

"It was. Both those things, and in spades. But that doesn't answer my question. Why do you care what I do with my life? What's it to you?"

Justine's thick, dark eyebrows drew closer together, and all her features seemed to quiver. "Oh, come on, Nick. You know."

He could see tears brimming in her lower eyelids. She was swallowing hard, too, in an effort to stop herself from crying. It didn't work, though. A tear splashed out onto her cheek, and while Nick felt a pang of guilt, he pushed on. "I'm starting to get an idea, but I still want you to say it."

A second tear landed, this time on Justine's other cheek.

"I think I might . . . love you," she said.

Nick came to sit beside her then. He reached out to cup her jaw with one hand and brushed a thumb gently across her cheek. "Well, that's all right then."

"It is?"

"Yes. Because I love you, too."

"You do?"

"And I am so sorry for being too stupid to know. Until now."

"Why now?"

"Well, that would be the long answer."

The sky was still a sparkling black when Nick Jordan began to tell Justine Carmichael the story of his night. He told her about the dog jumping out of the convertible and being hit by a car, and about the actor playing Romeo and the knocked-out tooth lying on the cobblestone stage, and about the vet and how she knew the dog from the Dogs Home, and about the stalled elevator and about Phoebe Wintergreen, who was as conversant in Shakespeare as Justine herself, and who was almost certainly in love with Luke Foster, who was a callow youth and didn't know what to do about the fact that he almost certainly loved Phoebe just as much, and about Blessed Jones and how the singer looked right into his eyes, and how the song she'd written because of a chance meeting in a bar had been somehow meant for him—Nick—and how he had said goodbye to Laura outside the Galaxy ballroom and how he'd been almost certain that there had been a look of relief in Laura's eyes, and how he'd thought about her—Justine—in the taxi, even before the dog jumped out of the car, and again when the moment came for him to choose whether to play Romeo or not, and again in the elevator, and he told her that he thought maybe everybody had some hidden shallows inside themselves but how he now knew—and perhaps this was to do with Neptune in Aquarius, and the spiritual forces of the universe converging, just as Leo Thornbury had said—that the shallows weren't going to be enough. And that was his New Year's resolution.

By now the sky was no longer black, but a shade that you might have called gray until you looked long enough to notice all of its other dimensions.

"So I got here the long way around," Nick said. "The very long way around. But now I'm here. And . . . can you just promise me that if ever you want me to know something, you will say it to me, straight out? Don't have an astrologer tell me, okay? And don't pretend to be an astrologer. It's all too confusing."

Justine made a small laugh. "It didn't even work," she said. "If you think back over it, almost everything I did backfired. 'Boldness be my friend! Arm me, audacity.' Could that have gone down any worse than it did?"

"And yet, here I am. And here we are."

"Only by luck, though," Justine said. "Only by . . . lucky, random chaos. I mean, if you hadn't seen some stray dog get hit by a car, and if that elevator had never stopped for long enough for that girl to quote Shakespeare at you, what then? There are choices within choices within chances. It's all so complicated and tangled. How does anything ever go the way it's supposed to?"

"I don't know how it works, Jus. I only know that it does."

"And wind it back further. What if Blessed Jones had never written that song, or if she'd never gone to that pub, or if her heart had never been broken, or—"

"Shhhhh," Nick said.

Brain: *I'm almost certain he's going to kiss you now.*

Justine: *I think you're right.*

Brain: *So, are we happy?*

Justine: *I think we might be delirious.*

"Happy New Year, Justine," Nick said.

He did kiss her then. And she kissed him back.

cusp

On the west coast of the country, New Year's Day had only just dawned when Joanna Jordan—having seen in the New Year with several glasses of sparkling wine—woke to the sound of the telephone ringing on her bedside table. Heat was already making its way into the bedroom in slices of sunlight at the edges of the blinds; the day was going to be a scorcher.

Mark Jordan, lying in the bed beside his wife, groaned sleepily and opened one eye for long enough to register the time.

"It's five-a-bloody-clock," he said, and then rolled over, burying his head under a pillow as he did so.

There was no need at this time of year for bedclothes, and little need for nightclothes either. In a flimsy silk slip, Jo sat up in bed and grabbed the phone. The call display showed an east coast number. Feeling a stretching in her maternal elastic, she thought immediately of Nick.

"Hello?"

The voice on the other end of the line was a woman's. "Jo? Is that you?"

"Who's this?" Jo asked.

"It's Mandy! Mandy Carmichael. Honey, I know it's early where you are and I'm so sorry, but I just—"

"Oh my God," said Jo, loudly enough to elicit another groan from Mark. She swung herself out of bed and padded along the hallway, squinting as she reached the brightness of the living room. "It must have been, what? Ten years? And every New Year, I promise myself that I'm going to track you down, and I never do, but—"

Mandy laughed. It was a familiar, bubbling, infectious laugh.

"I know, I know. I'm exactly the same. But this morning I had to look you up. I already woke up the other M & J Jordans in Perth. Poor bastards. But I couldn't help it. I had to ring," she said, sounding delighted. "I had to tell someone. I had to tell *you!*"

Jo was baffled. "Whoa, whoa. Back up the truck a minute. Tell me what?"

"So, I'm here at Edenvale, in the same old house, and this morning I opened Justine's bedroom door. I was just going to take her a cup of tea, but bless her heart, if she doesn't have *company.*"

"What?"

"Nick's here. Nick's *here.*"

"Are you saying . . . ?" Jo asked.

"Yes!" Mandy squealed.

"Do you really mean . . . ?"

"Yes!"

Jo waved a hand around at the side of her face in an ineffectual gesture that had something to do with feeling too much emotion all at once. She said, "I knew they'd been seeing a bit of each other . . . but I never thought . . . I didn't even dare—" she broke off.

"To hope," Mandy finished.

And then, for a brief moment, through a miracle of metal and magic that stretched the width of a continent, the voices of two old friends were joined together in high-pitched and slightly tearful squeals of joy.

✛

Late in the afternoon of New Year's Day, Daniel Griffin sat under a shady pergola in Jeremy Byrne's backyard and sipped on a tall glass of Pimm's while the Editor Emeritus of the *Alexandria Park Star* read the

contents of the manila folder that Daniel had brought to him. Jeremy
had been back from a month-long Pacific Island cruise for only a day,
and both he and Graeme—who was watering the flower beds—were
looking tanned and almost supernaturally relaxed.

Steadily, and with his spectacles perched low on his nose, Jeremy
had made his way through the documents in the folder: horoscopes as
submitted to the *Star* by Leo Thornbury, clippings from the *Star* with
Justine's alterations brightly highlighted. He had now reached the final
document: a letter from Leo, written on thick, pale blue paper, that had
arrived in a matching envelope, sealed with a blob of silver-gray wax.
The letter read:

Dear Daniel,

You will recall that I accepted with reluctance your commission to
provide an opinion upon Miss Carmichael's future with the *Star,*
and it has been with a heaviness of heart that I have carried this
responsibility.

It seems to me that Miss Carmichael's motive in adapting the
horoscopes to her own purpose was neither greed nor malice. Oddly
enough, her astrological vision was in at least one instance clearer
than my own. This has caused me to wonder whether, perchance,
my vision grows cloudy with my advanced age. I confess that it is
Miss Carmichael's perspicacity—she correctly identified that this is
a month of endings for those born under the sign of the archer—that
has led me to the decision that I must now share with you: I have determined to resign as the astrologer for the *Star.* Though it has been
my great pleasure to serve the publication these long years past, it
must fall to another to direct your readers in matters of the stars.

And so, my advice to you regarding Miss Carmichael is to err
on the side of generosity and forgiveness. I confess that the romantic
in me wishes that, all for the love of me, a woman might have been
moved to such rash conduct.

Warmly,
Leo Thornbury

Jeremy returned the letter to the folder, which he allowed to fall closed on his lap, and Daniel waited for the Editor Emeritus to look up with the kind of grave expression that he reserved for instances of serious misconduct. Instead, Daniel was surprised to see, when Jeremy lifted his head, that his eyes were full of laughter.

"Let me tell you a little tale," he said. "Back in the dim, dark, distant past when I was working at a daily newspaper, I was rather enamored of a young man. A musician, as it happened. Double bass, you know. Very talented. Shortly after I first met him, the newspaper ran a competition where the prize was a case of extremely classy champagne."

Jeremy paused to nibble on a mint leaf from his Pimm's.

"Go on," Daniel prompted.

"Well, you must remember that this is all a long time ago. Things were not so, ah, regulated, as they are today. When the competition entries arrived, I was simply given a sack full of envelopes with instructions to pluck one out. As I recall, I withdrew the entry of one Mrs. J. Phipps. Odd, isn't it, the things that stick in your head? Mrs. J. Phipps was the, ah, original winner. But, strangely enough, when the results of the competition appeared in print, the name of the winner was that of"—Jeremy gave an ostentatious wink—"a young double bass player from Alexandria Park."

Daniel was stunned. "But—"

"Of course, he may never even have entered the competition. But he was hardly likely to turn down a case of champagne," Jeremy said. "And *somebody* was going to have to phone him up to arrange for delivery of the prize."

"So, did you . . . and he . . . ?"

"Yes, yes. My little ruse was successful. For all the good it did me. The whole relationship was a disaster from start to finish! But after it was over, I took a little holiday to mend my bruised and battered heart. And next to whom, on the plane, should I be sitting?"

Jeremy looked over to where Graeme was showering water on the leaves of a thriving hydrangea bush.

Daniel stared at Jeremy. "You don't think what you did was . . . wrong?"

"From a certain perspective, yes, of course. But, in the broader scheme of things, Daniel, it's very hard to judge such matters. Maybe, in missing out on the prize, Mrs. Phipps was deprived of a night or two of bubble and romance. Or perhaps our Mrs. Phipps was a hopeless alcoholic and the champagne would only have served to hasten her death by cirrhosis of the liver. Perhaps I did her a kindness. Who knows?"

Daniel sighed. "So, what do you think I should do?"

"About Justine?" Jeremy asked.

Daniel nodded.

Jeremy smiled indulgently. "Give her another chance, Daniel. I don't think you'll be sorry."

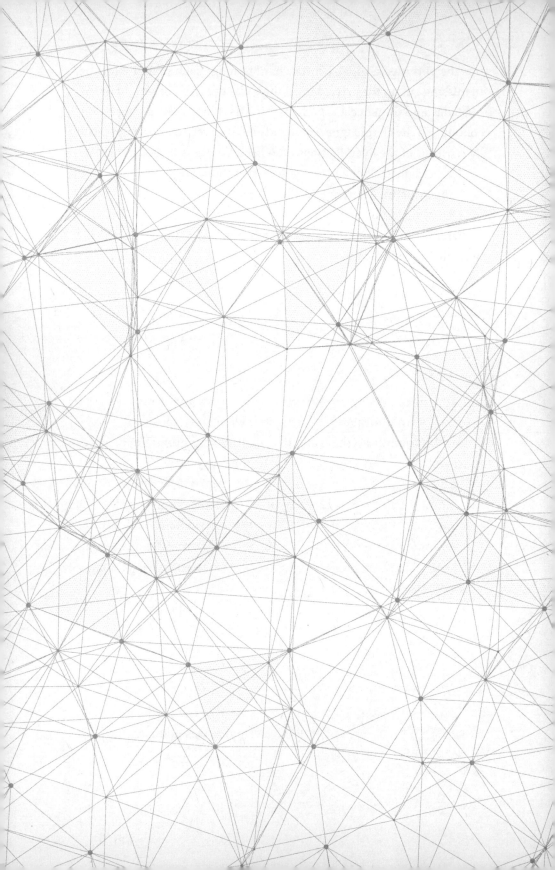

Aquarius

JANUARY 20–FEBRUARY 18

Margie McGee woke at first light on a sea of leaves, her boat a small timber platform hammered sixty meters above the ground into the trunk of a giant swamp gum. The date was February 14 and this was the 136th day of her tree-sit.

She crawled out of her sleeping bag and into a down-filled jacket, then set to work making herself a cup of tea. Although her nose was numb with cold, and her back stiff from the night on her thin mattress, Margie smiled at the joyful sound of the dawn chorus. As she poured water over the tea leaves at the bottom of her small enamel pot, a haiku suggested itself to her.

> pale mist of morning
> lifted higher by the notes
> of pink robin's song

Margie sat, swinging her feet off the edge of the platform so they dangled into the forest as if into water. No one was going to pave this paradise. Not on her watch.

~~~

Charlotte Juniper rode the rush-hour flow of humanity from the inner suburbs to the city, then walked the last few blocks to the office of Greens Senator Dave Gregson. Dave himself arrived half an hour later, and went immediately into the office's small kitchenette to make coffee.

Although they lived together, Dave and Charlotte thought it would be best if they arrived at work separately, left work at different times, and in every other way enabled the rest of the office's staff to maintain the flimsy fiction that Charlotte and Dave's relationship was a strictly professional one. But this morning, every other staff member was either out on errands, away on holidays or off sick. It was, Charlotte knew, a rare opportunity.

She slipped stealthily into the kitchenette and locked the door behind her. Though the sound of the latch alerted Dave to Charlotte's presence, she was too quick for him. He was still standing at the counter holding the coffee tin and a spoon when her hand shot between his legs, from behind, as accurate as a striking snake.

Dave could feel—through the fabric of his trousers—her fingernails on his scrotum.

"I just want you to know, Dave Gregson," she said, "that if you are ever unfaithful to me, the first thing I will do is apply to your bollocks one of those little green rings that farmers use for making wethers. It will only hurt for a little while, and then your balls will just shrivel up, and drop . . . *off.*"

"And the second thing?" he asked.

"Is," said Charlotte, "that I will start wearing underpants to work."

Early in the afternoon, Fern Emerson, having left Hello Petal in Bridie's capable hands, carried a heavy cardboard carton into Rafaello's Dufrene Street cafe. She set the carton on a vacant table and unfolded its flaps. There was a momentary flurry of bubble wrap.

"These," she announced to Rafaello.

Rafaello pursed his lips. Scratched his head. "You're sure? For your engagement party? You want the wedding china of Princess Diana and Prince Charles?"

Fern nodded happily.

Raf worriedly ran his hand through the remains of his dark, slicked hair. "But with the numbers we have talked about for your party, there won't be enough here. Not for everybody."

Raf seemed relieved to be able to point this out, Fern thought.

"Actually," she said, indicating Caleb's minivan, parked out the front of the cafe, "I have plenty more where this came from."

≋

In the Oxfordshire village of Fritwell, Dorothy Wetherell-Scott née Gisborne, former owner of the world's largest Charles and Diana wedding china collection, woke to find that her husband had already risen. She was puzzled, for Rupert was not, by nature, an earlier riser. She hoped he was not unwell.

At the base of the stairs, Flossie the border collie waited like a forward scout, and at the sight of Dorothy, she gave a conspiratorial grin before turning tail and trotting into the kitchen, her toenails clicking brightly on the linoleum.

Rupert was at the stove, cooking eggs.

"Well, good evening, Mrs. Wetherell-Scott," Rupert said, with a wink.

"Good morning, Mr. Wetherell-Scott," Dorothy said.

This joke had not, for them, grown tired.

Dorothy saw that Rupert had set the table with a white cloth, and got out the best silver. There was an envelope waiting at her place, and the dozen red roses on the table were beautifully arranged in a china vase. With a gasp, she realized that it was a Kate and Wills wedding vase.

"Oh, Rupert," Dorothy sighed.

"Happy Valentine's Day, love," Rupert said.

≋

The woman slid a fingernail, painted in a shade called Pixie Dust, under the flap of a large, white envelope. Then paused. To the ginger cat, sitting tidily on the kitchen table and watching her every move, she said, "Well, Shithead, here goes."

Inside the envelope was a magazine. Hastily, the woman shuffled through its pages. Then she stopped and stared, frozen in disbelief. The clock ticked. The cat's heart tocked. But the woman did not, for a time, breathe or blink.

Then: "Eeeeeeeeeeee!"

It was official. It was in print. There was proof of it in the small, square photograph: a profile shot, her neck long and elegant, her hair styled by city hairdressers to curl wildly out of the wrappings of a richly patterned headscarf. It was her. It really was. And she was Davina Divine, astrologer to the *Alexandria Park Star*.

Daniel Griffin let the February edition fall closed on his desk then leaned back in his office chair with a satisfied smile. It was a corker of an issue, even if he did say so himself. Jenna had scooped the press gallery on a new travel expenses scandal that was threatening to unseat a senior member of parliament, and a couple of quotes from Martin's excoriating column on the state of Australian rugby were going viral. As for Justine, Daniel had to hand it to her. She hadn't missed a beat since returning to work, and her piece on the retirement of a silver-tonsilled radio shock jock had been so delicately acidic that he'd laughed out loud in several places.

Just quietly, Daniel thought—as the telephone on his desk began to ring—he, too, deserved a pat on the back. Replacing Leo Thornbury with an unknown like Davina Divine had been a risky move, but if her first column was anything to go by, his punt was going to pay off brilliantly. Davina's writing was contemporary, spicy, just a little bit sexy and—what was more—her February horoscope had promised spectacular romantic opportunities for the lions of the zodiac. Daniel, still leaning back in his chair, let the phone ring three times, four. Lions, he reflected, responded to demands in their own sweet time.

"Daniel Griffin," he said, answering at last.

"Daniel, hello," said a woman's voice. "This is Annika Kirby."

Annika Kirby, Annika Kirby, Daniel thought, trying to place the name. It took him a moment, but then he got it. She was the deputy editor of one of those women's magazines that were wall-to-wall sex and fashion—except for the compulsory back-of-the book think piece about child marriage or land-mine clearances. But what did Annika Kirby want with *him*?

"I'm ringing because you've been named number seventeen on our list of the nation's top twenty eligible bachelors," she said, "and it is my happy responsibility to put together a few column centimeters on, well, on *you*."

Seventeenth, he registered. Seventh would have been better. But even so, he'd made the list.

"I see," Daniel said, trying not to sound as pleased as he felt. "So, Annika. What exactly would you like to know?"

≈≈≈

Len Magellan had been confounded to find himself in Heaven. For one thing, he'd always thought Heaven was bullshit. And then there was the fact that he'd hardly been a model citizen. Often, he'd been a total prick.

And yet, here he was, sitting in a very comfortable rocking chair, perched on the edge of a cloud. With Della beside him. Her hair was its youthful blonde and styled in the manner of Grace Kelly's, and she was wearing the pastel lemon skirt suit that she'd chosen as her going-away outfit for their wedding day.

He'd expected her to be wild with him about his decision to cut their three children out of his will. But, as things transpired, Della hadn't even mentioned it. Heaven was like that; stuff that had mattered on Earth seemed to matter a lot less up here.

Now she said, "Look, Len, there's our Luke."

Len could see Alexandria Park, stretching out like a map, with meandering pathways cutting through the green lawns, and the blue splotches of the lakes. Luke was waiting on a park bench, with a nervous air and a tissue-wrapped bunch of tulips partly obscured behind him.

A girl approached. She wore a pretty peasant dress with long, full sleeves and colorful embroidery, and was surreptitiously wiping her sweaty palms on the back of her skirt.

Luke, catching sight of her, hurried the tulips behind his back and stood to greet her.

"Hi," said Luke.

"Hi," said the girl, who was, of course, Phoebe Wintergreen.

Luke had spent most of January squeezed inside a hot car on a gruesome road trip with his family, and for the last couple of weeks Phoebe had been away at drama camp. Now that they were seeing each other again after all this time, they were—each of them—as nervous as hell.

"Happy Valentine's Day," said Luke, thrusting the bunch of tulips out toward her. God, he was a fuckwit. He'd nearly shoved them up her nose.

"Thank you," said Phoebe. "They're beautiful."

Having uttered that completely unremarkable line, Phoebe flipped over the page of her mental script, only to find that the following page was blank. Utterly blank. So she said nothing. Luke said nothing either. There was a silence. And it was an awkward one. In fact, Phoebe was sure it was the most excruciating silence ever in the history of excruciation.

Then they both, simultaneously, had the same swift and reckless idea. *Fuck it,* they thought. And kissed.

Luke kissed Phoebe just the way he had visualized kissing her, and it turned out that her perfume smelled of peppermint. And Phoebe kissed him back just the way she had imagined that she would, and the skin of his cheek felt ever so slightly raspy against her own. The kiss was long and sweet.

"Yesss!" said Len Magellan, in his rocking chair, as he punched the air of Heaven.

Back on Earth, Justine Carmichael walked down Dufrene Street. Even though the day's light was falling, she levered her sunglasses down from the top of her head to cover her eyes before making a casual-looking turn into the markets. She threaded her way through to the fruit shop at the back, and there it was. In big, black, bold letters: ADVOCADOS. Justine took a deep preparatory breath and reached into her bag for the brand-new Sharpie she had swiped from the office stationery closet. This time, it was red.

Conditions were risky, Justine observed, since customers were thin on the ground. Behind the counter was the grocer himself, wearing a long, striped apron that only just stretched around his formidable girth. Fortunately, though, the avocado stand had been positioned to the far left of the display, and after a quick assessment of the sight lines, Justine decided that she should be able to get in and out, unseen, using a towering pyramid of Granny Smiths as cover.

She approached, swift and decisive, uncapping the pen as she went. She reached the sign, but instead of crossing out the additional D in ADVOCADOS, Justine sketched a small, bright love heart beneath it. Then she was off, not looking back, out of the markets, across the road, through the wrought-iron gate and into Alexandria Park. Smiling.

On one side of the park's meandering path was a flock of tai chi practitioners. In their loose white clothes, and in perfect synchronicity, they flowed from one position to the next. On the other side of the path, down by the bandstand, a girl lay on her stomach, staring into the face of a young man lying on his back, a bunch of tissue-wrapped tulips on the grass beside him. Justine could not help but watch on as the boy reached up and took the girl's face in his hands, tenderly drawing her in for a kiss. Smiling as she went on, Justine wondered whether Nick would yet be home from rehearsals. She had nearly all of *A Midsummer Night's Dream* by heart.

When she was almost at the far side of the park, the path curved around so that she was looking directly at Evelyn Towers. On each side of its shallow front steps, young elm trees cupped the last of the day's light in the curves of their slightly yellowed leaves. Inside the arched moldings of the entranceway, a pair of leadlight doors glowed invitingly through glass wedges of pale pink, apricot and green. Justine quickened her pace.

In the living room, its walls newly decorated with theatrical production posters, Justine found a note lying on the dining table. In his scrawly capital-letter handwriting, Nick had written *COME UP-STAIRS*. Justine kicked off her work shoes and shoved her bare feet into a pair of Nick's old thongs. *You minx, you,* she thought, as the rubber soles made schlepping sounds on the steps that led to the rooftop.

When she opened the door, she saw all the parts of the scene at once and laughed with delight. The banana lounges were angled together under the wiry shade of the clothes line, which was hung with foil stars. There were a hundred of them, or more, dangling on lengths of string and twisting in the breeze, their silver surfaces sparkling, the floodlight having been angled just so.

On one of the star-spangled occasional tables were a bottle of sparkling wine and a pair of Vegemite-jar glasses. There was the wagging tassel-topped tail of Brown Houdini-Malarky as he ran on short, twisted legs to greet her. And then there was Nick Jordan—Aquarius, lover and friend—reclining in one of the banana lounges with a battered straw hat pulled down low over his forehead. At the sight of Justine, he struck a cheery chord on the ukulele in his grip.

As Nick sang the first few lines of "I Don't Care If the Sun Don't Shine," Brown pricked up his ears and joined in with a good-natured howl.

Justine swiped the hat off Nick's head and ruffled his hair before kissing him in the middle of the forehead. He put down the ukulele and shifted over, and she lay down beside him. But Brown wasn't going to miss out.

"Oooof," said Nick, as the full weight of a nicely fattened street terrier landed unceremoniously on his stomach.

"Sit down, you goofy dog," Justine said, and Brown flopped into a pose of utter contentment, his paws on Nick's chest. The bamboo lounge was not especially comfortable, and Brown's hot breath was not entirely pleasant to smell, but nothing made Justine want to move from where she was.

"So what do the stars say tonight?" Nick asked.

Justine squinted upward.

"They say, Aquarius, that your life has never been better."

"Is that right?"

"It is," Justine said.

Above Nick Jordan, Justine Carmichael and Brown Houdini-Malarky, a constellation of foil stars sparkled and spun. And above those scraps of brightness, beyond a layer of man-made fog and cloud, the real stars also turned.

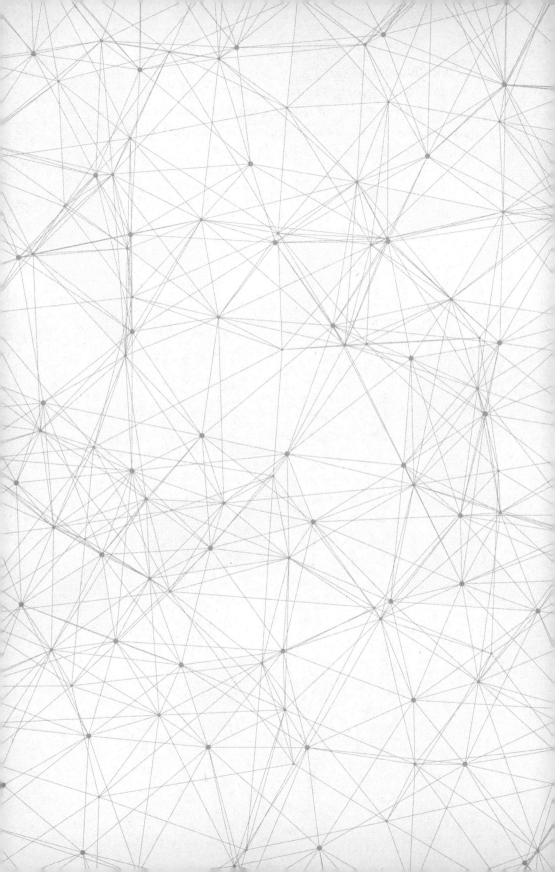

Acknowledgments

My huge thanks to Johnny Jones and Morris Jones, for penning the lyrics to "Hidden Shallows"; Wallace Beery, for advice on cryptic crossword puzzles; Sarah LeRoy, for advice on Shakespeare; the Picky Pen, for exquisite pedantry; Gaby Naher, for being this book's golden star; and Beverley Cousins, Hilary Teeman, Francesca Best, and Dan Lazar, for all their faith, hard work, and brilliant ideas.

Writing would be harder without: Freda Fairbairn (Taurus, best of all readers), Sugar B. Wolf (Leo, pathfinder and soul sister), Jean Hunter (Leo, Renaissance chick), Lagertha Fraser (Sagittarius, infallible compass), Pierre Trenchant (Scorpio, knight in shining iArmor), Marie Bonnily (Cancer, nurturer and true believer), Lou-Lou Angel (Leo, happiness-maker), the Noo (Canis Major, footwarmer and faithful companion), Alaska Fox (Gemini, luminous star of my sky), Dash Hawkins (Capricorn, hug machine), Tiki Brown (Capricorn, miracle), and, most especially, Jack McWaters (Aquarius, my love).

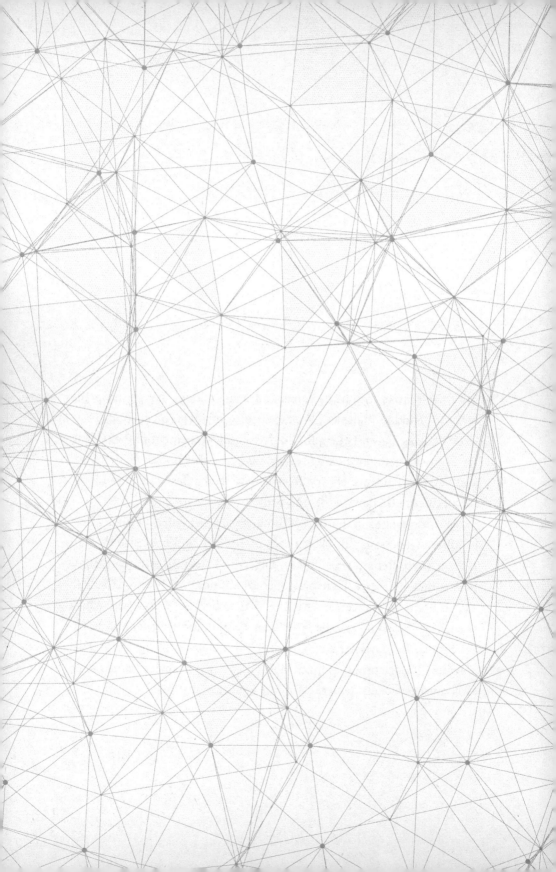

About the Author

Minnie Darke—Gemini with Virgo Rising, Scrabble cutthroat, knitter, and lover of books, freshly sharpened pencils, and Russian Caravan tea—wrote this book to amuse herself and to entertain you.